A RIVER RED WITH BLOOD

ALSO BY JOHN CONNOLLY

THE CHARLIE PARKER STORIES

Every Dead Thing
Dark Hollow
The Killing Kind
The White Road
The Reflecting Eye (novella in the Nocturnes collection)
The Black Angel
The Unquiet
The Reapers
The Lovers
The Whisperers
The Burning Soul
The Wrath of Angels
The Wolf in Winter
A Song of Shadows
A Time of Torment
A Game of Ghosts
The Woman in the Woods
A Book of Bones
The Dirty South
The Nameless Ones
The Furies
The Instruments of Darkness
The Children of Eve

OTHER WORKS

Bad Men
The Book of Lost Things
The Land of Lost Things
he: A Novel

SHORT STORIES

Nocturnes
Night Music: Nocturnes Volume II
Night & Day

THE SAMUEL JOHNSON STORIES (FOR YOUNG ADULTS)

The Gates

Hell's Bells

The Creeps

THE CHRONICLES OF THE INVADERS (WITH JENNIFER RIDYARD)

Conquest

Empire

Dominion

NONFICTION

Books to Die For: The World's Greatest Mystery Writers on the World's Greatest Mystery Novels (as editor, with Declan Burke)

Shadow Voices: 300 Years of Irish Genre Fiction: A History in Stories (editor)

Parker: A Miscellany

Midnight Movie Monographs: Horror Express

A RIVER RED WITH BLOOD

John Connolly

EMILY BESTLER BOOKS

ATRIA

NEW YORK AMSTERDAM/ANTWERP LONDON
TORONTO SYDNEY/MELBOURNE NEW DELHI

ATRIA

An Imprint of Simon & Schuster, LLC
1230 Avenue of the Americas
New York, NY 10020

Originally published in Great Britain in 2026 by Hodder & Stoughton Limited, an Hachette UK company

First Emily Bestler Books/Atria Books hardcover edition June 2026

EMILY BESTLER BOOKS/ATRIA BOOKS
and colophon are registered trademarks of Simon & Schuster, LLC

Manufactured in the United States of America

1 3 5 7 9 10 8 6 4 2

Library of Congress Control Number: 2026936674

ISBN 978-1-6680-8397-0
ISBN 978-1-6680-8399-4 (ebook)

For Nicholas Stuart

(1942–2025)

1

For all guilt is avenged on earth.

Johann Wolfgang von Goethe, *Wilhelm Meister's Apprenticeship*

CHAPTER

I

Moxie Castin and I were sitting in the Great Lost Bear on Forest Avenue. The Bear was quiet that evening; the after-work crowd had departed and there was no sign of any great rush to fill the chairs left vacant. But enough souls remained to lend more life to the Bear—"more" since the Bear was always alive, even when hibernating—and outside it might have been day or night, summer or winter, because the Bear didn't hold with windows and natural light. Inside, it was, and would always be, the Bear.

Portland was nearing the end of its annual period of transition: a gentle early fall easing into a cooler late one, soon to harden into winter. The smell of the city had been subtly changing since summer's close, the vegetal, arboreal essence fading as the temperature dropped. The streets were now less crowded, the tourists no longer so obvious, and the younger drifters, the troubled and the lost, were abandoning the Northeast, warned of the chill to come or feeling its approach in their bones. The ones who stayed were mostly older, with the knowledge of past winters to draw on, and were resigned to what must follow. The city, allied with charities and volunteers, would attempt to care for them, because no one with alternatives would choose to spend the season on the streets of Portland, and those months would be cruel enough without adding callousness and ignorance to the burden. But then, it seemed to me that we were living in callous, ignorant times.

Moxie was drinking wine, which was an odd choice for the Bear. It wasn't that the wine was bad, just that nobody went to the Bear for wine, only beer. Ordering wine at the Bear was like going to one of those fancy cheese shops with hundreds of varieties on offer, and asking for chocolate spread. It defeated the purpose of the exercise.

As usual, Moxie was wearing a tie to make the blind wince, and a suit that had started to wrinkle as soon as it touched his skin. Moxie could have been sitting next to a six-month-old and the kid would have creased out of sympathy. Only Moxie's bald head was smooth, gleaming under the lights like a great white egg waiting to be cracked. A couple of the cops at the bar might have liked to give that a try, as Moxie was the state's best criminal defense lawyer and thus a source of aggravation to the police, but they, like so many of his adversaries, wisely kept any feelings of hostility to themselves. Moxie would have taken it amiss, as would I, but more worryingly, so would Tony and Paulie Fulci, who were playing slapjack at a reinforced table reserved for their use. The zone around the Fulcis was conspicuously unoccupied, perhaps because anyone who didn't know them was afraid that should the card table break, the Fulcis might start pounding on them in its absence. The Fulcis weren't very tall, but they were very wide and very strong. It was hard not to feel sorry for the table. Even buttressed, it was difficult to see it lasting much longer.

And each time a massive flattened palm landed on the wood, the man seated with us flinched.

"Do they have to do that?" he asked.

"You could ask them to stop," said Moxie.

"Would they?"

"They might, but then you'd have to worry about what they did next."

The man sighed heavily. He was thin and bald, with a face built for sighs. His name was Allen Atwood Alcock, and unlike Moxie, he was far from being the best criminal lawyer in the state, even if he was always in steady employment—or had been until Maine finally instituted a system of public defenders after years as the only state not to provide them for the indigent accused. In their absence, it had hired private attorneys on a case-by-case basis, one of them Alcock, who did nicely out of the arrangement. In return, a lot of defendants had spent less time behind bars than they might have otherwise, because Alcock was the king of the plea deal. A poor performer in court, he was aware of the shortcoming and did his best to ensure his cases never made it to trial. This wasn't great news if you didn't want to cop a plea or, God forbid, you were innocent, but since Alcock's client base inclined toward the guilty, such conflicts rarely arose.

Alcock was still a contracted attorney, but he wasn't making as much as before, despite public defenders struggling with their workloads and a backlog of cases remaining to be cleared. This was because Allen Atwood Alcock—or Triple A, as nobody called him, Alcock himself excepted—had irritated someone at the Capital Region Public Defenders' office, or so he claimed, which meant any cases that did come his way were lousy.

"They hate me," he said. He took another mouthful of Brown Hound Ale and sighed again. Somewhere in Venice, a bridge debated relocating west to be closer to its kin.

"They don't hate you," said Moxie. "They just don't like you. There's a difference."

"What difference would that be?"

"The difference between some money and no money."

"That's easy for you to say," said Alcock. "You wear a Rolex."

"It's fake."

"Really?"

"No," said Moxie, "but that's what I tell people. I work with criminals. I don't want them to think I'm wealthy. They might try to rob me."

Alcock picked at the bowl of chips and salsa before us.

"If I don't get this business with the defenders' office sorted out soon, I'll have nothing left worth stealing," he said. "Any thief would take pity on me and feel compelled to give instead of take."

Moxie patted him on the back, causing Alcock to choke briefly on a chip. Allen Atwood Alcock really was a most unhappy man. He wore a wedding ring, and I could only imagine what his wife might be like. If she resembled her husband, only a pitchfork and a gabled window would be required to bring a Grant Wood painting to life.

I ostentatiously checked my watch. It wasn't a Rolex, fake or otherwise, and I wasn't interested in the time. I just wanted to signal that I'd now been sitting with Moxie and Alcock for ten minutes and still had no idea why Moxie had asked me to join them. I was also worried that sighing, like yawning, might be contagious at close quarters. If I became a sigher, Sharon Macy would smother me in my sleep, or leave me. Or both.

"I think Mr. Parker wishes to know why he's here," said Moxie.

Alcock regarded me with watery eyes, like a disappointed basset hound.

"I have a client who'd like to hire you," he said. "His name is Ward Vose."

"What's he done?" I asked.

"What hasn't he done? Robbery, burglary of a dwelling, theft of more than ten thousand dollars, theft by unauthorized taking or transfer, liquor smuggling, aggravated criminal mischief." Alcock sighed once more. "The list goes on. It's almost admirable in its variety. Curiously, Ward's not such a bad person. I've represented worse."

"Where is he now?"

"Where do you think? He's in Maine State Prison, and likely to stay there for the foreseeable future."

"Is this where you tell me he's innocent?"

Alcock made a sound like air slowly escaping from a balloon or the wheezing of an asthmatic kitten. It took me a moment to realize he was laughing.

"Good Lord, no," he said. "He's never denied any of it. For Ward, criminality is not so much an occupation as an unignorable calling. It's just a pity he's not better at it, though at least he represents a reliable source of income for the legal profession. I always feel a pang of regret when he receives a heavy custodial sentence: The sooner he gets out, the sooner I can begin earning again."

Alcock resumed looking mournful, but now he was feeling sorry for someone other than himself.

"Ward has had a rough time of it lately," he continued. "His son died and he wasn't permitted to attend the funeral."

If you were bereaved while in a county jail, and you hadn't antagonized the sheriff, they'd find a way to escort you to the service, even if they billed you for it later. But at Maine State, you had to pray for the deceased in your cell.

"The death made the papers," said Moxie. "Ward Vose's son was Scott Theriault."

Seventeen-year-old Scott Theriault had drowned somewhere up in the Kennebec Valley about a month or so back, close to a plantation in Somerset County known as The Plains, one of the smallest and least-populated communities in the state. The Plains was one of a number of plantations in Somerset County, the concept of a plantation being unique to Maine. While it dated from colonial times, referring to a state of development somewhere between nothing at all and not a whole lot more, the Maine iteration defined a region with a small population, limited self-government, and no real urge to change the status quo. Some plantations had religious roots, but as far as I knew, The Plains didn't. It was founded by speculators early in the nineteenth century. Lumber would have been the most reasonable assumption for the purchase, had the investors not cleared tracts of forest to leave the open spaces that gave the area its name. That suggested groundwork being laid for a settlement, but if so, it was never built. The Plains survived as an afterthought, an echo of a conversation ended more than a hundred years earlier. It featured on only the most detailed of maps, hooked northeast of The Forks plantation, and was otherwise absorbed into its larger neighbor for the sake of convenience. But it was its own entity, with residents who had been part of the landscape for generations, along with a handful of outsiders carried there by unknown tides, their habitancy marked by trailers left in place for so long that ivy had softened their lines, and RVs with tires so rotted that the rims were sunk into the ground.

Scott Theriault, however, had been an inhabitant of a different stripe, closer to an inmate than a dweller. His body was discovered floating in the Austin Stream, a tributary of the Kennebec, days after he'd run away for the third time from Spero School, the behavioral-modification facility in The Plains to which he had been consigned by his family, one of those "tough love" places favored by parents who didn't really understand the concept of love at all or saw it only as a synonym for blind obedience. All I knew about the drowning was what I'd read in the papers and heard on the news. Scott's mother and stepfather "enrolled" him after he'd started acting up at home and been expelled from a pair of more conventional schools. He hadn't settled, and twice made breaks for freedom, once getting halfway to Augusta before being apprehended and returned to Spero. The third time, he'd gone north instead of south, but he must have fallen badly before entering the water, as his right leg was broken when his body was found. His parents had asked for privacy in the aftermath, and that request was being respected. As for the school, it tried to counter any bad publicity by offering restricted tours of its facilities to the media and supervised interviews with some tamer students, all of whom claimed that being sent to Spero was the best thing to have happened to them since they emerged from the womb, and professed sorrow that Scott Theriault had disagreed. End of story.

"That death was investigated by the Maine State Police," I said.

"Aided by the Somerset County Sheriff's Office," said Alcock, "and the Office of the Chief Medical Examiner. It was ruled an accident. It went by the book, and neither Ward nor I are impugning the integrity of any of the officials involved."

"But?"

"Ward Vose is convinced that his son was unlawfully killed."

"On what basis?"

"Call it a feeling."

"A feeling and a conviction aren't the same thing," I said.

"Let's say that the first has hardened into the second," said Alcock.

I looked at Moxie. Moxie looked at me. He was giving me nothing.

"Do you have an opinion on this?" I asked him.

"Only that I don't like those schools, and I don't like parents who submit children to those regimes."

"So you want me to cause trouble?"

"Isn't that what you do?" said Alcock.

"Trouble may be a by-product," I said, "but it's not an end in itself. As I get older, trouble also costs extra, because it has a way of bouncing back on the troublemaker and hitting him in the face."

I pointed at my nose, recently broken by a man wielding a length of timber. The nose hadn't set right and now it hurt when I sneezed. That was what came of looking for trouble.

"Talk to Ward," said Alcock. "Listen to what he has to say. He has money: I can vouch for that. If, when he's done, you believe his son died accidentally, you can walk away with a clear conscience."

"I have a clear conscience already," I told him. "Are you suggesting that if I don't hear him out, I won't any longer?"

Alcock set aside his unfinished beer to regard the Bear and its clientele. If the sight made him happy, it didn't show. I doubted there was much that made him happy, beyond being a lawyer, and even that was relative.

"I met Scott a couple of times," said Alcock. "He wasn't a demon child. He wasn't even very difficult, not by the standards of some rebellious kids I've represented, and those kids' parents weren't talking about having them hauled off in the dead of night to a school that's only a step away from a correctional institution. Scott had a smart mouth, and he didn't like being told what to do, especially by an ambitious stepfather who might have preferred that he vanish from sight and a mother who wouldn't have shed more than the minimum of tears if he did. Some people, men and women both, shouldn't be permitted to raise children, and the law manages to intervene only in cases of violence or neglect. It can't do much about an insufficiency of love. It's my belief that Scott's mother and stepfather regarded him as more effort than he was worth. I would question that verdict."

"So Ward Vose and the boy's mother are divorced?"

"Ward Vose and Hailee Theriault were never married," said Alcock. "They were together for a few years when they were younger, and Scott was born in the middle of them. Only subsequently did Hailee marry Scott's stepfather, and she lives for her new family. Had Scott fitted in better, she might have been more patient with him, but he struggled to adapt. Her sorrow at her son's death may be diluted by a measure of relief.

"Ward Vose, meanwhile, was a lousy role model, but he did love his boy. He just couldn't stay out of jail long enough to look out for him. Ward is a deeply flawed, fundamentally undisciplined man with a wayward streak, but he has never been convicted of a crime of violence, nor do I believe he has ever committed one. He is also self-aware enough to accept that he bears some responsibility for his son's death, if only by his absence from Scott's life, and he will have to carry that guilt for the rest of his days. If hiring a private investigator to examine the circumstances surrounding Scott's death helps ease that guilt somewhat, or offers him the illusion of agency, I see no reason to hinder him. We will pay you for the time it takes to listen, and should you agree to act on Ward's behalf, we will meet your quoted rate. Should you choose not to pursue the matter further, no blame will accrue."

Allen Atwood Alcock certainly spoke like a man who charged by the word. Compared to him, Moxie was practically taciturn.

"Let me sleep on it," I said.

Alcock said he thought that would be acceptable. He even paid the check before leaving, though Moxie and I told him we'd stay where we were for a while. I watched Alcock as he departed. He walked with a peculiar stooping motion, like a heron or a stork, pecking his way through the patrons at the bar, shedding feathers of melancholy in his wake.

"Well?" said Moxie.

"I'm not being told the full story."

"When are you ever? If we knew the full story, there'd be no reason to hire you."

"Do you trust Alcock?"

"He's sincere. I can't speak for his client. That'll be for you to decide when you meet him."

"If I meet him."

"You know you will," said Moxie. "You're already picturing him in his cell, beating himself up about his boy. He's a father who couldn't save his child."

"Like me, you mean."

"No, not like you. Never like you. But you understand his pain."

"It won't bring his boy back."

"That's no reason to turn away."

"I said I'd sleep on it."

"Sure," said Moxie. "It'll take me a couple of days to clear a visitor's permit anyway. I'll book you an afternoon slot, knowing how averse you are to mornings. Let's say Wednesday. That means it won't intrude on your weekend."

"Why are you pushing so hard on this?" I asked.

"Because the troubled-teen industry stinks. If Spero School is part of it, then it stinks too. I like the idea of you rattling that cage."

Moxie was giving me an answer that was general, but behind it lurked the specific, and in the specific lay the personal. I was content to wait Moxie out. If waiting were an Olympic sport, I'd have killed at it.

"You're a pain in the ass," said Moxie, who has the patience of a child. "You know that?"

"That's why they pay me the big bucks. More important, it's why you pay me, big bucks or otherwise. So tell me: Who was the client who had a hard run at a behavioral-modification school?"

"There was no client," said Moxie. "It was me."

CHAPTER

II

It is odd, I suppose, how little one may know about one's friends. Moxie and I had grown closer since I'd become what he liked to describe, only half jokingly, as his "tame investigator," but even then, we didn't discuss our pasts. In Moxie's case, this was because he didn't care to be told anything about me that he didn't want to hear, and what he did want to hear, he already knew. As for me, I'd noticed early on that Moxie deflected questions of a personal nature with a joke before changing the subject. He didn't mind talking about the women in his life, and in eye-popping detail, but his own history was off-limits.

Now, at the Bear, he described without hesitation a nightmare childhood: alcoholic parents, physical abuse, desertion, foster care, and finally, his consignment to a troubled-teen school by a mother unable to cope and a father who was only a mistimed fist or boot away from killing his son.

"Where did they put you?" I asked, but I could guess the answer. Given Moxie's age and Maine upbringing, there was only one.

"Élan," he said.

THE ÉLAN SCHOOL WAS FOUNDED in the town of Poland in Androscoggin County, Maine, in 1970, on thirty-three acres that had once been the site of a hunting lodge. Later, the school added more campuses, including one in Parsonsfield, in York County, where the worst of the abuse was said to have occurred: beatings, sleep deprivation, public humiliation, and punishments for misbehavior that verged on torture. From the start, Élan was dogged by allegations of mistreatment, but serious flaws in the state's system of school supervision meant that investigations were stymied, when they occurred at all. The Parsonsfield campus shut down within a decade or so, but the Poland facility remained in operation until 2011, when it was finally forced to close because of declining enrollment. Throughout, Élan's owners denied accusations of misrule, claiming they were the victims of a smear campaign, yet students repeatedly attempted to escape. One had been raped and murdered while trying to return home. Another was reportedly beaten so badly in the school's boxing ring, where students were reputed to have been forced to fight one another as part of their therapy, that he later died of his injuries. He was buried in an unmarked grave.

"I avoided Parsonsfield," said Moxie. "But Poland was bad enough."

I didn't ask how bad. If Moxie wanted to share those details, he would.

"I hear someone tried to burn it down a while back, or what's left of it," I said.

"I'd like to shake that person's hand. If they'd told me what they were planning, I'd have paid for the gasoline."

"Does Spero have a similar reputation?" I asked.

"I doubt any school in Maine under such a cloud could function these days," said Moxie, "or not for long, but Spero is still no summer camp. Parents wouldn't send their kids there otherwise. It's a farming-out of discipline to strangers, and the moms and dads don't want to know the fine print of how that might be accomplished. All that matters is a difficult child is no longer in their hair and they can get on with their lives and take care of the kids who aren't such a pain in the ass. I can understand the reasoning but not the solution, because it's no solution at all. It's an abrogation of responsibility and the antithesis of what parenting should be."

Over at the Fulcis' table, the pounding had ceased. The brothers were sipping sodas while staring intently at a guy who looked to be giving a hard time to the woman with him. I couldn't hear what was being said, but I could see a finger jabbing, making hard contact with soft flesh. The Fulcis wouldn't like that. I didn't like it either. As for the woman, she was keeping her head down and staying silent, but the set of her jaw was firm. I'd seen my share of women broken by men, and this woman was some distance removed from them—for the time being. The finger jabbed again. It would leave a bruise.

And the Fulcis continued sipping and watching.

"I have no problem assisting with a personal vendetta," I said, "as long as it's acknowledged and the target is worthy. If you and Alcock want to point me at Spero, I'll go, but if the school hasn't broken any laws, there's a limit to what I can achieve."

Moxie finished his drink.

"Why would Scott Theriault have headed north from The Plains?" he asked. "He was just a kid. If he was trying to run away, it would make more sense for him to work his way south. Surely he'd have looked toward civilization again, not wilderness, if he wanted to escape."

"He might have wanted to be anywhere but Spero," I said.

Moxie studied me with eyes that understood the impulse.

"If that's true," he replied, "what does it say about the place?"

CHAPTER

III

Only one Fulci currently remained seated in the bar: Paulie, the younger brother. Alone, he represented more than enough Fulci to meet demand, but it was concerning that both his older brother and the finger jabber were absent. The woman was still at her table, gazing around like someone who didn't necessarily want to be where she was but didn't regard the options as any better. I watched Bird Dickson, one of the Bear's owners, walk over to ask if she was okay, Bird not being one to tolerate the bullying of women in her bar or anyplace else.

I asked Moxie for a minute and headed to the restrooms. Tony Fulci came out of the men's room just as I came within sight of the door. He was holding something in his right hand. I feared it might be a body part, but it turned out to be a driver's license.

"Did you make a mess?" I asked.

"Of what?"

"Of the guy who was too free with his finger."

Tony looked offended. He had recently informed our mutual friend Louis that he believed himself to be evolving as a person, which Louis took to mean Tony's knuckles no longer dragged along the ground with quite the same force as before.

"I just talked to him," said Tony. "And asked for his driver's license."

"Did he hand it over willingly?"

"No," said Tony. "But he handed it over eventually."

I wasn't surprised.

"So now you know where he lives," I said.

"That's right."

"And he knows you know."

"Yeah."

"What are you going to do with the license?"

"What license?"

Tony held up his hand, which was now empty. Maybe he was evolving after all, if only as a conjurer. As I prepared to move past him, he said: "I'd leave him be. He needs some time alone."

"Why?"

"To stop crying."

I held Tony's gaze.

"You're sure you just talked to him?"

Tony broke eye contact first.

"After I got his attention," he said. "By dislocating a finger."

I patted Tony on the shoulder. It was still progress, and progress was to be applauded.

"He has others," I said, and together we returned to the bar.

CHAPTER

IV

The men's names were Roger Teal and Edward Kenney. They were in their midforties and had known each other since adolescence. Both had grown up in Macwahoc, not far from Maine's border with New Brunswick, although Teal was born in New Hampshire and moved to Macwahoc following his parents' divorce, when his mother returned there to live with her parents. He had gone on to become a public servant, marry, and have a daughter, only the first of which brought him much happiness, and then more outside the office than in. Sometimes it wasn't what you did, but who you met while you were doing it.

Teal lived in West Sodriner, while Kenney resided farther north, in a suburb of Bangor, and ran a garden-supply company in Orono. Like Teal, Kenney was married, with a son and daughter. Unlike Teal, he was a contented man. From time to time, Kenney and Teal crossed paths in Maine, but rarely for longer than it took to exchange a few words in a parking lot or over a quick coffee. Theirs was not that kind of relationship, publicly at least. But once every three years, they would meet in a city or town outside the state, the arrangements made months in advance over burner phones. They never stayed at the same hotel and socialized in bars and restaurants where little attention would be paid to them and cash remained king. There they would eat, drink, and plan for the Game.

Teal was an averagely handsome man, Kenney less so; he had "gone to seed" both vocationally and physically, one might have said. He was a reader, and always had been, while Teal had only a passing interest in books beyond the odd business or educational text. On the out-of-state trips, Kenney enjoyed visiting art galleries and museums. Teal preferred to shop for clothes or, if bored, watch movies in his room. Their conversation was general, and in bars they would often end up sitting in semi-companionable silence, especially if there was sports on TV, because they shared that interest. They differed on tennis, which Teal liked to watch and play but which Kenney regarded as deeply tedious, and golf, on which their positions were reversed. However, these remained small points of contention, and sporting events were their preferred choice of cover, as on this occasion: Pistons versus Celtics at the Little Caesars Arena, in Detroit, Michigan.

Before each out-of-state reunion, one of the men would take responsibility for a reconnaissance visit, even if the location was one with which both were already familiar, because it was important to be cognizant of any changes to the terrain: new security cameras, recent apartment developments, a basement transformed into a nightclub, or a parking lot become a favored spot for police cars to lurk. Often, the opportunity to explore a city's possibilities arose in the course of their day jobs: conferences for Teal, and research or buying trips for Kenney. The final member of their triad also assisted, when circumstances permitted.

But they only ever hunted in twos, not threes. That was the rule. It could be challenging. Fallow years were difficult for the one who was excluded, but it was a question of learning to control one's appetites. Kenney found that yoga helped. Teal popped Valium. The other, the third, immersed himself in his work. Alcohol was better avoided. It made men bitter and careless. That was a lesson hard learned.

Because they had once been four.

THAT YEAR, KENNEY HAD BEEN RESPONSIBLE for the bulk of the preparations, but he typically took care of them when his chance came around. Kenney had an eye for detail, and attention to detail was what kept them safe, allowing them to continue playing the Game. For example, when they'd started out, they sourced their vehicles from rental-car companies. Minivans were best, or SUVs, something with space, but now many of the big companies routinely fit their rentals with GPS, which meant the vehicle's movements could be tracked. The addition of GPS was a shame, because at busy locations the rental companies turned their vehicles around fast, which meant they were cleaned inside and out within a matter of hours, wholly eliminating DNA evidence or contaminating whatever remained after the players had scrubbed it down. Smaller rental companies didn't use GPS as much, but the downside was that the renter was more likely to be remembered, and the players didn't want to be remembered at all.

Kenney's latest solution was for one of them to purchase, with cash, a used car during the initial scouting trip and pay to store it until it was needed. Craigslist was their source at first, later superseded by Facebook Marketplace, though they still had to be circumspect. It was difficult to buy a vehicle with fake ID and insurance, so they did their homework and picked the sellers who were most desperate. They always opted for popular models because it made the next part easier, the part in which Kenney was engaged on that particular evening. He was driving a Toyota Camry, consistently one of the bestselling cars in the United States. This one was a 2012, but Kenney had flown in a few days earlier to give it a new paint job, so that if someone didn't know their vehicles, they might have mistaken it for a more recent model. It bore an out-of-state (and out-of-date) dealer plate, but Kenney was diligent about keeping to minor roads, so the chances of it being spotted by a license plate–reader were small.

He drove to the Twelve Oaks Mall in Novi, where he prowled the lot until he found a similar Camry over by Nordstrom. He parked alongside and switched the license plates before striking the rear bumper of the other car hard with a hammer, denting it where the plate should have been. With luck, if the absence was noted, the driver would assume it had fallen off following a collision and would not immediately report the plate as stolen. Kenney and Teal had once come close to being caught in Indianapolis, when the owner of a Taurus noticed that their plate was missing, as someone nearby must have heard her talking and connected the theft to a man seen kneeling by the car moments earlier. Mall security arrived so quickly that Kenney and Teal could see the gumball lights in their rearview mirror as they drove off. They'd been forced to abandon the car in a Walmart lot before splitting up, and the Game was postponed; Kenney didn't think he'd managed to breathe properly again until he was safely back in his bed in Maine. That was a few years before COVID, which was a hard time for them, throwing the rotation into disarray. It was now back on track, but the enforced hiatus had caused disagreements when they spoke about resuming, since it meant one of them would have to endure a longer gap. In the end, Teal bowed out, but more from necessity than goodwill owing to a brush with prostate cancer.

The clock was ticking as Kenney drove away from Twelve Oaks. Should the owner of the other Camry spot the missing plate, they'd have to go to the DMV to replace it, and they'd have to report a possible theft to the police in case the plate was used in the commission of a crime. The cops would add the missing plate to a hot-sheet, which meant that plate readers and cameras would respond if it was spotted. Kenney and Teal probably had until the following morning to play the Game, at which point the stolen plate would be more of a hindrance than a help. In that case, common sense would dictate that they should walk away and try again at a later date, but deferred pleasures were for the young. The older a man got, and the more aware he was of his mortality, the more he came to realize that pleasure deferred would soon be pleasure denied.

In the early years, the players preferred to target prostitutes and junkies, because bottom-dwellers were easy marks and wouldn't be missed. A combination of factors, not least hookers seeking proof of ID before meeting, or electing to visit and work only out of hotels, led them to change their tactics. If they were desperate, they might still resort to a streetwalker, a drunk, or an addict—better something than nothing—but the thrill of the chase had a part to play, as well as the quality of the flesh. Their tastes had developed, and they now preferred unspoiled meat—not literally, they weren't cannibals—but "unspoiled" meaning women whose bodies hadn't yet slipped. As far as Kenney was concerned, the best ever was a freshman who Mike Hurvich—the late Mike Hurvich, back when they were still four—had spotted throwing up in an alley in Austin, Texas. She'd become separated from her friends and could barely stand without a wall to support her, so it was the work of a moment to get her in the back of the minivan. She scarcely struggled, and stopped doing even that when they assured her they were going to take her home. By then Kenney was going through her pocketbook to find her ID—and her smartphone, which he destroyed, because gone were the days when batteries were easy to remove. The girl was just nineteen and very clean. Kenney and Hurvich had a lot of fun with her. They made her last.

When they were done, they tossed a coin and Kenney lost, which meant Hurvich got to finish her off while Kenney held her feet. They then laid her on a sheet of plastic and scrubbed her from head to toe with bleach before burying her, after which they went over the interior of the van with handheld vacuums followed by more bleach, heavily diluted. Kenney always found that part a downer. In an ideal world, they'd have let someone else take care of the detailing, or hand it back to the rental company to be sanitized, but this world was far from ideal, as multiple women had learned to their cost at the players' hands. The reason they'd been able to keep playing was because they were careful and stuck to the rules: Only Out-of-State Games. One Fallow Year in Three for Every Player. Restricted Contact Immediately After. Clean As You Go.

And No Extracurricular Activities. That was the big one. You had to learn to control your urges. No escalations. You lived off the memories until your turn came round again. It wasn't easy, and some of the men found it harder than others, like Mike Hurvich. He'd made two mistakes: He'd killed a girl outside of the Game, which was the first, then admitted what he'd done, which was the second. Hurvich's car was discovered up by Presque Isle, far from his home in Greenville, but his body was never located, and only Kenney knew for certain where it was buried. As a token of gratitude, Teal and the Saint drew straws, the Saint lost, and Kenney took his spot that year. Ever since, they'd been three. Kenney liked it that way, Teal too. But the Saint—

The Saint was wavering.

CHAPTER

V

At the Bear, I waited for Moxie to finish his drink. Together we watched Finger Man return to his table, collect his jacket, and pay the tab. He used his left hand for everything, kept his right hand close to his chest. His face was pale; having a finger dislocated is painful, and Tony would have opted for strength over precision. The woman was gone. So, too, were the Fulcis. The woman had left with them not long after Tony had a quiet word with her.

"Does Tony do that a lot?" Moxie asked. "You know, help damsels in distress?"

"He usually does kittens in trees, but the damsels-in-distress guy called in sick today."

"Interfering in domestic disputes is risky," said Moxie.

"It worked out this time."

"Unless she goes back to him, in which case he'll take his misery out on her. Does that count as helping or hindering?"

"I don't want to think too hard about it."

"You might have more in common with the Fulcis than you'd like to admit."

"I don't mind admitting it."

Moxie picked up his coat.

"If Spero is implicated in the death of Scott Theriault," he said, "feel free to set the Fulcis loose on the place."

"I can try, but I should warn you: Tony is evolving as a human being."

"Says who?"

"Says Tony."

Moxie pondered.

"What does that mean in real terms? Does he now use tools?"

"I'm just saying that you might need to spring for a couple of sledgehammers," I replied.

"I have an account at Maine Hardware," said Moxie. "Tell them to spare no expense."

CHAPTER

VI

In Detroit, Teal was staying in one of the chain hotels over by the Riverwalk while Kenney was in an Airbnb in Hamtramck. Kenney liked Airbnbs, especially the crappy, midlevel ones: clean, but not fastidiously so, in buildings that were secure but didn't have cameras. Before Airbnb came along, one of the players would always stay in a motel, preferably a mom-and-pop operation where you could park your car directly outside your door and didn't have to enter via a lobby, but those places were thinner on the ground than in the past. It was, Kenney reflected, as though the country was set on taking anything individual or quirky and throwing it under the corporate bus. It was the Starbuckization of America. And, okay, Airbnb was a big business and played hell with the residential nature of cities, but it wasn't like the company was branding the exteriors of buildings. The places on offer still resembled homes, and Kenney, Teal, and the Saint were scrupulous about leaving them in the condition in which they'd found them, and frequently even tidier. A degree of self-interest was obviously involved, but it was also a question of being respectful of the property of others.

THEY TOOK THE WOMAN NEAR FISHKORN. They'd had to drive around for a while to find her, which was always hazardous, but the police didn't spend any more time in Fishkorn than they had to. Fishkorn was up there with Belmont, Von Steuben, and Petosky-Otsego as an area better avoided in Detroit, but Kenney had nixed Belmont and P-O because of the gangs, same with Greensbriar and Franklin Park. Teal was sure Fishkorn had gangs too—it had drugs, which traditionally meant gangs—but Kenney was insistent, and Teal went along because Kenney hadn't yet steered them wrong. Also, Teal liked Black girls, and Fishkorn was about as Black a community as a man could find without relocating to Africa. The problem, of course, was that Kenney and Teal were white, and two white guys in a car in Fishkorn screamed "police," but Kenney had gotten around that by removing the bulbs from the interior lights and adding a tint to the Camry's windows. The tint was a far-from-perfect job, most noticeably at the rear, which was all creases and bubbles, but it would suffice. Shortly before they reached Fishkorn, Teal got in the back of the Camry and lay down flat, so now it was just one guy in a murky car, and as far as any inquisitive residents of Fishkorn were concerned, he was probably trying to buy or sell something, even if that something was trouble. But nobody paid the Camry much attention at all, since folks in Fishkorn were too busy making trouble of their own, avoiding it, or simply being poor.

Kenney had done his homework, as expected, so they bypassed the stretch of West Warren between Greenfield and Wyoming, as that had a bunch of Middle Eastern joints and those people had a way of looking out for their own. They concentrated on the blocks around Fishkorn itself, which was where they spotted the woman walking west along Joy Road. When she turned down Freeland, she was theirs. Kenney pulled over—not too close or too fast—rolled down his window, and said he was lost, looking for the White Castle. He made no attempt to open the door and went out of his way not to alarm the woman, who was in her late twenties or early thirties; bigger than Teal preferred, though the color was right. By the time Kenney rolled to a stop, Teal had the rear door unlocked, and when the woman turned to point back toward Greenfield and the White Castle, Teal was on her.

In the past they'd used chloroform, but it wasn't like in the movies where someone has a pad pressed against their face and seconds later they're out. Two of the previous women had struggled, one of them like her life depended on it, which it had, and Teal took a bad blow to the cheek that was a bitch to explain to his wife when he returned home. After that, they'd pivoted to a gun or knife, the only difficulty being that some women froze at the sight of a weapon, which meant a delay in getting them into the car. But Teal now used a more direct approach, and as the target became aware of him, he hit her hard with a blackjack at the base of the skull, then one more time on the same spot to be sure. Even as she was falling, Teal was using her momentum to steer her into the back of the car, and once she was lying on the floor, he climbed in on top of her and closed the door. Only then did he apply the chloroform, but not before Kenney had rolled down all the windows, since chloroform didn't make distinctions between attackers and victims at close quarters.

"All set," he told Kenney.

Twenty seconds, give or take. They were getting very good at it. But then, they'd had plenty of practice.

CHAPTER
VII

The Airbnb came with a parking space in a basement garage, which was another reason Kenney had selected it. There was also a bellman's cart, which was an added bonus. From the trunk of the Camry, Kenney removed an open XXXXL wheeled canvas duffel bag, fifty-six inches long and twenty-seven inches high. He placed the bag on the cart and wheeled it to the back door of the Camry, and he and Teal folded the unconscious woman into it before zipping it half-closed—it wouldn't close any further because of her size—and draping a coat over the gap. By then Teal had taped her mouth and bound her hands and feet with cable ties, but they still needed to move quickly because the last thing they wanted was for the bag to begin making noise while someone was passing them in the hallway. Kenney added a suitcase for appearances' sake, and he and Teal maneuvered the cart into the elevator. Fortune was smiling on them, if not the woman: the elevator went straight to the top floor, no stops, and they encountered neither persons nor problems as they ran the cart into the apartment and closed the door behind them.

The apartment had two bedrooms, one of which Kenney was using. He had stripped the sheets from the bed in the other room and replaced them with a cheap set from Marshalls. More sheets were laid on the floor; sheets felt more comfortable underfoot than plastic, which was too functional for the first stage, though Kenney had put down plastic in the master bathroom, where they would wash the woman once they were done with her.

Kenney and Teal removed her from the bag and laid her on the bed. She was moaning against the gag, so Teal gave her another blast of chloroform while Kenney returned the bellman's cart to the basement. He didn't want anyone knocking on their door to find out if they had it, which would spoil the mood.

By the time Kenney returned, Teal was removing her clothes. Because they weren't yet ready to untie her, Teal used a box cutter, being careful not to wound her. Finally, when she was naked, they bound her arms and legs to the bed. Only when they were satisfied she was secured, and each had double-checked the other's work, did they strip. There was no awkwardness about it, not any longer.

"Go ahead," said Kenney. "I went first last time."

Teal didn't argue. Only a fool would.

IT WAS AFTER THREE A.M. when they finished and the woman was dead. Both men were tired, and it was tempting to sleep, even if for a few hours, but there was a process to be followed: *If we don't take care of ourselves, the law will take care of us*, as the Saint liked to say. They put on gloves and disposable aprons, tied nets around their hair, and cleaned the body thoroughly before triple-wrapping it in black garbage bags, which they sealed with tape at each stage. They returned the body to the duffel and removed the sheets from the bed and floor, folding each carefully inward so it formed a neat square, before sliding them into more fresh garbage bags. The following day, Kenney would take the sheets to a twenty-four-hour laundromat near Chandler Park, where he'd wash them himself before dumping them.

Only when all this had been accomplished did each man shower, both careful to remove any stray hairs from the drain protector afterward. Kenney finished first and retrieved the bellman's cart. They placed the duffel on the cart—a body always felt heavier dead than alive, which Kenney never understood—and rolled it to the basement. As a precaution, Kenney had oiled the wheels earlier, but he needn't have bothered because the other residents were either also Airbnbers or had grown used to visitors arriving and departing at odd hours. While it was still dark, they drove out of the garage. On a printed map, Kenney had marked the locations of several dumpsters, of which there was no shortage in Detroit and especially not in Hamtramck, which was also the location of the Metropolitan Transfer Center for garbage collection and transport.

This was the most fraught part of the operation, even more so than the abduction itself, because the victim was now dead, and there was a big difference between being charged with attempted abduction and being charged with murder. They found a big yellow dumpster over by French Road, but for some reason there were people milling about, even at that early hour, and as they drove away, they saw one of the crowd begin a deep dive. Teal declared it a good omen and Kenney chose to believe him. Finally, they came to a black dumpster full of construction waste, just north of I-94. They parked, Kenney hit the trunk-release button, and within seconds the bag was in the dumpster. Teal even had time to rearrange some of the detritus to cover it up. Kenney then swung by the Riverwalk to drop Teal near his hotel before returning to the Airbnb where, at last, he slept.

But not immediately. He'd thought about sharing what was on his mind while they were driving back from dumping the body, but Teal was fractious. He was always that way once the Game was over, just as Kenney got sad, but Teal was more quarrelsome than usual. It might have been because, while Kenney would have another turn next year, Teal wouldn't get to play for two years. As for Kenney, his melancholy was a product of a sense of anticlimax, made worse by the cleanup. He liked to fantasize about someone taking care of the bodies for them, but that was the preserve of wealthy Saudi sheikhs who could afford to pay to have journalists dismembered. Ordinary folks were forced to do the grunt work themselves.

He'd have to speak with Teal eventually, though. It would involve bending the rules, as once they were done with a girl they weren't supposed to see each other again in that city, but Kenney regarded it as forgivable for once. There were minor breaches and major breaches, but one rule was sacrosanct: No Extracurricular Activities, and that rule, Kenney feared, had been broken once again.

CHAPTER

VIII

Before visiting Ward Vose at Maine State Prison, I performed due diligence on the circumstances of his son's death, aided by a file from Allen Atwood Alcock and the coverage of the case in the *Maine Sunday Telegram* and elsewhere. I also steeled myself to trawl social media and a couple of local news websites that flirted with disreputability, even going so far as to read the comments under their takes on the drowning, which was like wading through raw sewage inhabited by lower forms of life. Some of the input came from people who were, or claimed to be, former students-cum-inmates of Spero School. I made a note of their names, though at least one had already been called out as a fantasist. The majority had nothing particularly terrible to say about Spero, and one or two even said it had helped them straighten out their lives. Only one user, Domenure2627, was explicitly hostile, stating that staff had not intervened to prevent him from being bullied, physically and psychologically, by fellow students. Perhaps unsurprisingly, his allegations resulted in a pile-on, leading Domenure2627 to be bullied anew, after which he ceased to post. Still, I added his username to the list of people to talk to before returning to the main business of Scott Theriault.

Scott was born during one of his father's earliest stints in prison, this one in the Northern State Correctional Facility in Newport, Vermont. All of Ward Vose's prison time had been served in the Northeast, and he could have produced a comprehensive guide to the regional penal system had he put his mind to it. Because Vose eschewed violence, and Maine and New Hampshire didn't have three-strike laws, he'd managed to avoid punitive sentences but had fallen foul of Maine's habitual-offender driving law having, at various points over a five-year period, eluded an officer, passed a roadblock, driven to endanger, and operated after revocation. That he was arrested for the last of these while attempting to reach his son, who had broken out of Spero for the second time in as many weeks and contacted his father for help, cut no ice with the judge, which was why Vose was languishing in MSP.

Scott's mother, Hailee Theriault, was just twenty when Scott was born, while Vose was six years older. The photographs of Hailee in Alcock's file showed a redhead with a sprinter's build and a face too hard to be pretty but interesting enough to be beautiful. She hadn't changed much over the years and was now married to a successful realtor and state senator named Jerry Rakestraw who had an eye on a run for Congress in Maine's Second District. The Second District, which encompassed more than 90 percent of the state, was overwhelmingly white, rural, and conservative, and it would be interesting to see how Rakestraw chose to frame the death of his stepson in light of his political ambitions. He was a natural politician, which wasn't necessarily a compliment. He was doing his utmost to cling to the center, alienating neither the right nor the left, which meant the committed on both sides were suspicious while the waverers saw him as one of their own. Then again, Maine was a difficult state in which to campaign, and what appealed to the liberals in Portland and Augusta went down like the *Hindenburg* with the more conservative elements elsewhere. But those same rural voters were also prone to voting Democratic in congressional elections and Republican in presidential contests, with the governorship a coin toss. In Maine, Janus, the god of duality, was also the god of politics, so Rakestraw might have been onto something by straddling the fence, even if lately he'd begun pitching for the Fearful White Vote, since that was the way the wind was blowing.

Rakestraw married Hailee Theriault when Scott was nine years old, shortly before Rakestraw was first elected to the state senate. Hailee had since given birth to three children with Rakestraw, all much younger than their half sibling. In those early years, Rakestraw made a big deal of his family, including his stepson, and was rarely pictured without them. But slowly, Scott began to vanish from photographs, and by the time he reached his teens he wasn't to be found in any. I noted the absence but didn't rush to condemn. When I was a teenager, I had no desire to take my place in family photos either, which caused my mother and grandfather no small amount of frustration. Having a stepfather whose political career depended on demonstrating a commitment to family values would have placed a strain on any adolescent, never mind one as purportedly rebellious as Scott Theriault. Perhaps Rakestraw and his wife decided it was better to excuse him than have him spoil publicity opportunities. But even in those earlier photographs, Scott stood out from his half sisters for a reason other than his age and height: Ward Vose was the child of a Black woman and a white man, and his son's biracial heritage was apparent.

Already I had quite the list of people to approach if I agreed to take on the investigation: Scott's parents, Spero students past and present, the police, the chief medical examiner's office—and that was just to begin with. According to Alcock's paperwork, the Somerset County Sheriff's Office and the Maine State Police had done what was required of them, and maybe more. The medical examiner's report stated that Scott had alcohol in his system when he died. While the ME couldn't be precise, Scott's blood alcohol content would have been in the range of .10 to .15 percent, which meant his muscle coordination and reaction times were reduced and his reasoning and judgment impaired. A flask of bourbon had been stolen from the principal's office on the night Scott left the school, and the operating assumption was that he had taken it, along with food from the kitchen, to sustain him. So what we had was a teenage boy becoming intoxicated and disoriented in the woods, before falling and drowning.

I called Alcock and asked him to advise the OCME that I was acting on behalf of a client, namely Scott Theriault's father, and any assistance they might be able to provide would be appreciated. I had always found a succession of state medical examiners to be cooperative, but it never hurt to have a lawyer smooth the way. Alcock said he'd make the call immediately, but I gave him twenty minutes before following it up. I was put through to an assistant to the deputy chief medical examiner, who located a copy of the same report I had in front of me. After a little to-and-fro, he put me through to the new DCME herself. Her name was Asmara Saputri, and she was, as far as I knew, the first woman of Indonesian heritage to hold significant public office in the state of Maine. I'd met her only once, in passing. Even then, she'd looked at me in a concerned manner, for which she could hardly be blamed. I liked to think I'd earned my reputation.

"Mr. Parker," she said now. "Don't take this the wrong way, but a call from you immediately raises a red flag, or so my colleagues have warned me."

"I have nothing but respect for the OCME," I said. "Should anything terminal befall me, I can think of no better people to perform my autopsy."

"That's reassuring, and I promise we'll do our very best for you. This is about Scott Theriault? If so, I should begin by saying that I did not perform the autopsy. That was my predecessor, the late Dr. Tutin."

Humberto Tutin had died suddenly a few weeks earlier, from a heart attack, at the age of fifty-nine. Actually, it was his second heart attack, as the autopsy revealed. The first one was asymptomatic, so Tutin, unaware of the danger, had gone to play his usual weekly match at the Augusta Country Club and collapsed on the court. He was dead before the ambulance could reach him. Tales of asymptomatic heart attacks in someone's late fifties were not destined to make me sleep any more soundly at night.

I told Dr. Saputri that I understood, and my question related to the break in Scott Theriault's right leg.

"What about it?"

"It was very clean," I said.

"Yes, a broken tibia. A person might not notice a hairline fracture of the tibia for a while, but Scott Theriault would have struggled to walk unsupported with that kind of injury."

"If I'm interpreting the autopsy report correctly, Dr. Tutin suggested the force was vertical and down."

"I see that."

"Could a fall really have caused it?" I asked.

"It depends on the fall: if the leg became trapped, for instance, and the momentum carried the victim forward. But off the top of my head, that type of fracture is more common following an impact or a collision. I've seen it on the football field following a bad tackle."

"You mean a boot landing on a shin?"

"Yes, just that," said Saputri. "But in this case, Dr. Tutin identified irregular abrasions on the skin. His opinion was that the blow came from a rock or stone, a large one. Scott Theriault might have slipped, dislodging debris, some of which impacted on his lower right leg."

"Unlucky for him."

"Very."

"Could it have been done deliberately?"

The pause that followed went on so long that I wondered if the line had gone dead.

"It's possible," said Saputri, "but I would be unwilling to go further."

"As was Tutin."

"I believe he was even more cautious about such matters than I am. I see no reason to contest the conclusion of accidental death. Do you have any evidence to suggest the injury might have been inflicted purposely?"

"None," I said.

"Then why do you ask?"

"It's what I do. If I didn't, I'd be forced to find a real job."

"That would be a bad thing, right?"

"It would be terrible. I'd have to set an alarm for the mornings."

"It's been interesting talking to you, Mr. Parker."

"And to you, Dr. Saputri. Good luck in your new role."

"And good luck with avoiding the autopsy table," she said.

Which was kind of her.

THE SITUATION WITH SCOTT THERIAULT was complicated by the fact that his death wasn't the only recent incident in the Kennebec Valley to occupy police time and the public imagination. A nineteen-year-old Bingham girl named Mallory Norton had gone missing shortly before the discovery of Scott's body, and had yet to be found.

It was in the nature of crime in the internet age that social media commentators, podcasters, and all manner of prurient observers now waded into criminal investigations, muddying the waters. Police appeals for information, always crucial to inquiries, drew more attention than before, not all of it helpful. I doubted harried detectives would welcome me also sticking my nose in their case, but that wasn't any reason not to do it.

While I was at my desk, I reached out to both the Maine State Police and the Somerset County Sheriff's Office. Neither had anything more to add to the file on Scott Theriault, and when I brought up Mallory Norton's name, I was told to mind my own business. But because I'm nothing if not obdurate, I called in a favor, which I might as well have left untouched. I learned only that Mallory's phone had not turned up, and that it had ceased sending out a signal somewhere between The Forks and West Forks on the night she went missing. The phone records were subsequently accessed with a warrant, including all calls and texts. The MSP found nothing in them to indicate that Scott Theriault's death and Mallory Norton's disappearance were connected, but they were "keeping an open mind," which was police-speak for a *dead end*, even if it hadn't stopped some of the internet sleuths from yoking one case to the other. It made for a better story, and story was all. Either way, nobody expected Mallory Norton to be found alive.

CHAPTER

IX

Roger Teal wasn't in his room when Edward Kenney dropped by the hotel shortly after ten a.m., but neither had he checked out. Kenney left a message in a sealed envelope suggesting they meet at the Lager House on Michigan Avenue at two p.m., though Kenney added that he'd be there from earlier in the afternoon. He hoped Teal would realize it had to be important if Kenney, the most vigilant of all of them—and a stickler for the rules, as Mike Hurvich had learned in his final moments—was prepared to breach protocol in this way.

The Lager House had been around since Prohibition, during which it operated as a speakeasy under cover of a furniture outlet. By night it was a loud music joint, but it was quieter during the day and the beer was about the cheapest Kenney had ever come across in a major city. At two dollars for a can of Hamm's, a man could get a decent buzz on for ten bucks and be close to incapacitated for twenty. But someone would have had to put a gun to Kenney's head to make him drink more than one can of Hamm's, let alone ten, so he ordered a Blue Moon and nursed it while watching YouTube and X videos on his phone and thinking about Nola Maddick, the woman from the previous night. In between watching footage of car chases and bar fights, Kenney browsed a few news websites, including the *Detroit Free Press*, *Bridge Michigan*, and *MLive*, but there was nothing yet about a missing Black woman.

The twenty-four and forty-eight-hour period before a person being officially acknowledged as missing was only so much baloney for TV shows and movies. Normally, any delay was due to friends or relatives assuming the subject would show up with a hangover or bedhead, looking either sick or sheepish; that, or they didn't give a rat's ass about the person one way or the other, unless they owed them money. Kenney hoped the latter would be true of Nola Maddick. They'd found nothing in her pocketbook but $23.92 in small bills and change, a driver's license, a receipt for cheap clothing at Nice Price on Greenfield Road, one of a chain of local discount stores, and another receipt for even cheaper food at the Ever Fresh Market in Dearborn. The driver's license gave her address as Dearborn, so she'd been out of her home territory when Kenney and Teal picked her up. She might have had a boyfriend or girlfriend close to the center of town, Kenney thought, or she could have been a hooker, as her body was more worn than he'd expected. Oddly, the pocketbook hadn't contained car keys, so however Maddick managed to get to Fishkorn from Dearborn, it wasn't in her own vehicle.

All things considered, Kenney was inclined to take a positive view, especially with no car to link Maddick to the area from which they'd snatched her. The Game had been played as close to textbook as they could manage. Like any sport, the Game involved an element of chance, and three or four times the players had been forced to leave a city unfulfilled, at which point the options were to reschedule or let the Game go for that year. Nobody had ever yet gone for the second choice, the risks associated with trying again only adding to the pleasure.

But one or two facets of the night's events nagged at Kenney. Until they'd really gotten into it, and the blood had begun to flow, his impression was that Maddick was more angry than frightened. She had a core of steel to her that took the two men time to break. Also, on reflection, *worn* wasn't the right word to describe her. Rather, she might have been older than her license indicated, which meant it could have been fake. She was muscular, too; well built for her height, but not fat.

Kenney was distracted by Teal's arrival. Teal looked weary; his exertions had caught up with him. Kenney wondered where he'd been earlier. He'd hardly gone sightseeing. The center of Detroit might have been undergoing a kind of renaissance, but that revival was progressive, and starting from a low mark.

Teal slumped into the chair opposite Kenney and ordered a Foggy Geezer, a fancy IPA in a can. The music in the background was set at the perfect volume for Kenney's purpose: loud enough for them not to be overheard, but not so loud that they couldn't hear each other. Kenney waited while the server went to get Teal's drink. The can, when it arrived, was a nineteen-ounce monster, and the beer came in at 7.3 percent ABV.

"That's strong stuff," said Kenney. "I'd need a ride home after."

"I walked here," said Teal. "I wanted some air."

"You won't be walking back, or not in a straight line. I can drop you."

Teal didn't jump at the offer, and Kenney knew why. They'd seen enough of each other, in every sense of the word, after what they'd done to the woman. It was one thing to get caught up in the moment, but another to come down from it. Even after so many years, it was better to process the backwash alone.

"Why are we here?" asked Teal.

"I'm worried."

"About?"

"The Saint."

No proper names. Better safe than sorry.

"Why?"

"Something he let slip a week or so back."

Teal glanced around. For a moment, Kenney believed he was checking that they were unobserved until Teal signalled to their server. She was young, and wide at the hips and chest but narrow at the waist. Kenney briefly entertained an image of her struggling against him.

"How's the food here?" Teal asked her.

"It's good. You like Cajun?"

"No."

"Well, it's still good. Have the Butcher Burger."

"I'll take it with fries."

Teal raised an eyebrow at Kenney.

"You?"

"I'm not hungry," said Kenney.

Teal shrugged.

"I'm not sharing," he warned Kenney.

"You're not listening either," said Kenney once the server departed.

"Just get to the point. I want to eat, pick up my bag from the hotel, and be gone from here. I never liked the Midwest. It's too far from the sea." Teal lifted his beer again.

"Hey!"

Kenney spoke with an edge, compelling Teal to focus, however much he might have preferred not to. Kenney looked soft, and more than one man had mistakenly judged him to be an easy mark, but he was rock solid, and ruthless with it. Teal had witnessed that with his own eyes, as recently as the previous night. But Kenney's wife and kids adored him, which meant he was very good at keeping this other side of himself hidden.

"Yes," said Teal. "I hear you. You're worried. About what?"

"Scott Theriault. And Mallory Norton."

Now Kenney had Teal's attention.

"Theriault drowned."

"So they say. And the girl?"

"Still missing."

"She's the Saint's type. He likes them slim and dark."

Teal knew that was true. Kenney liked them soft, while the Saint preferred the bones to barely have skin on them. He said it made them easier to snap.

"It doesn't mean he took her."

"Hear me out," said Kenney.

Teal did. When Kenney was done, Teal said: "Were you planning on asking him straight?"

Kenney didn't reply, because the server had come back with silverware for Teal and a second set for Kenney, "should you change your mind."

Kenny glared at her.

"I said I wasn't fucking hungry."

The server took the second set away, but not before giving Kenney the old stink eye.

"Why did you have to make a big thing of it?" Teal asked.

"Because she, like you, didn't listen the first time."

"You're going to give yourself a stroke, you know that?"

"No, other people are going to give me a stroke, but only if I allow them."

Teal drank his IPA. Kenney swallowed the last of his Blue Moon. They said nothing more until the food arrived. This time, the server didn't even bother looking at Kenney and didn't inquire whether he wanted another beer. As it happened, Kenney wasn't in the mood for another drink, but it would have been polite of her to ask. It was also what she was being paid to do. Kenney had another flash of the server in pain. These were dangerous thoughts. If he wasn't careful, he'd end up breaking the cardinal rule, which brought him back to why they were here.

Teal tried a french fry.

"I asked if you were planning to confront him."

"Not yet," said Kenney. "Not until I know more."

Teal had thought as much. Kenney might have looked soft while being hard, but the Saint was a different creature. Cut him, and what spilled out would come with a biohazard symbol. It was why Teal preferred the years when he was partnered with Kenney, because Kenney was better at pretending to be normal.

"So what if he did take her?" Teal asked.

"If he hurt her, he's endangering all of us. That's why we keep to the rules."

"But as long as no one finds out—"

"That's a slender thread on which to hang our freedom," said Kenney. "Or our lives."

They had played the Game in multiple states, which meant they were gambling with federal penalties if caught. This, too, added zest. The higher the stakes, the greater the pleasure.

Teal dug into his burger. Kenney watched him eat, making no effort to hide his distaste. Kenney's concerns about the Saint had affected his sleep and his appetite, though he hadn't allowed them to cloud his enjoyment of the girl. Teal, on the other hand, gave every impression of being untroubled by what Kenney had just told him. For a shrewd man, Teal could be a disappointment.

But as it turned out, Teal was thinking while he ate: about Kenney and how much the sight of his naked doughy body repulsed him; about the Saint and how he liked to order Teal around when they played the Game together, like Teal was his bitch; and about his future, because as much as Teal enjoyed playing the Game, he was a calculating person.

He used a napkin to wipe ketchup from his chin and took another swallow of beer.

"If you're right," he said, "it can't be allowed to slide."

"My view exactly."

"*If* you're right," Teal emphasized.

But he was already sizing up the challenge of killing the Saint without blowback. It wasn't just about silencing the Saint but disappearing him. The Saint wasn't some nothing girl in a decayed Midwestern city. He wasn't even Mike Hurvich, a self-employed handyman and borderline alcoholic. The Saint had a public profile.

Kenney spotted the change in Teal—the brightness in his eyes and the set to his mouth. It was the way Teal had looked as he choked Nola Maddick to death with her scarf, choked her while he was inside her so that he orgasmed as she breathed her last.

"Tell me more," said Teal.

THEY PARTED AFTER AN HOUR. Teal made Kenney leave a generous tip for the waitress—in cash—but didn't bother asking him to apologize; the money would be worth more to her, and its sincerity couldn't be doubted. They agreed to speak again once they'd both had time to think.

Like Kenney, Teal was now of the opinion that the Saint might have killed a girl outside the Game, and not unaided, because the Saint had apparently suggested to Kenney that they should increase the number of players from three to four, as it had been in Hurvich's time. It would break up the pattern, the Saint argued. Kenney had responded that there was no pattern, or none that extended beyond a couple of years, to which the Saint replied: "We're the pattern. We've been playing as three for too long. We need a fourth."

Then the Saint told Kenney who he had in mind to be the new player, which was when Kenney realized that the Saint, if he'd killed the girl, hadn't acted alone. But Kenney didn't voice his suspicions, not then. He was now potentially dealing with not only a rule breaker but also an accomplice, and two against one was bad odds. Two against two was better, right? That was why Kenney had brought Teal into his confidence, because a confrontation was looming, one that might well end in violence.

CHAPTER

Angel offered to join me for the trip to Maine State Prison, which said a lot about how dull his day might otherwise have been. To be fair, I agreed to detour via Rockland, where Angel could kill a few hours at the Farnsworth Art Museum, which he liked, while I went on to Warren. Louis was in New York—I didn't ask what he was doing there, on the grounds that there were some things I was better off not knowing—while his partner elected to stay in Portland. These days, the two men spent more time in Maine than New York. Portland had grown on them, but they were also older, and the pace of life in New England suited them better.

Before we left, Angel asked me to take a photo for his passport renewal. I took four, none of which met with his approval.

"Do you have to make me look so old? How about moving back a little?"

"To make you look younger," I said, "I'd have to be in a different zip code."

"Just try."

"You need to be more than a distant figure in a landscape. It's supposed to be your passport photo, not something by Caspar David Friedrich."

I made a few more attempts, and he finally conceded that one of the dozen was acceptable.

"It still reminds me of a mug shot."

"That's bitter experience talking," I said. "But thanks to my efforts, it's now the mug shot of a marginally younger-looking man."

I let Angel take care of the music for the ride, and he picked a playlist of yacht rock put together by the musician Questlove as a tribute to the late chef Anthony Bourdain. Louis wouldn't have allowed us to listen to it—he'd have sooner walked to Rockland—so it felt like we were thumbing our noses at him. While I drove, we spoke of my daughter Sam, who had recently commenced studying criminal justice down in Lowell, Massachusetts. Ultimately, she hoped to become a private investigator, though it was possible that her studies might open her eyes to alternatives. Private investigation was a hard way to make a living—even if done right, when it was just tedious. I'd never figured out how to do it right, which was why I had so many scars.

"That guy really did a job on your nose," said Angel, who'd been checking out my profile since we passed Bath.

"Macy assures me it adds character to my features." Macy and I had been seeing each other for a while. (She hated her first name, and didn't have a middle name, so Macy she insisted on being, even with me.) I was in love with her, and thankfully, she felt the same about me, otherwise it would have been awkward. "And there I was thinking I had enough character to be getting along with."

"Nobody needs that much character," said Angel as we crossed Montsweag Brook. "You get any more characterful and you'll be dead."

Angel finished the apple he'd been eating, wrapped the core in paper, and placed it on the dashboard to dispose of later. Discards from cars drew animals to the road, and animals drawn to roads eventually ended up as roadkill.

"How's Sam doing down there among the great Massachusetts' unwashed?" Angel asked.

"Holding her own," I replied. "I wish anyone who crosses her the best of luck. Plus, Lowell's an okay town."

"Yeah?"

"It has a quilt museum."

"Be still my heart."

Angel was quiet again for a time, then: "And Jennifer?"

Ah. Jennifer was my first child, who had died with her mother back in the 1990s. Jennifer still came to me. This Angel knew, but rarely mentioned. When last I'd heard her voice, Jennifer was frightened.

i should have hidden myself better

i should have hidden us both

And through her eyes, I'd glimpsed what scared her so: It was an angel, but one immense, curious, and deeply, coldly destructive. I had not spoken of this to anyone, not even Macy. I did not know what it signified. I hoped only that the angel's gaze would pass on, and that a young girl waiting by a lake for her father to join her could hold no fascination or represent no threat. Even if I was wrong, what could I do? I could not intervene. Jennifer was a dead child in a dead land. But if the angel persuaded her to go with it, she would be lost to me. The prospect was unbearable, which was why I chose not to think or speak of it. For now, I believed her to be safe. If it came for Jennifer, I would know: I would hear her screams. Still, I wasn't sure why she stayed there, waiting. I knew it was for me, but not so we could enter the water together and be swallowed up like the rest. We had another purpose, one that remained concealed from me. I could not say the same for Jennifer.

Now here was Angel, speaking her name. We were in uncharted territory, he and I, but the time for mapping it had come.

"Why do you ask?"

Another silence from Angel. Finally: "Because I've seen her. She came to me, like she comes to you. She still does, right?"

"Yes," I admitted.

"Lately?"

"I've felt her close, but she hasn't spoken, not since the spring. March, I think. Yes, March."

I tried to say it lightly, though I could have given him the day, the hour, the minute.

"Last night," said Angel. "It was like a dream, but I wasn't sleeping. Does that make sense? I was on the cusp, so just about awake."

"That's how it happens," I said. "When it happens."

They were known as hypnagogic and hypnopompic apparitions, images glimpsed on the cusp of sleeping or waking, and were more common than many people realized.

"I couldn't see her face," said Angel. "It was hidden by her hair. I was glad of that."

Jennifer's face was a ruin. When she crossed over, she appeared as she was at the end of her life, after the Traveling Man had had his way with her. On the other side, by the water, she was different, unmarked.

"Why did she come to you?"

"Because she says you're in danger, but not from anyone on this side. The threat is coming from where she waits, or beyond it. She said you've been forgotten, but because of her, it may be that you'll be remembered again. She didn't think that would be positive for any of us."

"Us?"

"You and her, but also Louis and me. We're at risk too."

And this she had shared with Angel, even as—again—she held back more than she revealed. Why wouldn't she just disclose all of it? The secrecy was maddening, and might even have been mistaken for a child's game, except I thought I was beginning to understand: For the man in the water, the difference between a flow and a flood is the difference between swimming and drowning. The torrent of information had to be controlled.

"When last I saw her," I said, "she wasn't alone. Something was watching for her."

A phrase came to me: *full of eyes within*. It might have been from Revelation, but it was as apt a description as any for the being by the water. It was all eyes.

"When you say 'something'—?"

"I mean something not human," I continued, "and it meant Jennifer no good. It was trying to draw her from hiding. I saw the Traveling Man in it. I saw myself. I think it was ransacking Jennifer's memories and reflecting them back at her. She did her best to hide them, but even the fact that she felt the need for concealment would have disturbed it."

"Which means it'll return," said Angel. He touched a finger to the passenger-side window, as though seeking to reestablish contact with the world beyond only to find his way blocked by the unseen.

"Yes," I said, "in time."

"What is this?" Angel asked. "What are we part of?"

"I don't know, but Jennifer does."

"And she won't say."

"No."

"What could be so terrible that she can't bring herself to speak of it?"

I glimpsed a dam about to burst, the wall cracking, then exploding. I saw a man not only washed away by the resulting deluge but torn apart by the force of the water, and he was not alone. Two others were sinking with him.

"I'm sorry," I said to Angel. "I'm sorry that I've put you in danger again, even if this time, I can't be sure from what."

"Don't be. We made the choice. And—"

A truck rolled by, loaded with logs, but the trunks were mature, not young. Perhaps they'd become infected and needed to be cut down; old creatures, their antiquity to be revealed only in death, counted in rings.

"Go on."

"I think," said Angel, "that it's one we've made before."

CHAPTER

XI

In New York, Louis was sitting on a stool in PubKey on Washington Place. He was sipping an old-fashioned and taking in the décor, which reminded him of *The Shining*, though not necessarily in a bad way. The walls were painted black, the ceiling was made of pressed tin, and the floors, tiled in blue and white, were overlaid with rubber-backed red mats. Tinsel hung both behind the bar and on the wall opposite, which, combined with strings of fairy lights, gave the place an all-year festive atmosphere at odds with the interior, like Santa's grotto after the old man had died. The drinks list included a lot of beers in cans, and the available snacks ran to nuts, Ruffles, and fried Oreos.

PubKey was a dive bar, occupying a space that had once housed Formerly Crow's, also a dive bar, which itself had taken over from the Stoned Crow. (Three guesses as to the last one's nature, and the first would surely be correct.) So PubKey was maintaining a noble tradition of unpolishedness, even if it was a twenty-first-century version of the same: PubKey was Bitcoin-friendly, and Louis mistrusted money that didn't rustle or jangle. He had also reached an age where he firmly believed mankind needed to think long and hard before inventing new stuff, given how many people were still coming to grips with the old. And while Bitcoin held a certain fascination for a man like himself, one who preferred his financial arrangements to remain private, he was uncertain how one went about spending it. He was aware that it might involve a smartphone, which immediately ruled it out, Louis regarding "smartphone" as a misnomer, being of the opinion that the dumber someone was, the more they lived on their phone.

Finally, Louis feared that some of PubKey's regular clientele had either been bullied too much at school or hadn't been bullied enough. A Bitcoin bar inevitably attracted tech bros, and as far as Louis was concerned, the reputation of tech bros, never very good, had recently suffered near-terminal damage from the ongoing efforts of Mark Zuckerberg and Elon Musk. When he'd first scouted the bar, a seminar was underway in a large, curtained-off area at the back, with a mostly young male audience taking notes on financial instruments and the growth of AI. Curiously, Louis also identified a smattering of old West Village radicals who, in common with the rest, were seeking ways to protect themselves from regulation while sticking it to the Man. Louis failed to understand how you could stick it to the Man by investing in crypto when the Man, in the form of the president and his family, was trying to sell you on a crypto of his own. Ultimately, Louis concluded, it was all a hustle, and if you weren't hustling, you were getting hustled.

On this particular afternoon, PubKey was quiet, with half a dozen drinkers along the bar or occupying the stools by the wall. Louis was seated at the far end of the bar and had a clear view of the only door, accessed by a set of metal stairs, PubKey being not only a dive bar but a basement dive bar, which was another factor in its favor. Behind Louis, illuminated signs warned against "Central Bank Digital Currencies," while a ticker displayed the latest Bitcoin price. Otherwise, it was admirably murky. Louis didn't think he'd want to be there when it was jammed, but on a Wednesday, he was prepared to concede that PubKey held no small appeal for someone who was happiest in the shadows.

The door opened and a young Black man entered. He was wearing a tan jacket that hung loose over a white button-down shirt and blue jeans. His sneakers were new, expensive, and very clean, and he carried an iPad in his right hand. He ordered a beer, set the iPad on the counter, and peered around the bar as though seeing it for the first time. But he'd given the impression of knowing exactly where he was headed when he entered, and that tan jacket, while loose, wasn't loose enough to conceal the gun he wore on his left side from an expert eye, and if there was one thing Louis knew, it was guns. He doubted the kid was right-handed, because that would have left him with a cross-draw, and cross-drawing was a good way to get oneself killed. If Louis was correct about the kid's identity, he'd been warned to leave the minimum distance between gun and gun hand, just as Louis had once instructed his employer.

A striking older female bartender leaned against the well, keeping a bored eye on the patrons. When the kid raised a hand to order a Coke, she served him without speaking, and when he thanked her she merely nodded and smiled before returning to her station. The kid's gaze followed her; she caught him looking, and he quickly gave his attention to the iPad. Over his left shoulder, two Japanese men played a rapid-fire game of chess on a miniature travel set, each responding as soon as the other completed his move. The kid, who considered himself an accomplished forward thinker as well as a reasonable chess player, concluded that either of these men would have handed him his ass within a dozen moves.

A second female bartender joined the first, this one younger, blonder, and friendlier, and the kid forgot the game. The second bartender leaned over to wipe away a moisture ring, revealing an expanse of cleavage that the kid was sure would come between him and his sleep. Nevertheless, he did his best to concentrate on his screen. Nobody else ordered a drink, and the hum of conversation was low.

So Louis didn't watch the kid, and the kid didn't watch Louis, and no one else watched either of them. Time passed. Louis kept his hands on the bar, moving them only to lift his glass to his lips. He listened to the music, which was the *Genuine Negro Jig* album by the Carolina Chocolate Drops—arguably not what one would expect to hear playing in a Bitcoin bar, but if the incongruity registered with the kid, he didn't let it show. He was focused on his screen, scrolling through emails and, Louis assumed, communicating with whoever was waiting outside.

Finally, after a good fifteen minutes had gone by, the door opened again and another man entered, this one older than the kid by about a decade, which made him younger than Louis by thirty years—if Louis remembered correctly, which he did. His skin tone was very dark, so dark that Louis's appeared almost sallow by comparison in their reflections in the mirror. The new arrival was first-generation American, his mother and father Nuer, from South Sudan, both long dead. His name was Kade, which had Hebrew origins in war and battle and proved, if nothing else, that nominative determinism was alive and well. Kade, like the kid who had entered the bar ahead of him, was wearing a white shirt, but his was accessorized with a gray knit-silk tie. His black trousers were well cut, the whole finished off with a black wool-mix blazer, black brogues, and a pair of round, steel-rimmed glasses that he didn't need, fitted only with clear lenses. His left wrist bore a tasteful but not overly expensive watch—Tudor, not Rolex—and he had a wedding band on his ring finger, though he wasn't married. He looked like a prosperous businessman in his thirties, or a successful young lawyer who didn't have any court appearances scheduled that day.

Everything about Kade was designed to discourage police attention, which was undoubtedly a good thing, since somewhere on his person he would be carrying a weapon, possibly more than one. This Louis had taught him, even though he did not regard Kade as a protégé any more than Kade considered Louis a mentor. But once upon a time, when Kade was vulnerable and alone, Louis and Angel had taken him under their wing. He had lived with them for just four months, but in that short span, Mrs. Bondarchuk, who had occupied the apartment below theirs since time immemorial, grew fond of him and made a valiant effort to put flesh on his bones, one destined to be defeated by his metabolism. Even Mrs. Bondarchuk's Pomeranians, who didn't like anyone not named Mrs. Bondarchuk, had taken to Kade. Back then, he seemed gentle and lost. Now, he was no longer either; the US military, and what came after, had made sure of that. While Louis had not turned Kade into a killer, he wondered whether, by protecting him, he might not have contaminated him, because a killer Kade had become. Not one like Louis, never that, but a killer nonetheless.

A third man entered the bar, this one overweight, white, and carrying a copy of the *New York Post*. He took the stool nearest the door and ordered a soda. Like the kid with the iPad, and Kade, he kept his jacket on. Louis knew there would be at least one more man outside, behind the wheel of a car, with a view of the entrance. The engine wouldn't be running—because that, too, was a sure way to attract the police—but the driver would be primed to act fast. Kade, trying to minimize the risks. Kade, failing.

Kade took the stool two down from Louis, leaving one seat unoccupied between them. He ordered a glass of Scotch before turning to acknowledge the man he had come here to meet, even to kill.

"No Angel?"

"He's back in Portland," said Louis.

"I've never been."

"You wouldn't like it."

"Too quiet?"

"Too white."

Kade's whiskey arrived. He raised his glass to Louis, who did not respond in kind.

"Yet I hear you now call it home."

"We still keep the place here," said Louis, "but I've grown to appreciate life by the sea. It's been a long time, Kade. You're looking well."

"You too. The gray suits you."

Louis ran his left hand over his scalp. He kept his hair shaved close, but still, the years showed. Now and then, at Duane Reade, he dawdled a little too long by the men's hair-care products, tempted by the possibilities of gray-reducing shampoos. He felt the companies missed an opportunity by not putting more Black men on the packaging; it was all middle-aged white guys with shit-eating grins. However you chose to parse it, the message being communicated was that this was a white-guy solution for a white-guy problem. They might have believed Black men to be less vain. If so, they were leaving money lying on the table.

"If I let it grow too long," said Louis, "I look like one of those old barbers I remember from childhood, the ones who always smelled of Barbicide and bay rum."

Louis noticed that Kade flinched when he lifted his hand. The iPad kid farther along reacted too, and the dumpy white guy peered up from the newspaper he wasn't reading. There were a lot of nervous people in the bar that afternoon, more than anyone except Louis might have guessed.

"I shave my own scalp," said Kade. "I don't like strangers standing over me with sharp blades. Blunt ones either."

Louis tapped out a cadence with his fingertips.

"Why are you here, Kade? Why did you want to see me?"

This was it. This was the moment.

"Because there's a contract on your life," said Kade.

"And who picked up the paper?"

"I did." Kade gestured loosely with his glass. "How many of these people are yours?"

Louis raised the index finger on his right hand and brought it down once, sharply, on the bar.

"All of them," he said.

And it began.

CHAPTER

XII

In a woodland that did not truly exist, by a lake that did not exist either, stood Jennifer Parker. She inclined her head and listened, as though the sound of Louis's finger tapping on the bar had carried to her even here, crossing the barrier between the living and the dead as easily as Jennifer herself.

Beside her, the dead priest named Martin waited, unwilling to disturb her concentration. Jennifer Parker frightened him, and not without cause, but he had allied himself with her nonetheless, because a war was coming. He could have elected to do what so many of the dead did while he and Jennifer watched from the woods: enter the water that was not water, immersing themselves until, finally, it covered their heads and they were gone. It must have been soporific, he thought, since the dead did not struggle. Some even smiled at the last.

There was a time, not long after he'd arrived in that place, when Martin was tempted to join them. The water called to him. It promised peace, and an end to any recollection of human suffering. When, in life, Martin had spoken at the funerals of men and women going to their reward, this was a version of what he imagined. So why, then, had he chosen not to embrace it? That was a question to which he still struggled to find an answer. The best he could offer was doubt, the same doubt that had plagued him during his years as a priest. It was not uncertainty about the existence of God—indeed, when violent death finally came for him, Martin was given dramatic confirmation of the reality of transcendental evil in the world, and if such evil was real, so too was its opposite—but he had qualms about God's nature. As part of his vocation, Martin was witness to the terminal sufferings of many and struggled to provide any meaningful consolation to them beyond the possibility of a divine plan, the purpose of which would become apparent only once their agonies ceased. Then, at the time of his own death, he endured appalling pain, and though he pleaded with God for the torment to end, it did not end soon enough. So it was that when he took his place by the lake, he heard the summons of the water less as a guarantee of eternal tranquillity than as a siren call, and whatever it promised rang hollow to him. In common with a handful of others, he turned away. He had never encountered any of his fellow exiles again, but they were out there somewhere. Like Martin, they were waiting; like him, they had seen the young girl by the water; but unlike him, they feared her too much to approach. Here, Martin had the advantage. He knew who she was, because he had once met her father, and if the daughter was troubling, the father was terrifying.

"What did you hear?" Martin asked. "One of them?"

They had not glimpsed an angel since the last of the three—a destroyer, a killer—had come to the lake, seeking to draw from the woods the girl so intent on keeping her distance. She was seen as a disturbance, an anomaly, but so far, not a threat. Were they to construe her as such, they would arrive in force, and while they could not compel her to go with them—free will endured, right up to the moment the waters closed over one's head—they could, in sufficient numbers, work on her so that the line between compulsion and impulsion was blurred, and she would yield, if only to make the voices stop.

"No," said Jennifer. "I heard Louis."

She had lately been visiting her father's confederates, Martin knew, just as she visited her father. As a consequence, she was more aware of Angel and Louis than before. She was preparing the way, but it was a delicate affair. The machine was out of phase, and it was important that it remain so. Were it to be jarred inadvertently, it might return to true, and all their waiting, all her efforts, would be for nothing. What would happen then? Would there be a punishment? Would he—they—be damned? Martin thought not, but he saw himself being led to the water, subdued by the whispering of angels, there to drown.

"Is he in trouble?" Martin asked.

"Someone is."

find me. It wouldn't make the pain of parting any less, but it would make the years without him easier to bear."

He worried at his lower lip.

"Except," he continued, "I feel—as sure as I'm with you here, in this car, on this road—that I never had that sense of a hidden past before now, only the pain, because the pain was the purpose. And I think you were there too, just as you've always been there, but as a shadow, unformed. Then you stepped into the light."

He studied me warily.

"Is this madness?" he asked. "Because if it is, it's a madness I endure with Louis, and he'll corroborate everything I've told you. He's shared my thoughts and dreams, been visited by Jennifer, and reached the same conclusions. The question is: Do you also share this particular madness?"

I could not reply, not at first. When I did, it came as a release.

"Yes," I said, "I share it all."

CHAPTER

XIV

In PubKey, all was movement. The kid with the iPad reached across his body for his weapon (he definitely hadn't paid attention to his elders) only to find himself staring down the twin barrels of a sawed-off shotgun, said shotgun held close to the body of the blond bartender who had, only moments earlier, been asking him about the Haskell syntax decorating the cover of his iPad: the code for the Fibonacci sequence rendered as a single line—*fibs = 0:1:zipWith (+) fibs (tail fibs)*—when other computer languages might have required multiple lines to communicate the same information. The bartender had seemed genuinely interested as he explained all this to her. The kid, whose name was Amir, had even considered asking her on a date. Now here she was, brandishing a weapon that could potentially remove his head from his shoulders if her finger twitched too hard on the trigger—not that her finger showed any signs of twitching, because it, like the shotgun, was very still. If she pulled the trigger, it wouldn't be by accident, and if Amir forced her to kill him, she would have few regrets. Amir was now glad he hadn't asked her out. The humiliation of the refusal would only have compounded an already difficult and embarrassing state of affairs.

"I'm going to move my hand to the right," he said, "away from my gun."

His voice shook. He received the barest of nods in response. In the mirror, he saw two guns pointing at the man by the door, Ulyan, who hadn't even had time to put down his *New York Post* before he was disarmed. Amir had never regarded Ulyan highly and now had confirmation of that opinion; but then, Ulyan hadn't respected Amir either, so they were both right. Farther along the bar, Kade was motionless, as was Louis, but Louis was more relaxed than Kade because two Japanese men were not leveling pistols at him. This disappointed Amir almost as much as the attitude of the bartender, since he had always associated the Japanese with politeness. He had never seen a Japanese person holding a gun outside of a war movie.

Behind Amir, another of what he had mistaken for the bar's regular clients locked the door and extinguished the neon sign in the window. Finally, the music was turned off, leaving them all briefly in silence, broken by the ringing of a cell phone. The man who had locked the door answered the call, acknowledged whatever was said, then hung up and signaled to Louis. In the mirror, Amir could see the rest of the bar's clientele were also holding pistols of varying makes and calibers. Either the tech industry was even more cutthroat than rumor suggested or Kade had walked them into a trap.

The older bartender came from behind the bar to relieve Amir of his gun. She approached him from the left side, keeping clear of the sawed-off barrels, in case Amir decided to do something stupid that necessitated his decapitation.

"Are you left-handed?" the younger bartender asked him, though Amir supposed it should have been her dark-haired colleague who asked, since the latter was the one doing the disarming.

"No, right," said Amir.

"Then why wear your gun on the left side?"

Amir blushed.

"I don't know."

But he did: because he thought it was cool, despite Kade having stressed, on more than one occasion, that it wasn't.

"Dumb," said the woman.

"I did warn him," said Kade. He continued looking at Louis, one hand resting by his Scotch, the other held away from his body. "But these young people, they just don't listen."

"They might not listen any closer after today," said Louis. "You haven't covered yourself in glory here."

"I didn't expect you to take over the whole bar. I didn't even think it was your kind of place, though I should have guessed from the shitkicker music."

"Black shitkicker music."

"Whatever."

"Your loss. By the way, we took your boy outside too."

Kade frowned.

"Pity. I had higher hopes for him."

"At least he's still alive to learn from the experience," said Louis. "In lower company, he might not have been so lucky. Same goes for the two here. As for you, I can't say. You always were hard to call."

"I'll take that as a compliment."

"Take it how you like, I don't care."

Louis got up from his stool and took three steps back. "You can stand now. One of my friends will frisk you, though it would help everyone breathe easier if you were to point him in the right direction. It's polite to show you're willing."

Kade stood.

"Belt, right side," he said. "That's all."

"Seriously?"

One of the Japanese chess players removed the nine-millimeter Mossberg from Kade's gun belt and ejected the magazine and the round in the chamber. He proceeded to search Kade thoroughly, all while his opponent continued to target Kade's head. But Kade was telling the truth and no other weapon was discovered.

Louis resumed his seat and indicated that Kade should do the same.

"I didn't come here to kill you," said Kade, "despite what you might be thinking. Even if I had, one gun would have been enough for the job."

"Yet you came in here with backup and more on the street."

"Consider it an understandable excess of caution, given what's just gone down."

"An excess, after you picked up a paper with my name on it? There isn't enough caution in the world for that. Did you really think you were going to make bank on the deal?"

"No," said Kade. "I figured you'd hear."

"And still you picked it up."

"You haven't asked why."

"There can only be two reasons," said Louis. "One is poverty, and you don't dress poor."

"I'm not."

"Then give me reason number two."

"I picked it up so that no one else would."

Louis regarded him thoughtfully.

"You know it's true," said Kade.

"Do I?"

"If I were going to follow through on the contract, I'd have shot you in the head from behind, up close and intimate. You wouldn't have known a thing about it."

"Assuming you could get up close and intimate with me."

"I liked my chances."

And Louis thought Kade might have been right, but whether he could have followed through was debatable.

"It didn't sound like your scene," said Louis. "Last I heard, you were a contractor of a different stripe."

"I still am. I like government work. It pays surprisingly well."

"Depends on the government. The worse they are, the better they pay."

"I'm not greedy," said Kade. "And I have a conscience."

This had always differentiated Kade from Louis. The former's morality had barely flickered from the start, while the latter's only slowly incandesced.

"It's what confused me when your name came up," said Louis. "Worried me, too."

"Because you wondered what might have been bad enough to cause me to pick up the paper," said Kade.

"If I had to guess, I'd say it was from way back."

Louis had left wreckage in his wake—it came with the territory, and with Parker—but anyone clinging to that flotsam wouldn't have attracted Kade's interest, not for any sum. He'd have been more likely to stamp on their fingers and watch them sink. In the right hands, morality was a double-edged sword.

"Because now you have a conscience as well," said Kade.

"Don't believe everything you hear. I'm a work in progress."

Louis picked up his glass, tapped it to Kade's, and both men drank, Kade more deeply than Louis because his nerves required more steadying.

"Did you really believe I'd accept money to kill you?"

"I wasn't sure," said Louis.

In truth, he trusted only three men in the world. Two of those were in Maine, and the third was himself. As for Kade, Louis had been only a fleeting figure in his life, and while they had parted on good terms, people changed, particularly when money was involved, with the degree of change being proportionate to the amount of money on offer.

"I owe you a lot," said Kade.

"You don't," said Louis. "And even if that was true, not everyone pays their debts."

"After all this time, I still don't fully understand why you took me in—and the rest that you and Angel did, all that came after."

Funds: sufficient for Kade to hold his head up in company, but not enough to cloud it; a private education; guidance, when asked for or required; and discipline, when necessary. But Kade saw Louis just once or twice a year, if that, and Angel more seldom still. And recently, Kade had not seen them at all, but it did not mean that he forgot.

Meanwhile, Louis might have dismissed the intervention as a whim, or if this were a Hollywood movie, he could have said that in Kade he saw a reflection of himself as a boy, for they had orphandom in common. But while there was truth to both statements, neither was sufficient to explain Louis's motivation.

It was Parker. He crossed my path and I was altered—or awakened. Had he not, I would, without hesitation or regret, have left Kade to the dubious care of the state or the brutality of the streets. And I would have been less than I am now.

Kade adjusted his tie and said: "This place is very subdued without music."

"What was playing wasn't to your liking."

"It didn't mean I wanted to join a silent order."

Louis gestured to the blond bartender. Curiously, she had continued to keep Amir under her gun. Amir concluded that she might like making people nervous and unhappy, especially him. But at Louis's signal she lowered the sawed-off and stored it under the bar. The older, dark-haired woman joined her, Amir's pistol tucked in her belt. Louis touched his right ear, followed by a circular movement with his right index finger, directed roughly at the speakers on the wall. The older bartender's fingers moved rapidly in response.

"Do you want the same?" said the blonde, translating the sign language.

"Softer, please," Louis replied. He faced the dark-haired bartender as he spoke, so she could read his lips, and seconds later classical music began to play: Bach, one of the Cello Suites.

"How can she hear music if she's deaf?" Kade inquired.

"She can't, not unless it's got a lot of bass. But she can read a Spotify playlist."

"Who are those women? Because if they're really bartenders, I've misjudged the challenges of the trade."

"Friends," said Louis. "More or less."

He swirled his old-fashioned, drained the glass, and raised it for a refill.

"Was there a plan B?" Kade asked.

"You're looking at it. Plan A was to kill you before you even got here, all 'up close and personal,' as you put it, but I was minded to give you the benefit of the doubt. I'm glad you didn't disappoint me, beyond the ease of rendering you harmless."

"How long have you known?"

"About the paper? A week."

"And how long have you had me under surveillance?"

"A week."

"I didn't spot it."

"That's the point."

"Damn," said Kade. "I got to ask you for some phone numbers when we're done, because you got more contacts than Bausch and Lomb. I may need to start a new address book."

"You've been playing a different game for a while," said Louis. "Speaking of which, how was Ukraine?"

Louis's research had traced Kade most recently to the war in Europe.

"Dangerous, even as an advisor." Kade touched a finger to his cheek. "Skin like ours makes a man a prime target for drone operators."

Some soldiers from African nations were serving on the front lines of the conflict, but most were fighting for the Russians, either as mercenaries or trafficked conscripts. Americans—whether Black, like Kade, or otherwise—were drawn to the Ukrainians, as was anyone else with a shred of decency. As far as Louis was concerned, those who didn't side with the Ukrainians deserved to be introduced to the Russians in person.

"And I've crossed paths with racists in my time, but you haven't met a true racist until you've met a Russian one," Kade said.

Louis, too, had crossed paths with racists, but didn't regard the Russians as worse than the rest. Ignorance transcended racial boundaries; ironically, to have believed otherwise might have made him a racist.

"Tell me about the contract," he said.

"What do you know?"

"Only that someone put my name to a paper and you picked it up."

"There wasn't a lot of competition, but it was better not to take any chances."

"Price too high?"

"Too low: fear of blowback." Kade extended his arms to take in the bar and its occupants. "You were known to be protected, but that wasn't the only reason."

"Go on."

"I read the small print. I dug deep."

Opinions differed on the wisdom of investigating a contract. Some considered it unwise, others irrelevant. But early on, Louis had learned the value of establishing the identity of one's ultimate employer and the reason they wanted a life to be ended. When things went wrong—and in Louis's experience, they went wrong more often than they went right—it was crucial to have an inkling of where the danger might lie.

"And?"

"I put together a file," said Kade. "It's on Amir's iPad, but it doesn't amount to much. The point of origin is a Boston businessman named D. Francis Sturgis, the D standing for Dawson. He's fifty-eight, and distantly related to the Boston Brahmin Dawsons. He has property wealth, all inherited, and a reputation as a philanthropist: children's charities, pediatric hospitals. According to the broker, he was also open about why he wanted you killed, which might be another reason the paper was treated like it might ignite if touched."

"So why did D. Francis Sturgis put a price on my head?" asked Louis.

"Because," said Kade, "an angel told him to."

CHAPTER XV

By the lake, Jennifer Parker's shape shimmered, momentarily to vanish—Martin blinked, and she was present again—but time had passed, though nothing had changed. He knew only that she had left him briefly, and he wondered what could have drawn her so suddenly away.

"AN ANGEL?" SAID LOUIS.

"The broker figured Sturgis was demented," said Kade. "But funds were deposited in escrow, so his lunacy was the solvent kind, and no one who puts a price on another man's head is ever completely rational."

"Did Sturgis elaborate?"

"No, and the broker decided, or wanted to believe, that Sturgis might have been speaking euphemistically, which freed him from any impulse to investigate further. Brokers prefer not to ask too many questions. They live longer that way."

"Who was the broker?" Louis asked.

"I can't tell you that," said Kade. "Anyway, you haven't told me how you found out I'd picked up the paper."

"I got it from someone who declined the contract."

"And he didn't name the broker either?"

"You know how it is," said Louis.

These were professional courtesies. Nobody named names unless they had to, but Louis had hoped Kade might be more forthcoming.

"Yeah, I know how it is," said Kade, "which is why I'm not saying."

Louis reckoned it to be one of three brokers. Once he'd dealt with Sturgis, he'd send a warning. For now, the paper remained active, even if Kade claimed to have no intention of fulfilling the contract. Tackling Sturgis might nullify it, but that depended on the truth or otherwise of his claim. Louis didn't know how one went about discouraging an angel from seeking one's death, but he was sure it wouldn't be straightforward.

"What about Angel?" Louis asked. "My Angel," he added.

"The paper related only to you."

pain, said a child's voice from nearby. Louis spotted her in the shadows: a girl, a ruined girl.

the reason is pain

Jennifer Parker.

they want Angel to suffer, continued Jennifer, *because it's his turn*

Louis almost responded, so clear was her voice, only to catch himself just in time.

his turn to watch the man he loves die

Then she was gone.

"Are you okay?" Kade asked.

Louis continued to stare at the darkness for a second or two.

"Why wouldn't I be?"

"You went elsewhere just then."

"It's a lot to take in," said Louis. "A man I've never met wants me dead on the word of an angel."

"I won't say I've come across stranger reasons for a contract," said Kade, "but I've come across worse. You sure you've never heard of Sturgis before?"

"The name doesn't register, but I'll need to see that file on your boy's iPad to be certain."

"Just tell me where to send it."

"He can print it. The one here is AirPrint-compatible."

Even with end-to-end encryption, Louis wasn't about to ask that a file on a man he might have to kill be sent to an email address. He and Kade sat in something approaching companionable silence while Amir did what was required, and a few minutes later the blond bartender handed Louis a sheaf of five or six pages. Louis was halfway through the second page when he paused.

"Damn," he said.

"You start swearing like that," said Kade, "and I'm going to hyperventilate. Want to share?"

"Sturgis is a member of a club."

"He's a white guy with money," said Kade. "That's a big club all to itself."

"A physical club," said Louis. "In Boston."

"And why is that bad? Because I'm guessing it's not good."

But Louis didn't elaborate. He skimmed the remaining pages before folding them in half and placing them in the inside pocket of his jacket.

"What's the time frame?" he asked.

"The client's instructions were 'as soon as is practicable,' " Kade replied. "I'd say I can hold Sturgis and the broker off for a week or so. Is that enough?"

"All I need," said Louis. He extended a hand to Kade. "You really didn't owe me, but if you ever thought you did, we're square now."

"Call if I can be of help. I've learned that you already have friends, but a man can never have too many of those."

Louis prepared to slip by Kade, pausing to rest a hand meaningfully on the younger man's shoulder.

"Why don't you and your associates stay awhile?" said Louis. "Have another drink. It's on the house."

"And your friends will keep us company, right? You still don't trust me."

"I wouldn't want you to feel abandoned and unloved in a big city."

"I can see now why you've lived so long."

"Longer than you might think," said Louis.

BY THE LAKE, ALL WAS QUIET. The lake was always quiet. Even the water made no sound as it lapped the shore, and the dead had no voice. The woods, too, were forever silent. It had taken Martin a while to spot that no birds flew through them and no insects buzzed. But above the clouds that forever lowered, there was movement. What was it that had once been written on the unknown regions of maps? *Here be dragons.* Dragons, and worse.

Jennifer sat on the grass that wasn't grass. She broke off a stem that wasn't there and observed it not being.

"Is there a problem?" Martin asked.

"I think so," said Jennifer. "An action has been taken. Either the machine is trying to reset itself—"

"Or?" Martin pressed.

"Or someone is recalibrating it."

CHAPTER

XVI

At PubKey, the music changed from classical to math rock. The door was locked behind Louis and the fake clientele kept an eye on Kade and his people, but the mood was less tense than before. Amir noted, with mixed feelings, that the cute bartenders were no longer behind the bar. They had been replaced by a heavily tattooed man in his thirties who was not cute but, on the upside, showed no signs of wanting to point a shotgun at Amir's head, though the night was still young, as the saying went.

Amir hadn't known the older female bartender was deaf until she began signing. He wondered if she was mute as well, because for him the two went together, even as he suspected he was probably wrong. Had he asked her, she might have gone ahead and pulled the trigger on him, and to hell with the consequences. Now Amir saw her emerge from an anteroom containing stacked cases of beer and a spare cooler. She passed Amir without acknowledgment, and the door was briefly unlocked before closing behind her again. Amir, who tracked her in the mirror all the way, saw Louis waiting for her outside. Amir was very glad Louis was no longer in the bar. The more time he spent in Louis's vicinity, the more aware he was of his own mortality. He had underestimated Louis because of Louis's age. It was a fallacy of youth.

Amir put his iPad to sleep. He had not worked for Kade for very long and feared he wouldn't be working for him much longer. But he had learned a lot from his short time in the Bitcoin bar, not least the absolute inadvisability of a cross-body draw.

"I'm sorry," he told Kade, who had accepted another glass of whiskey from the new bartender, but had not otherwise spoken since Louis's departure.

"For what?"

"For being taken so easily."

Kade swiveled on the stool to regard him.

"Do you think we came here to get killed?" Kade asked. "If you'd drawn your gun, that's what would have happened."

"To be honest, I'm no longer sure why we came here."

"I'll tell you why: If we hadn't come, we'd be dead."

Amir thought about this. "Because Louis would have assumed you'd picked up the paper in earnest," he said.

"That's right."

"You could have called to tell him otherwise."

"That's not how it works. He had to be able to look me in the eye. More than that, he had to know I was willing to put myself at his mercy."

"What will he do now?"

"He'll talk to Sturgis, forcefully. After that, the paper will be rendered null and void, unless—"

Kade raised an eyebrow at Amir, inviting him to contribute.

"Unless Sturgis isn't crazy," said Amir. "Then whoever used him to front the contract might try again."

"You don't believe an angel told him to do it?" Kade asked.

"No," said Amir. He was about to smile, until he noticed that Kade was doubtful.

"Wait," said Amir, "do you?"

"You weren't looking at Louis when I told him," said Kade. "He thinks it's true."

Amir took longer to reply this time. When he did, it was to say: "So, is Louis crazy too, crazy like Sturgis?"

"No," said Kade, "Louis is not."

"Then where does that leave us?"

"It leaves us in the middle of something we don't understand."

Us.

"Does that mean I'm not being fired?"

Kade sipped his whiskey.

"You did almost everything wrong today, but so did I."

"Almost? What did I get right?"

"You survived."

OUTSIDE THE BAR, THREE MEN SAT in a black SUV, but only two gave any indication of enjoying themselves, the exception being Kade's driver. Louis didn't even look in their direction. He had eyes only for the deaf woman, whose name was Liat.

The rabbi wants to see you.

She mouthed the words soundlessly, and signed reflexively. As for the rabbi, his name was Epstein, and Liat served as his assistant and bodyguard. She was also, as Louis had lately learned, his adopted daughter, which explained the bond between them. However, Epstein never referred to Liat as his child, no more than she called him "father." It was better that their relationship remain secret. Were it to become widely known, it might make Epstein more vulnerable, and he already had enemies enough. They all had that much in common.

"When?" Louis asked.

Now.

And Louis, having nothing more to do than deal with a contract on his life, shrugged and said: "Sure."

CHAPTER XVII

We had reached Rockland, where I stopped the car on Main Street. Not everything of which Angel and I needed to speak could be dealt with before I left for MSP, but there was more I wanted to share with him while there was time, because our conversation—our shared realization—explained a glitch in my recollections that had long disturbed me.

"I have clear memories of my father striking my mother twice," I said to Angel, "but I'm also certain he hit her only once. The first memory had to do with a small fire in the kitchen, which I think I might have caused, but the circumstances are blurry. The second time, I am clear on. My mother's pocketbook was stolen in a restaurant by the people sitting behind us, and my father slapped her for what he viewed as her carelessness, even though, as a police officer, he should have known better.

"For years, I thought I must have invented one of the incidents, or conflated the first with the second, so that each ended with him hitting when, in reality, he only became physical on one occasion. Obviously, that doesn't make it any less wrong, but it was always confusing to me. I could see and hear the blows land, and they were different blows, while all the time I knew I could say, 'My father hit my mother once, just once' and be sure I wasn't lying. That was my small madness."

"But it wasn't a mistake, right?" said Angel. "Because they were different mothers and different fathers. Only the child was the same."

That was the final piece. Yes, I could see and hear the slaps; they echoed still. But the faces themselves were clouded, or had been until now. Like condensation wiped from a mirror or mist dispersed by a breeze, what was formerly ambiguous became apparent. The incident of the pocketbook was the more recent. I saw my father hit my mother, saw the redness rising on her cheek, and saw the shock on his face as he realized what he had done, a thing that could never be undone and because of which he would forever after always be less to her and less to himself. The slap following the fire was much earlier, in a kitchen smaller, humbler, and older than the one I remembered from Pearl River. The house was only vaguely familiar, as though it might have belonged to grandparents long dead, visited in my early childhood, or was known to me solely from photographs. And the man and the woman, the one striking, the other flinching, were less recognizable too, so that they also might have been figures from a family album, creatures of sepia and deckle edges. I couldn't recall their names or his occupation. I couldn't bring to mind the city or the town in which we lived, and whether I had brothers or sisters, but had I been forced to guess, I would have said that I was an only child, always an only child. My surviving memory of them was a single incident of violence, and I suspect that had resurfaced because history had rhymed a generation or two later, one blow echoing another.

If that memory was real but buried, how many more were interred beneath it? I pictured lives layered, like flakes of schist or shale, impossibly old and hidden from view, though one could mine them, breaking each stratum to release a cloud of musty, sealed air, a zephyr of remembrance and pain, because as those nameless parents retreated from me, so also did I retreat from them. There was hurt, so much hurt, more than anyone could bear; loss upon loss upon loss that I was not yet ready to face.

This is a honeycomb world. It hides a hollow heart.

It hides the truth.

CHAPTER XVIII

Edward Kenney was back in the bosom of his wife and two lovely children, and Roger Teal was in the company of his soon-to-be-ex-wife—the clock had been ticking on the marriage for a while—and the teenage daughter he wouldn't miss after the divorce came through, though he supposed he'd have to put up a fuss about visitation rights for appearances' sake.

Lying in bed at night, fantasizing about a future free of the weight of family, Teal would speculate on whether the Game was providing an outlet for his intense dislike of the two females in his life. Without the Game, he might already have murdered both of them, for which he could have blamed his feisty Mediterranean heritage. Teal's late Italian grandmother, *che riposi in pace*, once remarked that the historic referendum of 1974, in which Italians voted to retain a law legalizing divorce, was passed by a large majority, even in the face of opposition from the Catholic hierarchy, because most sensible adults viewed divorce as preferable to poisoning and stabbing, the more traditional Italian methods of closure for troubled marriages. The apple, Teal accepted, never fell far from the tree.

But if Edward Kenney was right about the Saint's plans, and a fourth player was to be introduced, soon too many years might pass before Teal was permitted to play the Game again. In that case, a divorce would be for the best, because what Teal hadn't told Kenney—was reluctant to admit even to himself—was that as he slowly finished off Nola Maddick in Detroit, savoring the moment, he had briefly visualized both his wife and his daughter, Maddick's face transforming first into one, then the other; and rather than giving Teal pause, it only made him want to hurt Maddick more. If he was to retain his freedom and thus continue playing the Game, it was important that he distance himself from these XX chromosome sources of domestic aggravation as quickly as possible. As for what he'd do if forced to delay playing, he might have to look into some form of medication. He could ask his physician to prescribe a pill for anxiety, preferably one with the additional benefit of temporarily curbing his libido.

Yet should he have to go to all that trouble because the Saint wanted to increase the number of players from three to four? They were getting along fine as they were. They had a system. They looked out for one another, one for all and all for one, because if one fell, so might three. A new player would only complicate matters and put them at risk. Teal still hoped Kenney was wrong about the Saint, but his experience was that Kenney—chubby, hail-fellow-well-met, wouldn't-hurt-a-fly Ed—was rarely wrong, not when it came to the Game. If so, it meant the Saint was not only on the verge of introducing a fourth player, but might have embarked on a separate Game of his own. That would be selfish and dangerous.

Teal visualized killing the Saint. It turned out to be easier than expected. Easier, and surprisingly pleasurable.

CHAPTER

Liat drove Louis to the Lower East Side: Norfolk Street, south of East Houston, where she parked in front of a brownstone adjacent to the Angel Orensanz Center, once a Gothic Revival synagogue and now the studio and gallery of the eponymous Spanish artist, as well as a performance space. Incongruously, a statue of Lenin stood on the rooftop of one of the nearby buildings. It was either an art installation, thought Louis, or someone had despaired of even socialism providing an answer to the nation's ills and decided that full-tilt communism was the way to go.

Louis gathered that the venue for their meeting had not been chosen lightly. For a short time, the basement of the Orensanz Center had served as a holding cell for a killer named Kittim, and Epstein was one of his jailers. Back then, Louis had regarded Kittim only as an unusually disfigured criminal, a marabou stork in human form, but subsequent events caused him to revise that opinion, though he had remained reluctant to accept Kittim's nature as angelic, fallen or otherwise. But over the years that followed, the reservation fell by the wayside.

Now, less than an hour since Kade had spoken to Louis of Sturgis and angels, here was the rabbi, a cup of green tea on the table before him, a pot beside it, waiting to hold converse in a brownstone next to the Center. From across the street came the laughter of children in a playground, but Louis could not say whether he found the sound reassuring or disconcerting.

"May I pour you some tea?" Epstein asked, as Louis took the chair across from him. Liat positioned herself in a spot where she could read the lips of both men.

Louis, who regarded herbal tea as an abomination, declined, and coffee was sourced instead.

Louis took in the apartment. Its furnishings were old and very worn but spoke distantly of quality and expense. The art on the walls, both prints and originals, was uniquely German Expressionist; Louis identified at least one of the latter that might have been a Kandinsky, and another a Klee. The air smelled of soups and stews left sitting too long, and beneath that a sickly sweetness, like cheap spilled wine. He could see no books, and the environs said the owner was an older woman.

"The apartment isn't mine," said Epstein.

"I'd be surprised if it was."

"It belongs to an old friend, but she's frequently out of town. I find it calming in small doses."

"It's too somber for my tastes," said Louis.

"The owner is photophobic. She's also a depressive. I am not sure if one is a consequence of the other, and if so, which is cause and which effect."

Louis heard noises from farther back in the apartment.

"I thought you said she was out of town."

"She is. That's Reuven. He's a caretaker. You'll meet him momentarily."

Epstein plucked a tea leaf from his tongue and placed it on his saucer.

"I believe, when last we spoke, that our mutual friend Mr. Parker was still recovering from his brush with mortality—his most recent brush, I mean, unless I've missed one since. With him, it can be hard to keep up."

"Someone put him in the hospital last year," said Louis. "Broken nose, busted ribs, concussion. For him, that's like stubbing a toe."

"He has a remarkable capacity for endurance," said Epstein. "And a similarly remarkable need for it."

"I'll admit he's a magnet for misfortune."

"He must consider himself cursed."

Those bright old eyes regarded Louis closely, alert to the slightest response to words carefully chosen, but he received none and moved on.

"What did you learn from your former pupil?" Epstein asked.

"Kade wasn't my pupil. Angel and I looked out for him after his mother and father died. He wasn't with us for long."

"But he learned from both of you."

"He learned not to be like either of us," said Louis. "As for what he had to say, he claims a man named Sturgis wants me dead, on the orders of an angel."

Epstein pursed his lips.

"How curious," he said. "I wonder what Sturgis's reward will be. Perhaps he was promised salvation."

"For arranging the killing of a man he's never met? If I were Sturgis, I'd want that in writing."

"I agree," said Epstein. "There are all kinds of angels, and I wouldn't trust any of them. But it's also possible that this Sturgis is of unsound mind."

"Which is the general view, Kade's included."

"But not yours?"

"It might have been, were Sturgis not a member of the Colonial Club."

"Ah, that den of robber barons."

"Robber barons may be the least of them," said Louis.

The Colonial Club was an outpost of wealth and privilege on Boston's Commonwealth Avenue. It hid its secrets well, but Louis knew, from Parker's efforts, that among its members were individuals—"Believers"—committed to the search for an entity they referred to as the Buried God. The most dangerous of them were the Backers, wealthy men and women who, whether they truly believed in the Buried God or used it only as a flag of convenience, were engaged in the systematic corruption of private and public institutions, including local, state, and federal governments. From the wreckage of a plane in Maine's Great North Woods, Parker, Angel, and Louis had retrieved a partial list of conspirators in said corruption. They were fellow travelers, and compromised persons, many linked to the Colonial Club, if by degrees of separation, but so far Parker's efforts had failed to identify any of the Backers. The Colonial was discreet to the point of paranoia; some openly acknowledged being members, but most preferred not to, and there were those who had never set foot inside the club while enjoying the associated benefits of its business and political connections. A surveillance operation mounted on the Colonial Club, even over a period of months, might have yielded no useful information—indeed, *had* yielded no useful information, because the Federal Bureau of Investigation attempted just such an operation before finally admitting failure. But D. Francis Sturgis, of that same Colonial Club, was currently attempting to suborn an act of murder, seemingly on the instructions of an inhuman being.

Louis's coffee arrived, brought by a middle-aged man with prematurely white hair—Reuven, presumably—who did his best not to meet Louis's eyes, even when Louis thanked him. Louis saw that he made the man was nervous, but Louis was used to people being apprehensive around him.

"Traditionally," said Epstein, "angels have done their own dirty work, as demonstrated by the fate of the firstborns of Egypt. Why outsource?"

"It might be cheaper, like buying machine parts from China."

"Are you suggesting that God is a capitalist? His son, for those who believe, always struck me as a committed socialist."

"And look what happened to him," said Louis.

"He suffered the fate of so many who speak truth to power."

Again, Louis thought Epstein was weighing his words precisely before he committed to them. Louis was being tested, but to what end he had no idea. What Epstein was saying appeared to be open to more than one interpretation, but the variations were known only to him.

"We could always ask Kittim," said Louis. "He might have an opinion."

"Kittim? I haven't heard that name mentioned in years."

"We can go next door to his former cell if your memory needs refreshing. Isn't that why you arranged to meet me here?"

"Kittim is gone."

"Dead?"

"Gone," Epstein repeated. "We monitored his slow decay. We wanted to see what might happen at the end."

"And?"

"The experiment was inconclusive. There was a fire. It might have been started deliberately. Kittim—or a layer of skin over old bones, which was all that remained of him by then—went up in flames. Others burned with him."

"Meaning?"

"His essence, like theirs, was freed. In time, if we're right about his nature, he'll find another host and return to torment us."

Epstein spoke almost lightly, like someone discussing a dogged cold caller.

"I have a question," said Louis, "about the Orensanz Center."

"Ask."

"Did Orensanz know about Kittim? Was he aware of the use to which his basement was being put?"

Creamy late-afternoon light spilled viscously through the ancient lace drapes, the material so thick and its decorative holes so minute that Louis might have been witnessing the separation of curds and whey. Epstein dipped a finger to pull back a drape and expose the glass, as if to check the Orensanz Center was still present and nothing untoward had befallen it.

"You know, I have always considered evil to be antithetical to the creation of good art," said Epstein.

"So there are no evil artists?"

"Art being in the eye of the creator, even more so than the observer, I might have to accept the existence of a great many evil artists," Epstein replied. "But I would contend that, in the main, evil produces bad art. Good art—and great art, which is far rarer—is a manifestation of the divine, from which it draws its inspiration. Evil has no such wellspring."

"And what if you're an artist who doesn't believe in God?"

"All artists drink from the same well, whatever they choose to call it," said Epstein. "And the artist is always reaching for God, even if they do not refer to Him by that name, or any name beyond 'beauty' or 'perfection.' Mr. Orensanz is, in my view, a very fine artist. He and his late brother Al saved the synagogue from the wrecking ball, and in return, I like to think that the spirit of the place infused Mr. Orensanz's work. It would not have done so were he not, in addition to being a good artist, also a good man."

Which was, Louis accepted, as close to an answer as he was going to get.

"And now?" he asked.

"The Orensanzes' basement holds nothing that would raise an eyebrow. It served us when we had need of it, but that need has passed."

"Until Kittim comes back."

Epstein shrugged. "Then we'll find another basement, pending an alternative solution."

"To the problem of a reincarnating fallen angel?" Louis couldn't help but laugh. "I hope you've put your best minds on the case."

From his pocket Epstein removed a battered hardback notebook bound with elastic bands. He carefully undid the elastic, licked a finger, and searched the pages until he found what he was looking for: a line of text, entered by hand, in a language that resembled Hebrew:

לֵית מַלְאָךָּא דְיָבֵיל לְמְשַׁחֵת מַלְאָךָּא אֶלָא מַלְאָךָּא

"It's Aramaic," said Epstein. " 'None can kill an angel except an angel,' or that was how it was first translated—inexactly, as it turned out. 'Kill' wasn't the right word. The verb *me'abbad*—to cause to perish, or to annihilate—is open to mistranslation. A better interpretation might be *destroy* or *unmake*. Personally, I prefer *disincarnate*."

Epstein turned more pages of handwritten Aramaic.

"Where the sources agree," he continued, "is that human action against an angel may destroy the host body, but not the spirit inhabiting it. The latter is released, to seek a new host. The method of dispatch is also important. There has to be contact, a confluence between the assailant and the assailed. A bullet won't suffice, but a blade will, or bare hands. You'll be familiar with images of Saint Michael the Archangel vanquishing Satan? I favor the Reni over the Raphael, but you'll note that, in both, the saint is wielding a blade: a sword in Reni's case, a metal-tipped spear for Raphael. Those references to stabbing or cutting weapons are not a coincidence, but God speaking through the artists."

"And did Saint Michael vanquish Satan?"

"Since there's no agreement on who, or what, Satan might be," said Epstein, "I would wager that the saint did not. Like the ongoing ill-advised War on Terror, it's difficult to destroy an abstract concept. At its least theoretical, Satan might be a name applied to any or all of a collective: If they fell, they were Satan. Kittim, by that reckoning, would be Satan. At its most theoretical, it's a personification of evil, a means of making figurative, and therefore vanquishable, what is really only metaphysical. Having seen what I have seen, I find myself drawn toward the first interpretation. Whatever you elect to call them, the entities are real —and persistent. They return, over and over."

"And do they remember, these entities?" Louis asked.

"Their past hosts, you mean? Kittim did. He spoke of them, while he still had the power of speech. He was also aware of his own nature. He knew what he was, or what he once had been. Assuming we accept the veracity of his claims, he was a banished angel, but he did not resent his exile: he welcomed it. Kittim and his kind did not envy God; they envied man. They were jealous of flesh and all its capacities, even that of experiencing pain. In casting them down, it may be that God inadvertently gave them what they wanted: to think like angels, yet live like men. A better punishment would have been condemning them to become men in all aspects, so their suffering might be unalleviated by a conception of its novelty."

"Are you saying God erred?" Louis countered. "That sounds like blasphemy to me. And if I remember right, the preachers always claimed the angels were cast down for wanting to be like God. It was his power they envied, not man's. I'm starting to wonder if you're even a real rabbi."

"You wouldn't be the first to level that accusation," said Epstein. "It's why I now find myself somewhat alone, relegated to the peripheries of my tribe. As for rebel angels, yes, it may be that God's throne became an object of desire for some. But have you ever heard of Iblis? According to the Quran, he was a jinn raised among angels who refused to bow before Adam, which caused him to be flung down from heaven by God. Iblis's sins were pride and disobedience. He didn't want to be like God; he just didn't consider himself inferior to man. And who is to say Iblis—or Shaitan, as he is also known, because it's another telling of the same tale—wasn't right?"

"Now you're referencing the Quran," said Louis. "They're going to take away your skullcap."

Epstein toyed with his teacup and risked a glance at Liat, who had been reading the lips of both men. The expression on her face was one of amusement mixed with disapproval—and yes, Louis thought, a measure of concern. Were he forced to guess, Louis might have said that the conversation he was having with Epstein had been discussed beforehand between them, which meant that he, Louis, represented the unknown quantity in the room.

"I believe in the existence of one God," said Epstein, "so I have that in common with my Muslim brethren. It may be that I simply choose to call Him by a different name. Likewise, then, if we speak of angels and demons, we are giving diverse names to similar entities. It matters only that we accept their reality. Who is to say that the one the Quran calls Iblis does not have another name buried elsewhere, or did not assume a divergent form for the Incas and Aztecs? Iblis must, after all, have predated the coming of man if he witnessed man's creation—or evolution, if one prefers. Which, as it happens, being a man of both God and science, I do."

The afternoon shadows had stretched by increments across the room, and Louis had a strange urge to distance his feet from the encroaching dark that it might not touch him.

"You think they were there waiting for us all along," said Louis.

"I think they had knowledge of what was to come. If they were cast down, it was to a still-forming earth. Perhaps the time passed quickly for them—what is four and a half billion years compared to eternity?—or they slept through the millennia until the first biped became self-aware, which was the signal for them to wake. As a myth, it's as good as any other. But what I find fascinating about Iblis is what his fate implies."

"Which is?"

"Not one fall," said Epstein, "but many: a succession of acts of defiance. It posits God as a ruler confronting the same challenges faced by any king: rebels, rival claimants, traitors. Just because the Creator is perfect, it does not follow that His creations are. Since I am being open with you, and this is an exchange of ideas between intelligent men, I have never embraced the concept of a perfect deity. Even to skim the Tanakh is to perceive a wrathful God, a God who loses His temper. One cannot be perfect and impatient, or perfect and prone to rage. The New Testament, which I do not accept as divinely inspired, attempts to present God afresh through the prism of a gentler son, if one also prone to bouts of anger. But the New Testament is the work of men; only in the Tanakh do we glimpse the true face of God, and it is one to be feared."

"Why are you telling me this?" Louis asked.

Epstein began further unfastening his high-collared shirt, the top button being already undone. He usually wore a tie, but not today. Louis had not noticed its absence until now. With three buttons opened, Epstein pulled back the shirt to expose the skin at the side of his neck. Louis hissed involuntarily at the sight of the swollen lymph nodes.

"Because I'm dying," said Epstein.

BY THE LAKE, Jennifer Parker's features softened with pity.

"Oh, old man," she whispered. "I'm sorry. But we will watch for you when you come."

CHAPTER

XX

In the umbrous regions of the apartment, the oversweet odor became more pronounced to Louis, like ignoble rot, so that he might have been smelling the cancer itself. He looked away as the rabbi rebuttoned his shirt. His eyes turned to Liat, but her face was impassive.

"How long?" Louis asked.

"Months, if I'm lucky," said Epstein. "Or unlucky, depending on the pain. That has already commenced, but it is tolerable so far. It can be managed."

"Treatment?"

"Great effort would be expended for scant reward, and I do not want those extra days so badly. I have made my peace with death, there being little point to the alternative."

Louis did not say he was sorry. He did not say anything at all. Epstein leaned forward to place a hand on Louis's knee, the long fingers splayed like the talons of a bird.

"Listen to me," said Epstein. "Parker cannot remain hidden forever, not from others and not from himself. His nature is ambiguous, though I have not concealed from you the direction of my thoughts, but whatever the truth, his identity is the reason they are drawn to him, both those in pain and those who thrive on the pain of others. But is he good? This is someone with blood on his hands. He is capable of extraordinary violence, and he holds such wrath inside, but also such sorrow. Where does it come from? What is its cause?"

"He returned home to a dead wife and child," said Louis. "That's the cause."

"No," said Epstein. "I think it was there long before the Traveling Man arrived at his door. I think it's very old."

Louis felt his anger flare. He turned to Liat.

"Is that why you slept with him?" he asked. "Were you sent to find out what you could learn by sharing his bed? I hope you paid for breakfast."

Liat started signing, took a step forward. Epstein raised his other hand and she came to a halt against it, though her fingers continued signing rapidly. Louis would have understood none of it had her lips not formed words in unison. Most were profanities, but he could see the hurt in her eyes. He did not take back what was said because he was convinced there was a veracity to it, even as he accepted that Liat cared deeply for Parker. He wished only that he had kept his mouth shut. What he had directed at her should have been beneath him.

Louis's mind wandered elsewhere, drawn back decades to a labyrinth of cells beneath an ossuary in the Czech Republic where a creature named Brightwell—his nature, too, less or more than human—sought to free an angel imprisoned in a statue. Brightwell believed Parker to be like himself, one of the angels who rebelled against God and was punished with exile, the spiritual corruption of the worst of them reflected in a physical transformation, so they became blighted beings. Parker rejected this assertion and put a bullet through Brightwell's forehead, silencing him, and Louis had barely given him another thought, not until Brightwell returned years later in the guise of a boy come to seek revenge in the Great North Woods. It was not that Louis had failed to spot signs of the peculiar in Parker, which would have required a degree of self-delusion bordering on actual blindness. But what if Brightwell was not wholly in error?

"Parker has brought too much attention to himself," said Epstein. "There are others who now think as I do, and not all of them mean him well."

Epstein's hand loosened its grip on Louis. He sat back in the chair, his face suddenly gray with exhaustion.

"But for the moment," he said, "Parker can wait. You have more pressing concerns. If Sturgis is telling the truth, he has been made an instrument of vengeance. If this vengeance is empyreal, then we must ask why you have been targeted. You, Louis: not your lover, not Parker, but you."

Liat put a hand on Epstein's shoulder. He held it, stroking her fingers gently. But still Liat would not look Louis in the eye.

"I hope Sturgis is unhinged," said Epstein. "If he is not, then I hope he's lying to cover a more prosaic motive. After you speak with him, you might tell me what he says, no matter how self-serving."

"I will," said Louis. "Is there anything I can do for you, anything that might ease what's to come?"

"It is kind of you to ask, but no. I have money, which will pay for the best of care, and I have Liat. A man could have far less and be thankful."

The two men stood. Epstein embraced Louis, and for a moment, Louis, who could not recall when last he had been held by anyone but Angel, clasped Epstein gently to him. When they separated, Louis left without saying goodbye. For the first time since Angel's illness, he was afraid his voice might fail him.

AFTER LOUIS WAS GONE, Liat signed to Epstein.

What did we do?

"We sowed a seed," said Epstein.

Is he one of them?

"I can hardly ask you to sleep with him to find out."

He should not have said what he did.

"He regretted it. I could see it in his face. But I was pressing him hard, and he too has his wrath. It is cold and hard, but wrath nonetheless."

If he is of their nature, why did he fall?

"I hoped I might live long enough to find out," Epstein replied, "but I fear it is not to be."

CHAPTER

XXI

I left Angel at the Farnsworth, with a stern injunction not to steal anything, not even a pencil from the gift store. I then drove to Maine State Prison, about which the best thing that could be said was that it wasn't as grimly forbidding as the old institution at Thomaston, though it did lack much of the latter's character, even if that character was all bad.

Allen Atwood Alcock was waiting for me in the reception area. Despite his many years as a defense attorney, Alcock still looked uncomfortable in the confines of a prison, like a man who feared that a single phone call detailing his failings might be enough to prevent him from leaving. I might have looked the same way, and likely with more cause.

"I wasn't sure you'd come," said Alcock.

"I said I would."

"That doesn't mean much. Christ said he'd come back and we're still waiting."

"That's because he's busier than I am. Also, he wasn't being paid by the day. That was his father."

Because Ward Vose had been assessed as a medium-security inmate, and Moxie held some sway with the correctional services, I was to be permitted to meet him in a bare-walled private room. Alcock decided not to join us, preferring that I speak with Vose alone. Two paper cups of water were provided in advance, but otherwise the room contained nothing but a table, three chairs, a single security camera in one corner of the ceiling, and me.

Vose was led in ten minutes after I arrived. He was a tall man in his forties, with a thick head of gray-black hair, burnt-honey-colored skin, and curiously large hands. He didn't look to be carrying any prison weight, which was an achievement given how much of his life had been spent behind bars. He carried himself with confidence but not arrogance, which, if he hadn't learned it from repeated incarceration, was a trait that must have served him well during his time inside. He grinned as he entered the room, displaying wrinkles around his mouth and eyes. I wondered how many of them were recent, because it was shocking how quickly grief left its mark.

Having secured Vose with leg irons, the guard gave the impression of being tempted to hang around, if only out of force of habit or as a chance to sit undisturbed for a while, but he'd obviously been instructed to leave us in peace. He contented himself with advising us that he'd be watching, and pointed to the camera just in case we mistakenly assumed him to be omniscient. Vose thanked him politely.

"I appreciate your agreeing to meet me," said Vose once the door had closed.

"A favor for a third party."

"Yeah, Moxie Castin. Alcock told me. He's a terrible lawyer."

"Moxie?"

"No, Alcock."

"Then why let him represent you?"

Vose shrugged.

"Because I like him. He may be a lousy lawyer, but he's a good friend. Anyway, I've never been locked up for anything I haven't done. Alcock's best efforts have always been hindered by my guilt."

"And what happens if you get picked up for something you didn't do?"

"Then I may look for a different lawyer."

Vose drank half his water and smacked his lips like it was the best he'd ever tasted.

"How are you doing in here?" I asked. It might have sounded like a dumb question, prison being prison, but prisoners liked to be asked how they were and whether everything was as well as it could be. In that, they resembled the rest of us, but with fewer opportunities to act poorly with impunity; often, they held themselves to a higher standard of behavior. Incarceration brought out the best and worst in men and women, and an outsider made privy to its workings might have been surprised by how closely prisoners looked out for one another. You didn't steal from your own. You tried to protect the weak. You held on to your humanity. Sometimes you had to walk away and leave a body to the law of the jungle, because you always kept a piece of yourself apart, untouched. You were not Christ, but if you were convinced otherwise, the system would happily martyr you, though you would not come back from the dead.

"I've been better," Vose answered. "So has this place. Soon we'll be walking the Bloody Mile again."

The Bloody Mile was a term that dated back to Thomaston, where violence was so prevalent that the walkways between units were said to run red, and each year, when winter was over, younger inmates were incited to "spring clean" by beating up transgressors: sex offenders, thieves, snitches. The prison's move to Warren didn't end the violence, but it marked the beginning of an end, aided by the appointment of enlightened wardens who understood that brutality, like blood, trickled down. That era, according to some, had since come to a close. The system was alleged to be tilting back toward repression, with prison attacks on the increase, which would make it harder to retain good staff. The ones who replaced them would be less experienced and more fearful, which meant they'd favor further repression and be quicker to resort to force, a spiral that led only in one direction.

But there was no point in trying to explain this to people who advocated opening detention facilities for immigrants in alligator-ridden swamps, or cutting food and healthcare budgets for inmates. Maine spent about four dollars per prisoner per day on food, which was laughable, but only until one considered that most states spent less than three dollars. And why should this matter if you weren't a prisoner or related to one? The answer was self-interest: If the system can get away with doing it to the weak—and few are more powerless than prisoners—it'll eventually get around to doing the same to you, because the powerful always start with the most vulnerable and work their way up. Perhaps that was why, Moxie's wishes notwithstanding, I'd agreed to see Ward Vose. For better or worse, I stood between Vose and nothing.

Vose clasped his hands before him but otherwise did not move. Incarceration had taught him the virtue of stillness.

"You know about my boy?"

"I know what Alcock told me, and what I've read."

"In the newspapers?"

"And elsewhere. I've seen the autopsy notes. I have to say there's not a lot to make me doubt your son's death was accidental."

"I'd feel the same way looking at it from the outside," said Voss. "When you say 'not a lot'—"

"I'll admit it's odd that he headed into the wilderness and not toward civilization," I said, "or what passes for it up in the Kennebec. The break to his leg is uncommon but not inexplicable, especially since he'd been drinking. Like I said, it's not much. At the risk of sounding callous, there are better uses of my time and your money."

Vose said he understood, and took another sip of water.

"Here's what I'd say in reply. First, Scott knew how to survive in the wilderness. I taught him—when I was around, which I accept was less than I ought to have been. But when I wasn't there, my father did what he could to educate Scott about the woods. My pops died during the pandemic, but if he were still around, he'd confirm it."

"Anyone can have an accident in the wild," I said. "Bad luck is blind."

"And there's the alcohol, right?"

"There is."

"Scott didn't drink alcohol."

I'd heard that before from so many parents about their children that I could have set it to music and lived off the copyright.

"With respect, Mr. Vose—"

"Let me correct that: Scott couldn't drink alcohol. He had an intolerance. It was diagnosed when he was fourteen, after he took off with some buddies and a couple of stolen cases of Silver Bullets to go drinking. He'd sneaked a beer or two before and taken a sip from a bottle of hard liquor when no one was looking, but he'd never paid much attention to the effect it had, or blamed it on something else if he did, like a cold or hay fever. Because who knows about alcohol intolerance in their teens? I've got fifty in my sights and I didn't know about it until Scott was diagnosed after overindulging on the Coors.

"At first, they thought it might be asthma, because that's in my family on my mother's side. Some of the symptoms were the same: nose all blocked, trouble breathing, but then Scott also had real bad cramps, so severe that he collapsed and his mom was all set to take him to the emergency room. But one of her neighbors was a doctor, and by the mercy of God, she happened to be parking her car in her driveway when Scott hit the floor. She was the one who suggested the problem might be an intolerance."

"Was there a formal diagnosis?"

"I don't know," said Vose. "I just know that Scotty kept away from booze after. He never wanted to be that sick again."

"Or so he claimed."

Vose conceded the point. "Sure. He was a kid, and kids get tempted. I swore I'd never drink again after my first hangover, and I've lost count of the number of hangovers I've had since. There would have been more of them too, had the forces of law and justice not done their best to protect me from myself. But Scott was a smart boy; he didn't just look older than his years, he acted it too, when he chose. If he did drink, he'd have done no more than swill it in his mouth to fit in with the company he was keeping. He certainly wouldn't have drunk so much he could hardly stand. Even if he'd wanted to, he wouldn't have been able. He'd have started hurting badly long before he became intoxicated."

I let it go.

"And where were you when a possible intolerance was first identified?" I asked.

"Doing nine months at the Northern New Hampshire Correctional Facility," said Vose. "For receiving."

"What were you caught receiving, out of curiosity?"

"Chinese watches."

"Were they any good?"

"Only if you think *Rolex* is spelled with two l's."

The smile Vose offered could most accurately have been described as rueful. He might have been a loser, but he was a loser with no illusions about himself and few grudges against the system for repeatedly locking him up. Someday, he was destined to overstep the mark in a three-strike state where he'd already offended twice. He would then have failed himself, just as he'd failed his child. He might not have been able to save his son even if he hadn't been in jail so often, but at least he would have been able to give it a better shot; behind bars, he was no use to anyone. This too I had to factor into what I was being told. Aside from whether he was correct to be suspicious about the circumstances of Scott's death, Ward Vose was a father belatedly trying to atone for his shortcomings. If he couldn't help his son while he was alive, he'd do it now that the boy was dead, if only to salve his conscience, and he wanted to make me a device of his will, which I was disinclined to be.

"I can see what you're thinking," he said. "You're thinking that I'm clutching at straws. I'm looking for a reason for what happened to Scott, one beyond a dumb accident, because that way I can become some kind of hero in my narrative. Right?"

"Close," I said.

"And it's true. I want his death not to be his fault or mine. I want to be able to point at someone and say, 'He did it,' and I don't want to be looking in a mirror when I do."

I spread my hands. It was a gesture that was equal parts helplessness and an invitation to Vose to continue. Alcock was paying me for my time, and the smallest courtesy I could offer his client was to hear him out.

"This is what I believe," said Vose. "Someone force-fed my son hard liquor, crippled him by breaking his leg, then drowned him."

"Why?"

"I don't know."

"How often did you speak to Scott?"

"Once a month."

"Did he visit you?"

"Rarely. His mother and stepfather wouldn't bring him up here, but they didn't deny him permission to come. Alcock is an approved visitor, and he would bring Scott through when he came up from Kennebunk. Of course, once Scott got thrown in Spero, the visits ceased."

"How was your relationship with your son?"

"My mistakes meant we weren't as close as we might have been, but we got along, and lately much better than he did with his mom and his stepdaddy. And I was the one who discouraged him from visiting me here. He didn't need to see me locked up, and prison is no place for a boy, not even if he can leave after an hour. A phone call now and then was enough, or better than nothing, and preferable to forcing him to suffer the taint of this place."

Here was a flash of anger, the first since I'd arrived. Vose ran his hands through his hair.

"I wanted him to have a normal life," he said. "Find a good job, meet a girl, get married, have kids who saw their daddy for dinner every evening. Scott had made a start on some of it. He was seeing a girl."

"Where?"

"Up by Spero. He'd sneak out to meet her."

"What was her name?"

"He wouldn't say. It was a new thing. He didn't want to jinx it and I didn't press him. You know how it is with kids. He did have a nickname for her. He called her Smiles."

"So what happened with the girl?"

"She stopped coming to meet Scott. One day he was supposed to meet her, but she didn't show. The call I had with him the day after that was our last before he died."

"Was Scott concerned about her?"

"He was unhappy. It was hard for the two of them. Scott's phone had been taken from him for breaches of discipline, but he could only use it to call preapproved numbers anyway."

"Was the girl's one of them?"

"No."

"Why?"

"He'd have been forced to explain how he met her," said Vose, "or more to the point, how he expected to keep meeting her. The boys were permitted supervised visits to town, not that there's a whole lot to do in Bingham. A few times a month there might be an outing to Waterville, or even Bangor, but those trips were rewards for good behavior, and Scott rarely qualified. I don't know how he even took a leak without being watched, never mind got beyond the gates to hook up with some local girl. If I had to guess, I'd say she managed to get a phone to him and paid the bill out of her own pocket."

"How did he meet the girl to begin with?"

"On one of the few trips to Bingham he was allowed."

"And how did her parents feel about her seeing a kid from Spero?"

"It didn't come up because she didn't tell them."

Ward Vose had managed to dig quite a lot of information out of his son. But the story didn't flow right for me, even if I couldn't pinpoint the source of the disturbance.

"You got all that from him," I said, "but no name beyond Smiles."

Vose reached into a pocket and produced a newspaper clipping, which he unfolded on the table. It was an article from the *Portland Press Herald*, and I was familiar with the photograph that accompanied the piece. Most of Maine probably knew that face. The girl was Mallory Norton.

"What," said Ward Vose, "if this was her?"

CHAPTER XXII

Ward Vose finished his water and crushed the cup in his hand.

"May I ask about your daughter," he said, "the one who died?"

"No."

It wasn't the answer he was expecting, but I wasn't going to permit him that intimacy. Even among acquaintances, I was reluctant to speak of Jennifer. I liked Vose less for raising the subject, and since I didn't know him, I didn't greatly like him already.

"Okay," he said.

It didn't bother me if he considered it okay or not. He toyed with the ruined cup.

"My father once told me that people fragmented when they died," he said. "There was a separation of body and soul, but those weren't the only elements involved. He believed consciousness was a third, and distinct from the soul, so that a body might decay, and the soul be reunited with its maker, and still the essence of an individual might remain. To my father, ghosts were that remnant, and he was convinced of their existence. He claimed that an easeful death meant an easeful consciousness, one that faded away in the moments after the heart stopped beating. But even a hard death wouldn't necessarily leave a residue if it came as a welcome release. I like to think he was right about that, because he rotted away at the end, all eaten up by his own body turning against itself, and I feel he's gone. But an unjust death, or a killing, might cause a consciousness to not want to leave. Worse, it might not be able to even if it wanted to, because it died lost."

Vose gazed at his big hands, which had cradled his son as an infant.

"I think my boy is wandering," he said. "He died in dark country, killed by another, and whatever is left of him is frightened and angry. I sense his presence, even through these walls. If I could, I'd go searching for him up there in the Kennebec. I'd call out to him, so he could follow the sound of my voice, and once he came, I'd whisper that he didn't need to be afraid because I was there, and he wasn't lost because he was with me. And then I'd sing him to sleep, like I did when he was in the cradle, sing to him until he was at rest."

At no point while he spoke did he look at me. I might not have been in the room.

"I can't summon ghosts," I said.

Vose peered up.

"Can't you, now?" he replied, and I wondered what he had heard about me.

"I'll speak with Alcock," I said.

"And?"

"That's all. If he and I can come to an agreement, I'll give this a couple of days. If I haven't made any progress by then, I'll set it aside. Should anything change after that, by which I mean should fresh leads arise, Alcock will know how to contact me."

"It's as much as I could have asked for," said Vose. "The last thing I wanted for my son was for him to find himself trapped someplace like this. I held myself up to him as an example of everything he shouldn't be. I told him that this was what wasted years looked like. And what happened? Spero, that's what."

The door opened and the same guard appeared without being summoned.

"And I was wrong to try to bring your child into this," said Vose. "I apologize. I thought I could use her to talk you around, if I had to. In here a man can forget. You have to remember how to behave with decency."

The guard escorted him out, leaving me alone with the residue of Ward Vose's guilt.

CHAPTER XXIII

After a few minutes, a female guard came to escort me back to the waiting area.

"Whatever happened to Joe Long?" I asked her. Joe Long was the correctional captain, the senior guard, the last time I visited MSP. His skin was so tough, it could have been used to make saddles.

"He retired after an injury," she said. "He's taken over the family bar in Rockland."

"Bet you miss him a lot."

She managed to keep a straight face. "We're learning to live without him."

"What kind of injury?"

"Someone shot him in the foot."

Her voice and expression were devoid of anything approaching sympathy.

"Ouch," I said. "Did you put together a collection?"

"We tried, but it wasn't enough."

"For what?"

"For the guy to come back and shoot him in the other foot."

ALCOCK WAS SEATED ON A HARD CHAIR in the waiting area, working through case notes on his lap. We left the prison together. Only outside did we speak of Ward Vose and Scott Theriault, because the guards heard everything. Alcock lit a cigarette and smoked it while leaning against his car.

"Well?" he said.

"Would you like me to state the obvious?"

"It's as good a place as any to start. Going straight to the nebulous would be confusing for a simple man like me."

"Vose is consumed by guilt for failing his son. He wants to hire me to alleviate it, but that won't work. Vose will carry his pain with him for the rest of his life, and he should. He's a weak man, and he was a poor father."

"Spoken like a stern arbiter," said Alcock.

"Or one who knows," I replied. "That was why you came to Moxie and me, right? Because our respective pasts aligned with your case."

"We take advantage of the Fates when they smile on us," said Alcock.

"Did you tell Vose about my daughter or did he already know?"

"I told him. Ward isn't much for reading newspapers or even watching TV. He's fond of books, though." Alcock took a long drag on his cigarette. "All told, he's a perplexing, frustrating individual. So: Will you work on his behalf?"

"Like I told him," I said, "I'd prefer not to."

"Is there a 'but'?"

"More than one."

"Would Mallory Norton be among them?"

"Is there anything to prove she was the girl Scott was seeing?" I asked. "Assuming Vose hasn't just conjured the relationship out of thin air to draw me in. The police have come up with nothing so far."

"I haven't gone looking," said Alcock. "That's why I'm trying to hire you. For what it's worth, I don't think Ward would lie to you about anything Scott might or might not have said. He's too shrewd for that—and strangely, too honest. Ward would steal the eyeballs from his grandmother's head, but he'd never deny having done it."

Which didn't mean he was right about Mallory Norton and Scott Theriault being intimates, but it was another loose end, like the injury to Scott's leg and his decision to head away from civilization, not toward it, when he broke out of Spero. Bingham lay southeast of the school, and if Scott and Mallory had been an item, it might have made sense for him to contact her when he fled, but by then Mallory Norton had been missing for days. Could she have been so unhappy at home, and so smitten with Scott, that she'd agreed to rendezvous with him deep in the wilderness if he managed to escape? If so, why hadn't she returned to Bingham when he didn't show? Or maybe he did show, and what then? But that didn't square with what Ward Vose claimed: that a girl had missed her date with Scott, and without explanation. Unless, of course, Scott Theriault was lying to his father and knew exactly what had happened to Mallory Norton.

I thought about my current case load. It wasn't heavy, and neither was it very interesting: a trio of insurance investigations and some trial prep for Moxie, none of it urgent. Also, with Sam in college, I couldn't afford to turn down work, or not without resorting to passing off Cheez Whiz on crackers as dinner for two with Macy, and then it wouldn't be too long before I was sleeping alone again.

"I told Vose I'd give it a couple of days," I said. "If I hit a wall, I'll put together a report and step away."

"I'll pay you in advance for a week's work," said Alcock. "Expenses extra, to be receipted—not because I don't trust you, but no sense in giving the IRS more than it's owed. If you decide you're done before the money runs out, you can keep it. Those are my client's instructions, by the way. He has a rainy-day fund, and not a lot to spend it on."

Not even his boy went unspoken. Alcock stubbed out the cigarette, considered flicking the butt, and instead unlocked his car and dropped it in the ashtray.

"If I quit, you'll get a refund," I said. "That's how I prefer it."

"You don't strike me as the quitting kind." He handed me a business card. "Call anytime, day or night. I'm divorced, so the only person you'll be waking is me."

"You still wear a wedding band," I said.

"Force of habit. It's recent."

"Suppose you get lucky in the meantime?"

"The last time I got lucky, she married me," said Alcock. "After that, my luck ran right out."

CHAPTER XXIV

Louis spent that evening, as he had the previous one, at the apartment he and Angel owned on the Upper West Side. The building was also theirs, even if the title was hidden behind layers of accountants, lawyers, and dormant companies. Their sole tenant, the elderly Mrs. Bondarchuk, acknowledged Louis's return from her post by the window, a pair of Pomeranians asleep in her lap. The Pomeranians were the grandpups, or even great-grandpups, of Mrs. Bondarchuk's original dogs, Teffi and Anton, respectively named for a Russian emigrée humorist and a famous White Army general who fought the Communists in the civil war that followed the October Revolution in 1917. Louis was tempted to ask Mrs. Bondarchuk how she felt about large images of Lenin towering over Lower East Side brownstones, but that would have meant waking the Pomeranians, whose bark was worse than their bite only in the sense that their bite was fleeting while their bark seemed to go on forever.

Over wine, Louis slowly read through the entirety of Kade's file on Sturgis, making notes as he went. The file was incomplete, which wasn't the fault of Kade's people. Sturgis lived off his inheritance in a suburb of Boston, made the newspapers only in connection with charitable donations, had never married, and had no children. For a few years, he served on the board of the Colonial Club, acting as its spokesman when a reporter came asking about minority representation among its membership. Sturgis gave the reporter the party line: All were welcome, and the application process was the same for everyone, that is, challenging, even with money, but he declined to disclose how many of its members weren't WASPs, which pretty much answered the reporter's question.

Louis set aside his pen, made a cup of coffee for himself and a hot chocolate for Mrs. Bondarchuk, and went downstairs, steeling himself for the inevitable barking. Over rugelach from Zabar's, he gave her a heavily sanitized account of his meeting with Kade. Mrs. Bondarchuk clapped her hands in delight.

"Will he come visit?" she asked.

Louis replied that he was not sure, a polite way of saying no.

"But tell me, has he made something of himself?" Mrs. Bondarchuk persisted.

"He's been annoying Putin," said Louis.

"Good." Mrs. Bondarchuk raised her hot chocolate in a toast to Kade. "I knew the boy would do us proud someday."

CHAPTER

As I drove away from the prison, I wondered whether Angel had yet tired of the Farnsworth, before deciding that he almost certainly had not. There was now a quietude to Angel that had not been present before his illness. According to Louis, Angel could sometimes spend hours just staring at the sea, or watching the boats and ferries crisscrossing Casco Bay. To Louis, who loved him more than anyone, Angel had never been more unknowable. But it might have represented a kind of peace, in which case the Farnsworth could only have been good for his spirit.

"THE FUCK TIME DO YOU CALL THIS?" said Angel, as he climbed into the car and slammed the door with more force than was necessary. "I nearly died of boredom in there."

"I thought you'd like some extra time to feed your soul."

"I can feed my soul for an hour tops, and that includes restroom breaks and a turn around the gift shop. After that, my soul gets indigestion."

"I'm surprised you didn't text me."

I'd checked my phone as soon as it was returned to me at MSP and seen nothing from Angel.

"I would have, and it might have been a communication for the ages, except I left my phone back at the apartment."

"Well," I said, "let that be a lesson to you."

So that he wouldn't sulk all the way home, I offered to pay for an early dinner at Rustica on Main Street; if I couldn't successfully feed Angel's soul, I could do my best for his belly. Over pasta rossa and pan-seared bistro steak, I shared the substance of my encounter with Ward Vose. Angel listened without comment until the end, when he concluded that I was a soft touch, and someday I'd return home minus a cow but clutching a bag of magic beans. I told him that was questionable, since I didn't own a cow. Because dinner was on me, Angel decided to try both the boca negra and the tiramisu for dessert. I didn't object, so he might have been right about that soft-touch business. Only over coffee did he return to what we had spoken of in the car on the way up to Rockland.

"What I said earlier," he began, "about choices echoing themselves, and events repeating—"

He took in the figures walking along Main Street, rendered insubstantial by dusk.

"When Louis and I first met you, back when Susan and Jennifer were still alive, we felt like we could trust you, which made no sense, given that you were police and we were—"

"Not police," I finished.

"Definitely not police. Louis was more hesitant, but then, he had more to be hesitant about. Over the years, that trust has never wavered. If anything, it's grown stronger."

"Likewise," I said.

"I have no doubts that we knew one another before, we three," said Angel. "Louis and I were drawn to you more than thirty years ago, and you to us, but it wasn't the first time; and I think we've died for you, more than once, and we'll die for you again. Don't ask me how I can be sure of that, because the answer has to do with feeling, not reason. But I know it to be true."

"And Louis has had similar thoughts," I said, "independent of you."

"Not just similar thoughts. Jennifer came to him as well, the same night she visited me. Unless too many years of intimacy has led to us sharing dreams—and I sincerely hope that's not the case, because I know how darkly

Louis dreams—incidents are starting to come to the surface. Call them hidden memories. But when I try to focus on them, they submerge: not all the way down, but deep enough that I can only catch flashes. I think they need to rise in their own time. They can't be forced. If we push too hard, they'll sink all the way to the bottom and we may never be able to find them again."

Angel fixed his gaze on me. His eyes were very black. I could not recall them ever being so lightless, so old; and I thought that were I to be permitted to see my own eyes at the moment, they might have resembled his.

"Who are we?" he asked.

CHAPTER

XXVI

The empty coffee cups were set aside. We each ordered a glass of red wine. I would not finish mine, not with the drive back to Portland ahead of me, but I wanted the taste of it and the weight of a glass in my hand. Our server did not try to hurry us along, though the restaurant was almost full and I could see people by the door waiting for tables. At times, the intensity of a conversation will communicate itself to others and they will know better than to disturb its flow.

"This is a cycle," said Angel. "It repeats itself, over and over. We're trapped in it, and we don't even understand why."

"It's a punishment," I said, putting down my glass.

Jennifer had said as much, when last she spoke to me.

i should have hidden myself better

i should have hidden us both

Why?

because now they may try to reset the machine

What machine?

the punishment machine

"A punishment for what?" Angel asked. "What did we do?"

But when I asked Jennifer the same question, she refused to answer. I believed that Angel might be right, and the issue should not be forced. If we waited, it might emerge. But waiting required time, time we might not be given.

they may try to reset the machine

the punishment machine

"Something has changed," I said. "That's why you're starting to remember, and why Jennifer has visited each of us. The machine is out of sync. The cycle isn't repeating as it should."

"If that's true, what about you?" said Angel. "What else do you remember?"

I reached for my glass but my fingers missed it by a fraction, knocking it over. I watched the wine spread across the tablecloth as the spell over our table was broken. The server bustled across to deal with the mess.

"I'm sorry," I said.

"It happens," said the server. "I'll bring you another."

"There's no need. We're done. Just the check, please."

The server took a leather holder from his apron, the check already in place, and stood it far away from the spilled wine. Angel and I did not speak as I settled up, or as we left the restaurant. Only outside did Angel repeat his question.

"What else do you remember?"

"Falling," I said. "I remember falling."

CHAPTER

XXVII

We had spoken enough for one night, and I knew the ride back to Portland would be quiet.

I'd parked on Orient Street. Only as we reached the car did I spot the bar on the opposite side: Long's Ale House. A neon sign read: HOME OF THE IRISH WELCOME!

"One for the road?" I said to Angel.

"Seriously?"

"A soda. Out of curiosity."

Inside, Long's was quiet. I counted four customers, one server, and one bartender who, when last I'd seen him, was wearing the uniform of a prison guard. The bartender glared at us.

"You!" said Joe Long. "Get the fuck out of my bar."

"You don't mean that," I said.

"What about the Irish welcome?" asked Angel.

Long produced a heavy walking stick with a knob on the end and placed it on the bar.

"Here's your welcome," he said. "Come get it."

"I CAN SEE WHY SOMEONE SHOT HIM," said Angel, as we climbed in the car, light one anticipated soda each.

"At least he hasn't changed," I said. "In a volatile world, that's kind of reassuring."

2

The life of the dead is placed in the memory of the living.

Marcus Tullius Cicero, *The Philippics*, 9.10

CHAPTER XXVIII

Spero School was located on the site of a former National Guard training camp, which utilized buildings left over in turn from the Cistercians of the Strict Observance, better known as Trappists. The Trappists had raised a monastery on the plantation in the 1950s, intending it as a long-term proposition, since they constructed their church and a pair of other buildings from stone, not wood. Unfortunately, life in Somerset County proved too much even for the monks, plaguing them with insects from early summer into late fall, and tormenting them with ice and snow for winter and much of spring. Reluctantly, the Trappists admitted defeat in the 1980s, deconsecrating and abandoning the monastery, with the abbot opining that, with The Plains plantation, they had mistaken Edom for Eden, Edom being the biblical template for desolate wildernesses.

In the late 1990s, the Maine National Guard, undeterred by desolation—viewing it, in fact, as a means of toughening up doughball recruits—invested federal and state funds to transform the existing buildings into barracks, kitchens, classrooms, and indoor firing ranges, adding new structures as required. They succeeded only in creating a money pit, one that enriched a handful of local contractors to a degree still spoken of in hushed tones in The Plains, but that failed to serve its intended purpose beyond providing a few years of uncomfortable drill weekends and two-week summer training camps, exercises so legendarily unpleasant that they led to a noticeable drop-off in recruits completing the standard eight-year enlistment period.

And so the old edifices might have been allowed to decay or return to nature except, in the second decade of the new century, the property was acquired at a knockdown price by Spero School LLC, registered in Wilmington, Delaware, home to countless shady companies. Private money raised the existing infrastructure to the minimum level regarded as acceptable for a residential school, and so a location that had beaten monks from a reclusive order at ease with hardship and fasting, and led to threats of legal action from members of the US military, was deemed an appropriate place to house troubled youths. Spero was where children went when the traditional educational establishment failed them—or if you were the adult responsible for enrolling them, where children went when they failed the establishment, educational or otherwise. Those who could not or would not conform would instead be reformed. They would be laid low with firm but fair discipline before being encouraged to rebuild themselves in a new image, one more conducive to the requirements of a conservative American society. Yes, it would sometimes be challenging and tough, but these young people were themselves challenging and tough. While it would take a lot to break them down, it would be worth it in the end. They could handle it. They would not have been at Spero otherwise.

THE BOY'S NAME WAS ANTHONY MARSHALL, and he was not tough: challenging and complicated, yes, and prone to violent tantrums, but not tough, which was unfortunate for him. It meant he had all the flaws required of a candidate for correction without the physical, psychological, or emotional resources to withstand the process. He was fifteen years old and there were Department of Education commissioners who had seen the insides of fewer schools. His parents were decent people, if of a narrow-minded, deeply religious stripe, and had tried their best with their son, but for them he possessed a disposition inimical to guidance or household chastisement. Tell Anthony to turn right and he'd turn left. Warn him that to go left would mean being bitten by a snake, and snakebitten he would become. He was a lodestone for boredom and distraction, and out of this came destructiveness, yet there was no vindictiveness to his actions and his contrariness brought him no pleasure.

Anthony had three siblings—two older, one younger—who were as different from him as sheep from a coyote, and as their happiness and development was increasingly threatened by this creature of the id with whom they were forced to share a home, the decision was made by Anthony's mother and father to send him to Spero. If that experiment failed, the remaining options included a course of medication that would effectively zombify him, or so they had been informed. He would, his mother feared, end up like the Nilsens' boy, who was forty-three, weighed three hundred pounds, didn't work, lived in his parents' basement, and was once arrested for taking a dump on the floor of the local McDonald's. But medicating Anthony would also be an admission that there was something fundamentally wrong with him, and he had come out of the womb defective. If that was the case, would the ultimate blame lie not with him but his sires? If he was impaired, so also must his parents be, and those deficiencies could only be regarded as a judgment from God.

Had they been more enlightened, the Marshalls might have sought a more appropriate educational environment for Anthony than Spero, but they were at their wits' end, ground down by fights, suspensions, expulsions, and a fear of God. Also, they could not shake the view or abandon the hope that Anthony was "acting up," and under a firmer hand he might yet emerge from this adolescent storm as a young man to be proud of, or at least one that did not take dumps on the floors of fast-food restaurants. Ultimately, what the Marshalls wished for was a cure. But sometimes there is no cure, only ways of coping; to accept this is hard for everyone and impossible for a few. The Marshalls, regrettably for all involved, fell into the second category, which made them acutely susceptible to Spero's promises, because the easiest people to whom to sell hope are balding men and desperate parents. Spero School dangled a hook, and the Marshalls bit.

But what of Anthony himself? He had not been consulted about his transfer to Spero, because nobody saw the point. Anthony would only have objected or tried to flee, resulting in more trauma and greater embarrassment for the family. Anthony was bundled into a van in the dead of night by three male strangers while his parents watched and then driven two hundred miles north, into the Maine wilderness. Anthony had been terrified, but then, Anthony was always terrified. That was what nobody grasped and what he had never been able to explain: Anthony Marshall existed in a perpetual state of dread. The world was beyond his comprehension, just as he appeared to be beyond the comprehension of the world, and what people do not understand, they fear.

Anthony Marshall had never been more frightened than when the men locked him in the back of that van and drove him away from home. He believed he would never be as frightened again, but he was wrong. Now, in the dark of Spero's dormitory, he was so frightened, he thought he might die. He needed to go to the bathroom, but that meant venturing into the darkness.

And the darkness was alive.

Spero School had four dormitories: two large rooms, each containing ten beds, in one building; and two smaller rooms, totaling twelve beds, in a smaller building connected to the first by a tin-roofed corridor added during renovations. But the school never reached full capacity due to staffing issues: Spero's principal and founder, Dante Santopietro, adhered to a student-teacher ratio that maintained a minimum level of supervision while not overly depleting funds. (It had been touch-and-go for Spero during the first two years until student numbers firmed up, which Santopietro had never forgotten.)

In addition to the dormitories, a room containing two beds was located at the end of the classroom building, close to Santopietro's cottage. During the pandemic, it was used to house students required to quarantine, but had remained unoccupied since. At present, just eighteen students were in residence at Spero: fourteen in the larger dormitories and two boys each in the smaller rooms. The latter were older students deemed to have earned the privilege of not having to share space with their younger peers, who were noisier and, like Anthony Marshall, frequently more distressed. Some—again, like Anthony Marshall—were also prone to bedwetting, which was one of the great sins at Spero. While all the beds had rubber mattress protectors, an accident at night still resulted in damp sheets. Apart from the humiliation of having to strip the bed, wipe down the protector, and remake the bed with fresh linen, all under the eyes of one's fellow students, punishments included being deprived of treats for a second offense (everyone got one pass), which meant no soda, no ice cream, no TV for three days, and no phone for three days. Further breaches would result in the deprivation of privileges being extended to a week or more, with cleaning duties added, and nobody wanted to clean bathrooms used by eighteen teenage boys.

The school had a resident janitor and groundskeeper named Tim Sadlier who didn't like cleaning those bathrooms either, and was content for the task to devolve to one of the kids who had probably previously left pee on the bathroom floor as well as in his own bed, just as Sadlier was happy to supervise trash collection, paint stripping, and the planting or picking of vegetables while he snuck a smoke and read a fantasy novel or caught up with TV shows on his iPad. Sadlier had learned early on to arrive at Spero prepared, even if it was prepared to do nothing.

Sadlier was not an unkind individual. He felt sorry for a lot of the kids dumped at the school, because *dumped* was the operative word in many cases. He was less sorry for a handful, since it couldn't be argued that the worst of them were anything other than sonsofbitches, and Spero was just a taste of what they could expect in later life, when they'd like as not end up in prison. The nicer kids he'd supply with candy, or even a cigarette if he was in the right mood; the bad ones, he tried to steer clear of, as much out of what he feared he might do to them as of what they might do to him. Sadlier was a big, gentle man, but on more than one occasion he'd been tempted to educate a student the old-fashioned way about the importance of showing respect to one's elders. Yet even on the lousiest days, Sadlier could rely on being able to go home each evening and forget the school existed, which was more than any of the students could do.

Lately, Sadlier was happier than ever that he didn't have to spend nights at Spero, and he had been pretty darned happy about that already. Since the death of Scott Theriault, Spero was different. Sadlier liked Scott, who was among the better kids he'd encountered in a decade at the school, maybe even the best of them. What happened to him was a damn shame, and in common with the peace of God, passed all understanding. Whatever Scott's reasons were for striking out north, they'd resulted in his death, and it had cast a shadow over Spero that wouldn't lift. Wrongnesses that manifested after the sun went down: doors standing open that should have been closed, because Sadlier had locked them himself; the contents of closets thrown into disorder; faucets left running so that sinks overflowed; and most disturbing of all, holes ripped—clawed—in the seed bags he kept in his toolshed, which was Sadlier's personal fiefdom and to which only he had the key.

The natural response from staff was to blame the students, but none of them would admit to any wrongdoing, not even under the threat of collective punishment. For a week, all students were confined to the main dormitories, with the teacher on overnight duty required to sleep in a spare room instead of in one of the on-site cabins, and still there were incidents, including the smearing of honey on the main kitchen stove, and five panes of glass broken in the greenhouse. Had any better employment alternatives presented themselves, Sadlier might have handed in his notice immediately, but jobs were scarce in The Plains and Spero represented steady money. For the present, Spero it was and Spero it would remain. But as the fall days grew shorter, and night settled in earlier and earlier, Sadlier realized he had begun to fear the coming of winter, and Spero.

CHAPTER

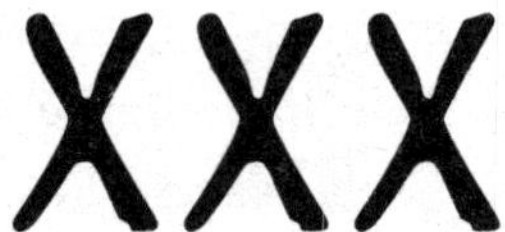

Anthony Marshall really, *really* needed to use the bathroom. Ordinarily, that wouldn't have been a problem. Each of the dorms—which were all named after Maine notables, Anthony's being John Ford—had a bathroom at one end, with a trough urinal and three stalls, but the ones in the main building were out of action because of a leak in the pipes, so the water had been shut off and the doors locked. It wouldn't have been such a big deal if Anthony only had to pee, because that was one of the reasons the Lord had created empty soda bottles and plastic chamber pots, but unfortunately the chili from dinner was disagreeing with Anthony in a serious way, and no bottle or pot was going to be up to the task, not at all.

The dorms were housed in what had formerly been high stone sheds built for the Trappists' livestock. While within sight and sound of the two cabins maintained for teachers on overnight duty, they offered a degree of independence from the staff and therefore scope for mischief, including the kind of bullying inflicted on Anthony Marshall since his arrival, especially after his second and third incidents of bedwetting. Anthony had asked to be moved to the old quarantine room, even temporarily, but at that stage he hadn't learned one of Spero's most important lessons: Hardship was character-building, so if you requested anything that might improve your circumstances, it would be refused. Being the target of bullying required the victim to find a way to deal with it, either by fighting back, which taught the virtue of self-sufficiency, or enduring it until his tormentors got bored and sought a new outlet for their sadism, which taught the virtue of stoicism. The third option was to kill oneself, as a boy had done back in 2020 when the restrictions imposed by the pandemic caused him to lose all hope. Since then, ropes and electric cables were kept under lock and key, and Sadlier marked off the lengths of each with a permanent Sharpie, foot by foot, so he'd notice if anyone was stealing.

But Anthony hadn't yet reached the stage of outright despair when it came to the bullying. Right now, all he wanted to do was empty his bowels, but that would mean leaving the dorm, going down the stairs, and crossing the campus to the gym, where bathrooms had been designated for day and night use pending the repairs. A door was left unlocked so students could enter and leave, and they were required to sign a sheet if they used the restroom after lights-out to encourage them not to make a mess or clean up after themselves if they did.

Anthony's bed was by a window that looked out on the green space between the dorm blocks and the main school building, with the pathway illuminated by four weak, solar-powered lamps. When he realized what he had to do would require leaving the safety of the dorm, he spent a good two minutes staring through the glass at the path and, more particularly, the blackness to either side. Having determined that the way was clear, he was about to kick back his sheet and slide into his Spero-issue Crocs when one of the lights appeared to flicker. Had he not been looking directly at it, Anthony might have mistaken this for a fault, or the waning of the battery.

But the light hadn't just flickered—it had been blocked. Then the obstruction moved on, or it might not have been there at all were a person disposed to call themselves delusional, though Anthony Marshall was not so disposed. He'd glimpsed a similar shape before, and he knew that at least three other students had too, but nobody wanted to say anything to the staff because it wasn't unknown for boys to be outside after dark, even if it was a serious breach of school rules, with penalties to match if they were caught. The likelihood of being spotted was greater since Scott Theriault's death, when motion-activated cameras were installed at the gates, on the cabins, and over by the main school building, a textbook example of barring the stable door after the horse had not only bolted but also broken a leg and drowned. On the other hand, Jamie Hanscomb, whose dad worked in security, claimed the cameras were just for show and the school's internet was too primitive to support that kind of system.

So Anthony regarded the dark, and waited.

WHEN THE SUBJECT OF SOMEONE MOVING about out at night was first raised among the students, no one would admit to being involved. This kind of evasion wasn't without precedent. Also during COVID, two boys were expelled for what Mr. Santopietro later described as "succumbing to unnatural urges," since being queer for another boy ranked one step below murdering a teacher on Spero's scale of wrongdoing.

"What if it's one of the local kids trying to break in?"

This from Kaspar Filipowski, who, at thirteen, was the second youngest of the boys and might have been even more scared of the world than Anthony was. Kaspar wouldn't reveal why his parents had sent him to Spero. Most of the other kids came up with some reason, even if it was just a shrug followed by "I hated my school," "I didn't get along with my mom's new husband/father's new wife/family's new dog," or whatever, but Kaspar gave them nothing.

"There are no local kids," said Jamie Hanscomb, "or none that give a rat's ass about us."

Which was true. You could currently count the number of non-Spero kids in The Plains on one hand. Everyone else, as far as the students could tell, was old, weird, or dead.

"It could be a ghost," said Troy Cafferty, but he sniggered as he said it. Troy was one of those who had set out to make Anthony's life as miserable as possible, but he was an instrument rather than the instigator. The real malevolence at Spero took the form of the boy who spoke next: Leonard Levesque, sixteen years old, with the face of a baby, the body of a mature man, and a quick mind that, were it not so damaged, might have destined him for a distinguished adulthood. Leonard was so good with numbers that Mr. Santopietro, who also taught math and science, now left him to his own devices during class, supplying him with workbooks that were checked as they were returned, all at Leonard's pace, which varied according to his mood. As for the rest of the curriculum, Leonard largely declined to participate, but he knew a lot about history, geography, and even literature, and if asked a direct question, he could usually answer it. But the teachers rarely so inquired, preferring to leave Leonard undisturbed. The shadow side of him was a morass of random acts of violence, destruction, and sadism, as well as an inability to view even the most modest exercise of adult authority as anything other than a personal affront. Since his features naturally assumed an expression of placidity, even when he was roiling beneath, gauging whether it was appropriate to involve him in lessons was a hard task, so it was deemed wiser to let Leonard decide.

Oddly, despite his volatility, Leonard and Mr. Santopietro had reached an understanding, one that extended to the rest of the staff. This understanding could be summarized thus: The dorms are your fiefdom and the students your subjects. Don't leave bruises and don't break bones. If you cross us, you'll suffer the consequences. The rest is up to you.

Now, in the recreation room, Leonard Levesque uncoiled from a chair and blinked once, slowly, at Troy Cafferty, who stopped giggling.

"If it's a ghost," said Leonard, "whose ghost might it be?"

"Stewie Daigle," suggested Austin Bernier. Stewie Daigle was the boy who'd killed himself during COVID.

Leonard blinked again.

"Any other bidders?" he said.

Nobody spoke. Leonard's gaze flicked to Anthony Marshall.

"What about you, Piss Boy?"

Anthony shook his head.

"Cat got your tongue?"

"No."

"No what?"

"No, Leonard, the cat hasn't got my tongue," said Anthony. "We don't have a cat."

Anthony didn't know where that one had come from. For a mad moment, he was usurped from his own body, his dominion contested by some rogue self. Unfortunately, he was back inside his body when Leonard Levesque's right hand slapped him so hard across the side of the head that his vision blurred. The second blow knocked him to the floor, so he was on his back when Leonard placed a foot on his balls and applied unwelcome pressure.

"You talk back to me like that again," said Leonard, "and I'll rip *your* tongue out and make you swallow it. Do you understand?"

"Yes, Leonard," said Anthony, and the weight on his groin eased. He stayed where he was for a few seconds, in case Leonard was tempted to hurt him again should he move. Only when Leonard turned his back did Anthony get to his feet. He was doing his best not to cry, but his eyes were prickling.

"There are no ghosts," said Leonard. "Not here, not anywhere. Either you're hallucinating like overexcited little girls, getting each other all worked up over nothing, or we have a liar in our midst. No one is going to drive all the way out here just to run around the grounds at night, so if someone is playing tricks, it's one of you. And you'd better cut it out, y'hear?"

Mute nods, followed by a silent dispersal. Anthony risked a peek, only to catch Leonard staring back at him, those infant features marred by confusion. Whichever of the boys he might have expected to smart-talk him, it wasn't Anthony Marshall, the little bedwetter. This meant Leonard had misjudged him, and action would have to be taken to maintain the status quo. Leonard Levesque would brook no dissent.

All this and more was communicated between the two boys in that look. Anthony, though he could not have said how, spotted that Leonard was worried. He wondered if Leonard, too, might have seen a boy at night but was reluctant to admit it. That little piece of theater, concluding with the naming of Stewie Daigle, was a distraction, or a test, because Leonard had relaxed slightly after Daigle's name was mentioned. What Leonard might have feared to hear spoken was a different name, one Anthony had been tempted to utter before discretion overcame valor, only itself to be overturned by a foolhardy impulse to get in Leonard's face.

You were afraid someone would name Scott Theriault. What did you do to him, Leonard? What did you do?

CHAPTER

As Anthony Marshall sat on the edge of his bed, his feet dangling inches from the floor, his bowels spasmed again. He had no idea what the punishment might be for shitting his sheets. Such an eventuality was not covered in the briefing he had received from Mr. Renders, the assistant principal, on arrival at Spero, or in the less formal introduction given to him by Jamie Hanscomb after lights-out. From this, Anthony could only conclude that bed-shitting was so unthinkable an occurrence as to be unworthy of mention.

Another spasm came, and this one sent a signal right down to Anthony's sphincter. If he waited any longer, he wouldn't make it to the toilet. He slipped into his Crocs and checked the other occupied beds, and saw his roommates were all sleeping. None of them moved as Anthony padded across the wood floor. He didn't make a sound, because another early lesson learned at Spero was which boards groaned, which doors squeaked when pushed too wide, and which windows opened while others remained stubbornly closed. This knowledge was added to the record of the personalities of the staff, their temperaments and trigger points, and the distinctive pattern of each one's tread. So much to be taught and remembered, even before one entered a classroom.

Anthony went down the stairs and paused by the main door, which was inset with a small panel of wired safety glass. Through it he could see the path and at the end of it, the door leading to the showers, the stalls, and blessed relief. Another of those sphincter testers gave him the impetus he needed to move. He didn't look left or right, but focused on the door ahead. Even had he risked a glance around him, he doubted he'd have been able to spot much beyond the path. Those solar lights might not have done more than illuminate a narrow stretch of white gravel, but amid the greater dark of the campus and The Plains beyond, they were enough to screw with a person's night vision.

Anthony reached the gym without incident and twisted the knob, but the door wouldn't open. He tried again, making more of a racket than he would have liked. The knob turned, but the door was stuck fast. He resorted to bracing his right foot against the frame and pulling back hard, with the result that the door opened outward unexpectedly, nearly knocking him on his ass. What that might have done to his bowels didn't bear thinking about, but seconds later, Anthony was sitting in a cold stall, and he wasn't thinking about Scott Theriault or Stewie Daigle or Leonard Levesque, only that disaster had been averted for the time being.

BUT IF ANTHONY MARSHALL WAS NOT THINKING of Leonard Levesque, the latter was thinking of him.

Although Anthony could not have known it and couldn't have done much about it if he had, not with nature calling so urgently, Leonard was currently smoking a cigarette outside the building that housed the two smaller dorms, Longfellow and Homer. Leonard Levesque was a nocturnal animal. He'd always struggled to sleep at night, which drove his parents to exhaustion during his infancy and early childhood, until it became apparent that sleep deprivation was just one of a litany of challenges with which their son would present them, and by no means the worst.

Leonard had formerly enjoyed his late cigarettes while sitting on one of the upper windowsills at Longfellow, leaning against the frame with a pillow for comfort. On cloudless nights, he would imagine himself adrift among the stars, like God before mankind was born; if the moon was bright, he would pick out the contours of The Plains and add castles, barricades, and knights, transforming a prison into a kingdom. When he was very tense or when he was concerned that the fury inside might be about to goad him into unwise actions, he ran figures through his head, calming himself by performing complex equations or searching for prime numbers, but that stratagem didn't work as well as it once had. He wasn't a kid anymore, and had enough self-awareness to recognize that whatever was wrong with him wasn't going to get any better as he got older.

But Leonard no longer smoked on the windowsill, not since the younger kids began whispering of a visitor who came at night. Leonard's window faced the woods, which, even in better light, were thick enough to prevent anyone seeing beyond the first rows of trees. Leonard believed an intruder would approach not through the woods but instead would come from the main road, and he planned to catch them when they did. As for talk of ghosts, Leonard knew that kids liked scaring one another with campfire stories, even if he'd never seen the point, but he had to admit that the conviction of those who claimed to have seen figures where no figures belonged was perturbing. He'd always taken Austin Bernier for normal, but Bernier was seriously spooked and had taken to keeping a small cross in one of his trouser pockets, fingering it obsessively. And while Bernier was among those who first suggested that Stewie Daigle might have come back, Leonard knew opinion was changing, and the name that came up more often now, if out of Leonard's earshot, was Scott Theriault's.

Everyone at Spero was aware that Leonard and Scott hadn't gotten along. Leonard viewed Scott as competition for top dog, and not without cause. Scott was as well built as Leonard, but neither as weird-looking nor remotely as unbalanced. Also, breaking out of Spero earned Scott bonus points for rebellion, as opposed to Leonard who, for all his infractions, stayed within the school boundaries. Leonard was glad when he heard about Scott's body being found, because it meant his rival was dead. As to how he got that way, Leonard chose not to speculate. Leonard Levesque could be blind, deaf, and mute when it suited him.

Nevertheless, it bothered him that any of the students might believe, seriously or not, in the return of Scott Theriault as a phantom. It implied Scott had unfinished business at Spero, and that kind of speculation needed to be nipped in the bud. One of those who was doing more whispering than most was Anthony Marshall, in part because Scott Theriault had intervened more than once to save Anthony from his persecutors, Leonard included. Leonard thought Scott did this to spite him. The idea that one person might intervene to protect another because it was the right thing to do was alien to Leonard. Stepping in as a demonstration of strength was comprehensible, or on a whim to see how it might feel, like trying on unfamiliar shoes, or even because it offered the prospect of an advantage gained or a favor to be held in reserve, but not because it was good or honorable. Like all those untroubled by conscience, Leonard Levesque saw the world purely in transactional terms. To be without a conscience was to be without a soul, which is why, in stories, the devil did not threaten, but sought to make deals with men. The devil was the ultimate transactional politician, and the damned nominated themselves.

So Scott Theriault had saved Anthony Marshall to thwart Leonard Levesque, and now Anthony, deprived of his protector, was attempting to resurrect Scott as an otherworldly guardian: Scotty the Unfriendly Ghost. Upon consideration of the matter, Leonard had determined on three linked courses of action: intimidation, to silence the whispers; observation, to locate the night visitor and reveal their true identity, like in *Scooby-Doo*; and finally, elimination, principally of the irritant represented by Anthony Marshall. Leonard would have enjoyed sending Anthony the way of Stewie Daigle, but if he couldn't make Anthony's life so miserable that he'd choose to end it, he could make him wish he was dead, which was the next best thing.

Leonard was just about to light a final cigarette from the butt of the previous and was thinking that, damn, the nights were getting colder, when whom should he spy, bent crooked as he scuttled along the pathway, but Anthony Marshall himself, little smart-mouth piss boy, all alone, and Leonard Levesque in the mood for devilment.

Leonard killed the butt and went to see what harm he might do.

CHAPTER XXXII

Anthony was shivering. The freestanding ablution block, as it was termed in a hangover from its National Guard days, was poorly heated, and the lighting was barely fit for purpose, so Anthony hadn't bothered to turn it on. He knew where he was going, and he didn't want to see what he was doing; he could hear, feel, and smell it well enough. More important, he didn't want to attract attention. He believed himself to have entered the block unobserved and by now was almost convinced that he had been mistaken about what he'd glimpsed from the dorm window. In case he wasn't, it was better to toil in the shadows. Lights drew insects, and other things, too. Enough moonlight shone through the narrow rectangular windows to content him.

He was just finishing up and was about to flush the evidence, when the stall door exploded inward, catching Anthony so hard that, with his pajama bottoms around his knees, he lost his balance and fell. He looked up to see Leonard Levesque standing in the gap, making a wafting gesture under his nose with his right hand.

"I think we're going to have to rename you," said Leonard. "Piss Boy isn't going to cut it anymore."

And Anthony Marshall managed a single cry before he was silenced.

CHAPTER XXXIII

James Renders, assistant principal of Spero School, sat up with a start in his cabin bed. He didn't know what had caused him to wake, but even deep in sleep, he'd registered a noise that was out of place. He listened but heard nothing more. He got out of bed, went to the window, and drew back the blind. He could see no lights in the dorms beyond those that always remained lit in case of emergencies and saw no sign of movement on the campus. Renders relaxed. It might have been the screech of a red fox that he heard. The animals were plentiful in the Kennebec, even if it was early in the season for females to be summoning a mate.

Renders was about to get back into bed when a rattling came from the cabin door. He looked over his shoulder to see the doorknob slowly turn, back and forth, though the motion-sensitive light outside had not come on. No one could have approached the cabin without activating the light, which was working fine earlier, and the grounds were empty when Renders had left the window moments before. Even a world-class sprinter couldn't have closed the gap between the nearest building and the cabin in that time.

Renders did not move. The door was locked and bolted from the inside, a precaution he'd begun to take in recent weeks. Patrick Elgot, who taught English, social sciences, and phys ed, admitted to doing the same when on night duty, even as he tried to make a joke of it. ("Sadlier tried locking up his seeds and that didn't help. I hope we're dealing with the ghost of a vegetarian.") Renders hadn't found it funny then and wasn't finding it funny now.

One of the kids has found a way to work around the sensor. Open the damn door and catch him in the act.

Renders didn't open the door.

You're a grown man.

Renders didn't feel like a grown man. He felt like a trapped child. But he wasn't going to let whatever was outside know it.

"Come on," he said. "It's just a door. If you want me that bad, you'll find a way. But don't think it won't go hard on you."

The doorknob ceased turning. Renders listened for teenage giggles, but none came. He returned to the window, this time lifting the blind on the opposite side to give himself a view of the doorstep. Nobody was there, the motion-sensor light remained dormant, and the grounds were quiet.

Renders retreated. His hands were shaking.

This school. This damned school.

CHAPTER

XXXIV

Leonard Levesque departed the ablution block and closed the door behind him. In his right hand he held Anthony Marshall's sodden pajama bottoms, which he tossed into the bushes with the boy's Crocs. Nearby, covered by a tarp, was stacked lumber of different lengths, which Sadlier, the custodian, planned to use to make repairs before winter set in. Leonard selected one that looked to be the right size and positioned it under the doorknob, kicking at it with his instep until it was lodged in place.

He stepped away and lit that last cigarette. He'd taken the time to wash his hands in the sink using the cheap soap from the dispenser, but he could still smell Anthony Marshall's waste on his fingers, or thought he could. Leonard dabbed at the blood on his white sleep shirt, not all of it his victim's. Piss Boy had caught him a few good ones before Leonard beat him down. Someone had taught him how to throw a punch, which Leonard wasn't expecting because Anthony had never fought back before; the kid must have been holding it all in reserve. The first two blows landed *smackity-smack* on Leonard's nose, and had he not been leaning back, he might well have broken it. As it was, he'd felt blood begin to flow, and was so shocked that Anthony nearly managed to slip by him—*nearly*, but nearly was worse than never, as Leonard's father often said, typically before he commenced landing some punches of his own. In common with Anthony Marshall, Chick Levesque didn't look like someone who knew how to use his fists—Leonard had inherited the bovine placidity of his features from his father, as well as the worst of what they concealed—but the old man was full of surprises, none of them pleasant. Leonard hoped to live long enough to see his father become sick and decrepit, at which point Leonard would step in to take care of him, like any good son should.

Leonard took a long, slow drag on the cigarette. He pictured Anthony Marshall in the ablution block, all naked and bloodied. Leonard tried to analyze how this made him feel, and concluded that he felt nothing.

Time for bed.

ANTHONY MARSHALL WAS SLUMPED NAKED on the floor of the stall, surrounded by water and his own filth. Distantly, he was aware of the sound of a door closing, then quiet. Anthony, too, was silent. He'd stopped crying a while back, because when he cried, Leonard Levesque hurt him more. As a result, Anthony had retreated so far into himself that he was barely cognizant of what was being inflicted on him, even as he struggled to understand what he could possibly have done to deserve it. Leonard's attack had progressed beyond any routine concept of bullying or degradation to become a sustained, ferocious assault on Anthony's very spirit, an attempt to reduce him to nothing but blood, shit, piss, and puke, an entity nameless and without consequence. What Anthony would specifically take away from the experience, retaining it unto the grave, was an impression of violation that was not alone physical but sexual, and the memory of Leonard Levesque's face, which barely altered in expression throughout, so that it might have been a mask worn by whatever demon it was that shared his body and revealed itself only in such moments.

Anthony's arms were wrapped around him against the cold. As he came back to himself, he knew he could not stay in the ablution block. He didn't think the night would freeze, not this early in fall, but the temperature wouldn't have to drop much lower to make him sick, and Spero was unsympathetic to illness. He would need to shower first; he couldn't return to the dorm like this. But the water would be cold and he didn't have a towel, just the now-soiled T-shirt he'd been wearing with his PJ bottoms, and he didn't want to dry himself with that. He'd have to use paper towels. He braced himself against the toilet bowl to get up, and pain made itself known in places that hadn't hurt before he moved. He was sure Leonard Levesque hadn't broken any bones—that wasn't the way Leonard operated—but there would be bruising and bleeding.

Since arriving at Spero, Anthony had tried not to think about his mom and dad because it made him sad and angry. He hoped Mr. Santopietro would allow him to call and tell them what had happened. They might then reconsider their decision to send him to Spero and come to take him home. If they did, Anthony would promise to try harder. He'd find a way to make regular school work. He'd keep his appointments with the counselor and swallow any pills they told him to. He'd do anything his parents asked, if only they'd get him away from this place and Leonard Levesque.

Through one of the high rectangular windows, Anthony could see the moon. He stared at it for a time, until a cloud drifted across its face, breaking the spell, followed by a *tap-tap-tapp*ing from above his head as a night creature ran across the roof: a raccoon, or a big owl preparing to take flight. Anthony commenced a slow shuffle to the stall door. He had his hand on the clasp when he thought he heard a noise from the other side: fabric brushing against ceramic, followed by what might have been a footstep. It was Leonard Levesque, it had to be. Leonard, who had gone through the motions of pretending to leave, closing the door behind him and rattling the knob, when all the time he'd been waiting for Anthony to recover from the first beating so he could deliver a second. But Anthony couldn't take another beating. He'd die. He was sure of it.

He found his tongue.

"Please, Leonard," said Anthony. "Please leave me alone. I'm sorry for whatever I did. I won't do it again, ever, and I won't tell anyone what happened, I swear. I just want to get cleaned up and go back to the dorm. Please, Leonard. Please."

But there was no reply.

Anthony pressed his forehead against the wood of the old stall. He was sure he was going to throw up again.

"Please," he whispered one more time, and opened the door.

CHAPTER

Anthony Marshall emerged from the stall to be confronted by his reflection in one of the small mirrors above the sinks on the opposite wall. The mirrors were barely worthy of the name, being so dirty and oxidized that even in daylight any image presented was barely identifiable, but the glass into which Anthony was staring was clear enough for him to be able to see his swollen eyes and damp hair, and the blood around his nose and mouth. He glanced to his left, toward the door. Anthony feared Leonard might be hiding in one of the stalls, waiting to spring out and resume hurting him. Painfully, he leaned down to peer under the stall and along the floor. He spotted no feet. Again, Leonard might have been standing on one of the bowls, but Anthony didn't think he'd go to that much trouble. One by one he checked the stalls, but each was empty.

He was tempted to make a break for the door, but if Leonard had somehow slipped by him and was now in the showers, Anthony didn't want him at his back. He risked a peek around the corner. The long shower stall, with its line of rusted heads, was also empty. For the first time, Anthony allowed himself to relax. Leonard had warned Anthony to stay where he was until daylight, but Anthony was banking on Leonard caring too much for his own comfort to hang around outside. No, Leonard was gone and Anthony was alone.

He could smell himself. He stank, and he wasn't only dirty but unclean, which was something different. Leonard had made him feel that way by the manner in which he'd abused him and the intimate places he'd chosen to target. Yes, the shower water would be chilly, but compared to what he'd just suffered, it wouldn't be so bad.

Anthony hung his T-shirt on a hook and turned on the nearest shower water faucet. The pipes protested, and at first the head spat it rather than sprayed it, but then the pressure kicked in. Anthony dipped his head under the flow. It was, as anticipated, fiercely cold, and he tolerated it only for a few seconds, which wasn't going to make him clean again. He took a deep breath and exposed the whole of his body, clinging to the exposed pipe for strength. The pain was worse where the water hit his injuries, but then it began to ease and a numbness descended. Anthony knew this was how people died of exposure. He liked to read about expeditions and adventures, and stories of polar explorers who'd become lost in the snow. Some of those who survived described the sensation of their systems shutting down, how they stopped noticing the cold and started to fall asleep, and had they done so, would never have woken again. Anthony would have liked that. He could sit in the shower with the water running, going more and more numb until he fell asleep, never to wake, and thus he would escape Spero. It was probably the only way he could, because his parents weren't going to come for him, no matter what. Mr. Santopietro wasn't going to let him call home to report a beating, and even if he could be persuaded to inform Anthony's mom and pop that an incident had occurred, Anthony was sure the principal would play down its severity. Tensions between students were always an issue in schools, and more so among the kind of teens with whom Spero was required to deal. *If they weren't quarrelsome, they wouldn't be at Spero to begin with. Am I right, Mr. and Mrs. Marshall? Huh, huh? Y'hear what I'm saying? Sure I am. Your boy will be fine. He's in good hands. What we have here are teething troubles . . .*

Teething troubles. Anthony tested one of his molars with his tongue and felt movement. He hoped he wouldn't lose it and add a gap-toothed mouth to his problems.

By now the shower had cleared his head and he smelled of nothing worse than the soap in the dispenser. With luck, his roommates would still be asleep and no one would notice him returning to the dormitory. He had a clean pair of pajama bottoms in his locker. He could put them on, climb into bed, and try to get some rest before wake-up at seven. He'd be stiff and sore by then, and what would he tell the others? The truth, he supposed, or as much of it as he cared to share. It wasn't as if he'd be able to hide the cuts and bruises to his face, but he wouldn't tell them about the rest of it.

Anthony turned off the shower and reached for his T-shirt. It wasn't exactly spotless, but he didn't want to leave without it, and he could use it to cover much of his nakedness. For once, he was glad the shirt was too big for him. But the T-shirt was gone. Anthony looked at the floor, expecting to see it lying where it had fallen, except it wasn't there either. Once more, Leonard Levesque loomed large in his mind. It wasn't enough to steal his pajama bottoms; Leonard had to come back for the shirt as well.

"Shit on you, Leonard," Anthony said aloud. He rarely swore—those kinds of words never sat comfortably in his mouth—but whereas before he'd been sad and scared, now he was furious. How hard would it have been for Leonard to leave him with his shirt? How low could a person stoop? Anthony wanted to kick the bathroom to pieces, and Leonard Levesque with it. Then, as suddenly as it had flared, the anger was gone.

"Oh, go to hell," Anthony added softly. Only much later would he identify this as a turning point, the beginning of his escape from the patterns of behavior that had led him to Spero. The old Anthony would have tried to yank a sink from the wall before going mute for days. The new Anthony, or the nascent one, wished only to sleep. Where once blind temper would have reigned, there was now disappointment and resignation.

Anthony left the shower and dried himself as best he could with paper towels. When he was done, he revisited the scene of the crime and used more paper towels to clean up the mess on the floor. It was possible that Mr. Sadlier might have taken care of it without mentioning it to Mr. Santopietro or one of the other members of staff, but if he didn't, questions would be asked, with someone obliged to accept the blame. Should no one confess, the punishment would be communal, and the innocent would exact their revenge on the guilty party. Taking care of business now would save Anthony from having to do it in the morning, avoiding unwelcome questions into the bargain.

He was shivering again, and any numbness from the shower had worn off, so he was hurting too. He went to the door but the handle wouldn't turn. He tried shouldering it, with no result. He didn't think the door was locked, since only staff had keys, so either the lock itself had failed or Leonard Levesque had jammed it to keep him inside. If Anthony kicked hard enough, whatever was blocking it might come loose. He stepped back and struck the door with the sole of his right foot, but succeeded only in sending waves of pain through his damaged body.

He was done. He needed help if he wasn't going to spend the rest of the night in the block. *You'll catch your death*: that was what his mom, who was born in England, would have said. To her, it meant you risked getting a bad cold, but Anthony was afraid it might have a more literal meaning in this case. He banged on the door, shouted, and listened. No response. He tried again—bang, shout, listen—with still no sign of anyone coming to his aid.

Something landed on the floor beside him, so softly that he didn't even notice it was there until his left foot brushed against it. He glanced down at the ball of wadded paper that he'd recently deposited in the trash can. He turned, his right leg raised to shield his groin from the blow he was certain was coming. He saw nothing, but Leonard Levesque had to be hiding somewhere. He had to be, because if he was not—

In the gloom at the far end of the block, close to the last stall, Anthony detected movement: a swirling in the dark, like smoke billowing in a breeze, and then it was gone, or not gone, not totally, because patterns shifted in the mirrors on the wall, gliding from one pane to the next, and Anthony realized that he was looking at a human form, the reflection of a shadow, but there was nothing to offer substance, no shape to be reflected. Yet something was drawing nearer. Anthony could follow its approach in the mirrors, could hear its breathing, and while it might only have been visible in reproduction, as if it possessed a more profound reality behind the glass than in front of it, some aspect of it was nevertheless present in the block.

Anthony tried the door again, keeping his back to it because he was afraid to look away from whatever was coming, and he mumbled words that had no meaning, even to himself. Then the presence was standing before him, perceived but concealed, while in the closest of the mirrors the darkness of it expanded, like ink diffusing in water; and Anthony knew it for what and who it was, though some atavistic part of his mind registered that it was not the totality of a person but one aspect of it; and he was right to be terrified because what had returned was a creature excised of rationality, retaining only an emotional purity beyond regulation, and what roiled in the glass was a manifestation of its hostility. The hair above Anthony's left ear rose as if by the action of static electricity. The strands were being handled—gently at first, then harder, so that he was abruptly yanked toward the presence, and he smelled mud and mold and the stagnancy of standing water. In the mirror only his face was visible, while all around him was enshadowed, and he feared that this blackness might flow into him and he would drown in darkness, drown like this boy had drowned. For the second time that night, Anthony pleaded.

"Don't hurt me, Scott," he said. "Please. I'm sorry for what happened to you, honest I am. Please, just let me go."

But as the presence embraced him, Anthony knew that this was not Scott, or not Scott alone. No, here were multitudes. The grip on his hair tightened as the room swam around him. The floor rushed toward him, and he wondered how it could be moving so fast, and only when his head connected with it did he think, *Oh, it was me all along—*

CHAPTER

XXXVI

Tim Sadlier woke alone in his bachelor bed. He couldn't recall when last he hadn't woken alone, but it must have been before COVID: two years before, if he was being charitable, three if not. The pandemic had blurred his concept of the passage of time, and he was no longer always sure of when it had begun—2019? 2020?—or even that it had really happened at all. It represented an unwelcome interregnum, a hiatus in reality.

The clock on the bedside table showed 4:08 a.m., but Sadlier liked to set the time ten minutes fast. It meant he was never late for anything, which made no objective sense because obviously he was aware, on one level, that all his timepieces were wrong. However, he lived his life as though they were not, just as he lived it as though the larger world was not itself out of joint. It had been out of joint for as long as he could recall. As a boy, he'd endured the fear of nuclear war, and later, the hole in the ozone layer. Now, as an adult, nuclear war remained a possibility, but he didn't know whether the hole in the ozone layer still existed. If it did, nobody was talking as much about it, probably because it had been overtaken by worse environmental threats. Sadlier was glad he'd never had children, as it spared him having to explain to them why everything was all fucked-up and no one seemed interested in unfucking it, or how children at summer camp in Texas could be washed away by a river swollen by months of rain falling in a matter of hours and the response from the authorities could amount to *well, shit happens*. All Tim Sadlier could say for sure was that a lot of people's grandchildren were going to be cursing their grandparents for being assholes.

Something had been nagging at him, something to do with Scott Theriault, Leonard Levesque, and Spero. In his sleep, he had almost figured out what it was, or thought he had, but awake, it slipped from him. He could try to drowse awhile in the hope of recapturing it, but he knew from experience that this would make it harder for him to get up in an hour or so. Chasing sleep was like chasing memories or motes of dust: the object only drifted farther off.

Sadlier lived in the same six-room Plains house in which he'd been born: two bedrooms, a kitchen, a dining room, a living room, and a bathroom. His elderly mother had shared it with him until 2015, when she could no longer look after herself while he was at work and he'd been forced to consign her to an assisted-living facility in Dover-Foxcroft. She remained there, telling him how much she hated it when he visited each week, and how she wanted to go home. He'd taken to popping a pill a few hours in advance to help keep him calm. If he took two, he even forgot what a bad son he was.

Sadlier went to the bathroom, showered in lukewarm water because the tank was only starting to heat up, dressed, and headed to the kitchen, where he intended to make a cup of coffee and read for an hour. He knew he ought to catch the early-morning news, but that was a penance he decided to shirk. A novel would offer him some escape from reality.

Tim Sadlier didn't have many luxuries; he couldn't afford them. He didn't have the internet for the same reason. When he did need it—which was less often than he wanted it, the two being easily conflated by the simple-minded—he had access to Spero's, or he could log on at the Bingham Union Library. He could also visit the Starbucks in Waterville for a change of scenery, but that required him to travel more than forty miles just to pay for a coffee, and he wasn't willing to give Starbucks money for what they put in their cups.

Which brought him back to the matter of luxuries, however modest. Sadlier liked to start the day by grinding beans bought at Jimmy's Shop 'n' Save in Bingham, brewing enough coffee for two cups in the Bialetti moka pot that someone had donated to the Goodwill in Windham, unused and still in its box, with a card inside from Chris and Irene wishing Daniel and Bethany every happiness on their wedding day. Sadlier's mother, had she known about it, might have warned that the pot would bring him no luck, and Daniel and Bethany were now either divorced or dead. But whatever had happened to Daniel and Bethany, the pot had brought Sadlier nothing but pleasure, from the grinding, the measuring, and the tapping to the smell of the coffee infusing the kitchen, and finally, that first sip.

But on this morning, with its sluggish dawn and the trees in the yard sticky with dark, Tim Sadlier would not have his coffee. When he entered the kitchen he saw that the coffee jar was overturned and his precious beans scattered across the counter, some of them spilling into the sink for the dripping tap to spoil. More of the beans lay on the kitchen table, where they had no business being, not if the rest were on the counter. Sadlier's first thought was that an animal must have gotten into the house and he'd have to hunt for an engorged rat or a hyped-up raccoon. He was surprised he hadn't heard anything during the night because he was a light sleeper and—

Sadlier stared at the bean jar. The jar had a screw-top lid, which stood beside it on the counter, and the glass was unbroken. Sadlier kept the lid screwed tight to save his beans, and while raccoons were dexterous enough to be able to manipulate a host of objects, no raccoon yet born was strong enough to open that coffee jar. Also, he couldn't see how the coon might have gained entry; the doors and windows were all closed, and Sadlier didn't pick up any hint of a draft.

He looked more closely at the beans on the kitchen table. What had first appeared a random sprinkling now revealed a pattern: letters, words.

SAD-LIER.

HELP.

CHAPTER XXXVII

Sadlier got to Spero an hour earlier than usual, which would ordinarily have pained him, a man who begrudged the school every minute for which he wasn't being paid—and doubly on this morning, when he was unfueled by coffee. After what was done with his beans, he'd given the routine a pass. And while there was much about the incident in his kitchen that justifiably gave him cause to be disquieted, it was the way his name was hyphenated that bothered him most: Sad-lier, or more correctly, *Saaaad-lier*, with the first syllable drawn out. Only one person at Spero had given it that emphasis, a person now drowned to death, so either someone was playing a very mean trick, or—

For now, Sadlier didn't care to dwell on that *or*.

He was still not sure why he felt compelled to get to Spero. Neither did he know who he was supposed to help, which brought him back to the *or*, the one he really preferred not to contemplate. For the moment, Sadlier was doing the only thing he could: arrive at the school and take a look around, which had the added bonus of getting him out of his violated home. He'd taken the time to search each of its rooms before he left, even looking in his bedroom closet and under the bed. He didn't mind admitting that he'd been on the verge of filling his pants as he opened those closet doors, and again when he went down on his hands and knees to get intimate with the dust bunnies, because all the windows were locked and the doors bolted from the inside—he'd checked those too—so whoever was responsible for spelling out the message with his coffee beans might still be in the house. If they weren't, then—

Screw you again, *or*.

But no one had looked back at him from inside the closet or under the bed, which was a relief, if a temporary one.

Sadlier parked his truck in his usual spot. To the right, behind a low hedge surrounding a neatly tended garden, was the residence of Mr. Santopietro, who lived on-site permanently. To the left were the staff cabins, one of which was currently occupied by Vice Principal Renders as part of the supervisory roster operated by the school. Staff rotations meant that for three nights in every nine one of the off-site teachers was required to reside on campus, where they were considered "on duty" and available to students. Santopietro could be called on for backup, but only in the event of an emergency. When not at the school, most of the teachers lived in rented accommodations in the area.

The school had a full-time teaching staff of just four: Santopietro; Renders; Patrick Elgot, who had arrived shortly before COVID kicked in; and Grady Bessant, though Bessant had been on medical leave since September and, rumor had it, was reluctant to return. He and Renders had never gotten along, which was not helped by the fact that Bessant had expected to be appointed assistant principal when Santopietro first announced the role, and it had instead gone to Renders, who had only been a short time at Spero. Elgot, by contrast, had shown no interest in being promoted, even though it would have meant a salary increase; however, like Bessant and Sadlier, he hadn't taken to Renders from the off. Sadlier believed Elgot to be biding his time and banking his money until something better opened up, avoiding any conflict with Renders while he was about it. Only Santopietro was tight with Renders.

Sadlier didn't think four full-time teachers was even close to enough to supervise and educate more than four times as many difficult teenagers, even if they were supported by recruits from a pool of retired local educators, each paid by the hour, but the truth was that education was not Spero's primary function. The school was a correctional facility in all but name, and education was merely one of the tools available to alter behavior. Nobody expected Spero to produce geniuses, and few of the students stayed long enough for anyone to be able to try.

The parking lot still bore faint traces of the distancing warnings from the pandemic. Spero had been more fortunate than many schools during COVID since it was already operating in its own bubble. Most of the students opted to stay—or more correctly, were not given a choice by their parents—so the pandemic caused only minimal interruption to its program. Spero managed to get through the whole of the first year without a single confirmed case of the virus, and the second with just two. A lot of that was down to location, but also a concerted effort to protect both students and staff from infection. Sadlier, too, had played his part. He supposed it was something to be proud of.

Sadlier noticed that Elgot's Jeep was already in place, which didn't surprise him; if the weather was good, Elgot liked to get in early for a run before breakfast. Sadlier spotted him warming up over by the main building. Elgot was lean, like a life-size human model assembled from pipe cleaners and twigs, but Sadlier wished he wouldn't wear such tight Lycra. It left little to the imagination, reminding Sadlier of someone trying to smuggle root vegetables in their shorts. But Elgot's appointment as the phys ed teacher had resulted in an improvement in the overall physical health of the students, and whatever helped the kids physically might, with luck, also aid them emotionally and psychologically, although they might not have felt that way while jogging or hiking in the rain. It surprised Sadlier that Elgot and Santopietro got on so well together, since the latter couldn't have run more than a few yards without stopping for breath, not even if pursued by wolves. Sadlier figured that, as opposites, they complemented each other. He'd heard of marriages that worked in a similar fashion.

Noticing Sadlier, Elgot detoured to say hello and make sure nothing was amiss.

"You're up with the dawn," said Elgot. "It's not like you to be here before you have to."

This was said with a grin, but there was an edge nonetheless. Elgot could be patronizing, but Sadlier forgave him because it was unintentional, a product of social awkwardness more than rudeness.

"Couldn't sleep," said Sadlier. "Thought I'd make myself useful, and if I couldn't do that, I'd make myself breakfast."

Spero employed a cohort of local women to look after cooking, cleaning, and laundry, but the pair on duty today wouldn't start for another hour. In reality, Sadlier wasn't hungry in the least, not with the morning he'd had, but he wasn't about to share with Elgot a tale of words spelled out in coffee beans or a fruitless search for an intruder in a house that was all locked up.

"Wait a little longer and someone will make it for you," said Elgot. "Yum. All that good stuff."

None of which Elgot would touch, of course, preferring to stick to a protein shake, nuts, and two poached eggs if he felt like spoiling himself. Sadlier knew observant Jews who were more likely than Patrick Elgot to eat a couple of slices of bacon for breakfast.

"Any sign of Mr. Renders?" Sadlier asked.

"His drapes are still drawn," said Elgot. "And you know how—"

But Sadlier was no longer listening. The door to the main dormitory building was ajar, which meant one of the students might be up. That in itself was unusual, since the boys, like Renders, never got out of bed until they had to. One of them could have gone down to use the facilities in the ablution block—Sadlier made a mental note to remind Santopietro about chasing up the plumber—but whoever it was should have had the sense to close the door behind him, because it was a cool morning. If Elgot spotted the lapse, he'd take time out from his run to do some shouting.

Now Elgot had seen it too, because he said: "Who left that damn door open?"

Together the two men went to investigate, but it was Sadlier who spotted the length of two-by-four rammed against the door of the ablution block. He felt his stomach sink. He broke away from Elgot and was already freeing the wood from under the doorknob by the time the teacher joined him. Yet even when the lumber was set aside, the door still wouldn't budge. The lock had been sticking for a while, but the wood had been jammed against the knob with enough force to knock the whole mechanism out of true. After a few minutes of jiggling, Sadlier was about to give up and fetch a crowbar when the knob finally turned and the door opened.

Anthony Marshall was sitting half-naked under one of the sinks. His eyes were squeezed shut and his face was so pale that had he not been shivering uncontrollably, Sadlier might have taken him for dead.

"Go fetch a blanket to cover him," he told Elgot, and to his credit, the teacher didn't hesitate or argue. Meanwhile, Sadlier removed his overcoat, eased the boy from beneath the sink, and placed the coat around his shoulders. All the time, Anthony kept his eyes closed.

"Can you stand, son?"

Anthony didn't answer. Sadlier tried to lift him, but Anthony's legs had cramped up and he would have fallen had Sadlier not put an arm around him. Not wishing to set him down again on the tile floor, Sadlier gathered him up and carried him from the block toward the dorm. By then Elgot was emerging with a blanket, as well as a pair of jeans, underwear, socks, sneakers, and a sweatshirt that he must have found in the boy's locker. Behind him stood two of Anthony's roommates, who'd been woken by the commotion and come to see what the fuss was about. Elgot unfolded the blanket and draped it awkwardly over the boy's lower body.

"Anthony," he said, "who did this? Who locked you in?"

Anthony Marshall opened his eyes and blinked against the early-morning light.

"It's not my fault," he said.

"I know that. Nobody is blaming you. We just want to—"

"I tried to tell him," said Anthony, "but he wouldn't listen."

"Who wouldn't?"

Anthony shook his head.

"Because it wasn't him," he continued, "not really."

His eyes darted madly.

Elgot looked at Sadlier, who said: "We should take him to the medical center in Bingham. I don't know how long he was stuck in there, but he's real cold. I can drive, but I'll need you to come with me."

"I can do that. I'll tell Santopietro, and then roust Renders from his bed."

Elgot ran to wake the principal while Sadlier carried Anthony to his truck. He put the boy in the back seat, buttoned the overcoat around him, got in the driver's seat, turned the heater up high, and closed the door. He glanced at Anthony in the rearview mirror. Anthony stared back at him.

"Who did it, son?" Sadlier asked.

"The dead boy," said Anthony. "And the ones with him."

CHAPTER

XXXVIII

The sun was streaming through the window when I woke, but it brought only light, not warmth. Beside me, Macy stirred. She'd come over on Thursday evening for dinner and decided to stay for breakfast on Friday.

"What time is it?" she asked, without opening her eyes.

"After eight."

"Five more minutes."

"You're not working today," I reminded her.

"Five more hours, then."

"How about splitting the difference?"

"How about going away and letting me sleep?"

I went away and let her sleep.

DOWNSTAIRS, I MADE A MUG OF INSTANT COFFEE and browned some toast. Out on the marshes, the grass had turned from summer verdant to fall gold. The greenhead flies were gone, so it was safe to leave the kitchen door open and let the salt smell fill the air. Over the water, a flock of shorebirds wheeled left and right, in their midst the larger, darker shape of a raptor hunting. I watched until the predator gave up the chase, its instincts warning it to conserve its energy for easier prey.

With my laptop open on the kitchen table and a notebook by my right hand, I considered how best to handle the Scott Theriault case. Having agreed to look into the circumstances surrounding his death, I was now faced with one of the challenges presented by any investigation in Maine that deviated from the I-295/95 corridor, namely the sheer size of the state. The Plains was a good six-hour round trip from Portland, so it wasn't as if I could just dip in and out of there on a whim. Planning was required.

I would have to talk to the staff at Spero about Scott, assuming they were willing—or permitted—to speak to me. I'd also have welcomed the opportunity to interview Scott's fellow students, but Spero was under no obligation to provide me with access. Unlike police, private investigators did not have a right to talk to minors without parental consent, and a worst-case scenario would see Spero's authorities telling me to take a hike. If they did, I'd be close to some good trails. Unfortunately, I didn't like hiking. I doubted I'd get much from Spero anyway, or not beyond whatever Santopietro had already shared with the media. The school wasn't going to welcome an unofficial inquiry into the death of a student just weeks after an official investigation had essentially absolved it of blame. More groundwork was needed before I set aside a couple of days for The Plains; a trip up there now would be wasted because I didn't know the right questions to ask.

But as soon as I began nosing around, it was possible that word would get back to Spero. Given too much time to think, even honest subjects begin trying to get their stories straight, and nothing is set to make a story more crooked than someone trying to straighten it. As for dishonest subjects, they grab a spade, literal or metaphorical, and get to burying. At least experience had taught me to spot the signs. It was another reason to let Spero stew.

In addition to tackling Spero, I might be interested in speaking to Mallory Norton's parents. I didn't think I'd have any difficulty persuading them to talk to me, because when a child goes missing, the parents typically open up to anyone who might be prepared to listen or help. If the parents don't open up, they may be part of the problem, and the search for the child needs to focus on the family's backyard. I had no proof that Scott and Mallory were an item, and the two occurrences—one death, one disappearance—might have been coincidental, but that ignored another fact about Maine: it was simultaneously sprawling and small, which made for improbable correlations.

I turned my attention back to Spero. Alcock's file didn't indicate whether the school was in receipt of public funds. If it was, it meant a commissioner from the Maine Board of Education would be required to conduct periodic inspections to ensure compliance with code. In other words, someone in authority, with knowledge of the field, might be able to provide an insight into the running of Spero before I went knocking on its door. A list of Maine private schools approved for public tuition funds was available on the state's website. What it revealed was that a) sending a kid to a private school in Maine could be injurious to your bank balance; and b) Spero had not received public funds for the current year.

But because I'm nothing if not tenacious and it had started raining and I didn't want to go out until it stopped, I worked my way back through a decade's worth of previous funding lists to discover that Spero had received public funding only for its first five years, presumably until it sourced enough students to be able to operate independently. So, during its development, someone at the department was responsible for monitoring Spero. The Maine Department of Education was in Augusta, which was only an hour away. I added "MDE" to my growing register of names.

I heard movement from upstairs. Shortly after, Macy joined me in the kitchen. She made herself a cup of tea, because she often couldn't stomach coffee first thing, stole the last of my cold toast, and slid my notebook toward her.

"Hey," I said. "That could be secret stuff."

"Secret, like what? The names of girls you moon over in biology class?"

"Lucy Bernstein is kind of hot."

"Who's Lucy Bernstein?"

"She sat in the front row of my biology class at Scarborough High."

"And you still think about her?"

"No, but I saw her yesterday at the Shaw's. She really is kind of hot. Still."

Macy kicked my shin under the table, but since she was barefoot, it hurt her more than it hurt me. She pushed the notebook back to me. She was aware that I was working on behalf of Ward Vose, but beyond that, we hadn't discussed the case. It was an agreement to which we tried to adhere, because my role as a private investigator might lead to ethical or professional conflicts with her job as an officer with the Portland Police Department. Unless asked, she would not involve herself in my work and I would not involve myself in hers, otherwise we'd risk our relationship falling apart, and we did not want that. Nevertheless, it was a loose agreement, since neither of us could completely ignore the other's vocation or the similarities between us.

"What do you see so far?" she asked.

I ran my finger over names and places.

"Unconnected dots."

"And if you join them?"

"A squiggle."

"But?"

"There are irregularities, and I don't like irregularity."

"That's unfortunate, given how much of it you live with."

Macy knew a great deal about me. She knew that I sometimes saw my dead child. She knew that my dead wife, too, used to seek me out, but mercifully no longer did so. None of this she doubted. Her experiences as a rookie cop on Sanctuary Island had taught her that this world lay alongside another and the boundaries between them were permeable. On that Maine island, Macy had learned uncomfortable truths about the universe.

I hadn't yet shared with her what Angel and I had spoken of on the journey to Rockland and in the restaurant after. Now I did. I told her all of it, including Angel's premonition that an end was coming. When I was done, she said: "Angel is a pessimist trapped in a pessimist's body."

"What about Louis? Because he feels the same way."

"I can't say what Louis is, beyond being an enigma trapped in a pessimist's body." She finished her tea and boiled the water afresh to make more. "Do you think they're right?"

"I hope not."

"So do I."

We didn't speak for a while. We were good with silence. It came with the trade.

When the second cup of tea was ready, Macy sat at the table again.

"What do we do?"

"We live our lives," I said. "What else can we do?"

"It's like breakfast with Samuel Beckett."

"Who said an education was wasted on you as a police officer?"

"I think they said that about my looks."

"Mine too."

She laughed.

"Let's go back to bed."

"Yes," I said. "Let's."

CHAPTER

XXXIX

The medical center in Bingham tended to Anthony Marshall's cuts and bruises, and the doctor on duty advised Elgot to make sure the boy got bed rest and stayed warm. Tylenol would help with any pain.

"That was a nasty beating he took," said the doctor. "Nothing's broken, but it was mean. It doesn't fall under the mandated-reporter law because I don't believe it's a question of abuse or neglect. However, if another kid at the school was responsible, you may have issues that need to be addressed."

"Did he tell you who did it?" Elgot asked.

"Nope. You?"

Elgot shook his head. He turned to Sadlier, who was seated nearby.

"Tim, are you sure Anthony didn't say anything while I was absent?"

"No names," said Sadlier, which, while not a lie, wasn't the whole truth either. Anthony hadn't spoken again to either of them on the ride down to Bingham, and he obviously hadn't mentioned anything about dead boys to the staff at the center. Dead boys didn't deliver beatings, but Sadlier was no longer certain even of that, because those coffee beans on his kitchen table hadn't arranged themselves into letters unaided.

Sad-lier. *Saaad*-lier.

A nurse escorted Anthony from the treatment room. He was wearing the clothes that Elgot had brought for him. Some of the color was back in his face, but he still looked shaken. Sadlier returned to the term the medic had used to describe the attack: *mean*. That word immediately brought to mind one person at Spero, which was Leonard Levesque, whom Sadlier had once caught killing hummingbirds with a slingshot. It was just like him to be unsatisfied with delivering a simple beating and add cruelty to the mix. Elgot might have been a jackass on occasion, but he wasn't a fool with it, so he must have been thinking along the same lines. Why, then, had Anthony talked to Sadlier of a dead boy? Shock might explain it, or perhaps there were two distinct components involved here, only one of them being Leonard Levesque.

The nurse produced the blanket and Sadlier's coat, both neatly folded. Sadlier took them from her. They smelled faintly of Spero soap. Elgot asked Anthony if he was good to go. Anthony nodded.

"Well," said Elgot, "let's head back, then."

Sadlier noticed that he didn't touch the boy, not even to pat him on the shoulder. He might have been worried about hitting a tender spot, even lightly, though Spero also had any number of rules regarding appropriate contact between staff and students. It might not have occurred to Elgot that what the boy needed most was a reassuring hug, because Spero wasn't a haven for hugs. Not for the first time, Sadlier speculated that were he a father, the last place he'd send a kid was a school like Spero, because no child was going to be better off by the end of it.

Sadlier followed Elgot and Anthony out of the medical center. Once again, the boy got in the back, and Elgot took the passenger seat. Sadlier put the folded blanket and coat beside Anthony in case he got cold again, even with the heater blasting. Sadlier started the engine and turned on the radio to give them something to listen to on the ride back, but Elgot immediately turned down the volume.

"Anthony," said Elgot, "you have to tell us what happened."

For Sadlier, there was a performative aspect to how Elgot spoke. Had Elgot and the boy been alone, the teacher might not have raised the issue, and not only because he already had a good idea who the culprit was.

"I fell," said the boy.

"You fell, then locked yourself in with a block of wood?"

"I fell," the boy repeated.

Elgot glanced at Sadlier and shrugged.

I tried. What more can I do?

Elgot restored the volume. They drove on.

AT SPERO, ELGOT AND SADLIER WATCHED Anthony return to his dorm. He'd be alone there, because the rest of the kids were already in class. After that, he'd have the weekend to rest. By Monday, he might be okay again.

"Leonard Levesque," said Sadlier. "That's who did it. No one else here is that kind of vicious."

"Unless, or until, Anthony opens up, let's not go pointing fingers," said Elgot. "I'd better bring Mr. Santopietro up to speed. You ought to have something to eat. You never did get that breakfast."

Elgot said nothing more. Sadlier watched him go. He looked to the dorm and saw Anthony at the window. Sadlier gave him a small wave, but the boy did not respond, only stepped away from the glass.

Sadlier went to the kitchen, where the women were preparing lunch. They asked him what had happened and he told them what he knew for sure.

"Some of those boys are no better than animals," said Lizbeth Cyr, the older of the two.

"Lower than animals," said her colleague, Jeannie Merrill. "No animal would torment one of its own like that."

She told Sadlier that she'd put a tray of food together for Anthony and take it to the dorm: cold cuts, cookies, soda, and candy too, things he could choose to eat now or save for later. Sadlier said he thought that would be much appreciated. He commenced scavenging from the refrigerator, but Lizzie Cyr made him sit down at the small staff table while she fried up bacon and eggs, and Jeannie Merrill poured him a cup of coffee that she'd made fresh, not poured from the Mr. Coffee stewing since breakfast.

"Which one of them did it, do you think?" Jeannie asked.

"The boy didn't say."

"That wasn't the question."

She was sharp, Jeannie. They both were, country-sharp, and wasted on their menfolk in Sadlier's view.

"Levesque, maybe," he conceded.

"Will he own up?"

"No."

"So what will Mr. S do?"

"What can he do?" Lizzie interjected. "He can't punish someone without proof, not even a little shit like Levesque."

Sadlier thought Santopietro might have a word with Levesque anyway, and without openly accusing him, let him know a line had been crossed that must not be crossed again. The women left Sadlier to eat in peace, or what would have to pass for it, and only when he had finished and was putting his silverware and plate in the dishwasher did they speak again.

"They're planning another search for Mallory Norton," said Lizzie.

Sadlier looked up.

"Who, the police?"

"No. Bennett Small is organizing it."

Bennett Small owned The Plains' sole convenience store, which also functioned as a make-do diner and social hub, thanks to four tables and some mismatched chairs. At election time, Small's was also where folks in The Plains went to cast their vote, although elections no longer represented opportunities to be sociable with one's neighbors, and Sadlier feared they never would again.

"When are they going?"

"Sunday, sometime after nine."

"I can spare a few hours," said Sadlier.

"Then we'll see you there."

They were looking for a body, of course, and had been for a while. But if the Norton girl was out there, she deserved to be brought back and given a proper burial. She was one of their own. As for the parents, Sadlier wasn't a believer in closure, and only someone who didn't understand the reality of suffering and loss would ever be foolish enough to use the word. But a burial would allow them to mourn the girl and give them somewhere to visit while they kept on mourning her, as they would for the remainder of their days.

Sadlier went to his toolshed and pulled together the equipment to replace the lock on the door of the ablution block. Afterward, he'd try to catch a minute with Mr. Santopietro and hear what he had to say about the morning's events. Depending on the outcome of that conversation, Sadlier might have to ruminate further on his future. He loved The Plains—it was the only home he'd ever known—but he wasn't confident he could spend many more winters there. He had a small sum of money saved, and the house was now in his name. Property in The Plains was hard to dispose of, so he didn't hold out much hope for a windfall, but he knew of people who'd fit out family homes for use as camps by hunters and folks from away. So he might not even have to sell up to make money, just settle for a semiregular income depending on the season. If he found himself a place in Skowhegan, where there were bars, stores, restaurants, and neighbors you could holler to from your front porch—hell, even women who might be lonely enough to settle for one of the scrapings from the bottom of life's barrel—he'd be close enough to maintain the property. He could even hold on to his job at Spero, if he wanted to—

But he didn't want to. He'd reached that conclusion as he watched Anthony Marshall being helped into the examination room by a nurse. First Stewie Daigle during COVID, then Scott Theriault, and now Anthony Marshall. Okay, the last of them hadn't died, but if he'd been trapped in that block in winter instead of fall, he might well have. Sadlier wished to have no more part of it. Spero was a sad, bad place, and if he remained there it would destroy him—not quickly, but slowly, like a cancer, leaving him a husk. So he'd listen to what Mr. Santopietro had to say about Leonard Levesque, and if Sadlier wasn't happy with what he heard, he might point out that a decent kid like Scott Theriault shouldn't have ended up drowned in the wilderness and the school should have done better by him, just as it should be doing better by all these kids. If he wasn't fired on the spot, he'd lay the groundwork for his exit and hand in his notice come summer, if not before.

With his toolbox in one hand and a new lock in the other, Sadlier returned to the ablution block. He'd disabled the old lock entirely before leaving for the medical center, and Elgot had left instructions that the boys were to use the toilets in the main school building until it was repaired, so Sadlier knew it was unlikely that anyone had been in the ablution block since. He placed a padded mat on the ground by the door—his knees were not what they once were—and went to work, so that shortly thereafter the facilities had a new lock that didn't jam. To be sure, Sadlier tried the knob a couple of times from both sides. Once he was satisfied, he filled a bucket with water and bleach to clean the area under the sink where Anthony Marshall was discovered, because the boy had smelled sour when Sadlier picked him up.

Sadlier kept the door open so he had more light to see by and commenced mopping, only to hear what sounded like pebbles scattering across the tiles. He stopped what he was doing and squatted to take a closer look. The pebbles were small and dark, not even the size of a fingernail, and all of a similar size. He gathered a few, held them in the palm of his hand, and stared.

Not pebbles. Beans.

Coffee beans.

CHAPTER

That Friday afternoon, Macy returned to her apartment while I met Angel and Louis in Portland, where we killed a pleasant hour wandering along Congress Street. Among other places, we browsed Moody Lords, one of the better used-record stores in town. It stood more or less across the street from the old site of Recordland, which had been the best record store in town before it closed in 1991. I used to haunt it in my late teens, so much so that Ruthie Baker, the owner and manager, must have wondered whether she might somehow have adopted me by accident. At Moody Lord's I bought a used vinyl copy of *New York Tendaberry*, an album I already owned but which I'd made the mistake of loaning to my daughter and now would never see again. But I didn't mind spending the money. I was content to support any number of record stores, used or otherwise, and by purchasing the album again, I managed to recapture a modicum of the pleasure of buying it the first time around. If picking up copies of albums I already owned became an addiction, it was a surefire way to go broke, but it would be an entertaining trip.

"Why don't you just ask Sam to give back the record?" Louis asked, not unreasonably. "If she's holding out, we could always threaten her on your behalf."

"I'm happy to see her displaying an interest in Laura Nyro," I said. "It shows good taste. Of course, Sam doesn't actually own a record player."

"Say what?"

"She doesn't own a record player," I repeated.

"Then why does she need the record?"

"She likes to look at the cover and read the insert while she streams the music. It's what the kids do these days. I admit it's odd, but it could be worse."

Louis took this in. His expression suggested that were the information a morsel of food, he'd have spat it out and shot the chef.

"The world," he pronounced solemnly, "is doomed."

"It was always doomed."

"Okay, more doomed."

I still hadn't asked him what he was doing in New York, and he still hadn't told me. If it was to do with his health, Angel would have shared it with me, which left two possibilities: it was illegal, or it concerned me, and potentially both.

We walked on. By now we were outside one of Angel's favorite stores, Pinecone + Chickadee on Free Street. If a man couldn't find something he didn't need there, he couldn't find it anywhere. We were about to head in and buy stuff none of us needed when a woman came out with a full bag, her hair and forehead concealed by a large wool hat. Louis, barely registering her, stepped aside to let her pass, but she stopped to stare. It was Angel who recognized her first.

"Well, well," he said, "if it isn't the human fortune cookie. If you tell me I'm going to meet a tall dark stranger, you're decades too late, and don't think I'm not resentful about the belated warning."

Sabine Drew smiled. It was an expression of genuine pleasure, but I didn't manage to return it. At one time, Sabine was the most famous medium in the Northeast, thanks to her involvement in the recovery of the remains of a missing girl named Verona Walters. Unfortunately for Sabine, she hadn't been so successful after, and she'd become known as one of the most famous fake mediums in the Northeast, assuming one was prepared to accept that not all of them were fakes to begin with. I'd been a skeptic until our paths crossed on a later investigation involving another missing child, after which I judged that whatever else Sabine might be, she wasn't a charlatan. But I wouldn't have called what she had a gift, and I doubted she would either. It brought her too much torment.

But none of that was the reason for my caution. I had cause to believe she might have killed a man with poison, a woman's weapon for a woman's revenge. This was the first time we'd met since his death, and only Angel and Louis knew of my suspicions. It wasn't for me to bring the law to her door, and anyway, as someone who stepped outside the law on occasion, it would have made me a hypocrite. However, few things dispose a man to be wary around a woman more than an aptitude for toxins. I couldn't say the same for Angel and Louis: Sabine's willingness to administer her own form of justice only seemed to make them admire her more, even if they did their best to hide it.

"They're still with us, I see," she said.

"They may always be with us," I replied, "like the poor. I've tried to get rid of them, but they keep finding their way back."

"You're not trying hard enough. With the stubborn ones, it can take time, but the effort is worth it in the end."

She peered at Angel and Louis, who regarded her with amusement, but not mockery.

"You know," she said, "it's like they understand every word you say. They're almost human."

Sabine was easy to dismiss, with her mismatched thrift-store clothes, the stray hair poking from beneath her hat, and a face she did her best to render unremarkable by making no effort at all to conceal it. At least one man was never going to make the mistake of underestimating her again.

Angel and Louis left us for the joys of the store, though not before Louis requested Sabine's assistance with locating a missing cuff link.

"Bribe Saint Anthony," she told him. "He takes all the small jobs."

She placed her bag at her feet. I asked what she was doing in Portland.

"Before I heeded the siren call of this place, I was out at Easy Aquariums in Westbrook." Sabine kept exotic fish. It was from these that she might have sourced her toxin. "You didn't stay in touch."

"I never said I would."

"I hoped you might."

"I thought it better to keep my distance."

A number of people had died in the course of the investigation that first brought us together—not all of them as bloodlessly as the poisoning victim, though certainly less agonizingly—and it made me the object of unwanted police attention. All things considered, Angel, Louis, and I were fortunate to not have ended up facing serious charges. Whether I was correct about Sabine or not, it was wiser not to give the law any excuse for taking a closer look at her. As it happened, Sabine was not in the mood for circumspection.

"The police asked me about him, you know, the man who died so unpleasantly."

"What did you tell them?"

"I said I'd only ever met him at a funeral, and we didn't speak, but I supposed he wasn't a very nice person if someone had gone to the trouble of poisoning him."

"He probably wasn't, but his death caused difficulties for his wife," I said. "In these instances, the police start at the home and work outward."

"But she was innocent, wasn't she? In which case she had nothing to worry about."

"They'd already tried to jail her once for a crime she didn't commit, so I admire your continued faith in the criminal justice system."

"I have no faith at all in the system. I have faith in you."

Which was flattering, even allowing for the source.

"Are you engaged in anything interesting right now?"

"A case in The Plains," I said.

I could almost hear the Rolodex in her brain flipping through cards.

"The missing Norton girl?"

"The dead Theriault boy."

"Yes, that was odd," said Sabine. "He must have hated the school a great deal if the wilds were preferable. Of course, there has to be more to it than that."

"Does there?"

"You wouldn't be involved otherwise, would you?"

As she picked up her bag and prepared to be on her way, I asked whether anything had changed in her life.

"I'm studying to become a psychotherapist," she said. "I was always good at listening, but I have to work on my patience. Meeting your two friends just now was good practice. I think I handled them with forbearance. 'The human fortune cookie'—I shall have to remember that. The drowned boy and the Norton girl, are they linked?"

"Only by conjecture."

"That's how it starts. You know, I've never been to The Plains."

"Are you offering to help?"

"Are you asking?"

"No."

"Not to worry," she said. "I won't take it amiss."

Bag in hand, she walked away.

INSIDE THE STORE, ANGEL WAS EXAMINING a Froot Loops–scented candle. Louis had found a brass Chinese ashtray, though he didn't smoke.

"What did she say?" Angel asked as I joined them.

"That she wasn't annoyed I didn't seek her help with the Theriault business."

"That's a relief," said Angel, "given what happens to people who upset her. Do you think she's nuts?"

"No."

"Me neither. I can't decide if that makes her more frightening or less."

"She's training to be a psychotherapist."

"For the living or the dead?"

"I forgot to ask, but I imagine the living pay better."

I took in the candle and the ashtray.

"You don't need a Fruit Loops–scented candle," I told Angel. "And you don't need a Chinese ashtray," I told Louis.

"Great," said Angel. "We'll pay for them, then we're good to go."

WE ATE AN EARLY DINNER at Boda on Congress. Angel opted for a beer, I had a glass of wine, and Louis ordered a margarita made to his own specifications, which turned out to be a combination of fruit, mezcal, and habanero tincture; heavy on the tincture, at his insistence, but not, he emphasized, too heavy.

"You need to taste it," he said, "not feel it."

"Feel it how?" I asked.

"So you get the burn on your lips, not lower down. You don't want to end up with, y'know, an ass like the Japanese flag."

"Thank you," I said. "That's an image to cherish."

The drinks arrived, along with wings on the house as a reward for Louis's regular custom. Once Louis's lips and tongue had returned to normal after the first sip of his drink, I told them of my plan to base myself closer to The Plains for a few days while I looked into the death of Scott Theriault.

"You think you're going to be given the red-carpet treatment at that school?" Louis asked.

"They may be smart enough to realize hostility won't help them. But from what I've seen in the newspapers and online, they've tried to be open to questions."

"Any sign of Spero being sued by the boy's parents?" asked Angel.

Trust Angel to spot a detail I'd missed. Ward Vose hadn't raised the prospect of litigation, and neither had Alcock, but if it was their intention to sue, I'd like to be told. Investigating how and why Scott Theriault died was not the same as establishing culpability that might assist in a civil action. I had no objection to working on either inquiry, but I didn't want to have to go over the same ground twice. If I was clear on what Alcock wanted from the start, I could ensure my questions were framed correctly, and whatever I gleaned from witnesses or interview subjects would cover everything. Of course, any decision on a lawsuit might not be Vose's alone to make. Even if he didn't want to sue Spero, Scott's mother and stepfather might. While I'd be talking to them soon, they weren't my clients and would have their own lawyer. Regardless, it was another complicating factor to bear in mind.

Over food we spoke of somethings and nothings, as old friends will. Angel told us of a man from Rochester, New York, named Miguel Himes who once dreamed of setting up an agency supplying minority individuals to serve as guests at the parties and dinners of WASP liberals, enabling the hosts to appear more inclusive and so impress friends and associates with their progressiveness.

"Himes had them all on his books," Angel said. "Blacks, Latinos, Asians, Jews—both Orthodox and Reform. He knew a lot of unemployed people who could hold a conversation. He figured he just had to give them a fake history based on interviews with the hosts and make sure they didn't drink too much, because that's when it all starts to go wrong at dinner parties."

"What about white guests for Black dinner parties?" I asked.

"Yeah," said Louis, "like anyone has ever said, 'You know what this party needs? More white people.' "

I told him he wasn't going to be invited to any more of my parties. He reminded me that I didn't hold parties, and even if I did, I'd struggle to find a suitable venue now that all the phone booths were gone.

"So what happened to Miguel Himes and his great idea?" I asked Angel.

"He went to jail in Florida," said Angel. "Can't remember why. I think it was for fraud. In Florida, it usually is."

And so a pleasant evening passed, and still Louis did not say what he had been doing down in New York.

CHAPTER

XLI

Sabine Drew spent the night in Portland. She stayed at the Inn at St. John, where a value room with a shared bath was within her budget and the parking was free. While she could have managed the round trip from Haynesville to Portland and back in a day, she preferred not to drive after dark because her night vision was poor. Also, an evening in Portland was a treat, so she took in a movie at the Nick and was out in time to order a Miller High Life for a dollar ninety-five at Dock Fore, the best happy hour in town, where she listened to the old geezers jawing while she read a magazine. She then ate a hamburger in Rosie's, drank another beer, and worked off some of the calories by walking the mile and a half back to the inn. In her room, she unpacked her purchases from Pinecone + Chickadee—she'd picked up a neat cotton bag featuring a seven-eyed cat—before watching some TV and going to sleep.

During all that time, she tried not to think about Scott Theriault or Mallory Norton. They were not her concern, or so she told herself—except they were, because even to care a little made them so. But the private investigator did not want her help, and she understood why, though she did not for one moment regret having poisoned that dreadful man, and neither had he ever troubled her by appearing in her visions. Unlikely as it sounded, it might have been that his soul was now at peace; that, or God, if He existed, hadn't liked him either, and consigned him to the void. Someone had once asked Sabine whether, with her gifts, she possessed any insight into the nature of

God. Sabine replied that she'd never caught sight of Him, only the pain He left behind, like coming across wreckage at sea in the wake of the storm that caused it.

Sabine slept soundly in her comfortable bed, and what dreams she had did not stay with her come morning. But as she watched the sunlight brighten the edges of the drapes, and listened to the sounds of stirring life on Congress Street, she thought of drowned boys and missing girls, and of Mallory Norton's parents waking to that same dawn, waking to unknowing. Sabine got up, showered, harvested free fruit and pastries from the breakfast buffet, and drove to The Plains.

CHAPTER

XLII

Santopietro rarely used the full version of his first name, Dante. To his friends, who were few, he was Dan. His first—and, so far, only wife—used to call him Santi, but she was dead and the diminutive had passed away with her. To the locals in The Plains, The Forks, and farther south in Bingham and Madison, as well as to the staff and students at Spero, he was Mr. S—unless they were in trouble, when he was very much Mr. Santopietro or, simply, sir.

Santopietro was currently in his office and intended to spend the rest of the day there, just as he would also spend much of Sunday morning in it. Spero required his daily attention. It might have been a fraction of the size of a regular school, but its students required more attention than the norm. Santopietro had learned a lot from his time as a pupil at Élan, including the inadvisability of condoning sadism. True, some Spero parents wouldn't have objected to their sons being beaten regularly with briars and left to hang overnight on a cross so long as they weren't causing an uproar at home, especially if the punishments resulted in permanent modification to the boys' behavior. One or two of the parents wouldn't even have given two shits on a nickel if their sons died suddenly in their sleep. But then, nobody sent a child to Spero out of love, tough or otherwise. At best, parents exiled them there because they couldn't cope, and at worst, because they didn't care. Santopietro might not have liked all of his charges either, but he found it depressing to think that he had more regard for them than some of their own mothers and fathers. He tried his best to ensure that the staff didn't compound the problem. Even if he didn't pay them enough to care a lot, he paid sufficient for them to care some.

Speaking of which, earlier that morning Patrick Elgot had reported to Santopietro that Anthony Marshall slept through the night and appeared to be recovering from the trauma of the ablution block—physically at least, though he remained more subdued than before. Elgot was about to go off duty for a couple of days to attend the Head of the Charles Regatta down in Boston, where his girlfriend was operating a food stall at the Riverbender. His absence required a certain reorganization of the schedule, but Santopietro didn't make a fuss because Elgot was obliging, kind to the kids, and had given plenty of notice, even if he did have a big sharp stick up his ass. Also, it suited Santopietro to have Elgot far from the school. Before he left for Boston, Elgot again raised the subject of Leonard Levesque and whether Santopietro had spoken to him about Marshall. It didn't do any good for Santopietro to point out, not for the first time, that Marshall hadn't named Levesque as the culprit.

"It was Levesque," Elgot said. "No one else here would do that to another boy."

"Regardless," said Santopietro.

"Regardless what?"

Santopietro didn't like Elgot's tone, but resisted the urge to tear him a new asshole, if only because Elgot might try to insert another stick up it.

"Regardless, we can't go making accusations without evidence." Santopietro really wanted Elgot gone, off to serve tofu, wheatgrass, or whatever else his girlfriend was shilling to the yacht crowd down in Boston. "But I'll speak with Leonard privately and advise him of the necessity of behaving respectfully toward the staff and students of this institution. To cover myself, I'll have to give a more general warning to the rest, but I promise you, Leonard Levesque will get the message."

Mercifully, Elgot had left it at that and they parted on good terms. Once Elgot was gone from the campus, Santopietro called Renders.

"Give me an hour or so to finish up what I'm doing," he said, "then get that bastard in here."

CHAPTER

XLIII

Hailee Theriault, Scott's mother, and her husband, Jerry Rakestraw, maintained two properties in the state: a cottage on Mount Desert Island, which would enable Rakestraw to meet the residential requirements for representing the Second District, should he someday choose to run there; and a home in Kennebunk, in the First District, where their children attended school. If he did want to get his name on the ballot, Rakestraw might have to make Mount Desert Island his primary residence, but for now he could keep a foot in both political camps: the blue of the first and the deep red of the second, all while mulling over a run for Congress.

The Kennebunk house was one of the more modestly sized on Beach Avenue, which meant it was worth closer to a million dollars than two. I'd called ahead—I wasn't about to intrude on grief unannounced—and spoken to Rakestraw himself, who agreed to give me some of his time on Saturday morning, though he couldn't guarantee his wife would do the same. "It has been very tough for her," Rakestraw explained. I told him I understood, and I did.

But as it happened, Hailee Theriault was seated in a window nook when Rakestraw showed me into the big kitchen, the gauzy horizon of the ocean visible through the trees. She was wearing a yellow cotton dress and her feet were bare. She was a small woman, made smaller by her husband, who had played point guard for the Black Bears in his college days. Rakestraw was dressed in chinos and an open-necked formal white shirt. Like his wife, he looked weary, but unlike her, his eyes didn't have the subdued glassiness of the sedated. He offered coffee, or soda or tea if I preferred. Since the coffee was already made, and they were each drinking a cup, I took coffee.

"The house isn't usually this quiet," said Rakestraw. "The kids are playing at a friend's place."

He made an odd, apologetic little gesture with his hands. I had only just arrived and he'd already referred to kids and uncommon silence, words he might have preferred to have avoided in front of his wife, especially when the subject at hand was her deceased eldest child.

Hailee Theriault didn't move in the alcove except to turn her head to regard me; we had not shaken hands, nor had she spoken. Only when her husband was pouring my coffee did she ask: "Why has Ward hired you?"

"He's unhappy with the verdict of accidental death," I replied.

"Does he blame us for what happened?"

"I believe he blames himself above anyone."

She snorted air through her nostrils in lieu of laughter.

"It's a little late for Ward to become a martyr."

"It's never too late for that," I said.

She shrugged. "You may be right. Perhaps I'll join him. Perhaps I already have."

She went back to looking out the window. Rakestraw sat next to her. She moved her bare feet so they rested against his thigh, but otherwise did not acknowledge his proximity.

"If you have questions," said Rakestraw, "we'll do our best to answer them."

I began by going through much of what Ward Vose had told me, including Scott's intolerance for alcohol. Hailee Theriault confirmed the diagnosis, but claimed it hadn't stopped Scott from fooling around with booze.

"Not hard liquor," her husband clarified, "only beer. And not much of that," he added.

"Not that we know of," said his wife, "but Scott was running wild by the end, and alcohol might have played its part. Who can say? That was why we had to send him to Spero."

"By running wild—?"

"He was mouthing off," said Hailee, "smoking pot, skipping school. He was impossible."

"He was difficult," said Rakestraw.

"Impossible," his wife repeated, but without feeling.

"Did he remain in touch with you after he arrived at Spero?"

"Only to ask us to allow him to come home," said Rakestraw. "When we refused, he cut off all contact."

"How long did you plan to leave him up there?"

"For as long as it took," said Theriault.

"For what?"

"For him to change."

"And suppose he didn't?"

"Then he'd have to stay at Spero."

"We could have sent him somewhere worse," said Rakestraw. "There's always somewhere worse."

"I'm not sure there is," I said. "Eventually, it all ends with a hole in the ground."

Rakestraw let it go.

"So when was the last time either of you spoke to him?"

"August, I think." Rakestraw looked to his wife for confirmation but received none. "Yes, late August."

"And no phone calls, texts, or emails since?"

"None, not from Scott. We reached out but . . ."

Rakestraw trailed off. I waited for his wife to contribute, but she didn't. Strike *mildly sedated* and substitute *heavily*. The silence rapidly became uncomfortable, even for someone who regarded silence as a weapon in the interrogator's armory.

"How was your relationship with Scott, Mr. Rakestraw?" I asked, when the sound of my own heartbeat began to bore me.

"Up and down. It started awkwardly when I married Hailee, improved for a couple of years, then deteriorated again. COVID didn't help, what with all of us cooped up together. We got through it, but the damage was done."

"Jerry tried hard with Scott," said Hailee Theriault, "but he didn't reciprocate."

"He was young," said Rakestraw.

"Not that young, not by the end."

The dynamic here was not what I had expected, but I didn't rush to judgment: There were as many ways to grieve as there were to be bereaved. But if this was as much as I was going to learn from the trip, it would be wasted.

"Is Ward planning to sue Spero?" Hailee Theriault asked.

"You'd have to ask his lawyer," I replied. "Do you intend to sue?"

"We could try," said Rakestraw, "but it would be difficult. We signed a liability waiver. It was a condition of Scott's acceptance as a student. We'd have to prove negligence, meaning the staff failed to meet the required duty of care. My lawyer isn't confident of a result, should we proceed."

"We're not going to proceed," said Hailee Theriault. "What happened to Scott wasn't Spero's fault. He brought it on himself. You can tell Ward there's no money in this for him, or for you."

I didn't bother telling her that I didn't think it was about money for Ward Vose. As for me, only the unimportant cases were about money. I liked being paid—sleeping on the streets had never appealed—but I was cursed with a conscience. I wanted to believe Hailee Theriault was similarly troubled, no matter what indications she gave to the contrary, but being in her company was trying. I hadn't anticipated a joyful encounter, but neither had I expected it to be so enervating. Here was toxic grief. I spent a while longer getting nowhere while the life was slowly sucked out of me before thanking Hailee Theriault and Jerry Rakestraw for their time and preparing to leave.

"Is that it?" Rakestraw asked.

"Yes, that's it."

I put my notebook in my pocket. I'd written about half a dozen words since arriving, and three of those were *Rakestraw/Theriault Interview*.

"I'll show you out," said Rakestraw.

"Goodbye, Mrs. Rakestraw," I said.

She continued to watch the sea, but I glimpsed my reflection in the glass, like a pale god rising above the waters.

"Aren't you going to tell me you're sorry for my loss?" she asked.

"Would you like me to?"

"Isn't it the done thing?"

"Not for me," I said. "Each loss is different."

"How very profound you are."

The level of misery and denial in the room was beyond measure. I had no desire to add to it by scoring points off a traumatized woman. I wanted only to get out, but first I made an attempt at conciliation.

"If it helps," I said, "I'm not working for Ward Vose. I'm working for your son."

"Then I have bad news for you," said Hailee Theriault. "You won't get paid."

Jerry Rakestraw's face was a mask, but behind it, his eyes were pleading with me not to engage further. I let him lead the way to the hall, where he opened the door and walked me to my car.

"Don't leave here despising her," he said.

"Was it her decision to send Scott to Spero?"

"Yes, but I could have argued more strongly against it."

I didn't bother asking why he hadn't. Hailee was Scott's mother, and Rakestraw might have seen the appeal of an easier life. If she was prepared to make the hard call, so be it.

"Would you consider it strange if I said I felt sorry for Santopietro and the staff up there?" Rakestraw asked.

"I have a high tolerance for strangeness," I said.

"The school did exactly what it promised it would, and that didn't include keeping Scott locked up in his room or chained to a radiator. When he ran away that last time, it turned into a tragedy for everyone."

"For Scott, most of all."

"I'm trying here, Mr. Parker."

I wanted to tell him it was too little, too late, but as with Hailee Theriault, those points were too easy to score.

"How much medication is your wife taking?"

"It varies between too much and not enough. Today, I'd say it's closer to the first."

I let my gaze pass over the neat house with Old Glory hanging from a pole above the porch, over the trimmed lawn and the beds of fall flowers, and heard the sound of the sea.

"Did Scott ever fit in here?"

"Not really," said Rakestraw. "Our girls sort of looked up to him, but the age gap was too big for them to be properly close. We all might have gotten along a lot better had he been able to live with his father instead of us, but short of sharing a prison cell, that wasn't an option. And once we sent him to Spero, any hope of a functioning relationship was blown to pieces. Maybe I was deluded. I had a vision of a happy multiracial family, but it was never that."

"Would the happy multiracial family have been more politically saleable?"

"That's quite the question to ask."

"If you're going to be all sensitive," I said, "politics may not be for you."

A more calculating Rakestraw showed his face.

"In the First District, perhaps, if we're talking congressionals," he said. "The Second is less predictable. For governor, it's a toss-up. You know, you ride a tall horse, Mr. Parker. The fall, when it comes, will be painful."

"Will your stepson's death affect your ambitions?"

"A few years is a long time in politics."

"It's a long time, period," I replied. "Long enough for people to forget, if you want them to."

"We'll see. I'd have preferred not to have to take that into account."

The politician departed, and the stepfather reassumed his place.

"You know, Scott screamed when they took him," he said. "He screamed, and he cried, and he begged and begged. He made so much noise that one of the men slipped a gag over his mouth because they were afraid someone might call the police. Scott kicked and fought so hard it took three men to subdue him, and they had to put cable ties on his hands and feet. I think letting it continue was the worst thing I've ever done."

"You could have stopped it."

"I could, but I didn't want to. That's my failing. Isn't that what you came to hear?"

"By now, I don't know why I came," I said. "I just wish I hadn't. What about your wife?"

"She repeats what you heard in there: that Scott brought it on himself, that it was his own fault. She'd like to believe it's true, but she can't, so she keeps saying it over and over in the hope that might make it true."

Rakestraw's voice dried up. He coughed hard. After, he was able to speak again.

"Scott was far from perfect as a son, but we should have been better parents. We were the adults and he was the child, so the onus was on us, not him. That makes us complicit in his death, however it occurred. Do you know what Santopietro told us when we first met him to discuss Scott's future? He said that we shouldn't blame ourselves for sending him away because we weren't trained to deal with troubled children. But what parent is?"

I had nothing useful to offer. Behind Rakestraw, Hailee Theriault floated to the front door.

"Jerry," she said, "let the man be about his affairs."

"If you learn anything—" he began.

"Alcock will let you know," I said.

"Not you?"

"No."

I got in my car and drove away. I tried to think of a child who had been failed so badly by more of the adults in his life than Scott Theriault, but couldn't come up with any. And I couldn't decide whether that was a good thing or a bad.

CHAPTER

XLIV

Sabine Drew arrived in Bingham shortly after noon. The town was quiet, but it was hard to imagine it any other way, except in the height of summer, and even then only as a throughway. Bingham was a functional community: three or four churches, some schools, a NAPA Auto Parts, a Dollar General—because where would the poor be without a Dollar General?—a few gas stations with convenience stores, and, because this was the new Maine, a cannabis dispensary. Faded signs on deserted or boarded-up buildings whispered of a departed Bingham with more appetite for the inessential and a supply to meet the demand. They reminded Sabine of the names found on tombstones or beneath pale pictures of the dead.

Thanks to the newspaper reports about Mallory Norton's disappearance, and aided by a Google search at the Inn at St. John, she had in her notebook the location of the building supplies premises owned by Mallory's father, Todd "T. K." Norton, as well as the address of the family home and much else besides, including prizes won by Mallory in middle and high school, both athletic and academic, and a selection of the more interesting comments about her on Facebook, Instagram, and Twitter. (Sabine would never call it X, not as long as breath remained in her body.) She had also assembled a short list of Mallory's employers since leaving school, which included the family business. Like a lot of residents in that part of the state, notably the younger ones who either opted to stay or felt they had no choice due to family commitments, Mallory Norton worked a couple of jobs, depending on the season: part-time hours for her father in late winter and spring, combined with shifts at a gas station or restaurant, or packing shelves as far south as Solon or Madison; but in the summer, when the tourists flooded the region and all the resorts and camps were scrambling for staff, she had greater latitude. She might still work two jobs, though out of choice rather than necessity, because what she earned would help her through any lean periods to follow. The opportunities tailed off some in hunting season, but the crossover with the winter sports crowd meant she could still bring in good money from waitressing through January or so. After that, it was a few months of hardscrabble.

Sabine was building a picture of the girl. This, she reflected, was not dissimilar to how the private investigator operated, though with a different aim. He would be looking for clues, but Sabine was looking for traces, like the scent offered to a dog before a search, just as the men and women who had scoured the Kennebec Valley for Mallory Norton might have done with their hounds. It wasn't enough for Sabine to arrive in a place, clear her mind, and wait for the dead to present themselves in the hope of identifying the one among them that interested her. That would be like opening the sluice gate on a dam and expecting to catch a single drop of water in one's mouth. For her to be of any help, filters were required.

Right now, Sabine had no sense of Mallory beyond what she'd read, which was why she'd driven to Bingham. She wanted to walk the streets the girl walked, see what she saw, hear what she heard, and smell what she smelled. She would stop by T. K. Norton's place of business and pass by the school, even go inside if it was open. Should anyone ask what she was doing, she might tell the truth, but more probably she would lie, inventing a daughter, a niece, the child of a friend, who might soon be relocating to the area. Finally, she would visit the street where the young woman lived and seek to enter her home, where all that was Mallory was so much more present. Of course, the Nortons might not appreciate a stranger arriving on their doorstep unannounced to spend time in their missing daughter's bedroom. Even if they knew who Sabine was, there was no guarantee they'd welcome her, but it would not be the first time she had invited herself into a situation rather than wait for an invitation to be proffered, and in common with the investigator, she understood the value of tenacity.

Sabine first went to T. K. Norton's warehouse and store where, on a small table inside the door, a votive candle was burning next to a framed photograph of the missing girl. Pinned to the table was a laminated notice containing a physical description of Mallory, the date she was last seen, and contact numbers for the Somerset County Sheriff's Office and the Maine State Police. Sabine placed the palms of her hands on the reception desk on the pretense of inquiring if the store had a restroom she might use. She would also have liked to touch the chair behind the desk or even to sit in it, but it wasn't really the kind of thing a visitor could ask of a receptionist.

She then went to Valley High School ("Home of the Cavaliers"), a redbrick building with tidy lawns and sports fields in the rear. The doors were all locked, the fields unoccupied, and she saw no one around who might have been persuaded to let her explore further. At the front door, beside a sign requesting that visitors and parents buzz for entry, a copy of the same photograph from the store had been blown up double size and taped to the inside of the glass, with a printed sign beneath that read MALLORY: IN OUR THOUGHTS, IN OUR HOPES, IN OUR PRAYERS. As at the store, Sabine ran her fingertips over a surface that Mallory might once have touched, and as at the store, she picked up nothing. But it was another step toward familiarizing herself with the girl's world by locating her in its precincts. The shape of a person was forming, but Sabine needed more than a bare outline if she was to have any chance of finding her, dead or alive. Sabine feared the worst—the disappearance of teenage girls from good homes rarely boded well—but she resisted allowing fear to become an assumption, because that would cloud her perception and judgment. Even the presupposition that the Norton home environment was good or safe was problematic, for who knew what went on behind closed doors? If she could get inside the house, Sabine might be able to come up with an answer, even if it was only to rule out the involvement of one or both of the parents. Abuse left a very distinct miasma, and sexual abuse a more specific one. A person didn't even have to be as unusual as Sabine to spot it. She had known police who could pick up on it within moments of entering a residence, especially if parent and child were present; abused and abusers had a shared spoor. So Sabine would have to go to the house, as she had always assumed she would. She could procrastinate no longer.

THE NORTONS LIVED ON THE NORTHERN OUTSKIRTS of Bingham, on the road to Moscow. It was a ranch-style home on about a half acre, but with no extensions to the original necessary to accommodate a growing family, since Mallory was the couple's only child. The front yard was planted with fall-blooming native trees—Franklin, Higan cherry, and witch hazel—while a single sugar maple stood at the eastern extreme, close to the road, a green ribbon tied around its trunk. The doors to the two-car garage at the right of the house were open, but only one of the bays was occupied. The vehicle inside was a Honda CR-V: more the choice of a wife than a husband, in Sabine's view. That was good, as she preferred dealing with women rather than men. It wasn't that women were necessarily more open-minded, only that they didn't feel the same need to pretend they weren't.

She rang the doorbell and watched samaras pinwheel from the sugar maple, the crown of the tree so bright with yellows, oranges, and reds that it might have been afire against the blue of the afternoon. But to the west, the sky was turbulent with cloud, and there was rain on the air. The door opened. Anita Norton stood in the gap; Sabine recognized her from the news reports. She was in her late thirties, so she couldn't have been more than twenty when Mallory was born, but looked older than her years. Her daughter's vanishing would have aged her, even in such a short space of time, though Sabine guessed that life might have been chipping away at her from before. The Honda in the garage was eight or nine years old, and the house showed signs of patching and mending in the absence of funds to make more meaningful repairs. The Nortons were managing to keep their heads above water, even as they felt it lapping against their chins.

Sabine wondered how many people had come to Anita Norton's door over the last month, or called her on the phone. A lot, she surmised, though it would have fallen off lately as the mystery of Mallory's disappearance dragged on. Anita would still have felt her heart skip and her stomach lurch every time the doorbell rang, but less so with the phone: if there was news, bad news, it would be communicated in person, and by someone in uniform. She might have been relieved to see only a woman of late middle age standing on her doorstep, holding a wool hat in her hands, a tasseled suede bag over one shoulder; relieved, and disappointed.

"Can I help you?" Anita Norton asked.

"I might be able to help you," Sabine replied. "I don't promise that I can, but I'd like to try."

She reached into the bag and produced copies of two newspaper articles, one from years before, the other more recent. Both related to the disappearances of children and, ultimately, the retrieval of bodies.

"I'm showing you these so you'll know who I am," she said, "not because I'm suggesting Mallory's outcome might be the same. My hope, like yours, is that your daughter is alive and may yet be found. In the past, I've been able to offer assistance in that regard—not always, not even more often than not, but I've had some successes."

She passed the articles to Anita Norton, who didn't read all the way through before handing them back.

"I've heard of you," she said. "What do you want here?"

"To see your daughter's room, if I may."

"Why?"

"Because I have no proper sense of Mallory, not enough to be able to recognize her."

Anita folded her arms: rarely a good sign, in Sabine's experience.

"There are photographs," said Anita. "Half the state knows what my daughter looks like."

"I wasn't speaking of her appearance," said Sabine. "I was talking about her essence. All that's the best of her, all that she is, will be present in her room." The breeze carried one of the samaras onto the step, where it landed by Sabine's right foot. She picked it up and sent it spinning toward soil. "But I understand if you'd prefer not to let me in. I don't make a habit of approaching people directly. They tend to come to me."

Sabine noticed that Anita was shivering. She was wearing a pink T-shirt over slim-cut jeans that might once have fit snugly but now had to be held up with a belt. How much weight had Anita lost since the girl had gone missing? More than she could afford. They didn't eat, the mothers of missing children; didn't eat, didn't sleep, struggled to concentrate, neglected their other kids, if they were fortunate enough to have any. It was different for the fathers, Sabine thought, neither easier nor harder, but dissimilar in the character of the suffering. Sometimes she felt sorrier for the men because so many lacked the vocabulary to express their pain and make it comprehensible, even to themselves. All grief consumed, but it might be that certain men welcomed the consumption more than women. They cannibalized themselves into oblivion.

"You should go back inside," said Sabine. "I'm sorry to have bothered you."

She stepped down from the porch.

"Will you know?"

Sabine looked up.

"If she's alive, I mean," Anita continued. "Will you know? Will you be able to tell?"

"I might."

The contrary held more true, Sabine being better attuned to the profundity of absence. This Anita Norton seemed to guess, because next she said: "And if she isn't?"

"Again, I might."

"What will you do?"

"I'll call her name," said Sabine, "and see if she answers."

It was that simple, and also that complex.

"And would you tell me if she did answer? Or if she didn't, but you knew she was dead?"

"Only if I was sure."

Sabine permitted herself the lie. When it came to what she did, certainty was a rare commodity, but even so, and should it turn out that Mallory was dead, it would not be for her to tell this woman that her child was gone. It would be for the police, and only when, or if, a body was found. For the present, it was too early even to conceive of such a conversation.

Anita opened the door wider.

"You can come inside," she said, "but—"

Sabine waited.

"Even if you're sure, don't tell me my daughter is dead."

She stepped aside to let Sabine enter.

"Do you have tea?" Sabine asked.

"All kinds."

"Which do you prefer?"

"Fruit."

"Then I'd like some fruit tea, please—if it's not any trouble, and you'll join me."

Anita closed the door.

"I'll show you to Mallory's bedroom," she said, "then I'll make the tea."

"No. Let's sit in the kitchen and drink it together."

"I thought you wanted to see the room."

"In time," said Sabine. "First, I'd like you to tell me about Mallory."

Anita Norton closed her eyes. Softly, she began to cry.

CHAPTER XLV

Leonard Levesque stood before Santopietro's desk with his hands in the back pockets of his jeans and a smirk on his face that Santopietro, for all his reluctance to repeat the sins of Élan, wanted to pummel into bloodiness. Santopietro remained seated, with Renders leaning against the bookshelves to his left. Renders was a big man, and by rights the combination of his physical presence and Santopietro's authority should have cowed the boy—it rarely failed to subdue others—but he remained resolutely unintimidated. Even when the subject of the attack on Anthony Marshall was raised, his expression didn't change. He displayed some mirth, but shallowly, as though he could easily tip into boredom.

"What about it?" Leonard asked.

"We think you might have had something to do with it," said Renders.

"Did he say I did?"

Renders didn't reply. Neither did Santopietro. Under ordinary circumstances and faced with an ordinary boy, they might have expected defiance, followed by a quick admission of guilt and some tears, crocodile or otherwise. But Leonard Levesque wasn't ordinary, which was why his parents were being charged a premium by Spero with their knowledge and consent. Mr. and Mrs. Levesque were under no illusions about their son.

The lull dragged on, the two men unwilling to lie to the boy but holding out hope that he might concede something, anything. It was Leonard who broke the silence, giving the slightest shrug of his right shoulder and saying: "Well, then."

Renders shifted position and audibly exhaled, like a bull preparing to charge. Leonard flicked a lizard glance at him, willing him to try. It was left to Santopietro to lift a finger of warning to Renders. They needed to be careful here.

"What was done to Anthony was brutal and cowardly," said Santopietro.

"I wouldn't know."

"I don't believe you."

Leonard stared past him, taking in the view of the playing field, the fences, and the landscape beyond.

"I was down to Small's yesterday," he said, "on my bike. They had a notice posted, about how they were going to search for Mallory Norton again tomorrow. I would have signed up, if I thought I'd be allowed out to help." He pursed his lips. "Maybe we ought to have the school offer its services. We could make a field trip of it."

His attention flicked back to Santopietro, who thought how disconcerting it was to find oneself the focus of such knowing eyes buried in embryonic, doughy features.

Santopietro didn't look at Renders. He kept his focus on Leonard.

"I'll bear the suggestion in mind," he said evenly. "But let's hope she's located safe and sound without our assistance."

"Yes," said Leonard, "let's hope. What with her going missing, then what happened to Scott, I bet everyone would appreciate some good news. Will that be all, Mr. S?"

"For now."

Leonard left the office. Without speaking, Renders followed him. Only when he was certain the boy was on his way to the dorm did he return to Santopietro. The principal was standing by the window, his hands clasped behind his back, and Renders knew he was thinking about Mallory Norton. They both were.

After all, they were the ones who had taken her.

CHAPTER

XLVI

It was just before three p.m. when T. K. Norton got home. He entered his daughter's bedroom to discover his wife seated at the end of Mallory's bed, clutching one of her stuffed animals, while a woman with wispy, graying hair stood with her back to the closet, holding Mallory's hairbrush in her right hand. The woman looked familiar to T.K., though he couldn't place her. It was only when his wife spoke her name that he made the connection.

Sabine guessed T.K. was at least a decade older than Anita. He was a handsome man with salt-and-pepper hair and soft, sad eyes. Any concerns about abuse that Sabine might still have entertained were immediately dissipated. She had felt nothing of it in the environs of the house or from Anita, but only in the presence of the husband could she be certain. Not surprisingly, T.K. was puzzled to find a medium in the bedroom of his missing daughter; puzzled, but not angry.

"I dropped by on the chance someone might be here," said Sabine. "I asked if I might see Mallory's bedroom, and your wife was kind enough to allow it."

"She wants to help," Anita told her husband. "No one else has been able to."

"And?"

It was the first word he'd spoken since entering.

"And now I feel I know your daughter better," said Sabine.

"You look for the dead, right?"

"The missing."

She might not have spoken.

"I don't accept that she's dead," said T.K.

"Nor should you. For what it's worth, I don't accept that she's dead either."

In the quiet of the bedroom, before T. K. Norton's arrival, Sabine had been reaching out, tentatively trying to pick up some trace of the girl while surrounded by her possessions. So far, all that she could say was that Mallory Norton, alive or dead, was not in Bingham.

She took in the parents. She was tempted to ask about Scott Theriault but decided against it. That would be for the private investigator when he finally made his way here. For her to raise the subject of the Theriault boy with the Nortons might do more harm than good. She picked up her jacket.

"Thank you for your hospitality," she said.

T. K. Norton asked: "What now?"

"As I told your wife, I'll call your daughter's name and listen for a response."

"And then?"

She touched his arm.

"Then we'll talk again."

CHAPTER

XLVII

In the principal's office, Renders continued waiting for Santopietro to speak. Even after what they'd done together, and what they'd shared, Santopietro remained his employer, and Renders was content to defer to him. Santopietro was easy to underestimate; it was a function of his appearance, his mode of dress, his slightly hunched way of walking, and the soft sibilance of his speech. But Renders, like Spero's more perceptive students, had come to appreciate that Santopietro deliberately cultivated a self-effacing air, particularly on the rare occasions when he was away from the school. Santopietro was a man who did not care to be noticed beyond Spero's confines and had constructed a persona to suit that end. So accomplished was he that no one even bothered to examine more closely this reserve, or conjecture what it might conceal. Renders could only speculate on how uncomfortable it must have been for Santopietro when Leonard Levesque, of all people, touched on the answer.

Santopietro began filing away the papers on his desk. He did not like unresolved business.

"This is an awkward position in which we find ourselves," he said.

"Levesque doesn't know anything," said Renders.

"But he suspects."

It was Levesque who had told Santopietro about Scott Theriault and Mallory Norton, ratting out his schoolmate to avoid punishment for some infraction that Santopietro could no longer recall. Were he to reveal this to another—say a loquacious classmate, or the police—Santopietro might be asked why he hadn't shared this knowledge following Norton's disappearance, especially after Theriault's body later turned up in a tributary of the Kennebec.

"The price of his silence," Santopietro continued, "is to be allowed free run of the school, for now. The beating of Anthony Marshall was a way of testing the waters."

"So let him be top dog," said Renders. "Top dog in a pound of mongrels."

"I said 'for now.' This is a form of blackmail, and blackmail escalates. An adult might grasp how far and hard one can push, but not an adolescent. Levesque will overstep the mark again—if he even knows what the mark looks like, which I doubt—and we'll be forced to rein him in. When we do, he'll bring up Mallory Norton once more, and we'll be right back where we started. And if he were to inflict serious harm on a fellow student, harm requiring a formal investigation by police, he could use the girl as a bargaining chip."

"I always thought Levesque was surplus to humanity's needs," said Renders. "It would be a shame if nothing happened to him."

"If something does, it can't happen here."

They'd just about gotten away with Scott Theriault. Losing two students in as many months would bring serious and unwanted attention: from the law, the media, and the handful of parents who gave enough of a damn about their children not to want to leave them in the care of an institution that appeared unable to keep its charges alive.

"Could Levesque have been the one who put Theriault's body in the water?" Santopietro asked.

It was certainly a possibility, thought Renders, if one he hadn't considered until Levesque started dropping nasty hints. Could the boy have been fucking with them from the start? Levesque tells Santopietro that Scott Theriault is seeing a Bingham girl who drives up to the school after dark, then he waits to see how the principal reacts. Maybe he's watching when Santopietro and Renders find Mallory Norton, and when she doesn't show up again, Levesque has a good idea why, so he starts tormenting Theriault by whispering in his ear that Santopietro and Renders may know more than they're saying about the disappearance of his girlfriend. Theriault reacts, forcing Renders to deal with him. Finally, Levesque somehow discovers where Renders has buried Theriault, but instead of calling 911, anonymously or openly, he puts the body in a stream to see where it ends up, like a kid playing with a stick on the current.

But that was where it fell apart for Renders. He couldn't figure out how Levesque might have known about Theriault, not without shadowing Renders into the wilderness. Yet somehow Scott Theriault's body, buried in a hole by the bank and covered with dirt, had washed downstream to be discovered.

"No," said Renders at last. "I'm still of the belief there must have been a collapse. I buried him within sight of the stream, so if the ground did fall in, the body could have tumbled down the slope to be taken by it. I mean, Levesque aside, what other answer is there? That someone else found Theriault and decided to give him a water funeral?"

Santopietro didn't reply. He had only Renders's word that Theriault's body had been disposed of properly. He didn't want to doubt the man, but it might be that without proper supervision, Renders flirted with negligence.

"So what do we do?" Renders asked.

"We wait. We control Levesque as best we can for the time being, until we find an opportunity to get rid of him—away from the school."

Renders didn't look happy, and Santopietro couldn't blame him. What he was proposing was less a solution than the kicking of a can down the road, with all the attendant risks of dealing with a creature as unpredictable as Leonard Levesque, but the reasoning was sound. The school couldn't afford any more dead students.

"Do you regret Mallory Norton?" Santopietro asked quietly.

"Not at all," said Renders. "I enjoyed it. I enjoyed her. I'd very much like for us to do something similar together again."

Which brought them back to the Game and Renders's potential introduction as a player. It would mean longer gaps between games for each player, but as Santopietro had explained to Edward Kenney, that might protect them in the long run by further disrupting the pattern. The other option was to continue what he had started with Renders: a separate game for two, meaning that Santopietro would no longer have to endure a time-out one year in three. But by taking Mallory Norton, he had broken one of the cardinal rules agreed to with Kenney and Teal, and they would be entitled to feel aggrieved. It might be better were they to remain ignorant.

"Let's see what we can do about that," said Santopietro.

CHAPTER

XLVIII

Edward Kenney was having a good day. Two potentially lucrative contracts that threatened to go south had instead soared thanks to a lot of effort on his part, and not only that, but the other parties involved were so happy with the outcome, they'd committed to further partnerships with him down the line, commitments to which he planned to hold them. Already he was assembling the deal memos in his mind, and with the application of only minimal pressure he might be able to get ink on paper within a week. To celebrate, he would book a table for a family dinner at the Tarratine on Park, one of Bangor's best restaurants, and pick up a shiny token of affection for his wife at Day's Jewelers.

Buying his wife a gift was something Kenney always did after playing the Game, though he took care to ensure he could offer a good reason: a bet that paid off, or like today, a business plan come to fruition. Unlike Roger Teal, Edward Kenney loved his wife and adored his children, but he also enjoyed every facet of the Game, from the planning to the resolution. He felt no guilt about raping and killing a stranger, but like many husbands who strayed, he found that his failings only made him value his home life more, which led him to increase the general store of his wife's happiness.

Kenney did not view his participation in the Game as an act of betrayal. He was not cheating on his wife by playing, and he felt nothing for the women involved beyond a passing lust. If he was addicted to the Game, it was a controlled addiction, which hardly counted as an addiction at all. It was, in spirit, closer to the pleasure he took in his biannual visits to the Hollywood Casino and Raceway, a small slice of Vegas glamour in Bangor. He loved waiting on the turn of a card, or watching the roulette wheel before the ball settled. In those moments, it wasn't about winning or losing but the possibility of both, held in perfect balance. (Schrödinger might have understood.) For Kenney, the Game truly was a game, but he cared about winning only because the consequences of losing were so grave. (Schrödinger's cat might have understood.)

The only shadow on the horizon was the one cast by the Saint's suspected extracurricular activities. Kenney wasn't due to visit Spero for a while, but he felt the need to confront the Saint face-to-face. With that in mind, he'd contacted the manager at Sworley's Garden Center in Jackman to let her know he was planning a road trip to catch up in person with valued, long-term customers, and a date and time for their meeting had been agreed on. To further support the road-trip story, Kenney made similar appointments as far south as Lewiston, Portland, and Portsmouth, New Hampshire, requiring a few nights away from home. The journeys wouldn't be wasted—nothing, with Edward Kenney, was ever wasted—because in some cases it was a long time since he'd pressed the flesh and picked up the tab for a lunch or dinner. It would be a way to revisit his early years, when he'd lived out of his car for days on end, and slept in it when money was tight. He'd let the Saint know he was coming to town only at the last minute. Kenney had contemplated bringing Teal along for the ride, but Teal had a habit of shrinking in the presence of the Saint, even at the best of times. Kenney couldn't picture him openly accusing the Saint of unsanctioned murder.

As for the most recent sanctioned murder, that of Nola Maddick in Detroit, it was a textbook example of the Game played well, which provided Kenney with no small satisfaction. He'd like to have awarded himself all the credit, but had to admit the snatch was the riskiest part and Teal had executed it expertly. Kenney might have set up the play, but Teal made the touchdown. Right now, all things being well, Maddick was lying in a pit, entombed by construction waste.

But it nagged at Kenney that no one had yet come forward to report her missing. Even whores and junkies had friends and family, people who cared about them, if not a lot. And should these dregs have been disliked or unloved, the agents of the state remained to be considered: social workers, mailmen—or police, because the good ones kept track of all the faces on their blocks; and that was before one took into account charity volunteers, landlords, creditors major and minor, and pimps. It was hard to pass through this world unnoticed and harder still to quit it with an involuntary version of an Irish goodbye.

Kenney tried to let it go. He was searching for problems where none existed. He and Teal had managed to abduct a woman from a city street, enjoy themselves with her, kill her, and dispose of the body, all without anyone paying the blindest bit of notice. It was as if the universe had wanted Nola Maddick excised from memory, and the agents of that erasure were not to be punished for doing what was required.

But Edward Kenney had lived too long to believe in a just universe. If proof of its nonexistence were needed, a just universe would not have allowed an individual like himself, a murderer of women, to thrive. Kenney's father, a gloomy man who would take a full glass and empty it to save life the trouble of doing it for him, liked to say that the world started every day by pulling on a fresh pair of boots with which to kick the unwary. The old man had been full of helpful sayings: If shit were wealth, the poor would be born without assholes. Be friendly to many and a friend to few. Never trust a man who gives you his phone number unbidden. (On women who did the same, Kel Kenney had not expressed a view, but doubtless he wouldn't have approved of them either.) All of which was to say that some of the father's fatalism had rubbed off on the son, because an optimist—and this was another of Kel's old saws—was someone yet to receive a proper schooling from reality.

Edward Kenney made the reservation at the Tarratine before browsing the Day's Jewelers website for a suitable gift. He then worked his way through a backlog of emails and performed a much-postponed tidying of his desk and office. Only when he was about to quit early, and with an eerie and mounting feeling of trepidation, did he check the by now familiar homepages of the *Detroit Free Press*, *Bridge Michigan*, and *MLive*. Each was running the same main story about a missing woman, using the same picture. From Kenney's screen, the face of Nola Maddick stared back, not dissimilar to how she'd looked as Kenney and Teal took turns with her.

But the name beneath the pictures was not the one on her driver's license. Instead, the pictures identified her as Gai Cotter. Or in full, Special Agent Gai Cotter of the Drug Enforcement Administration.

CHAPTER

XLIX

Sabine left Bingham feeling simultaneously unsatisfied and relieved: the former because, having gained access to the Norton home, she was no closer to Mallory—nothing had been awakened, and she could detect no echo of the girl beyond the house, even though Sabine was attuned to her now—and the latter because it would have saddened her to receive confirmation of Mallory's death, as her efforts would then have focused on helping to locate a body.

Sabine drove north, cutting through the backroads of The Forks into The Plains. The light was still good, and it was about two and a half hours from Bingham to her home; if she started out by three, she'd be back in Haynesville by six at the latest. She didn't plan to go walking in the woods, and if she did get out of her car, she would not stray far. From the media reports, she knew roughly where Scott Theriault's remains had been found. The current had carried his body to within sight of the road, where it was discovered lodged between rocks. She would drive to the spot and there she would stay for as long as she felt comfortable.

Just inside The Plains, she passed a convenience store and gas station on her left, with two cars and a truck parked outside. The tea she had drunk with Anita Norton was now pressing on her bladder. She should have asked to use the Nortons' bathroom before leaving, but she always felt awkward peeing in a stranger's home. She made a quick U-turn and returned to the store, which advertised itself as "Small's Gas & Provisions—The Big Heart of The Plains," whatever that meant. She put twenty dollars' worth of gas in the tank, because even though she didn't need to fill up now, she would by the time she got halfway home. Also, if she was going to use the facilities, it was only polite to put some money the proprietor's way.

As she went inside to pay, she saw another photo of Mallory Norton, but appended to it was a handwritten sign announcing a search scheduled for the following morning, to convene at ten a.m. from Small's. Sabine continued to the register, paid, and was directed to the bathroom. Once she'd done the needful, she asked the man behind the register if anyone was welcome to assist with the search.

"If you can walk and look around at the same time without tripping over your feet, we'd be happy to have you," he said. He introduced himself as Bennett Small, the owner. "Are you from around here?"

"No, Haynesville. But I know the family."

Which was true, as far as it went.

"You'll need a good pair of boots," said Small. "We'll supply coffee and pastries, but you might want to bring your own to-go cup."

Sabine told him she'd do that. Like a lot of Mainers, she kept a spare pair of old boots in her trunk and never went anywhere without a to-go cup. She returned to her car, and after a pause for reflection, turned south instead of north. If she still wanted to visit the place where Scott Theriault's body had washed up, tomorrow would do, after the search. And who knew what she might discover by participating? At the very least, she'd be able to gain access to regions that might have been inaccessible to her otherwise.

In Bingham, she booked a room for the night at the Motor Inn on Main, close to the banks of the Kennebec, her window looking out over Big Island. For sustenance, she bought a sandwich, a bag of potato chips, a Milky Way, and two cans of beer at Jimmy's, the gas station and convenience store a stone's throw away. As she walked back to her lodgings, that rain still threatening, she spotted an elderly woman watching her from the wooded island. Sabine shouldn't have been able to see her so clearly, not in the dusk, but the woman glowed faintly. She was wearing a nightgown that reached to her shins, and her feet were bare. A quadrant of her skull was missing, the edges impossibly neat, but the wound had stopped bleeding a long time before. Her head moved to follow Sabine's progress along the road, but Sabine ignored her. That was what came of being so focused on Mallory Norton, of calling in the hope of receiving a reply: if you sent out a signal, you didn't know who else might be listening. Sabine began the process of closing her mind. She'd been about to do so anyway in preparation for a night's sleep, but the woman's appearance made her act sooner. Sabine had learned early that going to bed with that damned faculty of hers active and engaged was a bad idea. At best, it made getting to sleep difficult, and at worst—well, she didn't want to wake in the night to discover that old woman with the ruined head standing by the side of the bed.

"Go on, now," said Sabine. "You're not the reason I came here."

She pictured shutters closing and fingers winding the wick on an old oil lamp, extinguishing the flame. She was grateful to see the woman's glow dissipate—and without resistance, because the dead commonly fought. They didn't want the shutters to close or the light to go out. They wanted to be seen and heard, but that was mainly the recent ones. Those who'd been dead awhile, such as the ruined woman, were more resigned, like starving people grown accustomed to the withholding of food. They began to give up until, at last, they faded away. If Sabine returned a year from now and called out to Big Island, perhaps no one would answer. Nevertheless, back in her room, and before she closed her eyes, she asked—no, label it what it was: prayed—that the woman would find peace.

CHAPTER
L

I was not a fan of early mornings—Macy shared that antipathy, which might be another reason we got along so well—but I was awake before seven a.m. that Sunday. I made a mug of instant coffee, took it to my office, and opened the floor safe. From it I removed the documents retrieved years earlier from the plane wreckage in the Great North Woods. The plane had been lost for years, but I'd found it, although people died along the way, died for what I was now holding. It was an early list of Believers, the compromised and the compromisers, those who had allied themselves, with varying degrees of willingness, to a specific cause: the search for the Buried God. It was, depending on whom one asked, a relic of a fallen angel, a representation of one, or the angel itself. The reality, objective or otherwise, didn't matter so much as the harm these people were visiting on the world with their activities: the accrual of wealth and influence untempered by moral, social, or environmental concerns, and the creation of a shadow rule of the wealthy and powerful over the poor and the vulnerable.

The head of the serpent was the Backers. If they could be dealt with, the serpent would be decapitated. Somewhere in these papers lay clues to the Backers' identities, a pattern of acquaintance and association waiting to be revealed. I had spent a long time trying to establish that pattern, whenever finances and opportunity permitted. Of course, I could simply have handed over the documents to SAC Edgar Ross of the FBI, but I didn't trust Ross to share with me whatever he might subsequently uncover. Ross knew I was in possession of the documents because I'd passed selected contents to him when any of those named in them were set to assume positions of especial prominence or authority. Once informed, the FBI, or Ross's particular dirty-tricks section of it, would move against them, exposing their failings to the light or using their misdeeds as material for blackmail: financial impropriety, assaults, affairs, forced abortions for younger lovers, rape, all were grist to Ross's mill. Fire was fought with fire as their own methods were used against them. This was a personal matter for me. For reasons I did not understand, I represented a threat to the Believers, yet they were reluctant to move decisively against me. They closed in, but did not strike. Sometimes, I felt they might even be frightened, though that could have been vanity on my part.

It might have been my recent conversations with Angel that led me to look again at the papers. In the years since their retrieval I had added notes, additional supporting documents, copies of bank accounts and affidavits, but soon, everything would have to be gone from my possession. I'd achieved what I could, and I accepted that others could do more. But I had a solution, however partial, to the puzzle of the Backers' identities, because the name of one institution recurred more often than any other: the Colonial Club of Commonwealth Avenue, Boston. But of course, Ross must already have known that because he, too, was a member of the Colonial Club, which I had learned only relatively recently.

Ross had been a part of my life for decades. I would not have called him a friend, and he would not put my interests before those of the bureau, but I'd never had cause to doubt his commitment to obstructing the Believers until I learned about his membership in the Colonial Club.

Ross, heeding. Ross, enjoining.

Ross, waiting.

3

There was a listening fear in her regard,
As if calamity had but begun . . .

John Keats, *Hyperion*

CHAPTER

LI

The rain that Sabine had intuited came down during the night. She woke to the sound of it on the roof above her room, at first mistaking it for footsteps, so heavy was it. She lay awake for a time, enjoying the novelty of being in a strange bed two nights running, before allowing the aperiodic rhythm to ease her to sleep for another hour. Later, she replenished a water bottle from the tap in her room, filled her to-go cup from the coffeepot at reception, just in case there was a line at Small's, and once more drove out to The Plains.

The parking lot was full by the time she arrived at the gas station, forcing her to park on the road, and all was bustle around the trestle table from which two women were pouring coffee and distributing doughnuts and Danishes. Next to it was a smaller table at which participants were required to sign up. Sabine saw, separate from the other cars and trucks, vehicles from the Maine Forest Service, the Somerset County Sheriff's Office, and the Maine State Police, along with a quartet of men and women in uniform. Their presence made her feel more comfortable about assisting with the search, so much so that she even liberated two of the doughnuts, one of which she ate and the other she wrapped in a napkin for later. She then added her name to the list.

Minutes later, one of the rangers used a bullhorn to call for attention. By then Sabine counted about forty people present, varying in age from teenagers to seniors, some carrying trekking poles and walking sticks. There were also four or five dogs. Most of those involved appeared to know one another, and the dogs likewise. She looked around to check whether Anita Norton or her husband was present, but saw no sign of them; their presence, she supposed, might have represented an awkward distraction.

The searchers were split into two groups, each under the supervision of a ranger, assisted by a state trooper or a deputy, and given a rendezvous point from which they would start out at ten sharp. Sabine was assigned to the second group, which was led by the ranger with the bullhorn and a state trooper who ticked off names as people confirmed they were clear on where they were supposed to be going. If, like Sabine, they were unsure, the rendezvous was pointed out to them on a map. Sabine put the location into her phone, though she didn't think she'd have trouble spotting a big group of cars gathered up by the Dead River, even without the help of the convoy that was already pulling out.

"You know where you're headed?"

The question came from a burly man with thick, graying hair and a beard that could have done with a good trim. His canvas field coat hung open, and under it he wore a zippered sweatshirt, also open, over a three-button undershirt, layers to be discarded as needed.

"I believe so," said Sabine.

"Good."

He resumed walking and she fell into step beside him.

"You come far?" he asked casually.

"Haynesville, but I stayed in Bingham last night."

"Just for this, or were you drawn by the bright lights?"

He squinted at her. She didn't need any great acuity to spot his caution. She knew there were those who would be thrilled not only by the idea of looking for a body, but also the possibility of finding one. Mallory Norton's disappearance would have drawn them from under their rocks. Sabine ought to have asked for the bullhorn to reassure everyone she meant well.

"I was up here anyway. I saw the notice about the search and decided to stay. I could spare the time. And you?"

"I'm from The Plains."

"Do you know the girl?"

"Only to see around," he replied.

He stopped by a battered Ford truck. "This is me."

Sabine pointed at her car. "And that's me."

"I'll keep an eye out for you. I'm Tim Sadlier, by the way."

"Sabine Drew."

"A pleasure, Sabine."

"Likewise. How about I just follow you, Tim?"

"Be my guest. I'd keep my windows closed, though. This old girl does cough some."

So Sabine followed the man named Tim all the way to the rendezvous—he wasn't lying about the exhaust—and once they arrived, she stayed with him. The forest ranger made everyone space out before they began, but ensured everyone kept within both sight and hailing distance of the searchers at either side, so Sabine found herself with Tim to her right and Bennett Small to her left.

"You see anything unusual," said the ranger, "you call out and look, but don't touch. Okay, let's move."

They'd been told to familiarize themselves with what Mallory Norton was wearing when she was last seen. Sabine had memorized the details and planned to do her best to pay attention to the physical surroundings, but really, she was engaged in an exploration of a different character. Already, she was reaching into the darkness of the woods ahead. In her right hand, plucked from the brush in the girl's bedroom, she held a tangle of Mallory Norton's hair.

CHAPTER

LII

As the morning wore on, Sabine learned why Tim Sadlier dressed in layers that were easily removable. Although the weather wasn't warm, the terrain they were searching was rough, with a gradual but discernible gradient, and after half an hour she'd had to take off her jacket to remove her sweatshirt. This had resulted in Sadlier and Small receiving a flash of red brassiere—and what it contained when the sweatshirt caught on the clip holding Sabine's hair in place, though Sadlier, unlike Small, had the decency to pretend not to notice. She tied the sweatshirt around her waist, put the jacket back on, and caught up with the rest, Mallory Norton's hair once more entwined around her fingers.

"Come on, honey," Sabine whispered. "If you're out here, give me a sign."

They were moving through woodland, which made it harder for Sabine both to hold her position in the line and maintain a clear mind, since she had to keep an eye on Sadlier and Small as well as watch where she put her feet. If she deviated too far east or west, she might overlook something important, and if she took a misstep, she could break an ankle. The last of the season's insects—mostly sluggish cluster flies—buzzed around her as she broke a sweat, and she picked up traces of stink bug on the breeze. Without stopping, she wiped her brow and drank some water. To her left was the Kennebec, visible through the trees some way distant, and to the right was a smaller tributary, flowing downhill. Now she paused to take her bearings, and thought the stream to her right might be the same one that had carried Scott Theriault's body. If so, the spot where the corpse had lodged was somewhere behind her. On the way back, she could change her position in the line so that—

What came at her was not utterly formless. It had shape but not fixity, its margins blurring and shading to gray, its core a deep, roiling black. It erupted from a stand of balsam fir, as if extruded by a rupture in some unseen membrane, like toxic gas expanded to the point of explosion. Sabine had just seconds to register it before it was upon her, and the forest, the extended line, even Sadlier and Small, were instantly lost from sight, leaving her in darkness. The force of the body's passage swept Sabine off her feet and she landed awkwardly on her back, causing a rib to pop, but the pain was the least of her concerns because the dark had both mass and intent. It was pushing against her face, suffocating her, and she was trying not to breathe because she didn't want it inside her, but nailed fingers were scratching at her lips, forcing them apart so they could enter her mouth, and even as she tried to clench her jaw they were scraping at the enamel of her teeth. She wanted to scream, but to scream would be to admit the dark, the dark with all its rage and loneliness, the dark that was many and one, plural made singular, so that even individual names were rendered fragmentary. Fear, desperation, hate, longing: all those were present, and love too, though the love was struggling to survive amid the rest. Suddenly the hands were gone from her face, and she felt them instead on her arms, her head. She pounded at them with her fists until a voice said: "It's okay, we're here. We've got you."

The dark retreated, reluctantly, and Tim Sadlier's features came into focus, Bennett Small beside him, and behind them, drawing nearer, the ranger, with the state trooper at his heels. The dark remained above, below, and around, swooping and diving, like the murmurations of starlings, but less a multiplicity acting in unison than a barely restrained chaos, and what kept it from dissolution was a distinct force of will stronger than the rest, but not strong enough to prevent damage being inflicted on Sabine to the point of death. Something in the dark was clinging to reason, but soon it would lose its grip. After that, there would be nothing to hold the rest back.

“Can you stand?” Tim Sadlier asked.

“With help, but I may have fractured a rib. Left side.”

“What about your head?” This from the trooper. “Did you hit it when you fell?”

“I’m pretty sure I didn’t,” said Sabine. “The pain’s only in my side.”

By now more of the searchers had come to see what was the matter, which meant Sabine was now both sore *and* embarrassed. With the aid of Sadlier and Small she managed to sit up, then stand.

“That’s your searching done for today,” said Sadlier. “We ought to have you checked out by a doctor, just in case you’ve done anything worse than break a rib.”

Sabine tried to demur, but the ranger and trooper were of the same opinion as Sadlier, if only to cover their backs. They had enough troubles without adding the blowback from an untreated injury incurred during a search they were leading. Sadlier volunteered to accompany Sabine to the rendezvous point, and from there to the clinic in Bingham. Once again, Sabine was about to protest, but managed to stop herself as the first syllables formed on her lips. She was shocked to find that she enjoyed Tim Sadlier’s company and he, on similarly brief acquaintance, gave every indication of liking hers.

Sometimes a person just had to get out of her own way.

CHAPTER

LIII

That Sunday afternoon, Walter and Lee Cole arrived from Vermont to spend the night with me at the house. The Coles' older daughter, Ellen, currently lived with her husband in Burlington, where they'd just had their second child, a girl. Walter Cole had been my partner and mentor during my unhappy years with the NYPD. After his retirement, Ellen went missing, abducted by a man many believed to be a myth, and together, Walter and I had found her. Now, Walter informed me, Ellen had named her daughter Parker.

"Personally, I think it's a dumb name," said Walter as we sat on my porch while Lee took a nap upstairs.

"You're only saying that because we named a dog after you," I replied. "Even if he was a very good dog."

We were keeping very still. In an area of grass at the edge of my property stood a little snow bunting, the first I'd sighted that season. Where one went, more would follow, and soon it would not be uncommon to see them swirling over the marshes, their color causing them to resemble snowflakes tumbling to earth. With the coming of spring they would be gone again, back to northern Canada and Greenland. They are cold-weather creatures. If I had a spirit bird, it was the snow bunting.

"Ellen would like you to say hello to the kid, when you have time," said Walter. "It may be a while before they're willing to travel with her. Leaving the house for a bite of lunch is like a military operation for them."

I told him I'd be happy to make the trip. I might even have Sam for company if she wanted a ride home from college. Rachel, her mother, also lived in Burlington, and Sam had grown up there. Walter asked after them both, and mentioned that Ellen sometimes spotted Rachel around town, most recently in the company of Jefferson Reid, her on-again, off-again, now on-again boyfriend. I didn't like Jefferson Reid. He was all money and mouth, but no manners. I also found it hard to accept that he could be as wealthy as he was and as dumb as he seemed. If so, Rachel would not have wanted to be with him, not unless she was very lonely, and nobody was that lonely, not even God.

"How are you and Rachel getting along?" Walter asked.

"Up and down," I said. "She's unhappy that Sam is studying law enforcement and talking about working as a private investigator after graduation."

"Does Rachel blame you?"

"Only for providing our daughter with an inappropriate role model," I said. "I'm not sure I could have been any other kind, but it wasn't like I encouraged Sam to consider a career in the sector."

"Has Rachel met your new girlfriend?"

"Not yet."

"Has Sam?"

"They get along like a house on fire. They may even be kindred spirits."

"So a more appropriate role model for Sam, then."

"Certainly better than me, but I'm not going to share that fact with Macy or else she'll have it printed on a T-shirt to wear around the house."

"Sam could do worse than inherit your conscience," said Walter. "Be good if she could avoid your habit of getting hurt, though."

"From your lips to God's ears."

Walter drank his Rising Tide copper ale, and I my wine. Lee came downstairs, poured herself a glass of wine, and joined us.

"What are you working on?" she asked me.

I told them about Scott Theriault, Spero, and Mallory Norton.

"That sounds like a full complement of hurt," said Lee when I was done.

"If it's not," I said, "it'll do until the rest of the hurt catches up."

I left them to enjoy the view together while I made a start on an early dinner. The first snow bunting had now been joined by a second, perhaps its mate. Out on the marsh, reflected clouds floated in dark blue water, and the afternoon was hushed. Walter took his wife's hand, and she rested her head on his shoulder, while I stood by the window and willed the world not to come apart.

CHAPTER

LIV

Sabine Drew had never fractured a rib before. In books and movies, it was passed off as a comparatively minor injury, like breaking a toe. A medic strapped it up and told you to rest, but otherwise, it had to be endured. What they didn't say was how difficult it was to walk with a busted rib, especially over rough terrain, even with someone to lean on, or how much it hurt even to breathe in deeply. By the time Sabine and Sadlier regained the rendezvous point, the pain was constant, and she was glad Sadlier was driving because she wasn't up to it, not with the nausea—and that was before she sat in the passenger seat of his truck and was sure she felt bone scrape against bone. The pain intensified, and she let out an involuntary yelp. Sadlier, all solicitousness, eased the truck as gently as he could from the shoulder and drove slowly all the way to Bingham, avoiding sharp turns and sudden stops. When they got to the urgent care center, he helped her out—which added another clockwise twist to the old volume knob of affliction—and walked her inside. He led her to a chair but she didn't want to sit again, so he left her leaning against the wall by the reception desk, within easy reach should she show any signs of tottering. Minutes later, he entrusted her to the care of a nurse, who recognized him and said: "Back again so soon?"

Sabine stared at Sadlier. "You make a habit of frequenting medical centers?"

"I was here recently," he said, "with one of the kids from the school I work at. I'm not on commission or anything."

“That’s a relief. And you don’t have to wait: I can call a cab when I’m done.”

“They’ll have to come from Skowhegan,” said Sadlier, “and it’ll cost you. I don’t have anything else to do, and I always keep a book in the truck.”

The way he said it stung her.

“Well, if you don’t have anything better to do—”

“Now, I didn’t mean it like that,” he replied. “I’d like to wait.”

Sabine thought: *He’s not an unattractive man. Unkempt, but that can be mended.*

Sadlier thought: *She’s a handsome woman. Kind of raggedy, but I’m no one to point the finger.*

The nurse coughed meaningfully.

“Can you resume this later?”

Both Sabine and Sadlier blushed, and said “Sorry” simultaneously.

CHAPTER

LV

Tim Sadlier managed to get through eight long chapters of the fantasy novel he was reading before Sabine Drew reappeared. He put it away as soon as he saw her, storing it in his jacket pocket. He really didn't want her to ask what he was reading.

"What are you reading?" she asked.

"How are you feeling?"

"I asked first."

He removed the book from his pocket and showed it to her. She took it from him and read the synopsis on the back cover.

"Do they actually have sex *on* the dragons?"

Heat rose to Sadlier's cheeks.

"Not in this one," he said. "Not yet."

"One can only live in hope, I suppose." She handed the book back. "I've always believed that escapism is underrated and we should never feel guilty about our reading pleasures, within reason. If I'd discovered you reading *The Protocols of the Elders of Zion*, I'd have been obliged to call that taxi after all."

Sadlier didn't know what *The Protocols of the Elders of Zion* might be, but was now determined to avoid it, or them, at all costs.

"So how are you feeling?" he asked again.

"Sore, and wrapped up like a mummy, but there's no internal damage, the fracture apart. I've been instructed to rest, ice the area a couple of times a day, do my breathing exercises, and take ibuprofen for the pain. I'm also supposed to cough regularly." She coughed, then winced. "But I may interpret 'regularly' loosely."

"What about driving?"

"I'm okay to drive."

Sadlier did his best to hide his disappointment. His best wasn't good enough though, because Sabine noticed.

"But," she added, "I'm going to hold off on heading home until tomorrow. It's been a long day, and I'm too tired and achy to drive for hours. I took a room last night at the Motor Inn, and I doubt they'll refuse me a second night. I'm worried about my car, though."

"It'll be safe where it is," said Sadlier. "But if it'll make you happier, I can ask someone in town to head out there with me and drive it back. I know a few people who'd be happy to do it."

Sabine said that she thought she might prefer to have the car where she could see it. Sadlier told her that he'd drop her at the inn and take care of the car after.

"And then I'd like a stiff drink," said Sabine, "and something to eat. Perhaps you might care to join me? The least I can do is buy you dinner in return for your assistance. We might have to dine at the Motor Inn, though. I don't really feel up to another long ride."

Tim Sadlier grinned like a Halloween jack-o'-lantern and said he thought that would be fine, just fine.

"But my treat," he added. "You're the visitor. And the patient."

Sabine didn't argue. She was, she thought, getting rather good at staying out of her own way.

CHAPTER

LVI

Once she was settled at the Motor Inn—she'd even been given the same room again—Sabine undressed slowly, filled the bathroom sink, and bathed with a washcloth. The nurse had instructed her on how to wrap the bandaged area in plastic when she showered, but it was too much trouble to go to, even without worrying about the potential consequences of slipping while getting in or out of the tub. Her jeans were muddied, and one of the knees was torn, so she set them aside and put on her pajama bottoms and sweatshirt. She'd have to wait for Sadlier to return with her car and overnight bag before she could finish dressing.

She sat on the bed. From her jacket pocket she removed the strands of Mallory Norton's hair, held them to her nose, and inhaled. She closed her eyes and tried to bring to mind the mass of emotion and negative energy that had sent her sprawling in the dirt, but no, she could not recall any hint of Mallory's presence. In the quiet of the motel room, she sifted through her memories of the incident. Yes, the Theriault boy was definitely in there somewhere, but he was not the one who worried her. It was the Other, and even as it tried to conceal itself from her, it could not disguise its nature or its name.

Sabine lay down for a while, until woken by a knock at the door, followed by Tim Sadlier's voice. She set aside any further thoughts of the forest and opened the door to him. He had changed his clothes, brushed his hair, and put on aftershave. In one hand he was holding a plastic bag with what smelled like a roast chicken inside, and in the other was a second clear bag containing a six-pack of beer, a bottle of wine, a quarter pint of vodka, and what might have been cans of tonic water.

"How many more people are we expecting?" she asked.

"None, I hope."

Sabine invited him to step inside. When he did, she kissed him.

CHAPTER

LVII

The Maine Department of Education in Augusta occupied part of the Burton M. Cross Office Building, a structure that wouldn't have looked out of place in Nicolae Ceauşescu's Communist Romania, right before the dictator and his wife were put up against a wall and shot. The building dated from the fifties, and despite being renovated in the twenty-first century, still dated from the fifties.

I'd made an appointment to speak to someone who might be able to answer questions about private schools in the state and was directed by the receptionist to the commissioner's office, where Jenny Berrien, assistant director of public affairs, was said to be waiting for me. I ended up waiting for her, which evoked uncomfortable memories of sitting outside the principal's office at Scarborough High, trying to come up with a plausible reason why I'd been caught killing time at the Big 20 Bowling Center when I should have been running indoor track.

Berrien, when she eventually showed up, turned out to be a tall, platinum-haired woman who, if she'd run track, would probably have wiped out the competition at anything over half a mile. She apologized for the delay and led me to an office that would have been small for just one and was intimate for two. I accepted coffee, which she made using a Nespresso machine perched on the windowsill in the absence of any other unoccupied space, the office being a shrine to paperwork.

"We don't get many private investigators visiting us," she said as she worked on the coffee, "or not with your reputation."

"For charm and good humor?"

"I may not have read that far," she said. "I might have gotten caught up in all the gunfire."

"If it's any consolation, I found waiting for you kind of intimidating. I kept expecting someone to tell me I was suspended for a week."

"Didn't like school?"

"Not a lot," I said, "but the feeling was mutual."

"I hated it too. I think anyone whose school days were the best days of their life ought to sue God for shortchanging them on the rest."

"Strange that you ended up in the Department of Education, then."

"I might have been trying to change the system from within, but those days are coming to a close. I have a few good years left in me, and a hankering to spend them in an advocacy role."

By now she had two small but admittedly fragrant cups of coffee prepared, in matching maroon cups. As she handed over one of them, the cuff of her shirt rose to reveal the edge of an intricate sleeve of tattoos on her right arm. I glimpsed ivy and eyeballs, and what might have been a serpent. She was an interesting woman.

She took the chair behind her desk, tasted her coffee, and said: "So: private schools."

"Yes."

"Any private school in particular?"

"Guess."

"Spero."

"Got it in one."

"Color me relieved, since I believe Spero doesn't fall under our authority beyond a requirement to supply an annual letter to our commissioner stating its intention to operate as an equivalent instruction school, which the commissioner duly acknowledges."

"Meaning?"

"Spero has satisfied the basic requirements for an approved private school under Title 20-A, Chapter 117, of the Maine Revised Statutes. May I ask who you're working for?"

"A lawyer named Alcock. His client is Ward Vose. Vose is Scott Theriault's father."

"Without wishing to sound judgmental," said Berrien, "it's a pity Ward Vose wasn't more concerned about his son before he sent him to Spero."

"Vose didn't send Scott to Spero. He was in prison at the time. Vose happens to be in prison a lot of the time."

"And I didn't believe I could pity that boy more. Then you come along to up the ante."

"Does the department have a problem with Spero?" I asked. "More to the point, do you?"

"Was it my tone?"

"Your tone, expression, and general demeanor."

"As these places go, Spero is reasonably well run, but 'as these places go' is a significant qualifier. Subjectively, I'm not in favor of the model as a way of dealing with troubled or traumatized youths. My instinct is to blame the parents, not the child, but where a child is unusually difficult, consigning them to the equivalent of an old reform school isn't the solution. It's an abrogation of parental responsibility, hence my comment about your client, whether he was behind bars or not. The same goes for Scott Theriault's mother."

"Vose didn't have much say in the matter," I said. "Scott's mother and stepfather made the decision to put him in Spero, which is not to absolve Vose of responsibility for the boy. He admits he was never in the running for father of the year, but that doesn't mean he's not entitled to ask questions about what befell his son."

"Is he going to sue Spero?"

That question was coming up a lot. If I set up a school, my first hire would be a good lawyer.

"The conversation hasn't arisen," I said. "What interests him is how and why his boy's broken body ended up in a river."

"Scott Theriault ran away from Spero," said Berrien, "and had an accident. That's death by misadventure, or whatever the legal equivalent is in this state."

I didn't reply, just drank my coffee. It was already almost gone and I'd barely started on it. No wonder the Nespresso people could afford to employ George Clooney as a point man.

"Which is what you've been hired to confirm or disprove, right?" Berrien pressed.

"In a nutshell."

"Well, as I told you, there's a limit to how much help we can be, given the independence of equivalent instruction schools, which I've mentioned. The department hasn't had significant contact with Spero for some years."

"But you must have had dealings with it at the start, when it was still in receipt of public funds."

Berrien's mouth twitched. I'd touched a pressure point, and pressure points were good. The important thing was knowing when to press, and how hard. Berrien might not be averse to sharing, but she wouldn't care to be harried. Gently would do it.

"What should I know?" I asked.

"That if I ever write my memoirs," she said, "I may title them *Accounts and Accountability*, with apologies to Jane Austen. But I doubt I'll ever write them. No one would publish them, no one would read them, and most of all, no one would thank me for the effort. Some people might be especially ungrateful."

I could almost see her finger hovering over the red button, waiting to press self-destruct on what remained of her career. The Maine Whistleblowers' Protection Act provided safeguards for employees who reported suspected violations, and Berrien had a strong union behind her, so her pension would be secure if she shared any concerns about financial malfeasance; and this wasn't an official exchange, so nothing she shared would have any legal consequences. But Berrien was obviously possessed of a conscience, and something had been bothering her for a while or else she would not have spoken as she had.

"You have suspicions," I said, "but no proof."

"That's right. It's a difficulty."

"Not for me. I'm in the suspicion business."

"I also intensely dislike the person concerned," said Berrien, "and the feeling is reciprocated."

I imagined that Berrien could rub a lot of people the wrong way. That might be why I was inclined to trust her: Like knows like.

"I assume your antipathy toward each other is recognized within the department," I said.

"It is."

"Is this person a superior?"

"No," said Berrien. "We occupy similar levels, but only in terms of salary. On every other scale, I'd regard him as my significant inferior, and I'm no angel."

I took out my notebook and uncapped my pen.

"Neither am I," I said. "Gossip away. I'm all ears."

CHAPTER

LVIII

After listening to Jenny Berrien for the best part of half an hour, I reached three conclusions. The first was that she'd been wise to keep her suspicions to herself, because she was operating on little more than unease, hearsay, and personal grievance. The second was that anyone in authority wishing to audit a private educational establishment that didn't wish to be audited had their work cut out for them. And the third was that something at Spero School probably stank.

I closed my notebook. I'd taken down so much information that my handwriting had deteriorated badly by the end, but I could reproduce most of what I'd heard based on key words, and it wasn't as if I'd be submitting my notes as evidence in court. Basically, Berrien's claims amounted to collusion between the authorities at Spero and the person at the Maine Department of Education originally responsible for ensuring that the money provided to the school by the state was not being misused.

"Well?" Berrien asked.

She was standing, because she liked to walk as she talked. I'd remained seated throughout.

"It's interesting that you're not alleging widespread financial mismanagement or misappropriation of funds," I said. "Your assertions involve just one person."

"By 'interesting' do you mean 'a relief'?"

"Maybe," I said.

"Almost everyone I work with in this department cares deeply about education and the needs of the young," said Berrien. "A lot of us could have found higher-paying jobs elsewhere, but we stayed because it allowed us to do some good—so you know, fuck Elon Musk and fuck Linda McMahon. That's why Spero bothers me so much. If I'm right, the actions of one individual threaten to make all of us look bad, even if any wrongdoing is historical, not current."

I could have reminded her that Scott Theriault's death wasn't historical, but it would have been glib, and Berrien's was a different crusade.

She took a breath, then added: "Wait, why did you say 'maybe' when I offered my interpretation of 'interesting'?"

"Because there's no proof of fraud."

"You could try to find it."

"That's not why I was hired," I said.

"But it could be relevant to your case."

"Maybe."

"You know, I'm starting to hate that word."

"I can switch to 'perhaps' if it helps."

Berrien dropped heavily into her chair.

"I feel like I've unburdened myself for nothing," she said.

"Unburdening is an end in itself."

"This gets worse. It's like being trapped in a room with the Buddha." She rubbed her face before cupping her hands in front of her mouth, her elbows resting on her desk. She might have been at prayer. "You know, I hate to admit it," she resumed, "but it does feel better to have put it in front of an independent listener. My only regret is that it sounded so thin, even to me."

"It's not thin," I said. "I didn't come here looking for legally binding proof of anything, because that's not how it works for me. I spend my days asking questions and being unhappy with the answers, even the honest ones. Generally, I leave a room no wiser than when I entered, and frequently more confused. Occasionally, someone tries to hit me. Sometimes"—I pointed to my damaged nose—"they succeed. But today I learned a lot. Frankly, I'd have been disappointed if I hadn't, this being the Department of Education and all."

Behind Berrien, the skies looked dark and heavy. The weather services were hedging their bets, warning of the possibility of heavy rain, even thunderstorms. In my bones, I felt they were right.

"So what now?" Berrien asked.

"I'd like you to make an introduction," I said. "It's time to close the circle."

CHAPTER

LIX

Berrien walked me through the building, which was already half-empty as the working day drew to its close.

"You're sure he'll still be here?" I asked.

"He never leaves before six. As far as appearances go, he's a model employee. Also, I think he prefers the office to home. The scuttlebutt is that his wife hates him, which puts her in good company, even if the rest of us had the common sense not to marry him."

I told Berrien I'd reconsidered, and she didn't have to come with me if she'd prefer not to, in case it caused problems for her later.

"I'm happy to come," she said. "I want to see his face when I tell him who you are and what you do. All set?"

I felt a little bad for her. She wanted me to ruin a man I'd never met on the basis of suspicion and personal antagonism, and I'd probably have to disappoint her. She knocked on a closed door and was already opening it before a voice inside had finished saying "Come in."

"Sorry for disturbing you," said Berrien, with what might have passed for sincerity if someone had never encountered actual sincerity. "Let me introduce you to someone. This is Mr. Parker. He's a private investigator. He'd like to talk to you about Spero School."

She turned to me and grinned.

"Mr. Parker, this is Roger Teal."

CHAPTER LX

Edward Kenney stayed in his office as his employees headed home. He wished a pleasant evening to those who said goodbye and thanked them, as always, for their efforts. None of them, not even his secretary, would have guessed anything was amiss, because disguising his feelings came easily to Kenney after so many years of hiding an entire self. Over the course of the weekend, he had eaten a fancy dinner at the Tarratine with his family, presented his wife with a pair of diamond earrings, collected book donations as part of his efforts for the Friends of the Bangor Public Library, and visited his elderly but still mentally alert father at the senior living facility, all without giving any indication of inner turmoil.

Kenney finished reading the latest about the missing DEA agent on the *Detroit Free Press* website but then continued browsing unconnected material, dropping down rabbit-hole links that did not interest him. Kenney used Brave as his default browser to minimize tracking, combined with a VPN, but he knew enough about forensic computing to accept that no browser was ever completely secure and every interaction left a trail. The best an amateur could do was limit the risks and clean as they went; in that sense, Kenney supposed, it was not dissimilar to the acts of abduction and murder. Always at the back of his mind, like the reality of death, was the prospect of the police arriving at his door with questions to be answered.

Now he knew why the disappearance of Nola Maddick—no, Gai Cotter—initially garnered no attention: It wasn't that nobody cared; it was that certain people cared too much. The reports didn't specify the nature of the investigation in which Cotter had been involved, but operating deep undercover might have required her to be out of contact with her handlers for days, even longer. When she dropped off the radar, those handlers couldn't be sure it wasn't for reasons pertinent to the investigation, but safety procedures must have been built into the system. Cotter might have missed a meetup or failed to make a call, or surveillance could have picked up a worrying conversation in which her name was mentioned. Whatever the cause, alarm bells had gone off, and now the DEA would be retracing her steps to establish when and where she was last seen, which might ultimately bring them to Fishkorn, and Joy Road.

While Kenney was anxious, he did not panic. His focus narrowed and his concentration grew, as when he was faced with a particularly thorny crossword clue in the Sunday edition of *The New York Times*. The Game had progressed to another level and the challenge was to adapt accordingly. Kenney had confidence in his own adaptive abilities, but was less convinced of Roger Teal's. Kenney would have to talk to him, calm him. No purpose would be served by Teal's getting spooked at this stage. Their victims had made the front pages of newspapers before, and police—good, smart police—had investigated the disappearances. On four occasions bodies were recovered. In one of those instances, the car used by Teal and the Saint was traced to a junkyard in Illinois, and footage was obtained of the vehicle being driven from Lincolnwood into Skokie, with the body of one Melba Roehr in the trunk. Nothing had come of any of it, and so the Game continued. Gai Cotter was another variation on the same theme, Kenney would assure Teal, one that always faded into irresolution. He sounded so persuasive, he was almost tempted to believe himself.

CHAPTER LXI

Roger Teal looked up from his desk to see a man in his late fifties of slightly-above-medium height, his dark hair graying at the temples, his face set in what only a fool would have regarded as an unthreatening expression. Without the benefit of a name and occupation, Teal would still have been on his guard; with both, he began actively shoring up his defenses, even as he did his best to hide his disquiet.

That it was the Bitch Berrien, as Teal called her (rarely aloud, and only when he was alone), who had brought this man to his door made him doubly wary. It wasn't so much that Berrien wouldn't have pissed on Teal if he was on fire, but that she would happily have pissed on him, and not to put out the flames. For years, she'd been nipping at his heels, asking for clarification on this and paperwork on that, which Teal had come to regard as an attack on his integrity. This was even before she moved to Public Affairs, which gave her wider latitude to apply pressure and more excuses to spread rumors about him. The fact that Teal was dishonest, and his moral principles would hardly stand up to the most modest of scrutiny, was beside the point. What annoyed him was that Berrien had assumed the worst of him from the start, and then set about trying to find evidence to support her convictions, which was tantamount to persecution. Teal didn't mind people taking a dislike to him, but he preferred that they make an effort to get to know him first.

Now, on top of everything else, Berrien was bringing a private investigator into his office, an investigator with questions about Spero. Teal had hoped this particular bugbear of Berrien's was laid to rest, since his formal involvement with Spero came to an end when the school ceased to draw on state funds. But why would a PI be interested in the quondam funding of a private school? The answer was that the investigation wasn't about money—unless, of course, the department had employed a specialist financial investigator to look into certain matters, but then a) Teal would have heard about it long before anyone arrived at his door, because a mayfly had a longer life than a secret in the department, and b) from what he could recall of Parker from the newspapers, his specialty wasn't forensic accounting but thuggery. So, definitely not a money matter.

Which came as a relief to Teal, who had managed to siphon a five-figure sum—okay, shading into six figures—during his time as the departmental inspector for the school, his cut of the deal he'd made with Santopietro. But if the investigator wasn't here to ask about misappropriated funds, why was he here? It couldn't be about the Game—

Could it?

All this went through Teal's mind in seconds, after which he spread his arms, palms raised upward like the Merciful Christ, and said: "Uh, why is the department employing a private investigator?" even if he was 99 percent sure that it wasn't.

"Mr. Parker isn't here at the department's instigation," said Berrien. "He's working on behalf of another client."

Teal looked confused, and his next question was genuine.

"Then what am I permitted to share with him?"

"I'll leave that to your discretion," said Berrien. "As far as the department is concerned, we have nothing to hide, so feel free to be as open with Mr. Parker as you'd like."

With that, she closed the door, leaving Teal alone with the investigator.

CHAPTER

LXII

I kept a close eye on Roger Teal as Berrien made the introductions, his features running the gamut of emotions from annoyance, through fear, before settling on muted defiance. I didn't know what he was guilty of, but he was guilty of something; if he hadn't been caught with his hands in the cookie jar, he remained worried about the possibility of crumbs trapped under his fingernails.

"Mind if I take a seat?" I asked, taking a seat.

"Why bother asking," Teal replied, "if you're going to do it regardless?"

He spoke mildly, but with a flash of teeth; not a church mouse, then, but closer to the cat that stalks it.

"My apologies," I said. "I can stand if you'd prefer. But personally, I don't like looking down on someone during a conversation, or having to look up to them. It might be the socialist in me."

Teal backed off, but marginally.

"The workday is almost over," he said. "I was worried that if you got too comfortable, I'd be caught in traffic."

"I'll try not to take up too much of your time."

I opened my notebook to a fresh page.

"May I ask who you're working for?" said Teal.

"A lawyer. His name is Alcock. I imagine the schoolyard was hard for him."

Teal registered the joke.

"I went to middle school with a kid called Seeman," he said. "His parents ended up homeschooling him."

I noticed that Teal had a stillness to him. After the initial disturbance caused by my arrival at his door, he was now sitting back to watch and wait. Even the exchange over the chair had an air of contrivance to it: he'd spoken only to see how I'd react. But in everything he did, however slight, he would give himself away, which was how it worked.

What could I have said already about Roger Teal? With certainty, only this: He didn't have a high opinion of people who weren't named Roger Teal.

"And who is the lawyer Alcock working for?" Teal continued. "Lawyers don't work for themselves. Like clockwork toys, they need winding."

I had no reason not to share the identity of the client with him. I'd be visiting Spero soon enough.

"Alcock has been engaged by a man named Ward Vose. His son was a student at Spero School."

"Was?"

"He drowned."

"Scott Theriault," said Teal.

"You're aware of the death?"

"How could I not be? It was in all the papers, for those of us who still read them. Also, anything to do with the school stands out for me. I feel proprietorial about it. I was engaged with Spero for years as a departmental inspector, which is presumably why you're here. I think it's trying to do good work. What happened to Scott Theriault will be used against it—is being used against it."

"Have you remained in touch with the officials at Spero?"

"Yes."

"Is that usual, an inspector keeping tabs on a school with which the department is no longer involved?"

"Who says I'm keeping tabs on it?"

"If not, then what?"

"I provide advice," said Teal. "And I help out on a voluntary basis. I was asked to join the board of trustees, but I felt it would be a step too far, and I doubt the department would have agreed anyway. I'll wait until I retire."

"What kind of advice and help do you provide, Mr. Teal?"

"Whatever is required. When the school stepped down from state funding, I guided administrators through the transition, beyond the general departmental assistance offered as a matter of course. At the school itself, I've painted dorms, put up fences, aided in the transfer and transportation of students—"

"Midnight abductions?"

Those teeth flashed again.

"I wouldn't call them that."

"What would you call them, then?"

"I've already answered the question: transfer and transportation."

"It doesn't strike me as a healthy way to deal with troubled children. It sounds like a recipe for trauma."

"Your observation contains the answer," said Teal. "They're troubled. Some of them have shown violence toward parents, siblings, teachers, and fellow students. Yes, they're teenagers, but frequently housed in adult bodies. Spero is a last resort, or next-to-last, and not one they're keen to embrace, not at first. And who can blame them? I wouldn't want to leave my family, my friends, my refrigerator of food on demand, my computer games, to be sequestered in rural Maine, where even the privilege of watching TV for an hour in the evening has to be earned. Few of them accede willingly, and at the other extreme, a number fight hard against it. So yes, there are times when the school authorities have to come in the night and take a boy when he's tired and disoriented, but only minimal force is ever used, and restraints if there's no option, as much to prevent the boy from hurting himself as anyone else. Is it traumatic? Yes, but we explain what's happening to them throughout, and they calm down soon enough."

Teal was the soul of reasonableness. But then, the worst men had the ability to make even the unconscionable sound acceptable, and it always ended the same way: with dead children.

"Do you enjoy it?" I asked.

"No, Mr. Parker, I do not. I have a daughter of my own and would hate for anything similar to befall her. That's one of the reasons I stayed involved with Spero. I wanted to develop a system that worked for all, but primarily the students, beginning with their first encounter with the school. That means being in the van with them, especially in the most challenging of cases, and later on-site as they adjust to their new circumstances. I view it as an extension of my work with the department. With luck, what I learn may subsequently be applied at similar schools."

I let it go. I'd never tried to force a terrified teenager into the back of a van in the dead of night, so the mechanics of the operation were beyond my remit. I just knew it wasn't something for which I'd volunteer. I expect there were those who were prepared to do it for money. You can get people to do anything for money, assuming you have the right people and the right money. It's harder to get them to do dirty work for free, especially if it involves inflicting suffering on others—unless they don't find it dirty at all, but instead kind of like it. We have a name for those people: sadists.

"And how does the department feel about the assistance you provide to Spero?"

"I'm not being paid for what I do," said Teal, "so it's not a concern. I'm not the only person here who volunteers at a school."

It was notable that Teal was making no effort to hide his ongoing links to Spero. Nevertheless, he was hiding something. He was too open not to be.

"Were you part of the team that took Scott Theriault from his home?"

"No."

"Any particular reason why you weren't?"

"I was otherwise engaged. I have a full-time job and a family. I assist Spero when I can, but I'm not on call."

"Did you ever meet Scott Theriault during your visits to Spero?"

"I might have. I don't recall."

"What about the principal, Dante Santopietro? How closely do you work with him?"

"We speak regularly. Dante is Spero. Without him, it wouldn't exist."

"I hear he was once a student at Élan. That wasn't a great place to end up."

"No, apparently it wasn't."

"Were you there as well?"

"Thankfully not, but I have a friend who wasn't so fortunate."

"Was Santopietro the friend?"

"No, the friend—he went missing some years ago. He struggled greatly after Élan. The assumption is that he took his own life. But I'd really prefer not to talk about that. It's very painful."

"I'd still like his name."

I pressed because Teal was now being openly evasive.

"Mike Hurvich."

The words came hard to him.

"What about Santopietro? Does he speak much about his time at Élan?"

"He has talked about Élan, but it's not for me to share those confidences. I can say that his experiences colored his views on behavior modification for troubled teens. Spero doesn't tolerate violence in any form."

"Outside of nocturnal abductions."

"On which we've agreed to differ."

"I haven't agreed to anything," I said. "However, violence must occur. Even the best of schools have to deal with fights between students."

"There are processes in place at Spero, systems of punishment involving denial of privileges, treat restrictions, extra chores, ascending in severity according to the nature of the infraction. Even striking a staff member isn't automatically an expulsion offense. It's discouraged, to put it mildly, and the penalties are severe, but every dog is allowed one bite. Spero can't change these kids overnight, and some of them it won't change at all, but the ethos of the school is to keep trying until forced to admit defeat, and such defeats are rare. A lot of the students are looking for discipline, but they don't know it. Spero is tough only because it has to be. Ultimately, it's built on care, and frequently Dante and the staff show more tenderness toward those boys than their own parents ever have."

And you know, I believed what Teal was saying, or I believed that he believed it, which was close enough. He spoke of Spero with messianic zeal.

Teal made a show of looking at his watch. "Is this conversation heading toward a conclusion? I have no desire to be unhelpful—in fact, I'm trying hard to be as helpful as I can—but I don't know what you want from me."

I glanced down at my notes. So far, I'd written only a handful of words and doodled a dangling man. I closed the notebook.

"I'm not sure what I want from you either," I said. "But when I figure that out, I'll come back."

"What did Berrien tell you about me?" Teal asked.

"That you were the person in the department most closely associated with Spero."

"Is that all?"

"All that's relevant. Why do you ask?"

"Because she doesn't like me. She never has."

He sounded hurt, like a child rejected by the pretty girl in the schoolyard.

"How do you feel about her?"

"You expect me to admire someone who doesn't like me?"

"I don't expect anything," I said. "That way, life is full of pleasant surprises."

But Teal didn't seem in a hurry to embrace this as his new philosophy, and once again a career in greeting-card messages remained tantalizingly beyond my reach.

"What I'm saying is," he continued, "you shouldn't believe everything you hear, especially when it comes from someone who's bitter."

"And why would Jenny Berrien be bitter?"

"She's been promoted as far as she can rise," said Teal. "She had leadership ambitions, hopes of a management position in the commissioner's office, but she's not the leader type. The public affairs job was a sop, a sideways move because she didn't make director of communications. And there were complaints."

"What kind of complaints?"

"About her attitude and the language she used. Her competence."

"Were you one of the complainants?"

Teal swerved to evade the question. "I just know that complaints came from various sources."

Which I took to mean yes. Some of what Teal was claiming might have been true, and Berrien herself admitted to feeling discontented, but those scales rarely balanced perfectly. I'd been doing what I did for a long time, and I'd learned that my instincts about people were more often right than wrong. Roger Teal couldn't have made my skin crawl any worse had he been made of bugs.

I thanked him for his time and placed one of my cards on his desk. Teal offered his hand and I shook it. I counted my fingers when he was done, and they were all present and accounted for.

I took a moment at the door. All those years spent watching *Columbo* weren't wasted on me.

"I was just wondering how long it will take," I said.

"For what?"

"For you to call Santopietro and tell him I've been asking questions about Spero."

"I won't lie to you," said Teal. "It won't take me any time at all."

"Why?"

"Because he has a right to know."

"A right, really?"

"He's a good man. What happened to Scott Theriault wasn't the Saint's fault."

"The Saint?" I said.

"A nickname," said Teal, "among friends." He waved it away. "Am I the first person you've spoken to in the course of your inquiries?"

"No."

"And were any of the others favorably disposed to Mr. Santopietro and the school?"

"Some more than others," I allowed.

"Then he knows you're on the way. He'll be open with you, just as I've been. We have nothing to hide."

We.

"This isn't a criminal investigation, Mr. Teal," I said. "I don't have the same legal powers as law enforcement. I can't perform an arrest, demand information, or conduct searches. All I can do is ask questions, collect evidence, and then, if it's deemed necessary—whether by a client, a lawyer, or me—present it to the appropriate authorities. The internal politics of this department don't hold much fascination for me, and as for your relationship with Spero and Principal Santopietro, it would be of relevance only if you knew anything about Scott Theriault that could shed some light on the circumstances of his death. You've assured me you have no such information. Should you later recall anything that might help, you have my number."

"I'll keep the card close," said Teal.

I opened the door.

"And Mr. Parker?"

Huh. Maybe Teal had watched *Columbo* too.

"Yes?"

"Tell Jenny Berrien to go fuck herself."

CHAPTER

LXIII

Berrien was waiting for me in the parking lot when I emerged from the main building.

"Well?"

"You're right," I said. "He doesn't like you. He asked me to pass on a message, but I don't have a nickel for the swear jar."

"That fucking prick," said Berrien, who obviously had a dime. "Did he reveal anything useful, apart from a fondness for expletives?"

Call me cold, but I wasn't about to tell Berrien anything more than I had to. On the other hand, I was curious to see any paperwork she might have gathered concerning Teal and Spero. I was sure she had such material, quietly copied and filed away.

"He claimed it's common knowledge in the department that he volunteers at Spero," I said. "Is that true?"

"I guess so. I mean, Teal doesn't advertise it by wearing a Spero baseball cap, but if anyone asks, he's up-front. No conflict of interest exists because the department is no longer funding the school."

"Did it strike anyone as odd?"

"In what sense?"

"Teal admitted to being part of the snatch squads that forcibly remove teenagers from their homes. It's not an activity most of us would sign up for."

Berrien's scowl deepened.

"I didn't know that about him," said Berrien. "It doesn't make me feel any warmer toward him—and they call them 'transport teams,' but 'snatch squads' sounds more appropriate."

The air was growing appreciably colder as the sky darkened further. Now I wished I'd worn a warmer jacket.

"If you're right," I said, "and Teal was skimming from the department, how much money might be involved?"

"That's hard to gauge," said Berrien. "Conservatively, a mid-five-figure sum, but it could be higher. However, for Teal to have engaged in fraud, someone at Spero would have been required to collude. We knew how much money was going to Spero, and the authorities there knew how much they were meant to receive, so no funds could be siphoned off before they reached the school. But we couldn't keep close tabs on how the money was spent when it got there, or if it was spent at all. We saw financial plans and were provided with details of disbursement, but Teal was the only means of guaranteeing their accuracy."

Until 2011, Berrien explained, the Maine Department of Education had insisted on annual audits of private academies receiving public funding. That requirement was then repealed for a decade or more, covering the period during which Spero was in receipt of funds. Now private schools needed only to give details of total expenditure, and in the case of nonprofits, like Spero when it first opened, no distinction existed between public and private funding, which made it even harder to track spending.

"If I'm right," she said, "and Teal was taking a cut, it was with the knowledge of someone at Spero."

"And by 'someone,' " I said, "you mean Santopietro."

"Even if Santopietro wasn't directly involved, he'd have known about it when the figures didn't add up. But why would Santopietro stay quiet unless he was one of the beneficiaries?"

And why stop claiming departmental funding if he and Teal had a good thing going? If Berrien was correct, the skim was modest, especially given the latest overall statewide audit, which revealed systemic mismanagement and a lack of oversight amounting to billions of dollars across multiple departments. As long as Santopietro and Teal didn't get too greedy, they could probably have augmented their respective salaries for years to come.

"How much do you think Santopietro is making from the school?" I asked.

"He keeps numbers low," said Berrien, "but he's probably averaging four or five thousand a month for the handful of longer-term students, and more for those whose parents are hoping a short, sharp shock will cure them. I don't think he's ever accepted more than twenty kids, so a hundred thousand a month would be my rough estimate."

That was a lot of money. A parent could send their child to a good university for less than an academic year at Spero might cost.

"So your department effectively subsidized him while he found his footing?"

"It did, but back then Santopietro's model emphasized education over correction. I'm not sure that holds true any longer. I judge the quality of these places by the number of counselors and therapists they retain, and Spero isn't big on counseling or therapy."

Teal had stayed in contact with the school even after it cut ties with the department. Setting aside altruistic motives, because Teal didn't come across as the type, it meant he had to be getting something else out of the deal. It might have been that Teal really did enjoy terrorizing kids, or watching them being terrorized by others, which brought me back to Scott Theriault, who had hated Spero enough to try to escape multiple times. Was Teal lying about not knowing him? It would be hard to prove, and more so after our recent conversation, since there was a good chance Teal was already sharing with Santopietro all that had transpired. If they were concocting a story between them, now was the time to get it straight.

I hit the unlock button on my key fob and my headlights lit up.

"If you want to share any paperwork that sheds light on your suspicions, I'll take a look at it," I told Berrien, "but only to satisfy my curiosity. Teal could be piling the department's furniture into a moving van on weekends and it wouldn't cost me a minute's sleep. His office chair looked so much nicer than mine, I might even be tempted to make him an offer."

"Who said I had paperwork?" Berrien asked.

"Don't you?"

"I might have paperwork," Berrien admitted, "but the majority relates to procurement costs, renovations, and operating expenses. Teal signed off on the bids and expenses, and came up with plausible excuses for everything being at the upper end of the scale. Basically, it was down to the price of doing business in The Plains, but there were also finders' fees—effectively a bounty for locating students—as well as mileage, overtime, and Lord knows what else. It was a dripping tap, but a dripping tap will fill a bathtub eventually."

I found another of my business cards and gave it to her so she'd have the email address to which to send the documents, but I wasn't hopeful. Also, if I kept handing out cards at this rate, I'd be out of them by—well, by the end of the decade, given how many of the damn things I had. One of Moxie Castin's guys had run the order for me, but a couple of zeroes had been added in error somewhere along the line and now I could have built a house with them.

I wished Berrien good luck with her retirement, in case I didn't see her again. She thanked me, said she hoped our paths might cross, then added thoughtfully: "Did you see how shocked Teal was when I told him who you were? Not just surprised, but really shocked, even scared. I've never seen him look that way before, no matter how awkward the questions we asked about Spero money were."

"Meaning?"

"I'm not a detective—"

"But if you were?"

"I'd say he was afraid you'd come about another matter. He's not a good man, Mr. Parker."

"Not being a good man isn't against the law, Ms. Berrien."

"It should be."

She wasn't about to get any argument from me. I could trace a lot of the world's problems back to men who were worse than they had any right to be. The same could be said of some women, but they were fewer, and had less power.

"I'll work on it when I come into my kingdom," I told her.

"You and Jesus Christ both," said Berrien. "And after two thousand years, we're still waiting on him to get back to us."

CHAPTER

LXIV

Roger Teal watched the investigator walk across the parking lot to where Berrien stood waiting. He saw Berrien glance up at his window as Parker drew nearer, which caused Teal to take a step back, though he knew he couldn't be seen from outside. Did Berrien suspect he might be standing there? She was in no hurry to hide that she was conspiring with Parker against him. Just the opposite: She wanted Teal to know. She was rubbing his face in it, nasty pussy-eating bitch that she was. Teal so wanted to teach her a lesson, the kind of lesson Nola Maddick learned at the very end, a lesson only a man could teach a woman. Berrien was no looker, but Teal could work up an appetite for her if he had to. He would hurt her, humiliate her, and finally, choke the life from her, and he'd do it in front of a mirror, from behind, so she could witness her own dying. He'd laugh her into the next world.

Unfortunately, that would mean stepping outside the Game, unless he could persuade the Saint or Kenney to make Berrien a target. Under ordinary circumstances, there'd be little hope, but if he were to advise the Saint that Berrien was being sly and had the bit between her teeth when it came to Spero, to the extent that she was willing to assist a private investigator, then Teal could see the Saint coming around to his way of thinking; Kenney, not so much, but the Saint was a practical man, and he really did enjoy hurting women. Teal thought the Saint might be even more open to despoiling a woman who was in a position to damage him, and there remained the not-insignificant question of the whereabouts of Mallory Norton, the girl missing up in The Plains. If, as Kenney feared, the Saint was responsible for her death, he had another reason for silencing anyone who could aid an investigation into Spero.

The more Teal thought about it, the more he wanted to skin Berrien alive and dump what was left of her into a hole in the ground. But if she was to be taken, it would have to be by hands other than his own. He'd need a sound alibi, because he could see the private investigator returning after her disappearance, this time with the police in tow. Teal would have to go away for a day or two while Berrien was being lifted, taking his wife and daughter with him. He could frame it as a reset, a chance for them to see if a change in environment might lead to an improvement in family spirit. Even if they were suspicious, they'd agree if he picked somewhere they wanted to go, with a promise of luxury thrown in for good measure. He could use some of Spero cash he still had squirreled away, his personal rainy day fund, and when he got back, the Saint would have Berrien waiting for him, and they could play with her together.

Teal walked away from the window, leaving Berrien and Parker to their confab. He was no longer alarmed by the investigator, but he didn't dismiss him either. If worse came to worst, they could deal with Parker as well. They'd grown practiced at making bodies vanish, and whatever his reputation, Parker was no longer a young man. That was the thing about reputations: They were always predicated on the past, and in due course the present gave the lie to them.

Teal was flicking through his cell phone contacts to find the Saint when a text message came through. The message looked like spam and read: VEHICLE TO SELL? WE BUY ALL MODELS FOR $$$$$ NOT ¢¢¢¢¢ INC. WRECKS, INSPECTION FAILURES, AND MORE!!!!! CALL NOW WITHOUT OBLIGATION!!!!! OPEN 24/7!!!!!

Teal had received similar messages only twice before, each time when an urgent problem had arisen with the Game. The message, he knew, came from a burner phone, one that would not be used again, and the sender was Edward Kenney, because only Kenney used car spam as an alert. (The

Saint's alert asked for clothing donations, while Teal's referenced antiques.) Teal had a couple of burners of his own but was reluctant to activate them without good reason because burners cost money, and Teal was careful with his pennies so the dollars would look after themselves. He was also rightly paranoid about cell phones, burners or otherwise, and where possible preferred to use pay phones. In a notebook, he kept an updated list of pay phones between Kittery and Houlton, a list that, to his sorrow, grew shorter every year.

Teal set aside any thoughts of calling the Saint for the time being, packed his briefcase, and left the building. Berrien and the private investigator were nowhere to be seen. Teal got in his car and drove to the Citgo gas station on State Street, where he used its pay phone to call Edward Kenney.

"We have to meet," said Kenney.

"When?" asked Teal.

"Now."

CHAPTER

LXV

I was sitting in my car, catching up on email and missed calls, when Roger Teal came out of the building, moving like a man on a mission. Either Berrien was wrong about his home life and Teal couldn't wait to be reunited with his wife and daughter, or he had a more pressing engagement in mind. I waited for his Toyota Highlander to pull out before starting my ignition and following him to the Citgo on State. For a moment I feared I'd tailed him for nothing and Teal just needed to fill up, but he got no farther than the pay phone.

In this day and age, the only people who use pay phones are the very abject or the very wary, and Teal wasn't yet among the wretched. Whoever he was calling, he didn't want to risk leaving a record. I whistled a few bars of the theme from *Columbo*, since nothing makes a detective feel happier than following what we in the trade call a "hunch"—stop me if I get too technical—and striking it lucky. Of course, if I continued to follow Teal and he went straight home from the Citgo, I'd have wasted my time and fifty cents' worth of gas, but Alcock was paying for both, so I wouldn't be much poorer.

Berrien had told me that Teal lived somewhere in West Gardiner, which was south of Augusta, but instead Teal drove north, which meant that wherever he was going, it wasn't home. I stayed with him for forty miles, listening to Classic Rewind on Sirius, until we got to Pittsfield, roughly halfway between Augusta and Bangor. Teal turned off at Somerset Avenue and drove south toward Main Street, where he entered a self-storage lot and disappeared behind the back of the single-story units, where I couldn't follow without alerting Teal to my presence, and I preferred him to remain blissfully unaware. I drove by the lot, made a U-turn, and when I passed by the second time, a silver BMW X7, a fancier family vehicle than Teal's, was pulling in. The BMW also drove straight to the back, but I wasn't quick enough to make out the license plate. I didn't want to head in there on foot, not only because it wouldn't do much good unless I possessed the hearing of a bat, but also because wandering around poorly lit storage lots is a good way to get shot or arrested. The next-best option was to pull into Frost's Mobil across the street and get to waiting again, which is what I did. While I sat there, I called Macy.

"Where are you?" she asked.

"Pittsfield."

"Nobody goes *to* Pittsfield. They drive through it on their way to somewhere else."

"I like to buck trends, and I'm easily amused."

"And what are you doing in Pittsfield to amuse yourself?"

"Sitting at a gas station, waiting."

"You're not selling me on the hidden joys of Pittsfield. Waiting for what?"

"A BMW to come out of a lot so I can follow it."

"Who does the BMW belong to?"

"I don't know. That's why I'm going to follow it. Duh."

"Duh yourself. Is this still Spero thing?"

"I think so. At least, it's Spero, but it may not be the same thing."

"Messy, but you wouldn't have it any other way. You free tomorrow night?"

"Unless I find another gas station to hang out at, so you'll have to make a tempting offer."

"I'll get naked."

"I don't know. Some of these gas stations have pretty good hot dogs."

"I'll also pick up barbecue from Wilson County."

"Hot damn," I said. "Sold to the nekkid lady with the fried chicken."

"Clown. And don't get shot in the meantime, or hit in the face with another block of wood. I don't want to overorder."

She hung up. What a thing it is to be loved.

CHAPTER

LXVI

To his credit, Teal didn't panic when Kenney told him about the undercover DEA agent they'd killed, but not unexpectedly, he wasn't pleased about it either. Already he was working through the implications and, as Kenney had done, going back over their interactions with Cotter, from abduction to disposal.

"Her cell phone will lead them to Fishkorn," he said.

Cotter had been carrying a Samsung phone, which Teal destroyed as soon as she was safely in the car. He'd put the phone in a cloth bag and used the heel of his boot to smash it to pieces before tossing the battery and SIM card out the window at intervals. As far as Teal could determine, the DEA would be able to trace its last-known location to the general Fishkorn area, if not the specific street from which the woman was taken, although they might get close enough depending on the distribution of the local cell towers. But they'd need a warrant to obtain that information, which would take time. As for Teal and Kenney, neither had brought phones with them that night, not even burners; they were too practiced to make that kind of mistake. To track them, the police would have to knock on doors looking for eyewitnesses—Teal wished them good luck in Fishkorn—and try to access footage from fixed security cameras or any dashcams that might have been in the area that night. He and Kenney would have to ride their luck on that score, but they'd ridden it before and come away unscathed. The main complication was that the searchers wouldn't give up, not with Cotter being a federal agent. But for the present, they'd be operating on the assumption that she might still be alive. Cotter was a missing person, not a murder victim.

All this he and Kenney went through as they sat in their respective vehicles, each with the driver-side window down, Teal's hood pointing toward the storage units, Kenney's outward, so they could speak softly and still be heard.

"If they find a body," said Kenney, "we're screwed. They won't ever stop."

"I wonder what she was working on," said Teal.

"If she was a decoy, they'd have been on us before she hit the ground."

"So she was working alone, and then they let days go by before they lit the beacons. Must have been something, or someone, big."

"Meaning that's where they'll start," said Kenney, "with the target of the investigation. I'd say that it buys us more time, but it's not like we can do anything with it. All we can do is hope."

"What about the Saint?"

"What about him?"

"Do we tell him?" asked Teal.

"That we raped and killed a DEA agent? Like hell we do."

Teal was silent.

"What?" asked Kenney.

"Uh, I spoke to him on the phone, a couple of days back. Spero stuff."

"And?"

"He asked how Detroit went. You know, in passing."

"What did you say?"

"That it was good. Clean. I told him she was colored."

"Is that all?"

"I think so."

"You *think* so?"

Teal hesitated again.

"I might have mentioned a name," he said. "I can't be sure."

Which meant he was sure but didn't want to say. Kenney's eyes fluttered closed. The Saint knew, because Cotter's dual identity had been revealed to the media as part of the ongoing efforts to locate her.

"I didn't think anything of it," Teal continued. "We've always been open with one another before now." He assumed a hurt expression. "I mean, I always like to hear how the Game went for others. Even if I didn't get to play, I get to experience it vicariously."

Kenney couldn't chastise Teal for that. He'd done the same himself, but he wished Teal had kept his mouth shut this once. In the past, they'd all been playing by the same rules, which bound them together. But if the Saint was playing a game of his own, it meant the rules had changed without consultation. Kenney recalled the glance that had passed between the Saint and Renders at the school when Kenney mentioned Mallory Norton's disappearance. Kenney had been up to Spero for one of his biannual visits and gave no sign that he'd spotted the interaction between the Saint and his assistant principal, but he'd filed it away nonetheless, and Renders's expression in particular. He was familiar with that look because he'd seen it on his own face in the days immediately after the Game. If the Saint had killed the Norton girl, Renders had helped him do it.

So the Saint had played close to home, which was a transgression all its own, and then hadn't even invited his old friends to join in the fun, which was, you know, selfish of him. Instead, he'd shared her with Renders. If the Saint was no longer abiding by the rules and was additionally shortchanging the original players, how could he be trusted about anything? Should the police connect the Saint to Mallory Norton, they'd begin tearing the rest of his life apart, digging in corners better left unexplored, and hiding in one of them would be Edward Kenney and Roger Teal. What if the Saint offered to sell them out in return for a better deal? Twenty-five years, the minimum for murder in Maine, was better than a life sentence.

But that was a worst-case scenario. Each man held the fate of the others in his hands, which was one of the beauties of the Game, and one of its guarantees. Just as the Saint could theoretically offer testimony against Teal and Kenney, so too could Kenney turn on Teal and the Saint, or Teal seek to save himself by sacrificing the others. If it came down to it, they'd all sink together, right? In theory, perhaps, but now there was the Renders factor to be taken into account.

"Did Mallory Norton come up in this conversation?" Kenney asked.

"Not then," said Teal. "But I've been thinking: She may have come up before, indirectly."

"How?"

"Way before you and I went to Detroit, the Saint mentioned that one of the boys at the school was sneaking out to meet a local girl. He said something would have to be done about it."

"And?"

"I think you're right," said Teal. "Something was done."

"You're only telling me this now?"

"It didn't register then. Nobody had died or gone missing, and you hadn't said anything about being worried."

But Kenney wasn't annoyed. He was grateful to Teal for confirming any remaining doubts about the Saint's activities.

"I still haven't spoken to the Saint about her," said Kenney.

"I'm starting to think you shouldn't."

"Because if we forget about Norton, the Saint might not lie awake at night worrying about whether our dead DEA agent is going to damn him? We forget if he forgets?"

"I didn't say nobody should talk to the Saint. I just said it shouldn't be you."

"Why?"

"Because you're the one who killed Hurvich when he stepped out of line."

Kenney absorbed this.

"And what I did once, I might do again?"

"Wouldn't you be thinking the same, in the Saint's shoes?"

"Are you scared of him?"

Teal stared at Kenney.

"Aren't you?"

"Not scared. Wary."

Kenney didn't enjoy playing the Game as much with the Saint. There was always more suffering when the Saint was involved, and Kenney couldn't even look the women in the eyes toward the end. What he saw there drained the Game of any pleasure.

Kenney spotted that Teal was toying with his wedding band. Teal never took off the ring, not even when he was deep in the Game. He was afraid he'd forget to put it on again afterward. Kenney, by contrast, always left his ring in the next room, on top of his clothes; that way, he'd only forget it if he also forgot to get dressed. Kenney supposed that the men's differing attitudes toward their rings reflected disparate attitudes to their marriages: Teal's showed how little respect he accorded his vows, whereas Kenney tried to keep his marriage and the Game separate.

While Teal played with the ring, he was debating whether to inform Kenney of the visit from the private investigator. Teal had never told Kenney about the misappropriation of departmental funds, or the deal he'd cut with the Saint to divide the proceeds. It was none of Kenney's business, and anyway, it was in the past, or had been until Berrien made one last attempt to screw Teal over by bringing Parker into his life. But if Teal didn't tell Kenney about Parker, and Kenney found out about it later, there'd be hell to pay. Kenney surely had a right to know, because what threatened one of them—or, in this case, two—threatened all.

"There's another problem," said Teal.

CHAPTER
LXVII

At Spero, Patrick Elgot was checking the dormitories. All the boys were supposed to be at movie night in the main hall, where this week's presentation was another minor superhero flick that bombed at the box office before being rushed to streaming and physical release. Elgot had picked up the Blu-ray used at Bull Moose in Bangor just days after new copies first appeared on the shelves. Even if it was garbage, it would keep the boys entertained for a couple of hours and bring a bit of joy into their lives. Elgot had taken Spero job hoping he might be able to do good, and it paid better than some of the positions he'd been offered in regular schools, but Spero was sapping his spirit. He feared that if he stayed much longer, he might lose any sense of vocation. Scott Theriault's death was the clincher in that regard, allied to the growing influence of James Renders.

In Elgot's view, there was a badness to Renders. It might have been that Principal Santopietro didn't see it, or did but chose to ignore it because Renders knew his subjects, could control the boys, and whatever the badness was, it didn't impact on his work. The third possibility, one that Elgot had begun to embrace as he paid more attention to how Renders and Santopietro interacted with each other, was that Santopietro had some of the same badness in him, and Renders might have been hired because of, not despite it.

In the main hall, Elgot had done a head count to discover that one boy, Kaspar Filipowski, was missing, and none of the others could say where he was. Even Leonard Levesque professed ignorance of Kaspar's whereabouts. If anyone was a candidate for inflicting harm on Kaspar Fillyourpantski, or Kaspar Shitstain as he was also known, it was Levesque, but the latter hadn't been out of Elgot's sight for hours. So Elgot left the boys in Renders's care, with the start of the movie delayed, to go looking for Kaspar.

Technically, Elgot was supposed to report even the most minor breaches of the rules, which included unpunctuality, but he tried to let as many of them slide as he could, the boys having enough to contend with as it was. The school's prospectus promised expert psychological care, but what it meant, in reality, was that Santopietro had taken a couple of online psychotherapy courses from a college operating out of a strip mall in Laconia, New Hampshire. He'd even had the certificates framed and hung on his office wall, which suggested, worryingly, that he regarded them as consequential, even if one suicide and one more recent fatality offered compelling evidence to the contrary.

Elgot found no trace of Kaspar in his dorm, in the ablution block, or in any of the other rooms. Lord, he hoped the boy hadn't tried to run away. He wouldn't get far, not after the Scott Theriault mess, but he'd be in a world of hurt when he was picked up and returned to the school, and Elgot would be forced to share the pain because Kaspar had wandered off the reservation on his watch.

Elgot stood in the hallway of John Ford and called Kaspar's name.

"It's Mr. Elgot. I came to see if you were okay. You don't have to be worried. It's just me."

He listened. Nothing.

"Goddamn it, Kaspar—"

Then he heard it: a whimpering, like a puppy separated from its mother.

"Kaspar?"

He listened harder, following the sound, eventually tracing it to the laundry closet at the end of the hallway. It was always kept locked to prevent the boys running riot with towels, sheets, and pillowcases. Elgot noticed now that the padlock was gone and the door, although closed, was unbolted.

"Kaspar?" said Elgot again. "Are you in there?"

He opened the door and smelled urine. Kaspar Filipowski was curled up at the bottom of the closet, between the floor and the lowest shelf. Even though he was small, he could only have managed to fit in there with difficulty. He was crying, but softly, as if afraid of being heard.

"What in God's name are you doing?" Elgot asked. "Never mind. Let's get you out."

But Kaspar didn't move, and he wasn't looking at Elgot but past him, over his shoulder. Elgot followed the direction of his gaze and saw nothing. He reached for the boy, who tried to shrink away, even though he couldn't have retreated any deeper unless he went through the wall. Kaspar spoke, but so quietly that Elgot didn't catch what he said.

"What did you say?"

Kaspar repeated himself, and this time Elgot heard him.

"I'm hiding."

"From who?"

Kaspar's eyes found Elgot's.

"From the dead boys."

CHAPTER LXVIII

Teal's Toyota came out of the storage lot first, followed shortly after by the BMW. Both headed for the highway, but Teal went south, presumably toward home, while the BMW took the exit toward Bangor. It was possible, of course, that both Teal and the owner of the BMW happened to have storage units in Pittsfield and experienced simultaneous urges to visit: One had to try to think the best of people. But there isn't a lot of money to be made from thinking the best of people, not in my line of work, and rarely was I hired because all was well in someone's world. So, operating on the theory that the driver of the BMW—who appeared to be male—might potentially be of interest, I decided to follow him instead of Teal, because I knew where to find Teal again.

The BMW had Maine plates. I got close enough to make a note of the license number as a precaution, then dropped back a few cars. Back in the good old days, I'd kept a couple of contacts at the Bureau of Motor Vehicles in Portland and Augusta. Patently, it was illegal for them to access owner information for non–law enforcement officers, but what was a boy to do? Both contacts were now retired and I hadn't tried to make new friends at the BMV. My PI's license was always hanging by a thread and I didn't want to give anyone in the Maine State Police's Special Investigations Unit, which licensed investigators, an excuse to decline my quadrennial renewal, or worse, seek to have my license revoked. Also, keystrokes were now logged, and state and federal employees could get fired for accessing personal information without cause. That made them reluctant to help private investigators, even for money. Finally, Moxie Castin had made it plain he preferred me not to source data in a manner that wouldn't stand up under cross-examination in court. If I did, he didn't want to know about it, and if called to give evidence, I'd better have alternative ways to support my testimony without perjuring myself. In desperate situations, I could call on David Southwood, who didn't know the meaning of the word *illegal* and could dig up any intelligence, albeit for eye-watering fees. But again, Moxie, the old spoilsport, indicated that he wouldn't pay for Southwood's services, not even if I included them under "Stationery and Other Incidentals" in my final bill. All of which meant that, on an evening when I could have been doing something more fun, I was following a fancy BMW while listening to 1st Wave on Sirius, because Classic Rewind was making me feel too old.

The BMW stayed on I-95 until after the highway crossed the Kenduskeag Stream in Bangor, where the driver took the exit for Outer Essex, which was a nice family suburb close to Essex Woods, heavy on big lots with a country vibe, a porch, a dog, a tire swing on an old oak tree, and kids who didn't swear. I couldn't vouch for the dogs or the kids, but the property at which the BMW finally arrived did have the rest, right down to the tire swing. The BMW stopped in the driveway and a man got out. He was short, running to plump, and paused for a few moments to gather himself before heading into the house, which was all lit up inside.

While vehicle records might have been difficult to access legally, the same was not true for property records, because property purchases left a bigger paper trail. Within minutes I had a valuation for the Outer Essex home—over $400,000, thanks to a recent barn conversion—and the names of the owners, Edward and Mia Kenney. A further search revealed that the Kenneys were joint proprietors of the Smiling Seed Company, a garden-supply business in Orono, with a focus on organic, sustainably grown, and non-GMO products. The couple featured on the homepage of the company's website, grinning organically in matching bib overalls, and it was definitely Edward Kenney I'd seen getting out of the BMW.

So why, following a conversation about Spero School, had Roger Teal made an eighty-mile round trip to rendezvous briefly in a Pittsfield storage lot with the owner of a seed store in Orono? I could have knocked on Edward Kenney's door to ask, but there was no point in alerting prey if you didn't already have snares in place to catch them. I called Jenny Berrien and asked if Edward Kenney's name meant anything to her, but she said it didn't.

"What about the Smiling Seed Company, out of Orono?"

Nope, that didn't ring any bells either. I thanked her and let her get back to whatever it was that whistleblowers did when they weren't blowing whistles. Then, not very much wiser than when I began, I drove home.

CHAPTER

LXIX

Elgot accompanied Kaspar Filipowski to the ablution block, where he waited while the boy showered, dried himself, and changed into fresh underwear and trousers. Elgot put the stained clothing in a bag and told Kaspar he'd take care of it. He'd add it to his own laundry, which Elgot always did himself, and nobody would be any the wiser. Elgot tried to press Kaspar on what he meant by "dead boys," but Kaspar had clammed up. Elgot decided it might be better to leave him be and broach the subject again the following day.

Once Kaspar was dressed and ready, Elgot walked him to the hall, where the film was playing, even though he'd asked Renders not to start it until the boy was located. The others peered curiously at Kaspar, but nobody made any smart remarks, and a space was cleared for him at the end of the back row. The students appeared to Elgot to be almost solicitous of Kaspar. Even Leonard Levesque wasn't sneering, and a sneer was his default expression. Renders wasn't around, and when Elgot asked where he was, Jamie Hanscomb, the oldest of the current intake, said that Mr. Renders had pressed play on the Blu-ray and left him in charge.

"Well, you're still in charge," Elgot told him. "I'll be back in a few minutes."

While it wasn't unusual for a teacher to assign one of the older boys to supervise, Elgot was irritated. Why couldn't Renders have just stayed where he was? Elgot decided not to waste time finding him. Better that he speak to Santopietro first. Elgot's encounter with Kaspar Filipowski had unsettled him, coming so soon after the trouble with Anthony Marshall. But the latter hadn't said anything about dead boys, not that Elgot had heard, and Kaspar, unlike Anthony, hadn't suffered any injuries.

Because he managed to hide in time.

Hide from whom, though? Elgot wasn't a superstitious man and immediately dismissed a literal interpretation of what Kaspar had said. However, he was prepared to accept that one or more of the older boys might have found a way to terrorize some of the younger ones. Half the city kids, marooned far from home in an alien environment, were already scared of the dark. It wouldn't take much more than some ghost stories and a couple of Halloween masks to tip them over the edge. Again, Elgot would have nominated Leonard Levesque as a prime suspect, but unless Levesque had added bilocation to his skill set, he wasn't the one who'd made Kaspar hide in a closet and wet himself from fear.

As he neared the closed door of Santopietro's office, Elgot heard voices inside: Santopietro and Renders. Elgot was about to knock, then paused. He heard just one word clearly, the one his mother used to refer to as the "c-word," and another that might have been a name but was more muffled. Elgot experienced a similar sensation to what he'd felt when, as a child, he heard his parents giggling behind their bedroom door, followed by sounds that might have been expressions of pain, pleasure, or some adult combination of both. The two incidents, distant and recent, coalesced as he heard Renders laugh filthily. Elgot started to walk away, but he was only halfway along the hall when Santopietro's office door opened behind him. Elgot had the presence of mind to turn on his heel so that when Renders emerged, Elgot appeared to be walking toward the office, not away from it.

"Everything okay?" Renders asked as Santopietro poked his head around the frame.

"Not especially," said Elgot. "I found Kaspar Filipowski in a closet over in Ford, scared half to death."

"Did one of the boys do something to him?" Santopietro asked.

Elgot wasn't sure how to reply. Eventually he settled for: "The rest of them were in the hall, waiting for the movie to start. But something frightened Kaspar enough to make him want to hide."

Elgot watched a shadow pass over Renders's face, but it was Santopietro who spoke.

"Like what?"

"Intruders, maybe?" Elgot suggested. "Local kids with too much time on their hands?"

"Is that what Kaspar said? Did he tell you it was boys who had scared him?"

Elgot decided to tell the truth, if not the whole truth.

"He did."

The shadow, Elgot saw, had now settled on Renders. The man was unnerved.

"I accept that the rest of the students might have been in the hall when Kaspar was discovered," said Santopietro, "but we don't know how long he spent in hiding before then. It's possible that some of the others were picking on him before movie time was called."

Elgot didn't bother arguing. He didn't believe it, and by the look on his face, he didn't think Renders believed it either.

"I'd better be getting back," said Elgot.

"I'll make a general address to the school in the morning," said Santopietro. "We can't have any escalation, not after all that's happened."

Elgot nodded. Renders seemed about to follow him when Santopietro held him back.

"A minute, Mr. Renders."

Renders returned to the office with Santopietro, closing the door behind him.

"Could this be Levesque acting up again?"

Renders replied that he didn't think so. Since the incident in the ablution block, the staff had been keeping tabs on Leonard Levesque, Renders more than most.

"And what Elgot said about intruders?" Santopietro persisted. "I saw your face. Is there something you haven't told me?"

Renders shifted uneasily.

"A few nights ago," he said, "I thought I heard noises outside my room, in the yard. It sounded like voices whispering—boys' voices—but when I went outside, there was no one."

He didn't mention the separate occurrence on the night Anthony Marshall was attacked, when he'd watched from beside his bed as someone tried to open his locked door, someone who had managed to evade a motion-activated light so sensitive that a big moth could set it off. Nor did he speak of a darkness that was too dark, and a conviction that whatever waited in it wanted Renders's curiosity to get the better of him, wanted him to come closer, close enough for it to be able to take hold of him and draw him to itself.

"What time was this?"

"It was after one," said Renders. "I remember looking at the clock."

Santopietro was dubious.

"We haven't experienced that kind of intrusion in a while, not since the Shackfords moved away."

The Shackfords had been what passed for bad news in The Plains, their property resembling a junkyard, the extended family scattered over two or three decaying cabins and subsisting on welfare and minor criminality. Some of the younger Shackfords had taken to taunting Spero's students, even dealing out a cursory beating when they caught any of them outnumbered, or better still, alone. Then, six months earlier, someone had burned the Shackfords out, the fire spreading so fast, thanks to a northerly wind, that it was a miracle no one died. The Shackfords weren't short of enemies and had no friends at all, so few tears were shed outside the immediate clan, and its members subsequently scattered. An investigation by the Somerset County Sheriff's Office and the Maine State Fire Marshal concluded that gasoline was the accelerant, but no obvious suspects presented themselves; in fact, there were so many potential candidates that it was less time-consuming to identify the innocent. Santopietro assisted with the sheriff's inquiries as best he could and attested to the noninvolvement of the students under his care. He decided not to bring up the beating Leonard Levesque had taken from Emile Shackford and two of his cousins a week or so before the fire. After all, boys would be boys.

"I might have been mistaken about the voices," said Renders. "I'd had a long day."

But he didn't think he was.

"And Kaspar Filipowski?"

"He might have been mistaken too."

"He does have a nervous disposition," said Santopietro. "The kindest thing we can do is strengthen him. In the meantime, talk to Levesque, see if he can shed any light on the situation."

Renders examined his fingernails.

"The boy really is more trouble than he's worth," he said.

"He is," said Santopietro. "Someday soon it may be the death of him."

CHAPTER

LXX

Edward Kenney ate a quarter of the beef pot pie his wife had baked for dinner, she and the kids having already eaten. He'd warned her that he'd be delayed—paperwork to catch up on at the office—but could tell she was annoyed. Unless he was away from home for the night, she preferred him to be present for the evening meal. She'd grown up in a household where the kids were left to fend for themselves, less from neglect than a consequence of struggling parents working long hours, and she hadn't liked what it did to her family. As soon as she and Edward began talking seriously about marriage and kids, she'd laid down some ground rules, and household dinners were among the first.

She asked whether he wanted to watch a movie on TV later, but he told her he had to go over one or two more bits of business while they were still fresh in his mind, and she didn't argue. While Mia Kenney was a registered owner of the Smiling Seed Company, she left the day-to-day running of it—the finances, the tools and supplies side, the farm seed—to her husband. Her aptitude was more hands-on, and the land on which their home stood functioned as both a nursery and testing bed for the new varietals she bred each year. Together, they made a good team.

Kenney poured himself a bourbon and retreated to his small home office. He turned on the desktop computer and reopened the most recent Excel spreadsheet for the sake of appearances, but didn't glance at the figures on the screen. He was going back over all that Teal had told him, and what he, in turn, had shared with Teal, because the threats to them were multiplying. Not only had they murdered an undercover DEA agent, but a private investigator was now sniffing around Spero, drawn by the death of Scott Theriault. Worse, the private investigator in question had a deserved reputation for tenacity, resilience, and violence.

According to the *Bangor Daily News* website, detectives were not ruling out the possibility that Theriault and the missing Mallory Norton might have known each other. Some of the more downmarket media outlets had even concocted a Romeo-and-Juliet scenario in which the star-crossed lovers, instead of falling prey to poison and daggers, fled into the wilderness, where one of them died. Kenney might even have been tempted to believe it was true, if only to ease his mind, were it not for what Teal claimed to have heard the Saint say, back before Teal and Kenney left for Detroit.

The Saint mentioned that one of the boys at the school was sneaking out to meet a local girl. He said something would have to be done about it.

Which was why Teal said he was so against the idea of Kenney confronting the Saint. It was one thing to accuse the Saint of something he hadn't done, and quite another to accuse him of something of which he might be guilty. The former would arouse justifiable anger, but the latter could lead the Saint to seek to protect himself. He already had reason to move against Kenney and Teal because of what they'd done in Detroit, assuming Teal was right and he had, in fact, inadvertently let slip the name of the dead woman, a name now revealed to have been part of Special Agent Gai Cotter's cover.

That element of Teal's story rang true to Kenney, but at the same time he had long harbored suspicions that Teal was not being completely honest about his earlier dealings with Spero. Of the four original players, only Teal was not a former student of the Élan School, though he had grown up with Kenney and Hurvich, both of whom were at Parsonsfield. Later in life, Teal had reconnected with Kenney, but only after Teal was appointed by the Maine Department of Education to liaise with and inspect Spero. After three years, the Saint nominated Teal as a fourth player ("He's like us, and he'll break the pattern"), supported, after only minimal hesitation, by Kenney. Out of caution, Hurvich made some cursory objections, but was outvoted by the others, who vouched for Teal's bona fides—or, since they were talking about someone they believed capable of committing crimes of rape and murder while concealing the same, his absence of it.

Once, when drunk the night before a Game, Teal had spoken to Kenney of Jenny Berrien's animosity toward him while skating over the reasons behind it, but one or two hints indicated that she suspected him of financial impropriety. When Kenney asked if she might have cause, Teal got all self-righteous and Kenney immediately dropped the subject, but the strength of Teal's reaction signified that Berrien might have been right about sticky fingers.

Now Parker was nosing around Spero's affairs, and thanks to Berrien, Teal was on the list, making him susceptible to pressure if, as Kenney feared, he'd been skimming department funds as part of an earlier arrangement with the Saint. Meanwhile, if they kept digging, they'd find proof of a relationship between Scott Theriault and Mallory Norton in a region as sparsely populated as the Kennebec Valley, where the ties between people were more apparent than in a big city. That would return the focus of their inquiries to Spero. If the police or Parker managed to obtain evidence linking the Saint to the disappearance of Mallory Norton, it wouldn't take much more work to uncover details of his trips outside the state to play the Game, which in turn would lead them to Mr. Smiling Seed himself, Edward Kenney, and Ride-Along Roger Teal, who got his kicks from dragging terrified kids from their beds in the dead of night, tightening the old cable ties, and shipping them to Bumfuck, Maine, for some serious attitude adjustment.

And then there was Renders, the new player the Saint wanted to introduce to the Game. Kenney didn't know how much the Saint might have shared with him, but if he and Renders had together killed Mallory Norton, after first taking their pleasure with her, Kenney feared the postcoital pillow talk might have included the Game and its existing players. If so, Renders owed nothing to Kenney and Teal; if he was allied to anyone, it was to the Saint.

Kenney sipped his bourbon. The top two buttons of his shirt were undone, revealing the tip of a long vertical scar on his chest, a souvenir of a heart procedure in his teens. He touched an index finger to it, following the route of the old incision. Were his wife present, she would have identified it as a sign of anxiety. Rubbing his scar was Edward Kenney's tell; had he been playing poker, his opponents would have commenced raising their bets.

Kenney kept a small safe in his office, concealed behind a panel in the closet. In the safe was stored ten thousand dollars in cash for emergencies, as well as five one-ounce gold American Buffalos and eight quarter-ounce American Gold Eagles, together worth about another thirty thousand dollars, in case the economy tanked, temporarily or otherwise. The safe also contained a Taurus Raging Hunter .38 Special with a micro red dot mounted on the rail machined into the top of the barrel, which gave Kenney the assurance of being able to see where his shots would land. He stored a similar model in his office at the seed company. Kenney didn't plan to end up in prison for life, or sweating out his days in a federal penitentiary while he waited for the needle. If the police came for him at home or work, he was confident he could get to a gun in time to kill himself before anyone could lay hands on him. Neither did he have any doubts about his willingness to pull the trigger. He'd rather die than witness the disappointment on the faces of his wife and children. Teal, Kenney knew, also owned a firearm, and for similar reasons, at least when it came to the police.

Kenney opened the safe and removed the gun. He cleaned it regularly and kept it loaded, with the hammer resting on an empty chamber. Only he and Mia had the combination, but his wife never went near the safe. She tolerated the gun as a last line of defense, but preferred it to be out of sight and out of mind. As for the cash and coins, she was aware that her husband held emergency reserves in the safe, but had no idea of the amount. Kenney could use it as an escape fund, if given the chance to run, but he didn't see himself blasting all the way to Mexico. He doubted he'd get as far as New Hampshire. No, if the Game concluded badly, the final taste in his mouth would be of metal and gun oil.

Kenney sighted along the barrel as the shake-awake tech activated the micro dot.

Teal: vulnerable, unreliable.

The Saint: vulnerable, unreliable.

Renders: unreliable, and an unknown quantity.

What worried Kenney most was that, over in The Plains, the Saint might be engaged in a similar process of risk assessment.

Teal: vulnerable, unreliable.

Kenney: vulnerable, unreliable.

Renders—

Reliable. The Saint's new best friend, he and Renders bound together by Mallory Norton—and Scott Theriault too, because whatever the police said, Theriault must have been the kid at Spero who was meeting up with her.

Kenney felt this phase of the Game drawing to a close, but it didn't have to be an ending, more a pause before a new beginning. He could reboot, but this time as the only player. It would be risky without a second pair of hands, but if he picked the right victims, it would be okay. He might have to plan differently and select his targets in advance, but he'd try to be open to chance as well. Yet he kind of liked Teal. They played the Game well together. Why not keep it as two? And Teal might well be thinking along the same lines. . . .

Kenney put the gun away, locked the safe, and went to check on his children. Oliver was in bed reading. It was past lights-out, but Kenney wasn't about to bitch at him for reading a book. Even if he did, Oliver would just use the light on his phone to resume once his dad had gone, potentially damaging his eyesight, and Kenney didn't want his son to blame him later in life for having to wear glasses. Kenney kissed him, warned him not to be up too late, and went to the next room, where Suze was working on a project for school—"working," by her definition, involving watching videos on her phone, messaging her friends, and listening to music, despite a next-day deadline for delivery. But she'd get the project done, because she always got things done, even by the skin of her teeth, and the resulting grades would be better than they had any right to be since she had brains to burn. If she ever decided to apply herself, Kenney believed she could be president, though that wasn't the high bar it might once have been, given the quality of some recent incumbents.

Kenney kissed Suze on the top of the head. He considered suggesting she turn off the phone but then thought better of it. From discussions with other fathers of teenage daughters, Teal among them, thinking better of getting into any kind of confrontation was part of the job description. But Kenney loved his daughter deeply, so much so that Mia was of the opinion he could be overprotective. Suze, Mia would tell him, needed her space. She was nearly sixteen ("So she's fifteen," Kenney would reply. "Fifteen!"), and if her father thought he could keep her locked up until a suitable candidate for marriage presented themselves—assuming such a creature existed, which Kenney questioned—he was destined for disappointment. Kenney could only nod along and reply that all fathers, or all fathers who cared, felt the same way about their daughters.

What he couldn't add was that he had a special insight into the kind of predator who would target a young girl walking home alone because he was that predator. The only way he could play the Game and enjoy it was by closing a door on his wife and daughter and pretending they did not exist; by not thinking of the unwilling third party in the Game as someone else's daughter, someone who might be loved by her father as much as he loved Suze. And if there was a foul, uncontrolled corner of Kenney's imagination, one that smelled of blood and intimate fluids, one in which, despite his every effort, the features of a woman in the Game would occasionally transmute into those of his daughter, he chose to avoid exploring it. It wasn't unlike what happened when you tried too hard not to think of a song, an animal, or an image: It forced its way in. It was a nasty trick of the mind and nothing more.

Kenney left the kids to join his wife and their dog on the couch. The movie was one he and Mia had seen before, but he was happy to watch it again because the movie, like her, represented the familiar. This was what was meant by home, by family: the same faces, the same experiences, day after day, yet each time subtly different. "Family" and "familiar" even had a common origin in *familia*, the Latin word for "household." To be a family man was not only to accept the commonplace but also to take pleasure in it, and thereby achieve contentment. It was the Game that had enabled Edward Kenney to reach this accommodation. In an unexpected way, it had made him a better father and husband, if not a better man.

CHAPTER

LXXI

Leonard Levesque was crouching by the supply closet when Kaspar Filipowski passed, his toothbrush and toothpaste in one hand, a towel in the other. Leonard caught Kaspar before he made a sound. While the two boys walking behind Kaspar could not have failed to notice, they acted as though nothing had happened and Kaspar Filipowski was never there. Leonard Levesque was a law unto himself.

Leonard closed the door with his foot, hit the LED light, and pushed Kaspar against the wall. He put the heel of his right hand against Kaspar's neck and pressed gently: not hard enough to choke or hurt, but hard enough to let Kaspar know that choking and hurting were not far away.

"What did you see?" he asked.

Kaspar shook his head. Leonard increased the pressure, causing Kaspar to splutter, inadvertently spraying Leonard with spittle.

"Do that again," said Leonard, "and you'll get worse than spit from me."

He relaxed his hold. He wanted the boy to be able to talk.

"Tell me," said Leonard.

"You won't believe me."

"That's for me to decide. I won't ask you again."

Kaspar accepted that any victory here could only be relative, and leaving the closet unhurt would be a triumph against the odds.

"I saw three boys," he said, "two short, one taller. But they weren't there, not really. They were like shadows with no one to cast them. And they smelled."

"Of what?"

"Rotten stuff, like old roadkill."

Leonard leaned in.

"Who were they?"

"I don't know."

Leonard Levesque's fingers, unwashed and uric, reached into Kaspar's mouth, gripped his tongue, and twisted.

"Liar, liar," said Leonard. "Little Shitstain speak with forked tongue. Tell. Me. The. Truth."

The pain brought tears to Kaspar's eyes, but more than that, there was the humiliation of being bullied once again by Leonard Levesque, and the pain of being abandoned to this boy's whims by parents who should have cared for him, who were supposed to love him but did not. Yes, Kaspar had lashed out, but not at them, not really. The world was very confusing to Kaspar, and if it got really bewildering he had to retreat from it, retreat fast, fighting all the time at what was coming for him; when he did, he forgot who and where he was, so that when he came back, it took a while to readjust, and he reentered the world as scared and confused as when he'd left it. The last time it happened, he had blood on his hands when his vision cleared, and his stepmom was holding her nose, redness dripping through her fingers, while his father had gashes on his face where Kaspar's nails had gouged parallel paths. And no matter how often Kaspar said he hadn't meant it, or how hard he tried to explain about the scariness of the world, they wouldn't listen, which is how he'd ended up being driven to Spero and left there. That was weeks ago, and he'd had no word from his dad or stepmom since.

Fucking Leonard Levesque. Fucking Mom and Dad. Fucking Spero.

Leonard released his tongue and Kaspar Filipowski screamed. His small, hard fist struck Leonard close to the left eye. Had it impacted directly, it might well have burst the eyeball, but instead Kaspar's thumbnail snagged on the corner, close to the sensitive tear duct. Leonard stumbled back and his right foot caught the leg of a chair, sending him sprawling. Then Kaspar was on top of him, punching and yelling, while Leonard held his left hand to one eye and tried to fend Kaspar off with his right. Even as he struggled against the smaller boy, Leonard thought: *First Anthony Marshall clocks me a good one, now Kaspar Shitstain. I just can't catch a break.*

As suddenly as the attack had commenced, it was over. Kaspar Filipowski got to his feet, brushed himself off, and calmly stared down at Leonard.

"If you ever touch me again," he said, "I'll stab you in your sleep."

And Leonard believed him unhesitatingly. Leonard Levesque might have been rotten and recognized himself as such, but Kaspar Filipowski was patently nuts.

"But maybe I won't have to," Kaspar continued. "You're right: I lied when I said I didn't know who the boys were. I know who one of them was. It was Scott Theriault, or what was left of him."

Kaspar's eyes sparkled with delight.

"And I don't think he was looking for me," said Kaspar. "He came for you."

CHAPTER

LXXII

Roger Teal's wife had gone to bed early. She always went to bed early these days, and was either asleep, or pretending to be, by the time her husband joined her. Teal didn't care. They rarely screwed, and then only when they'd each drunk enough to allow lust to overcome mutual distaste. As for Teal's daughter, she was staying over at a friend's, which she also did as often as she could, preferring other people's homes to her own. When the trigger was finally pulled on the marriage, it would come as a blessing to them all.

Teal drank first one beer, then another. He thought of Edward Kenney, the Saint, and Renders. He pictured Mike Hurvich's body moldering wherever Kenney had buried it, and the Saint and Renders taking turns with Mallory Norton. He knew he'd have to tell the Saint about the visit from the private investigator. He would have done so sooner, but he wanted time to think. Kenney was right: Lines had been overstepped and trusts breached. Teal and Kenney had kept to the rules while the Saint had not. It was the Saint who was most at fault. But would that count for much if he decided to hold them to account for the death of the DEA agent? And suppose the DEA traced Cotter's abductors back to the Airbnb, rented in Edward Kenney's name? Could Kenney be relied on not to implicate his associate? And what of Jenny Berrien? Kenney would never agree to harming her, not with all that was going on, but the Saint might. What it came down to was, Teal would have to pick a side.

He drank a third beer, brushed his teeth, and went to wake his wife. He still had needs, and if he kept his eyes closed she could be anyone he wanted, even Mallory Norton, the same Mallory Norton whom the Saint, through his selfishness, had denied his friends.

And so the side was picked.

4

Hell hath no limits, nor is circumscrib'd
In one self place, but where we are is hell,
And where hell is, there must we ever be.

Christopher Marlowe, *Doctor Faustus*

CHAPTER

LXXIII

The morning after I followed Teal to Pittsfield, I met with Moxie Castin and Allen Atwood Alcock at Moxie's office. But first, Alcock and I were forced to wait in the reception area while Moxie dealt with State Representative Ricky "Goody" Carmichael, whose Ecuadoran gardener had been picked up in Saco by immigration officials, after which the gardener vanished into the system. Ironically, Goody Carmichael was one of those advocating for greater collaboration between Immigration and Customs Enforcement and local police departments in Maine, even though businesses across the state, including home care and farming, relied on ten thousand seasonal and temporary immigrant workers simply to function. ICE arrests in Maine had already soared 50 percent in a year, agents sweeping up legal and illegal laborers alike, and the state was hurting. It was all about creating a climate of fear, regardless of the damage to families, towns, and the local economy.

"So who did Carmichael think they were going to come after when he started cheerleading for immigration raids?" I asked Moxie, once the representative had left the building.

"Other people's gardeners," said Moxie, "not his. Worse, it wasn't ICE that lifted the gardener but Customs and Border Protection, and CBP takes the view that it doesn't have to provide access to family or counsel to detainees, so nobody knew where the gardener was for a week. We filed a habeas corpus petition in federal court, naming CBP officials as respondents, which was when they transferred him to ICE custody, so it was ICE who informed us that he's currently under lock and key in Massachusetts. Now we need to get him released and prepare for a hearing with an immigration judge. The man's been here for twenty years, his children are citizens, and he's been trying to get a green card since 2007."

"Where does that leave Carmichael?"

"I think the term is 'on the horns of a dilemma,' " said Moxie, "not to mention doing his own yard work. Goody's paying my fees, but I'm salving my conscience by telling myself I'm working for the gardener, not him, and I'll charge Goody a premium for being the agent of his gardener's misfortune."

Moxie was dressed for a federal court appearance later in the day, which meant he was wearing a tie that was less of a cry for help than usual, and had left his jacket in a closet so it wouldn't look like he'd slept rough in it. Alcock, meanwhile, was even more hangdog than ever. I wondered if his manner was partly contrived, an effort to garner leniency from judges and juries by evoking pity for clients afflicted with such counsel.

Over coffee and bacon cheddar doughnuts from the Holy Doughnut on Commercial, I updated them both on my progress. When I was done, Alcock said: "I think we may have differing concepts of what 'progress' entails."

"If it helps," I replied, "I don't eat much, so the subsistence payments will be low."

"He works how he works," Moxie informed Alcock. "You're always free to go elsewhere."

I coughed politely to remind them of my presence. Moxie was my lawyer, and often my client, but not my spokesman. Alcock backed down, partly if not wholly.

"I'm grateful to Mr. Parker for taking on the inquiry," he said. "I'm just curious as to why he hasn't yet visited Spero. I would have thought that might be among his first ports of call."

"I wanted to find out as much as I could about the school before going up there," I said. "Then I got sidetracked."

"By Roger Teal," said Alcock.

"And Edward Kenney."

"You have no proof that their meeting was precipitated by your visit to the Department of Education."

"No," I admitted, "but the odds favor it. What I do involves following trails that turn out to be dead ends, or picking at leads that come apart in my hands, but it's never a wasted effort because I'm narrowing the focus with every step. In addition, there's no ticking clock here. Without wishing to sound callous, Scott Theriault's problems are over, and easing his father's conscience may be beyond my powers. I'm still not convinced Scott's death was anything other than accidental, but neither am I convinced that Spero is beyond reproach."

"If Scott was killed by someone connected to Spero," said Moxie, "it's not because he spotted anomalies in the accounts."

"People who are financially suspect are also, by extension, morally so," I said. "Look, Teal acknowledged that he planned to contact Santopietro to tell him I'd been asking about the school. Shortly after I left him, Teal used a pay phone to make a call, and an hour later he was sitting in a storage lot in Pittsfield waiting for Edward Kenney to arrive."

"Why a pay phone?" Alcock asked. "Why not a burner, or the phone in his office? I mean, who's going to check those records?"

"Even burners leave a trace, like where they were purchased, and where and when they were subsequently used. As for an office extension, it isn't private, so you never know who might be listening, and as you pointed out, there may be a record of its use. Teal is either very careful or very paranoid, and any distinction between them is purely a matter of perspective. What isn't in dispute is that Teal has something to hide, and not just a fetish for pay phones. He contacted Edward Kenney immediately after I asked about Spero, which means that whatever he's concealing involves both Spero and Kenney. And if Spero is involved, so too is Santopietro, because he runs Spero, which in turn yokes him to Kenney."

"Maybe Kenney also snatches kids for Spero," said Moxie.

"I might ask Santopietro about that," I said. "By the way, did you know Santopietro had been at Élan when you asked me to get involved?"

"He doesn't hide it."

"You might have told me."

"I didn't want you making judgments about him based on it. It's not as if you don't have enough judgments to be getting along with."

The next time I billed Moxie for work, I'd be upping my rates.

"And Mallory Norton?" asked Alcock.

"It's Ward Vose who reckons she could have been the girl his son was seeing," I said, "but the police have flown that kite with no result. I can't see where her disappearance fits, other than as part of a pattern of Kennebec Valley oddness."

"So where does that leave us?" Moxie asked.

"I'll drive up to The Plains tomorrow or the next day, and base myself in Bingham or Madison." I gave Alcock a meaningful look. "It'll involve a motel bill, but I'll try to keep room service to a minimum."

"As long as you provide receipts," said Alcock, "and restrict yourself to two drinks."

Which concluded our meeting. Alcock headed off to make somewhere else look drab, while Moxie ran a couple of jobs by me, both of which could wait a week or so. He then folded his hands over his enviable belly and said, "What is it?"

"What's what?"

"Whatever's bothering you."

I could have shrugged it off and told him it was nothing, but he'd only have worried. For all his bluster, Moxie maintained a sensitivity and solicitude toward others. It made him a better lawyer, but also helped explain why a long line of ex-wives and former girlfriends retained affection for him. You might not have wanted to be married to Moxie for long, or even at all, but you still wanted him in your life.

"A conversation with Angel," I told him, "on the day I visited Ward Vose. It's hard to explain the substance of it."

"Try."

"I may have buried memories. They're starting to resurface."

"What kind of memories? Childhood?"

"No," I said. "Other lives."

Moxie's expression did not alter, but neither did he speak.

"Is this the point where you tell me you're going to have to hire another investigator?" I asked.

Moxie checked his watch, removed his jacket from the closet, and put it on. Immediately, wrinkles appeared in the material, like magic.

"That explains a lot," he said, and his eyes were sad and serious. "Who else have you told about this?"

"No one."

"Keep it that way."

"Because they'll think I'm crazy?"

"No," said Moxie. "Because some of them might think you're not."

CHAPTER LXXIV

Louis arrived in Boston, availed of an early check-in at the Four Seasons, and ordered lunch from room service: steak, medium, accompanied by a bottle of Prunotto Barolo. (Had Allen Atwood Alcock been presented with that bill, he might have suffered a coronary.) He showered while he waited for the food to arrive, drank one small glass of the Barolo with his steak, and saved the rest for later. He then took the T to the Wellesley Square station, where he enjoyed a stroll in the afternoon air, pausing by Fuller Brook Park to take in the birdsong. He returned to the T station, went back to the Four Seasons, and poured himself another glass of Barolo.

Louis had now seen for himself the Wellesley colonial home of D. Francis Sturgis, which was modest compared with some of its neighbors. On Grove Street, a buyer could drop $7 to $8 million on a family home with nine bedrooms and ten bathrooms, if they were so minded, but Sturgis was satisfied with four beds, three baths, and just under three thousand square feet—ample, and more, for a man who lived alone. When Louis passed the house, lamps were lit in the topmost rooms against the fall gloom. The specifications Louis had acquired for the property included details of a security company, with cameras and alarm monitoring. They would have to be dealt with before Louis could think about confronting Sturgis.

Unlike Moxie Castin, Louis had no qualms about engaging David Southwood, and didn't even regard his fees as excessive. When it came to illegal activities, one wasn't paying for the service alone, but also the aftercare. Remembering was cheap but forgetting was expensive, and the more consequential the business to be forgotten, the higher the price. Louis sent Southwood a message from a temporary email address. Five minutes later, the phone in the room rang, even though Louis had not told Southwood where he was staying.

"What is it?" asked Southwood.

"All your friends have gathered for a surprise party in your backyard," said Louis. "They were worried about you."

A few seconds went by before Southwood said: "There's no one in my yard."

"Like I said, all your friends."

"Funny."

"Don't say it if you don't mean it. I need an address isolated."

"Give it to me."

Louis did.

"When?"

"Tomorrow night."

A minute's silence followed while Southwood did what Southwood did, breaking any number of laws along the way.

"I wouldn't," he said at last. "BPW and NGrid have a gas relay project scheduled to begin in Wellesley tomorrow: Grove Street, Cameron Street, and Hampden Street are all in the affected area. It'll take a week or more. They'll be working nights to get it finished, and there'll be a police presence."

Louis couldn't afford to wait that long, even if Kade managed, as promised, to hold off the broker. Right now, he knew someone was at the Sturgis house.

"Tonight, then."

Southwood named his price. Louis was about to agree when Southwood added: "That's basic, without penalty payments."

"Why would there be penalties?"

"You want me to ask what you plan on doing once you're inside?"

"You never ask that kind of question."

"When it comes to you, that's why there are penalties. I'll also have to postpone other pressing work."

"How much?"

"Fifty percent on top, the total payable in full immediately. But for that, you get the premium service, including access to his computer, if that's of interest. I can also install spyware, if you'd like to know who he'll be talking to from now on."

Louis said spyware wouldn't be necessary, since he didn't think Sturgis would be talking to anyone again after tonight, although he didn't mention this to Southwood; and Southwood didn't argue the point, almost certainly because he guessed the reason for the refusal. But Louis did ask him to search Sturgis's computer for any references to angels or associated words and terms, and any mention of the Colonial Club. Southwood said he'd get right on it.

"I'll be in your ear from the moment you reach the house," said Southwood, "with eyes on local and state law enforcement. How's the Four Seasons, by the way?"

"Reassuringly expensive," said Louis.

"Just like me. I'll send you my payment details via Threema. And just so you know, that crack about my friends was hurtful. I could have friends. I just choose not to."

"Well, if you change your mind, Angel and I will be your friends."

"Really?"

"No."

"It's for the best," said Southwood. "All your friends end up dead."

CHAPTER

LXXV

At Spero, Santopietro summoned Renders to his office.

Santopietro had just gotten off the phone with Roger Teal, who had informed him of the visit from the private investigator. Santopietro wasn't overly worried and did his best to reassure Teal. Parker, said Santopietro, wasn't interested in school finances, only in Scott Theriault. Regarding the latter, Santopietro's conscience was clear, since he hadn't killed Theriault; that, like Mallory Norton, was on Renders. Santopietro had simply identified the problem and left it to his subordinate to solve. The next thing Santopietro knew, Theriault's body was discovered in the water, a case of accidental death, which was certainly for the best: for Spero, where Scott was a disruptive presence; for Santopietro and Renders, because of what they'd done to Mallory Norton; and finally, for Scott himself, since his character flaws were too ingrained for the school to remedy.

What Teal hadn't mentioned, or not until Santopietro raised the subject, was Nola Maddick, aka Gai Cotter, the undercover DEA agent missing in Detroit. When Santopietro asked Teal straight out if Gai Cotter was the woman he and Kenney had killed, Teal at first expressed doubt and tried to end the call, but Santopietro had long had the measure of Roger Teal.

"Roger," he pressed, "was it her?"

"I think so." Then: "Yes."

"Which is it? Possible, or certain?"

"Certain. We couldn't have known what she was, but it was clean, very clean."

"What does Kenney say?"

"He agrees."

He would, thought Santopietro.

"Kenney hasn't been in touch," said Santopietro, "not with me."

"He will."

"He told you so?"

"Yes."

"Over the phone, or in person?"

"In person," said Teal, who was starting to wish he'd never made the call. "We met yesterday evening. That was when he told me that Maddick, Cotter, whatever, was DEA."

"What else did you discuss?"

"Parker's visit."

"That's all?"

"Yes, that's all."

This spoken with too much conviction: *a lie*.

"If you and Edward say the kill was clean," said Santopietro, "then it was. As for Parker, he'll find nothing here. Scott Theriault's death was a dreadful mishap, and his mother and stepfather have accepted it as such. His father is lashing out impotently. Take a pill tonight, Roger. It'll help you sleep."

"I might do that," said Teal.

But he didn't hang up.

"Is there anything more?" Santopietro asked.

"Mallory Norton."

"She's still missing," said Santopietro. "Hope is dwindling."

Teal was silent.

"Roger, are you there?"

Teal was.

"Is she missing like that DEA agent is missing?"

"I couldn't say," Santopietro replied.

"Because Kenney may ask the same question."

"If he does, he'll get the same reply."

“I’ll tell him,” said Teal. “It might save him a trip.”

“That’s up to you—both of you.”

“Well, we’ll see.”

“Yes, I’m sure we will.”

They said goodbye, which was when Santopietro contacted Renders. Santopietro then went through everything with him, point by point.

“The DEA won’t ever stop looking for one of their own,” said Renders, when Santopietro was done. “It could be they’ll find her eventually, or what’s left of her.”

“Even if they don’t,” said Santopietro, “they’ll keep hunting for whoever took her.” He shook his head. “Clean, there’s no such thing as ‘clean’ when it comes to killing law enforcement.”

“So Kenney and Teal are at risk,” said Renders, “and know they are.”

“Kenney more than Teal, because his name was on the Airbnb rental, but yes. If Teal was aware of how exposed he was by association, he’d never have revealed so much to me.”

“Or he was open with you because he was frightened.”

“I suppose so.”

“Which means he still trusts you.”

“Unwisely,” said Santopietro. “I’m in jeopardy as long as they are.”

“Did Kenney put Teal up to asking you about Norton?”

“Kenney might have planted the idea in his head, but Teal decided to run with it.”

“So Kenney believes you murdered Mallory Norton,” said Renders.

“I didn’t murder her,” said Santopietro. “You did—for which I’m not ungrateful.”

“Kenney doesn’t know that.”

“You can be sure he’s wondering.”

“Either way, he thinks you may be jeopardized too, and he’s at risk as long as you are.” Renders grinned emptily. “Four men, all with blood on their hands, and all suspicious of one another. That’s quite the pickle.”

“All suspicious of one another?”

“Don’t worry, I’m on your side. What about Kenney?”

"He's on his own side," said Santopietro.

"Teal?"

"Wavering."

"If he's worried about Parker and the school," said Renders, "he may side with Kenney."

"Or kill him," said Santopietro. "And once he gets started—"

"Does Teal have it in him? He likes killing tied-up women, but could he kill a man?"

"I wouldn't want to bet my life that he couldn't," said Santopietro.

In Santopietro's experience, it never paid to misjudge weak individuals because their weakness made them vicious. When he and Teal played the Game together, they egged each other on. Santopietro was crueler when he played it with Teal, and vice versa. Teal contained hidden depths, and what swam in them had long, sharp teeth.

Santopietro said: "Curiously, Teal was wondering if we might consider abducting a woman for him."

"In the middle of this?" Renders asked.

"It's Berrien, the one who set Parker on him. She's gotten under Teal's skin. He'd like to hurt her, but he also fears she may have material that could be used against both of us. Mostly, though, it's about the hurting."

"It would be madness."

"It's all madness," said Santopietro. "Mallory Norton was madness. The Game is madness."

Renders thought about it.

"Is Berrien good-looking?"

"Teal says not."

"Pity. But in the dark, who can tell?"

"She doesn't need to be good-looking," said Santopietro, "not for bait. In fact, we don't even have to take her."

"We just tell Teal we did?"

"That's right. Kenney too. We call her a goodwill offering."

"And then?"

"Then," said Santopietro, "we kill them."

CHAPTER

LXXVI

Louis did not like acting faster than he judged prudent, and without doing the groundwork. But if Southwood was correct, the chances of gaining access to Sturgis's property unobserved, and more importantly leaving it the same way, were set to decrease dramatically by morning. Southwood asked if Louis could source an untraceable burner at short notice, but Louis said he didn't know many people in Massachusetts because, well, #Massachusetts and #NobodysFriendButTheirOwn. Southwood told him to stay put, and an hour later a call from the front desk advised Louis that a package had arrived. The envelope, when it was delivered to his room, contained a flip phone manufactured by a company Louis had never heard of, and that probably no longer existed. As per Southwood's instructions, he did not turn it on but slipped it into his pocket. The phone was to be activated only when he was within sight of Sturgis's home.

Louis left the hotel shortly after nine p.m. This time, he didn't go to the T station but instead walked to Newbury Street, where he browsed for ten minutes before hailing a cab. He directed the driver to take him to Captain Marden's Seafoods on Linden Street in Wellesley, which was walking distance from the target. When he reached Sturgis's house, lights were on downstairs as well as on the top floor, and a porch lamp was burning. Louis powered up the flip phone, inserted the earpiece that had come with it, and waited. Seconds later, Southwood's voice was in his ear.

"A male left the house an hour ago," said Southwood. "No suitcase or bag, and he didn't take a vehicle, so he may not have been going too far, or for too long. The alarm was activated before he left and the cameras are motion sensitive. Are you proceeding?"

"Yes," said Louis.

"Okay, then I'm killing the systems: one, two, three—now. If you want me to stay with you once you're inside, I will, and I won't even charge you extra for my company. But if you think I might be a distraction, keep the earpiece in place and be sure to answer if I call."

Louis took the second option, because any potential for distraction aside, he wasn't convinced that Southwood's company was preferable to no company at all. He didn't bother double-checking with Southwood before entering Sturgis's property through the open gate, Southwood not appreciating doubters. At the rear of the house, he placed a folded newspaper against a windowpane and used the butt of his pistol to break the glass. When he was sure that no jagged edges remained, he reached in, twisted the latch, and raised the window. Once inside, he used the newspaper to stuff the hole in the glass; he didn't want an unexpected night breeze to warn Sturgis of an intruder.

Louis was standing in a large formal dining room that didn't look like it had been used to entertain in years. Even by moonlight, he could make out a patina of dust on the table, chairs, sideboard, and mantel. He turned on a slim Fenix Tactical Penlight, allowing him to take a closer look at the paintings on the wall: works from the first and second generation of Hudson River School artists: Cole, Durand, Church, Kensett, and more. These, too, had not been dusted in some time.

The dining room door was closed, but thankfully, not locked from the outside. It led into a dreary hallway, furnished with a sideboard and coat stand, and a Persian carpet so worn it could only have been expensive. The rest of the floor consisted of a living room—again, more paintings, more dust; a library, which showed signs of use; and a huge kitchen, with a four-seater table, an island, and bright Le Creuset kitchenware in orange and yellow. The cupboards and refrigerator were well stocked, and the EuroCave cabinet against the far wall was dominated by European wines, mainly Spanish and Portuguese. Sturgis might not have held many parties, but either he knew a lot about dining or employed someone who did. Louis inclined toward the former because of the dust elsewhere; this was the home of a very solitary man.

On the second floor were the bedrooms, two with master bathrooms and all with bare mattresses on the beds. Only the main bathroom showed signs of use. At the end of the hallway was a staircase to the third floor, and it was here that the lights burned. Louis ascended carefully, even though Southwood had assured him the house was unoccupied. For Louis, old habits died hard, in the hope that by embracing them, killing him might prove similarly difficult.

The top level of the house, which might once have been a high-ceilinged attic space, was now a single living area, with the exception of a small room containing a toilet, shower, and sink. The room smelled stale and sour, like male seed spilled and left to fester. One corner held a single bed, unmade. Open shelves, and a long steel rack on wheels, were used to store clothing that was exclusively male. Against the shorter wall was a large-screen TV, with an easy chair in front and a small side table nearby. To the left was a desk with a computer and high-end printer. On the floor, a trash can overflowed with scraps of paper.

Every space on the walls was adorned with pornographic images, many of very young boys and girls, at most in their midteens. Of the rest, there could be no doubt that the subjects were underage, with their teenage years ahead of them. Up close, the arrangements appeared random; only when viewed from a distance did patterns emerge. Louis discerned figures human and bestial, dominated by one image that took up the main gable wall, where genitalia, heads, nipples, and pubic hair combined in collage to create a dark angel seven feet tall, its wings extending to the side walls. Particular pain had been taken in constructing those wings: the scapulars and marginal coverts were nippled breasts, the primary and secondary coverts vaginas, and the primaries and secondaries below them erect penises. Louis could smell the paste used to glue the images to the wall; the angel was a recent addition to the décor.

The flip phone rang, startling him. He used the button on the earpiece wire to accept the call.

"Courtesy contact," said Southwood.

"I'm in. The house is empty."

"Can you see a computer?"

"Yes."

"Then it's probably the one I've accessed. Would you like to hear what I've found so far?"

"If it involves naked children, I'll decline."

"How did you know?"

"He's covered his walls with pictures of them."

"Guess he does his own housework," said Southwood. Then: "He's been accumulating videos and photographs for a long time. He uses the dark web, probably because he's under the false impression that it protects his anonymity. He's not just looking either: He's an abuser. If it's all the same to you, I'd prefer to leave everything intact, meaning I don't want to attempt to copy his caches to a secure server. Even I have my limits, and if I'm ever apprehended by law enforcement, however remote the prospect, I don't want child pornography coming back to bite me. But if you decide you want to sic the feds on him, I'll happily direct them to his door."

Louis said he'd think about it.

"Heads up," said Southwood. "You have a man entering the property, the same one who left earlier. He's just come through the gate."

"Description?"

"Tall, thin, balding."

Sturgis.

"Understood," said Louis, killing the call. He found a place in the shadows, the angel looming behind, and made himself unseen.

CHAPTER

LXXVII

Sabine Drew had returned to Haynesville to feed her fish, do some laundry, and consider everything that had happened in The Plains—which included, distractingly but pleasantly, a couple of bouts of lovemaking with Tim Sadlier at the Bingham Motor Inn. Sabine, who hadn't had sex in so long that she feared she might have reattained virginhood, was surprised by just how joyful being with Tim made her feel. She'd been alone for years—or not quite alone, given the immanence of the dead to her, but certainly deprived of close contact with the living—and it was only in embracing another person, physically and emotionally, and allowing herself to be embraced in turn, that she recognized just how isolated she'd become. At one low point she'd even investigated becoming a nun, after learning that the number of Catholic nuns in America had dropped by 80 percent over the past fifty years, with the average age of those who remained also being eighty. Sabine had been baptized Catholic but lapsed in her teens—coincidentally or otherwise, when her gift/curse, whichever was appropriate, began manifesting in earnest, proof of an afterlife not necessarily corresponding to proof of the existence of God. Nonetheless, she wagered the nuns needed her as much, if not more, than she might need them, and so wouldn't be in a position to quibble over details. What finally put Sabine off, apart from the prospect of having to rise before dawn to pray and chant, followed by solitary Bible study and reflection, was that she'd be required to spend the rest of her days contemplating the ultimate unattainable male. This struck her as adding unnecessary fuel to the fire.

She had, therefore, been living with a low-level hum of depression for years. When her seclusion was shattered by Tim Sadlier, and the hum fell away, she was able to appreciate the quietude, broken by the breathing of the man lying next to her in a motel bed. Strange, she thought, that she should use the word *lovemaking* about sex with a man she barely knew. Sabine disliked profanity and used it sparingly, but even allowing for her sensitivities, words other than the "f" one were available to describe what she and Tim had enjoyed. That she did not reach for them might have been dismissed as sentimentality, the impulse of a foolish woman falling head over heels in late middle age, a prelude to handing over the contents of her bank accounts before learning that her beloved had families in three states and a criminal record for fraud. But Sabine was not foolish, and her abilities made her acutely sensitive to those around her. She could pick up quickly on lies, evasions, hostility, but she was also attuned to their opposites: truth, openness, kindness. Love. In Tim Sadlier, she perceived only decency, and a kind of idealism. Life might have disappointed him, yet he was not a disappointed man and there was no bitterness to him. He had shared with her his ambition to leave Spero and The Plains, and while he might not have been speaking of moving to Europe and becoming an artist, or venturing into the Amazon to work with threatened tribes—he didn't even want to leave Somerset County, never mind the state—it was a big step for him. It spoke of a man who was not prepared to give up hope, however modest it might be. In like manner, Sabine had suspended, if not abandoned, her dream of companionship (stopping short of love, which was where hope entered the realm of fantasy), while isolating herself against regret should it prove elusive. Life, it seemed, had surprised both Tim and Sabine, rapidly and unexpectedly binding each to the other.

But the incident in the woods had stayed with her, and she discussed it with Tim before returning home, she in his arms, her face against his chest, breathing in the strong man-smell of him, all sweat and earth and grass. She shared a great deal about her past that night because she wanted to be up-front with him from the off. Were he to google her name, he'd find out the truth anyway, at least about the children, the living and the dead. That she was also a murderer who had killed a man by poisoning his wine was a morsel she'd keep for a deathbed confession. Murder was a lot to take in on a second date, and represented the kind of overshare that might militate against a third, even if the man in question deserved what he got. (Sabine's lack of doubt on that issue surprised even herself.)

"So you're a medium?" Sadlier asked.

"I don't call myself that," Sabine replied brusquely. "I don't even know what it means. Do you?"

Sadlier admitted that he didn't, but it was the only word in his vocabulary that approximated what she was telling him.

"I'm sorry," he said. "I didn't mean to offend. I'm trying to understand."

"Well, good luck with that. I've been trying to understand it all my life, and I can't say I'm very far from where I started."

"So when you came here to help with the search, it wasn't just to pull on your hiking boots and walk a grid?"

"I hoped I might have more to offer," said Sabine.

"Did you, um, pick up on something before you got here? Or see anything?"

"Like Mallory Norton's ghost, soaked in blood, pointing a finger into the far distance? *'Yonder lies the man!'* "

"Yes," Sadlier replied seriously. "Yes, I guess so."

"No, I didn't see Mallory Norton. I've seen others, but not her."

"Up here? You've seen others here, in the valley?"

They were coming to it now, coming to what she'd experienced out in those woods. Sabine first told him of the woman on Big Island, she with the cleft skull, and Sadlier rubbed his chin, the thick bristles making a sound like logs hissing softly in a fire, which brought Sabine close to tears for reasons that could not be explained beyond the beautiful ordinariness of it; and she did not speak further, nor did she move, but remained motionless against him, for though she had more to say, so much more, it seemed to her that her future, their future, rested on how he might respond; that here was the moment where words weighing less than feathers and more than a soul would tip the balance, either for or against, and nothing said after could ever undo it.

“Well,” said Tim Sadlier, “isn’t that a thing?”

His voice and eyes were all wonder, like a child encountering magic for the first time, and accepting it without reservation as itself alone. He peered down at her from the heights of the pillow, and a calloused finger stroked her cheek.

“But what,” he said, “made you fall in the woods?”

So this, too, she revealed to him; and when she was done, he told her of coffee beans arranged on a kitchen table and scattered on a cold floor, and seed bags torn in a locked toolshed, and she knew she had found the right man.

NOW, AT HOME IN HAYNESVILLE, she filled a bag with fresh clothing to last a week, replenished her toiletries, and made a final check on her fish. A neighbor, one of the few she trusted for the task, was looking in on the house while she was away, but the automatic feeders took care of the needs of the fish, and mercifully, none of them had died.

She both did and did not want to return to The Plains. She wanted to because of Tim Sadlier, but she did not want to because of everything else: a drowned boy, a missing girl, but most of all, the storm of anger and suffering that had engulfed her during the search, fragments of the lost coursing through it like debris, their names and the names of others, with the place and manner of their dying, but so confused that the associations between them could not be made with certainty and all deaths became one, a babel of voices speaking in tongues known only to the extinct, intelligible to her solely as emotions, colors; a synesthesia of agony. Scott Theriault’s voice was among them, but it was both him and not him: Scott, but not Scott entire. The best of him was gone, and the storm had gathered up what remained to add to its strength.

But the heart of the storm was the Other that spoke an older language still, a creature—because its nature was not human—concealed in the tumult, inciting the dead to extremes, using their pain to feed its own and its intent to focus theirs. It was both present and absent; Sabine was aware of entrapment and an enforced limit to its range. It resembled a prisoner whispering persuasions from his cell, making agents of disorganized others, so that what was once chaotic was channeled into purpose; or a wolf hunting with hounds, binding them with fear of the alpha, but also with the prospect of bringing down bigger prey through its leadership.

And the Other had a name, one it could not bury from Sabine, because as the storm passed through her, so too was she briefly of it. The Other's name was unfamiliar to her, but allied to it, like a twin star, was another name she knew very well. She'd held off on acting on it only because she wanted to be sure her mind wasn't playing tricks, conflating her memories with those of the Other.

Sabine called the private investigator. The call went straight to voicemail, so she left a message. She kept it simple.

"I've been to The Plains, Mr. Parker," she said. "Call me."

She closed her bag and went to bed. The next day, she would return to the hunt.

CHAPTER

LXXVIII

Louis listened to the noises downstairs but did not move: patience, patience. At last, he heard footsteps ascending and Sturgis entered the attic room carrying a half-full bottle of wine, a wineglass, and a plate of cold cuts and cheese. Sturgis put the glass and plate on the side table, pulled the cork from the bottle, and poured himself a generous measure. He picked up the remote control and turned on the TV, which came alive to CNBC. The noise of gunfire in some benighted part of the world masked Louis's approach, from behind, but as the screen darkened briefly, his reflection became apparent and Sturgis reacted. He stared first at Louis, then at the gun in Louis's hand, the suppressor doubling the length of the barrel, before returning his attention from the weapon to the man.

"I know who you are," said Sturgis.

"Likewise. Put the glass down slowly and sit in that chair."

Sturgis did as he was told.

"How did you find me?" he asked. "I was assured of discretion."

"You should have paid better," said Louis. "You might have been guaranteed it."

"What do you want?"

"The name of the person who told you to have me killed."

Sturgis's face lit up, transformed into the countenance of a fanatic.

"It wasn't a person," he said. "It was an angel."

"An angel with membership of the Colonial Club? So an angel can get on the books but not a Black man? Brother King must be turning in his grave."

"It's nothing to do with the Colonial. I'm no longer a member."

"I thought it was a lifetime deal."

"I'm about to be indicted," said Sturgis. "Receipt and possession of visual material of a child depicted in sexual conduct, with a mandatory minimum sentence of five years and up to twenty on each charge. I admit, I do like them very young, but we all have our weaknesses. I'm not optimistic about the prospect of leniency, and that's before the authorities begin digging deeper into my activities. I'll be an old man by the time I get out, assuming I survive long enough to be released, which I doubt. Pedophilia arouses the moral indignation of the general prison populace, or so I've been informed."

He might have been discussing unpaid tickets for traffic violations, so casual was he.

"And how does the Colonial fit into this?"

"My former friends and associates, learning of the misfortune that was about to befall me, deemed it best to sever ties. I was asked to resign from the club. I chose not to."

"Why?"

"That's none of your business."

Louis fired a single shot. The wine bottle exploded, showering Sturgis with glass and merlot. Tiny wounds began to bleed, but Sturgis took it in stride.

"I repeat," he said. "It's none of your business."

"What is my business is who instructed you to have me killed."

"I told you: an angel. He came to me in a dream. He told me I couldn't be saved from punishment in this life, but everyone was capable of being forgiven in the next. The sinner only had to prove himself worthy of salvation. He said God was merciful."

"And the name of this angel?"

Sturgis pointed at the vast, obscene representation on the wall.

"His name is Brightwell."

CHAPTER

LXXIX

As promised, Macy arrived at my house with barbecue from Wilson County, enough of it to induce a coronary in the dead. I put the food in the oven to stay warm while we fooled around; by a certain age, one doesn't want to be exerting oneself on a full stomach. Afterward, we split a half bottle of wine over dinner and I told her about Scott Theriault's parents, the encounters with Jenny Berrien and Roger Teal, and what subsequently transpired in Pittsfield.

"But you still have no proof that Scott Theriault might have been seeing Mallory Norton?" Macy asked.

Macy was wearing one of my T-shirts. She looked better in it than I ever had.

"If I did, I'd share it with the police," I said. "You know that."

"Sorry, of course I do. Some things you'll keep hidden, but not anything that might help trace a lost girl."

"And her disappearance may have nothing to do with Spero," I said. "That's what bothers me. We could be looking at two, even three, unrelated incidents: the death of Scott Theriault, the vanishing of Mallory Norton, and whatever Teal, Kenney, and potentially Santopietro have been up to at the school, which might be nothing worse than embezzlement—not that I'm condoning illegality, Officer, but we all have to choose our battles."

"Except you don't believe they're unconnected, do you?"

"It would be easier to accept in a city. But in a township of forty square miles in Somerset County with a population that only nudges eighty or so thanks to a residential school? Even allowing for a circumference that encompasses Bingham, that's the kind of range where coincidences wither and die."

"They're odd places, aren't they, those old townships?" said Macy. "They're too close to the past for comfort. The lines become blurred."

In cities, the past was buried; the present built over its bones. Fragments of the bygone remained in the form of structures or names that had survived for generations, yet frequently the past was a phantom, existing only as memories. But in somewhere like The Plains, where the marks left by men were minimal, the distinctions between past and present broke down, the existing landscape not dissimilar to how it had once been. In The Plains, it was possible to feel the persistence of antiquity.

Macy finished her wine, put the glass by the sink, and asked if I was coming to bed. I told her I'd follow in a few minutes.

"Don't be too long," she said. "I'm tired, on account of all that physical activity you just put me through, so I can't promise I'll be awake if you tarry."

I watched her leave. I was glad she was with me and I with her. But as she went, I felt an intimation of loss that was at once both premonition and remembrance, a feeling familiar from when Rachel was the woman with whom I shared this house. I used to think it was because of what happened to my wife: Having lost before, how could there not be the fear of losing again? But I now realized that I had also feared losing Susan, and not in the generalized way of one who loves and does not wish to be without the object of that love, but more specifically. A chain of losses snaked back into obscurity, into forgetfulness, but that opacity was no longer complete: Shapes were emerging, faces, incidents. A cycle of grief, a cycle of punishment.

CHAPTER

In the attic room, Louis shifted position to keep both Sturgis and the image of the angel in his line of sight. Only recently, after many years, had Brightwell returned to mind, in the company of Epstein and Liat in New York. It occurred to Louis that by remembering him, he might somehow have reconjured Brightwell into existence. But had Brightwell ever truly ceased to exist? He had disappeared, yes, but he had not died. What was it Epstein said? *None can kill an angel except an angel.* And there had to be a particularity to it: a hand, a blade . . .

"I can see by your expression that you believe me," said Sturgis. "You know that name, just as he knows yours. The angel is sage and mighty." Sturgis grimaced. "Of course, the angel is also insane."

"And what does he get from this arrangement?" Louis asked.

"An end to his pain. Forgiveness. He and I have that aspiration in common."

"Where is he?"

Sturgis waved a hand at the night, at the north.

"Far from here, but, to paraphrase the poet, his reach exceeds his grasp, or what's a hell for?" His shoulders sagged. "I'm not going to be saved, am I?"

"I wouldn't depend on it."

"It's not fair. I declined to fall on my sword at the Colonial because those who condemned me were guilty of crimes at least as appalling as mine. I wanted to be the mirror of their guilt. I wanted them to confront their own hypocrisy. But they defenestrated me with a letter."

"And who might *they* be, these hypocrites?"

Sturgis tapped the side of his nose with his right index finger.

"Wouldn't you like to know, you and your friend Mr. Parker? What will you offer me—my life in return for their names?"

"Would you trust me?" Louis replied. "Would I trust you?"

"*No* is the answer to both questions," said Sturgis. "I'll give you this for free: The one you should be most concerned about remains close. He's very determined."

"I could hurt you," said Louis. "I can make it last until you give up the name."

"And I'd tell lies to make it stop," said Sturgis, "which puts us at an impasse. But if I stay silent, hell may be more forgiving than heaven."

He picked up his glass and raised it to his lips.

"I'd like to finish this, please," he said. "It will be my last."

But Louis killed him before the first drop could touch his lips.

LATER THAT NIGHT, EPSTEIN—who, in common with the rest of the dying, no longer slept well—received a call.

"He gave me a name," said Louis.

"What name?"

"Brightwell."

"Did you believe him?"

"I did."

"What will you do now?" Epstein asked.

"To be honest," said Louis, "I have no idea."

5

And as for these spirits which are living, imprison them and hold them fast in the place of condemnation, and let them not bring destruction on the sons of thy servant, my God; for these are malignant, and created in order to destroy.

The Book of Jubilees, 10:5

CHAPTER

LXXXI

In Detroit, Michigan, life was proving challenging for Vincent Bergsma, and it showed no signs of getting any easier in the immediate future.

The disappearance of the DEA agent named Gai Cotter had come as a shock to Bergsma, not least because he had known her as Nola Maddick, formerly a minor dealer who could apparently turn product around as fast as it could be supplied, with the result that Bergsma had recently given the nod for her rise within his organization, a promotion further necessitated by a series of moves against him involving, in no particular order, his rivals, the Detroit PD, the DEA, the FBI, and probably the Vatican, the Screen Actors Guild, and the Girl Scouts as well, because why should they miss out on all the fun? That these misfortunes might have been a result, in whole or part, of Cotter's infiltration of his operation was conceivable. But whatever problems Cotter had caused Bergsma in life were nothing compared to what her unexplained departure had brought down on him. His people were being pulled from the streets, his clubs raided, and his legitimate business interests targeted by the IRS, who made the Black Mafia Family, from whose shadow Bergsma had emerged in the early part of the century, look like ragdoll pussycats.

While Bergsma himself was not yet personally threatened, it was only a matter of time before the combined efforts of the law enforcement agencies brought him to his knees, and all because they were convinced that the blame for whatever had befallen the DEA agent could be laid at his door. Bergsma wasn't above sanctioning murder or making his enemies vanish—

the illegal distribution and sale of narcotics was a dangerous business—but he did so only after every alternative had been exhausted, since bodies and disappearances attracted investigations. Even had he discovered the truth about Cotter, he'd have found a way to cut her loose without drawing federal heat. The cartel, with which Bergsma was required to deal as part of his chosen profession, might have taken a different approach, but what the Mexicans didn't know couldn't hurt them.

Unfortunately, the Mexicans were now well aware that Bergsma's operation had been infiltrated by the DEA, because Cotter's picture was all over the internet. And while Bergsma wasn't being named as a person of interest, the agent had penetrated at least two levels of his syndicate and was set to progress higher before she vanished. The result was that Bergsma was under pressure from all sides. He couldn't continue with his criminal endeavors because the cartel had turned off the tap pending an assessment of his vulnerabilities, and even had it been willing to supply him, Bergsma couldn't have moved the product because every law officer in the Midwest wanted to act as his proctologist. Meanwhile, the cash flow from his enterprises had slowed to a trickle, and like any businessman, Bergsma had debts to service, salaries to meet, and rents to cover, not to mention a couple of mortgages, alimony payments, and child support.

And it wasn't as though Bergsma could walk into the local DEA office on Howard Street to protest that he didn't do anything to their agent because he hadn't known she was their agent, as that was precisely what someone who had quietly removed an agent from the board would say, not to mention that he would effectively be confessing to a host of other crimes. The only solution that presented itself was for Bergsma to determine what had happened to Cotter and funnel this information to the authorities via back channels in the hope that it would be enough to exonerate him. Bergsma wasn't such an optimist as to believe the law would then walk away, allowing him to pick up where he'd left off, but the boot might be lifted from his neck. Once he could breathe again, he'd try to cut a deal; that or look into early retirement. Asia, Europe, the Middle East—Bergsma didn't care, as long as he wasn't behind bars or dead.

Now, finally, Bergsma had a crumb to offer his persecutors, a small but tasty one, which was why one of his lieutenants, Hollis Raines, was currently sitting at a table in the back room of a bodega in Delray, accompanied by a tame lawyer named Pfeffer, across from a pair of DEA agents named Solomon and Moyers. None of the four was overjoyed to be there, and the meeting was so far off the books that life after death would have been less deniable.

Pfeffer placed a manila envelope on the table.

"A goodwill gesture," he said.

Moyers reached for the envelope, but Pfeffer kept his fingers pressed down hard.

"Call off the dogs," he said. "Please."

He lifted his hand. Moyers took the envelope. Raines looked at Solomon, who was the senior agent.

"It wasn't us," said Raines. "We want her found as badly as you do."

"I doubt that," said Solomon.

Moyers opened the envelope and removed the contents: three photographs, each labeled with a time and location.

"What's this?" Moyers asked.

"That," said Raines, "is the car used to abduct Gai Cotter."

CHAPTER

LXXII

My efforts to pack for my stay in The Plains were hindered by a series of calls over the course of the morning, not all of them welcome. Of the ones that were, or comparatively so, the first came from Angel to say that Louis had returned to Portland from Boston and the three of us should meet, urgently. The second came from Moxie Castin, who informed me that Alcock had consulted with his client Ward Vose, and they would continue to pay me for as long as I was willing to look into Scott Theriault's death.

"But you'd have continued regardless, right?" he asked.

"It's Spero," I said. "It's piqued my interest."

"If Vose and Alcock decided to save their money, I'd have ponied up," said Moxie. "Knowing you're irritating Santopietro helps me sleep better at night."

"Roger Teal told me that Santopietro was intent on not going down the Élan road. He was trying for something better."

"Then he shouldn't be in the troubled-teen business at all," said Moxie, and hung up.

The final call, from Sabine Drew, was the one that fell conclusively into the Unwelcome category, if only because of my continuing reservations about her character.

"I left a message for you," she said.

"I've been busy, but you were on my list."

Which was close to the truth. She was on it, but I was in no hurry to get to her.

"Are you still looking into what happened in The Plains?"

"That depends," I replied neutrally. "The situation is complex and unfolding."

"My, how you weaponize vocabulary. It's almost like you don't trust me."

"I don't think you'd ever lie to me, but there are questions I'd prefer not to ask you, for precisely that reason."

Sabine dropped the matter. "I've been spending time in the Kennebec Valley," she said. "I went searching for Mallory Norton."

"And?"

"I could find no trace, and I looked hard. She may be gone."

Someone not paying attention or unfamiliar with her ways might have concluded that Sabine didn't care. I didn't make that mistake. We both knew that a person could bear only so much of the pain of others. One insulated oneself as best one could.

"Anything else?"

"I'm driving to Bingham right now," she said. "I don't know when I'll be returning to Haynesville. I've met someone."

"That's . . . nice?" It came out more like a question than I'd intended, and also more skeptical.

"You sound ambivalent," said Sabine, "though whether you're more concerned for him or me, I wouldn't like to speculate. Regardless, it's important that you and I meet. I'd encourage you to make it sooner rather than later."

I saw no point in hiding my travel plans from her. "I'm leaving for The Plains today."

"Then let's meet."

"Sabine, I—"

"Listen to me," she said. "Something up there knows your name. Something very bad."

CHAPTER

LXXXIII

I offered to meet Angel and Louis at one of our usual haunts—the Bear, or Bayou Kitchen—but Angel said they'd prefer to speak somewhere more private, so I told them to come to the house.

I knew something was wrong from the moment they stepped from the car. It was in the way Angel was keeping his head down and Louis was looking anywhere but at me. I was worried I might somehow have caused them hurt until I noticed Louis was not so much refusing to acknowledge me as he was checking the surroundings for potential threats. Louis rarely behaved this way when he came to my home. In the years after a gun attack in my yard almost took my life—had taken my life, as my heart stopped three times on the operating table—I had cut back much of the undergrowth and installed a monitoring system capable of detecting the presence of any creature larger than a possum. If an intruder, animal or human, approached the house, it would also be captured on camera, day or night. A stranger might have regarded this as paranoia, but a stranger would not have known of my wounds, or the pain with which I woke first thing in the morning and with which I went to bed at night, and I wanted to make it as difficult as possible for the next person who came for me. Then again, I only had to look in the mirror to see my recently busted nose, and I could trace with my fingertips the scar that the same block of wood had left on my scalp. As any expert in close protection will tell you—or won't tell you, especially if you're a client paying through the nose for it—if someone wants to get to you badly enough, they will. The rest is delaying the inevitable.

We sat at the kitchen table as Louis spoke of the contract that had been taken out on him; of Kade and the broker; of Epstein and his reflections; and finally of Sturgis, with his pornographic angel and false hope of redemption, false because if a man like Sturgis could be absolved of sin through murder, the very concept of redemption was rendered meaningless.

"And Sturgis named Brightwell," I said, when Louis was done.

"He did."

I saw a goitered child, Brightwell reborn, being swallowed by the Great North Woods. We had once thought Brightwell dead, and not without cause, since I could still see a chunk of his skull detaching as the bullet exited his head. But Brightwell's figure had been a recurring one for centuries, an imp of the perverse captured in text and art, so while the form of his return might have been a shock, the fact of it should not have been. However, back then we were still learning, and a lot had changed in the interim. We were now dreaming the same dreams.

"Did Southwood pull anything useful from Sturgis's computer?"

"He did a lot of reverse engineering based on the pornography," Louis replied. "Sturgis's contacts and suppliers will soon begin receiving visits from the FBI. But if you're referring to the Colonial Club, then no, nothing beyond confirming the rescindment of Sturgis's membership."

"So they learned of his tastes and tried to distance themselves from any potential fallout," I said.

Angel spoke, he who, as a boy, was abused like Sturgis's victims.

"Southwood says they must have known about Sturgis for years, but as his addictions grew, he got careless, and that carelessness became a liability."

"We need to look again at all the material you've gathered," said Louis, "including that list of names salvaged from the plane. Somewhere we've missed a connection, or we spotted a gap but couldn't identify the link. What if it's Sturgis? What if he's the key?"

"His name isn't in the documents," I said. "I've never even heard it mentioned until today."

"We could ask Southwood," said Angel. "He can run everything you have against what was on Sturgis's computer. Let him tear Sturgis's life apart, from the moment his mother purged her womb until Louis silenced him."

"I don't have that kind of money," I said. "Also, I've never met Southwood. He's just a voice at the end of a phone, and a mercenary one at that. I don't know that he can be trusted."

"He can," said Louis. "I guarantee it. And he'll help for free, or payment in kind."

"What kind of payment?"

"We offer to buy him dinner," said Angel.

"We send him a gift card for Domino's?"

"No," said Louis, "we meet him. We spend an evening in his company."

I could think of few things I wanted to do less, short of losing a toe.

"Why?"

"Because he's lonely," said Louis.

"With good reason," I replied.

"Don't be like that," said Angel. "We're all on the spectrum."

"But we're not all way out there on Southwood's end of it. He's like those colors only birds can see."

Angel and Louis regarded me impassively. I tried to wait them out, but like the poet, I had miles to go and promises to keep.

"Fine," I said. "But nowhere expensive, and if an awkward silence drags on for longer than five minutes, I get to leave."

Thus it was agreed, even if the mystery of Brightwell's involvement persisted. Then it became my turn to talk. I told Angel and Louis about Spero.

"You think they killed Scott Theriault to hide fraud?" Louis asked.

"It doesn't fit, but neither does Scott's death make sense as an accident. First, he goes north instead of south. He might have been trying to get to Canada, which is thirty-five or forty miles, but if so, why consume a quantity of alcohol he knows will render that impossible? No, I'm coming around to Ward Vose's way of thinking: Someone force-fed Scott Theriault enough hard liquor to incapacitate him, then drowned him, but it wasn't over money."

"So what does it leave?" Angel asked.

"If I had to guess," I said, "it leaves Mallory Norton."

CHAPTER

LXXXIV

Louis and Angel returned to their apartment. They'd offered to help with whatever was happening in The Plains, but while I would have welcomed their company, I didn't see what dragging them all the way up to the Kennebec Valley would achieve beyond making the locals nervous. Which might have been fun, but so far the locals had done nothing to deserve it.

The relationship between Roger Teal and Edward Kenney continued to worry me, though keeping eyes on them would be dull, time-consuming work. The Fulcis would take it on—they were remarkably stoic men, until they weren't—but although Alcock could be persuaded to sign off on their hours, I'd end up knowing only where Teal and Kenney went and perhaps who they met, not what was said. Also, the Fulcis were suited to surveillance that allowed them to work from a fixed position, like a house or a stationary vehicle; once they began to move around, they attracted attention. Only a blind person could be followed by the Fulcis and fail to spot them, and even then it would have to be a blind person without a guide dog. Finally, properly monitoring two men required hiring four to six people, which Alcock was certainly not going to sanction.

After some thought, I came up with a solution, which was to track the vehicles, not the men. Back in the not so dim and distant past, tagging a car was a complicated, costly, and unreliable affair, but thanks to advances in technology, illegally monitoring someone's vehicle had never been cheaper or easier. The most recently purchased car trackers in my collection cost three hundred dollars each, used 4G connectivity and a mobile app, had a fifty-day battery life if set to ping at five-minute intervals, and could be mounted without tools on any metal surface via three high-strength neo magnets. I still wouldn't be any wiser about conversations between Teal and Kenney, but it's better to know something than nothing, and I might be able to piece together a lot based on where they went.

I called Tony Fulci, explained what had to be done, and asked him to come pick up the trackers as soon as he could. He said he'd be there within the hour and he was as good as his word, arriving after forty minutes dressed in a sports jacket, a pressed white shirt, khakis, and brown Sperry top-siders. His hair was freshly cut and he smelled of cologne that, if not expensive itself, was based on a fragrance that might have been. He looked like someone who was trying desperately not to get thrown out of a country club.

"You didn't have to get all dressed up for me," I said. "Flowers would have been enough."

"I'm going to lunch," he said. His face, red at the best of times, darkened toward beetroot.

"In Kennebunkport, with the Bushes?"

"No, with Faith. You know, the woman from that night at the Bear. The night of the, uh, altercation."

"You mean the dislocation," I said. It was an unusual dating tactic, but it must have worked. "How has her ex taken the rejection?"

Tony jammed his massive fists into the pockets of his khakis as though storing hams.

"He left town."

"Willingly?"

"Sure, after Paulie and I packed up his stuff and put it in his car. He could go or watch it burn."

"And does Paulie like Faith?"

I'd never known either of the Fulcis to date anyone. Until now, their loyalties were solely to their mother and each other.

"He thinks she's nice," said Tony, beaming.

"And your mother?"

The beam died.

"Faith hasn't met my mother yet."

"Saving it for Thanksgiving?"

"Thanksgiving some year," said Tony, who could be droll when the mood struck.

I showed him the two trackers, which were encased in dark shrink-wrapped covers to blend with the underside of a car, and provided him with a printout of the home and work addresses of Roger Teal and Edward Kenney and the license plate numbers and makes of their vehicles.

"I'd like this done today," I said. "It'll take two people, one to tag the cars and the other to keep watch and run interference if required. I don't want to spoil your date, but if you pass this on to Paulie, Angel might have to go along with him for the ride."

Paulie was solid, but his capacity for lateral thinking was less well developed than his brother's.

"We're taking Faith to Otto's on the River," said Tony. "We can swing by Teal on the way and afterward drive north to do Kenney."

Otto's was an upscale waterside joint in Augusta. "That'll work," I said. "Wait, who's *we*?"

"Paulie and me," said Tony.

"Paulie's going with you on your date with Faith?"

"I never said it was a date. I said it was lunch. You said it was a date."

"But it is a date." I paused. "Isn't it?"

"I want to take it slow," said Tony. "I don't want to, you know, scare her off by coming on too strong."

Tony had dislocated her now ex's finger and railroaded him out of town, and soon both Tony and Paulie would be sitting down to lunch with this woman between bouts of illegally tagging cars with tracking devices. If that didn't scare her off, nothing would, and we'd all be choosing hats for the wedding before the year was out.

"Make sure you and Paulie bill me for your hours," I said. "And add the lunch at Otto's to the tab. Alcock's good for it. And if not, Moxie will pay."

Moxie would cover lunch just for the pleasure of hearing the story.

"These two guys," said Tony as he prepared to leave, "what did they do?"

"I don't know. I've only met one of them, but I didn't like him."

"Then I don't like him either," said Tony.

Which was about as solid a definition of loyalty as one could get.

CHAPTER LXXXV

Sabine Drew returned to the Bingham Motor Inn. Sadlier met her there, and together they drove out to his home, but they did nothing more energetic than drink take-out coffee and share a pastry while Sabine told him of the imminent arrival of the private investigator to The Plains.

"Will you help him?" she asked.

"Of course."

"Because of me?"

"And because it's the right thing to do."

"It might cost you your job."

"I'm as good as done with it anyway."

"When it's over," said Sabine, "let's not come back here."

"I'm okay with that. Did you have somewhere in mind?"

Sabine regarded him over the rims of her spectacles.

"How do you feel," she said, "about fish as pets?"

IN AUGUSTA, TONY ATTACHED THE TRACKER to Roger Teal's car without a hitch, after which he, Paulie, and Faith enjoyed a lunch of fettuccine Alfredo, seafood quiche, and steak medallions, respectively, at Otto's. They then drove north to Orono, where one of Edward Kenney's employees at the Smiling Seed Company took an immediate dislike to the Fulcis, keeping an eye on them from the moment they arrived, so it was left to Faith to tag

Kenney's BMW. As a token of his gratitude, Tony bought her a bouquet of roses, zinnias, and dahlias, and the three of them drove contentedly back south.

Paulie, showing some discretion, waited in the car while Tony walked Faith to the door of her condo building in Cumberland.

"Thank you," she said. "I had a really good time. I've never put a tracker on a car before."

"Me neither," said Tony. "It was a day of firsts for both of us."

She looked past him to where Paulie was seated in the back seat of the Fulcis' monster truck. He waved at her. She waved back.

"Your brother's sweet," she said. "But maybe next time—"

Tony nodded in understanding. He'd expected this, even wanted it some, but it still made him sad. He loved his brother.

"I just didn't want him to feel left out," said Tony. "We've done everything together, right from when we were little. Even our time in jail we did together. But I don't want it to be awkward between us, so I'll tell him that next time he should stay home."

Faith touched his arm.

"No, that wasn't what I was going to suggest," she said. "I was afraid it would seem weird, that's all."

"What would?"

"You see, I have a sister . . ."

CHAPTER

LXXXVI

In Detroit, the DEA, aided by the Detroit PD, began the process of tracing the Toyota Camry in the pictures. That it had been used to seize Gai Cotter, as Raines claimed, was not in doubt, because the angle of the second photograph showed a woman slumped on the floor of the vehicle, a man's feet on her body, and the image, when magnified and cleared, confirmed her identity. The evidence of foul play meant that the investigation into Cotter's disappearance was transferred from the DEA's Office of Professional Responsibility to the FBI, since the Bureau had jurisdiction over crimes committed against federal officers, and now its agents were trawling footage from security and traffic cameras as they attempted to piece together the likely route taken by the car. Their resources were greater than those of Vincent Bergsma, though even the FBI had to concede that Bergsma's people had done well. The investigators were helped by the City of Detroit's expansion of its police camera network, all of which were fitted with license plate readers, and web resources such as the Detroit Traffic Cam Archive and Michigan's Department of Transportation's Mi Drive initiative.

Within hours, the FBI had obtained a semi-obscured image of the driver and a profile shot of the man in the back seat, neither of evidentiary quality, and the license number of the vehicle, which information eventually led them to the apartment building containing the Airbnb rented by Edward Kenney. But the Camry was not registered to any of the residents; it belonged to one Meherwan Khanna, who lived in Novi. Khanna's wife had reported the license plate missing three days after the DEA lost contact with Gai Cotter, but the photograph on Khanna's license bore no resemblance to the Toyota's driver, though it was harder to be certain about the passenger in the back, the one with his feet on Gai Cotter.

A meeting was convened, attended by Solomon, the DEA agent in charge of the Bergsma investigation, two members of his team, and Solomon's supervisor. Also present were two FBI agents, a representative from the Detroit PD, and an assistant US attorney. It was decided that, regardless of the police report filed about the missing plate, a search warrant should be obtained for the home of Meherwan Khanna and any vehicle present on the property. The FBI had approached the super of the building in an effort to establish which space the Camry had occupied and which apartment, if any, was linked to it. But the super told the investigators that the vehicle wasn't known to him, and as many as a third of the units were used as Airbnb rentals, so the car might have belonged to someone who stayed only a night or two. That meant another warrant would be required, this one to be submitted to Airbnb's law enforcement portal, so that booking information for the units rented in the building on the night of Cotter's disappearance could be released.

With the assistant US attorney on hand to advise on the optimum wording, Solomon and an FBI agent worked to compose the affidavits. They handed them to the attorney for a final check, then presented the warrants and the affidavits for both the Khanna and Airbnb searches to a waiting magistrate, who had been briefed on the urgency of the situation. The FBI agent was sworn in by the magistrate and signed the affidavits in her presence, and the magistrate, content that the affidavits supported the warrants, signed off on them. All this consumed valuable time, but the magistrate agreed to keep herself available in expectation of a further warrant to be signed once the apartment rented by the driver was identified.

Unfortunately for the investigators, the Pistons-Celtics game was taking place on the night Cotter disappeared, so Airbnb submitted booking information for no less than twelve apartments in the complex that were rented through its portal during the event. Nine of those renters required parking spaces, although this didn't mean the others didn't have a car, only that they might be prepared to take their chances on the street. Three of the twelve rentals were for parties of four, seven were for parties of two, and two were occupied by solitary male renters, and all the renters stayed at least two nights. None of these guests was Meherwan Khanna. Further, all twelve apartments had been rented twice or more since the game, which meant they had presumably been cleaned and the sheets changed. Right now, according to Airbnb, five of those apartments were being rented. As long as the warrants were in order, the rest could be searched without delay. Regarding the occupied units, Airbnb did not have the authority to remove guests for law enforcement purposes, so any search would have to wait until the following day, when the guests were scheduled to depart.

While all this was going on, agents were checking the information on the booking forms against vehicle registrations, but they found that none of the guests at the complex was the registered owner of a Camry. Now the federal investigators ran into yet another difficulty, as if they didn't already have a healthy surplus: Meherwan Khanna had a cast-iron alibi for the night Gai Cotter was taken. Mr. Khanna, who was fifty-two and overweight, had suffered a heart attack at the Twelve Oaks Mall on the night of the basketball game and died in an ambulance on the way to DMC Harper University Hospital. So whoever it was with his feet on Gai Cotter's body, it wasn't Khanna. Furthermore, Khanna's Camry was cream, not dark, and was still in the mall's parking lot when Cotter vanished.

The DEA members of the team briefly reconvened in the supervisor's office. The absent FBI agents were contacting field offices in Texas, Idaho, Utah, Massachusetts, Florida, Minnesota, New York, and Maine in preparation for interviews with the Airbnb renters, while the Detroit office would deal with the tenants in the building. They would all have to be interviewed to see if they recognized the car, even though the super hadn't. Other agents were seeking to track the movements of the Camry in the hours and days after Cotter's abduction.

"They just switched the license plate," said Solomon as he grabbed a cup of water. "A different car but the same model, in case police ran the plate."

"But why target Cotter?" asked the supervisor.

"Bergsma's man says it wasn't their work."

"And you believe him?"

"I do. He gave us the car."

"What about the Mexicans?"

"If they'd found out Cotter was an agent, they'd have let Bergsma take care of her, though we're not ruling them out. But what if she wasn't targeted? What if it was just bad luck?"

"But the switched plate indicates planning," said the supervisor. "They set out to take her."

"Or they set out to take someone," said Solomon, "and settled on Cotter."

"So where is she?"

"Obviously, we're staying on the car," said Solomon. "There's no camera on the garage door of the apartment building because the super says the one they put up kept getting vandalized. We're back to scouring traffic cameras and archives, but it may be that Cotter never left the complex."

The supervisor stood, bringing the meeting to an end. Everyone in the room could be more usefully employed elsewhere.

"Tell the magistrate to get her signing hand ready," he said, "and let the FBI know that DEA agents will be present when they enter that building. We're going to tear that fucking place apart."

CHAPTER

LXXXVII

The Kennebec River was the artery that nourished the Kennebec Valley, rising in Moosehead Lake to the north, connecting with the Dead River, and picking up minor streams and tributaries on the way to joining the Androscoggin to enter the Atlantic at Merrymeeting Bay. Before the settlers came, the Kennebec Valley was Abenaki country; after the settlers came, it was still Abenaki country, but with visitors, and following a brief period of tentative commerce with the new arrivals, the Abenaki decided they'd been better off without them and reclaimed the valley for the best part of seventy-five years. But the region held too much potential wealth for that arrangement to be allowed to continue, so the settlers returned. The old Cushnoc trading post was resurrected in the improved form of Fort Western, Revolutionary veterans were offered land to farm, and the days of the Abenaki as the dominant force in the Kennebec Valley came to an end.

In the nineteenth century, textile and lumber mills were built along the banks of the river, and around them congregated flourishing communities. In the spring, logs from the winter cuts would be floated downriver, thousands and thousands of them, so numerous that in places they formed a solid floor over the river and a man could walk from one bank to the other, were he so minded and so skilled. As a boy, my grandfather took me to watch one of the last of the river drives, which must have been in '75 or '76, and we spent the night in a big room at the faded Solon Hotel, because my grandfather knew the manager and the hotel was only a quarter-full anyway. Now the lumber was transported by road, and it was leisure that sustained the Kennebec: fishing, hunting, rafting—which, ironically enough, was what the Abenaki had been doing when the first settlers came along. Everything comes full circle, if one is prepared to wait long enough. Even the Solon Hotel had reopened.

As I drove to Bingham, some of the fall coloration was still apparent, like the embers of fires that formerly burned brightly: the yellows of elm, birch, and maple, the reds of hornbeam and black oak, and here and there, the faded purples of white ash and witch hazel. Soon only the greens of the conifers would remain, and interspersed among them, like sketches unfinished or abandoned, the bare branches of the rest. I caught flashes of water as I neared the Kennebec, and I thought again of that last river drive, and the way the logs had come together to make the water vanish; and I thought also of the dead of the valley, Scott Theriault among them, so that the two combined to form an image of a river thick with bodies, thousands and thousands of them, and the water, when it became visible again, red with blood.

It was dark by the time I reached Bingham. Cell phone reception could be spotty, but so far it was holding up and I had 4G coverage. The trackers placed on the vehicles owned by Roger Teal and Edward Kenney were working, and at that moment I had movement on Kenney—he was driving south from Orono—while Teal's car was still in the lot in Augusta. I picked up some supplies at Jimmy's Shop 'n Save, checked into the Motor Inn, and let Sabine Drew know I'd arrived. She said she was out at her new boyfriend's house in The Plains for the evening, and we agreed to meet the following day. I watched TV for long enough to decide that a book would be more improving and less depressing, so I read a Bernard Cornwell novel until my eyelids began to droop, then drifted off to sleep.

I showed her a copy of my PI's license on my phone and assured her that I hadn't even liked hanging out with young people when I was young myself.

"Is this about Mallory Norton?"

"Do you know her?"

"Not well, but it's a small town," she said. "Everyone knows everybody."

"Where does she go for fun? And please don't say *someplace else*."

"I guess she did what most of us do: hang out at friends' houses when their parents aren't around or head down to the river."

With a few beers went unspoken.

"Does," I said gently.

"What?"

"She *does* what most of us do. Not *did*, not yet."

It took a couple of seconds for her to grasp my meaning. "*Does*—right."

"You said you guessed that's what she does. I'd say you were close to her in age, and like you told me, this is a small town. . . ."

"She kept—*keeps* to herself. Some kids just do, you know? Mallory's nice, but quiet. I think that's what most people here would say about her."

The peace was broken by a flurry of arriving customers. I thanked her for her time, told her I'd hold off on buying a house in the area, and ate my sandwich by the water. I opened the tracking app to check on Kenney and Teal, but their vehicles hadn't yet left home. I was going to be occupied in the Kennebec Valley for a day or two, so I called Tony Fulci and instructed him on how to upload the app to his phone. I gave him my log-in and password and asked him to keep an eye on Kenney and Teal. I assured him he didn't have to walk around with the app open, since it would advise him of any movement. But if they deviated noticeably from their home-work-home routine, or if the two men met, I wanted him to call me in case I was working and missed the alert.

"How's Faith?" I asked once we were both satisfied that he knew what he was doing with the app.

"She has a sister," said Tony.

"What does that have to do with anything? Wait—you're not going to try dating both of them? I'm no expert, but that strikes me as a recipe for domestic disharmony."

"Not for me, for Paulie," said Tony. "They haven't met yet, but Faith and I are working on it. I'd like Paulie to find someone, like maybe I have, and Faith thinks her sister is lonely."

"And it also means you won't have to face your mother alone when you tell her you've got a girlfriend," I said.

"You know, I never thought of that," said Tony in the offhand manner of a man who had indeed thought of that.

"Your mother might even be happy for you."

"Stranger things have happened," said Tony, this time in the manner of a man who couldn't conceive of what those things might be.

Of course, there was always the possibility that Faith and her sister would take one look at Mrs. Fulci, make their excuses, and leave, but Tony would have taken that into account too. It was why he'd wait as long as possible before any introductions, in the hope that Faith's affection might have deepened enough that she would not be terminally rocked by her first contact with Mrs. Fulci. I wished them all the best of luck.

CHAPTER

XC

Sabine Drew had advised me against visiting Spero during teaching hours. Based on what she'd learned from Tim Sadlier, staff at the school were stretched as it was, and there was no point in my presence being more disruptive than necessary. It seemed redundant to tell her that I made my living being disruptive, and necessity was in the eye of the beholder, but I'd wait until later in the afternoon before driving out to the school. I had plenty to occupy me in the meantime.

The Somerset County Sheriff's Office in Madison had initially dealt with the cases of both Scott Theriault and Mallory Norton, since missing person reports fell under its jurisdiction. Only when criminality was suspected or a formal request for assistance was made did the Maine State Police's Major Crimes Unit step in. Scott's death had been investigated, and that case was effectively closed. Mallory's disappearance, meanwhile, was currently a joint operation between the sheriff's office and the MSP's Troop C, based in Skowhegan, though Troop C was working closely with the MSP's Major Crimes Unit in Augusta. Searches of the area, like the one in which Sabine had recently participated, were continuing, and registered guides were instructed to remain vigilant, but the unspoken assumption was that Mallory Norton would not be coming back to Bingham, not alive. To reduce any friction with law enforcement, the smart move on my part was to let both the Somerset County sheriff and the MSP know I was in Bingham and would be asking questions, so I drove first to Madison, which was about twenty-five miles south, and then to Skowhegan, a little farther on, to present my credentials like a visiting diplomat.

It had been a while since I'd had cause to visit Somerset County for work, but attitudes toward private investigators—or this private investigator—remained unaltered. Officers were first coldly polite, edging toward suspicious, then grew distinctly chilly and downright unwelcoming once calls were made and my reputation for leaving messes was confirmed. The Somerset County lieutenant I spoke to in Madison wasn't so bad, since he could hand me off to the MSP and blame them for any turmoil that followed, but a Sergeant Byers from MCU-Central, who happened to be in Skowhegan when I arrived, was all for running me out of the county, then the state, then into the Atlantic to drown. Only the intervention of a detective named McKibben who was working the Norton case prevented the sergeant from giving it the old college try.

"Byers is old-school," said McKibben. He lit a cigarette as we stood in the parking lot, which was safer ground for me. "He thinks private investigators, like children, should be seen and not heard or, better still, neither seen nor heard. That goes double for you. When you show up, the noise level rises."

"And there I was," I said, "trying to be polite."

"For Byers, your being here is impolite. You remember Gordon Walsh? He and Byers are tight. That might have something to do with it."

Detective Gordon Walsh of the MSP and I had once been close, but not any longer, not since Walsh became convinced I had lured a man to his death.

"I'd prefer not to be here either," I said, "but duty called."

I gave him a rundown on what I'd been up to so far. I mentioned that I'd spoken with Jenny Berrien about Spero and touched on the red flags she'd raised about possible financial mismanagement, but I didn't name Roger Teal. Neither did I tell McKibben that Sabine Drew, local celebrity medium, was in Bingham; I was afraid he'd feel obliged to mention it to Byers, who would then have two people to run into the sea.

"It sounds like you have a lot of nothing," said McKibben. "And that's being generous."

"Right back at you," I said.

"We're following leads."

"Where?"

"Nowhere so far, but we haven't given up."

"Ward Vose told me his son had started seeing a local girl, but Scott had to keep quiet about it because it was against Spero rules."

"Yeah, I'm familiar with Ward," said McKibben. "I helped put him in jail a few years back. I felt bad about it. Even the judge felt bad because Ward's an okay guy."

"Could Mallory Norton have been the girl Scott was seeing?"

"We had it from her mother that Mallory might have had a boyfriend, but the mother didn't know who it was and no one else did either. I find it hard to picture it being a kid from Spero. Santopietro keeps a close eye on his students, and they're not allowed into town unsupervised, not after dark."

"It doesn't mean someone from town couldn't have gone out there."

"No, but neither does it mean that that someone was Mallory Norton."

"Did you ask at Spero?"

"We got blank stares. Have you been?"

"Not yet. It's on my card for later today. What's it like?"

"Like somewhere else you don't want to be," he said. "I couldn't wait to get out."

"So what's the working theory on Mallory Norton?"

"Unofficially, we don't think she's going to be found by Lake Parlin." Lake Parlin lay between Bingham and Jackman. "We've been over that ground more than once, with dogs."

"But that was where her car was found, right?"

"It might have been driven there by whoever took her to put us off the scent. The way things stand, she might as well have been beamed up into space."

I thanked McKibben.

"For what?"

"For not voting in favor of drowning me."

"Don't do anything to make me regret it," he said.

"If I find myself walking in your tracks, I'll try not to step on your heels. But I don't want to give up on a link between Mallory Norton and Scott Theriault just yet, if for no other reason than Ward Vose will ask me about it next time I see him."

"Are you going to speak to the Nortons?"

"If they'll speak to me."

"They might if you ask your psychic friend to put in a word for you. You do know her, right—Sabine Drew?"

There was no point in denying it. "Yes, I know her."

"Is it just a coincidence that she's up here at the same time as you?"

"Not completely," I said. "But she has her own reasons."

"And you didn't see fit to bring this up while we were talking?" He tutted in mock sorrow, killed his cigarette, and tossed the butt into the trash. "One step closer to drowning, Mr. Parker, one step closer."

CHAPTER

XCI

In Detroit, federal agents examined images on a screen. The search of the apartment building had turned up nothing so far but would resume once the Airbnb renters had moved out of the remaining units.

"That's the car."

"Can we follow it?"

The images changed—new cameras, new angles.

"Here. And here. Now we lose it. Wait, wait . . . and it's back, but look at the times. Where we lost it is a dead end with no cameras. But even allowing for a U-turn, the car must have stopped there for a couple of minutes. Then—" More images. "Back to the Airbnb."

"What have we got on the dead end?"

"Permission for demolition of an old grocery store, three floors, with planning for a condo."

"Get someone out there. See if there's security on the site or cameras. Same for residences, businesses, cars with dashcams." A pause. "And ask if they had a dumpster there that night."

CHAPTER

XCII

On the way back to Bingham, I stopped again in Madison to speak to Roy Colburn, one of the owners of Colburn's Rib Shack, the restaurant where Mallory Norton was working a couple of shifts a week, mostly weekends, before she disappeared. The rest of the time, she was helping out at her father's place of business; the resort at which she'd been waitressing during the summer had closed early after a slow season.

Colburn couldn't tell me much more than the kid at the Shop 'n Save in Bingham had, which was that Mallory was quiet but well liked and a hard worker.

"Does she have friends among the staff?"

"Mallory hadn't worked here for long," he said, "and we never have more than two servers on duty, including on weekends, when we're at our busiest. By the time we finish cleaning up, everyone's usually too tired to do more than head home, even if there were anywhere else to go around here, which there isn't."

Colburn's wife, Bea, who was co-owner and chef, chimed in.

"Mallory sometimes took food home with her instead of eating during her break. I figured she'd have it for lunch the next day. I'm proud of my cooking, but even I wouldn't be filling up on it before bed."

She returned to the kitchen to continue her prep. Roy Colburn gave me names and phone numbers for the restaurant's other servers but added that he didn't think Mallory would have been socializing with them since they were all twice her age, with kids. The ubiquitous picture of Mallory was pinned behind the host's station next to a print of Christ surrounded by adoring children.

"I might reconsider the location of that print," I told Colburn.

"We're all praying for her safe return."

"Which means praying she's not with Jesus yet."

He took in the two images.

"I'll put Jesus in the office," he said.

SPERO SCHOOL'S LOCATION WAS INDICATED only by a single small sign at its access road. The sign read SPERO. PRIVATE. It was easy to miss, which might have been the point. The access road was itself a tributary of a tributary of the main road through The Plains, all without houses, as far as I could tell. But then, it wasn't as though The Plains was overcrowded, and the kind of people who lived there preferred not to be troubled by neighbors, or anyone else.

Spero was not what I'd anticipated, meaning it didn't resemble Stalag 13 from *Hogan's Heroes*. It was a borderline bucolic combination of old and new structures, some made of stone, others wood, surrounded by a shoulder-height white fence, freshly painted. Two paddock gates, also white, stood open, without a barrier. Five cars were parked in a stony lot immediately inside the gates, but much of the rest of campus was green lawn, dotted at regular intervals by beds planted with fall-flowering asters and chrysanthemums. Over to the right and some way distant from the main buildings was a cottage with a garden of its own. Two smaller cabins, without yards, stood equidistant to the left. I could see a couple of security cameras but no staff or students, and the campus was quiet. I understood how easy it might have been for Scott Theriault to run off but also why the school did not see—or had not seen, before his death—any pressing reason for higher fences, locked gates, or heavier security. A boy could leave, but where would he go? No buses ran out here, and I'd passed no other vehicles once I left The Forks. If a student had access to a bike, he could cycle, but it was twenty miles or more to Bingham, and if he was gone too long, the alarm would be raised and the police alerted. Scott had learned this to his cost, but it hadn't stopped him from trying again, and the third attempt had killed him.

I parked on the road and walked through the gates. As I did, a bell rang in the newest of the buildings, a red-brick structure more modern and utilitarian than the rest. A door opened at the eastern end and boys began to appear, some running, some walking, some in groups, some alone, and a handful, older than the rest, indulging in horseplay. At first glance they resembled any regular bunch of students at the end of the school day, if distinguished by their paucity, and only by looking closer did one notice how few of them were smiling. Speaking as someone who'd wiped the dust of school from his feet at the first opportunity, I could understand their unhappiness. I'd been able to leave school behind when the bell rang, but for these kids, it was all there was, and its discipline lasted twenty-four hours a day, seven days a week. They also had to live with the knowledge that they were at Spero because their parents didn't want them around. Kids sent to fancy boarding schools might have sympathized, but boarders weren't being punished, and for all its lawns and flower beds, Spero was a punitive institution.

The last of the students filed out, followed by a tall man carrying a leather briefcase in one hand and a sheaf of papers in the other. He wore a navy blazer with shiny buttons, a blue turtleneck, and navy pants, like a sailor who'd taken a wrong turn at the ocean and got lost in the woods. His dark hair was cut very short and so faded at the sides as to resemble a Mohican, while the ends of his mustache curled past the corners of his mouth to dangle halfway to his chin. I didn't like mustaches. I associated them with men trying to sell me things I didn't want to buy.

When he spotted me, he stopped by a window, placed the briefcase on the ledge, opened it, put the papers inside, and closed the briefcase. This kept his hands free as he walked toward me, flexing his fingers. It wasn't the typical reaction of a teacher responding to a visitor. At the risk of sounding conceited—heaven forbid—I could tell he knew who I was.

"This is private property," he said. "No visitors without an appointment."

"I know," I replied. "I saw the sign."

"And you ignored it."

He spoke as though the consequences of this would be unpleasant, mainly for me. Here was the big man on campus, in every sense. I ran up against people like him a lot, but it was more entertaining when Louis was with me because he enjoyed hurting them more than I did.

"Ignoring signs comes with the job," I said. "I'd starve otherwise."

I took a business card from my wallet and offered it to him. He made no immediate move to take it, and I made no move to pull it back, and thus we might have remained until winter set in. But I was more at home with awkwardness than he was, and he buckled first.

He took the card, looked at it, and handed it back to me.

"You can keep it," I said. "If I reuse them, they get shabby."

I could see him thinking about crumpling it in his fist or tearing it to pieces and scattering it to the wind, but it would have made him look petty, and here was a man who stood on his dignity. It might have been a small hill, but he was prepared to die on it.

"My name is Renders. I'm the assistant principal here. And you still need to make an appointment."

I saw five or six students gathered at the entrance of what might have been a dorm building, drawn by the prospect of trouble between adults, one of them unloved, because I couldn't imagine Renders inspiring much affection. He glanced back, caught the kids looking, and told them to get inside. After a short delay for the sake of rebelliousness, they did as they were told, but not before the oldest gave the finger to Renders's back.

"We seem to have gotten off on the wrong foot," I said.

"I don't see it that way," said Renders. "The wrong is all on one side."

"Because I didn't make an appointment and ignored a sign?"

"Because you mean us no good. I know why you're here. You want to lay the blame for Scott Theriault at our door."

"He was under your care."

"And there are limits to that care. The boy absconded on multiple occasions, and he'd been warned of the dangers. Are you an ambulance chaser, Mr. Parker? Have you been promised a cut?"

"I get paid a daily rate plus expenses. I don't need more than that. You seem to be taking this very personally, Mr. Renders."

"I care about the school," he said.

He was leaning into me now, using his height and bulk to intimidate. I didn't care for it, but I didn't step back, though he was close enough for me to smell both his breath and his cologne. It might have ended badly had one of us brushed against the other, but the situation was defused by a voice asking what was going on. I looked away from Renders to see a small, balding man approaching from the direction of the cottage and beside him a younger man dressed in a casual jacket and jeans, carrying a plastic document folder. The older one was Santopietro. I recognized him from his appearances on TV after the discovery of Scott Theriault's body.

"Can I help you with something?" Santopietro asked when he was near enough to be touched by Renders's shadow. Renders answered before I could.

"This is Mr. Parker," he said, "Mr. Vose's private investigator."

Santopietro conjured up a smile and offered his hand. We shook, and Santopietro said: "I'm surprised it's taken you so long to get to us. I feel as though I've been listening to your footsteps without catching sight of you, which I suspect might have been your intention all along. Still, you ought to have called ahead. You would have made a wasted journey had I not been here."

"Are you often absent?"

The smile broadened. "Hardly ever."

"Well, then."

Santopietro introduced the man with him as Patrick Elgot, who taught phys ed and a few other subjects that washed over me without leaving a trace. Elgot said hello but didn't hang around. Renders, by contrast, gave every indication of wanting to remain, but Santopietro told him that he'd take things from here. We watched Renders retrieve his briefcase and walk to one of the cabins. It wasn't much of a show, but it was all there was.

"Were you and Mr. Renders arguing?" Santopietro asked. "You gave that impression."

"A difference of opinion."

"On what?"

"On whether I should be here," I replied, "and on what more might have been done to prevent Scott Theriault's death."

"It's been very difficult for us all, staff and students alike." Then: "Are you recording this conversation, Mr. Parker?"

I showed him my phone so he could see I was not.

"We've taken legal advice, obviously. We have to protect ourselves, and the school."

"Neither Mr. Vose nor his lawyer has indicated that they're contemplating suing."

"I'm glad to hear it," said Santopietro. "However, it pays to err on the side of caution. As for Scott's death, I will say only that the loss of any child is appalling, and we should have done better by him—would have done better, given time, but that was denied us. Scott did not want to be here, and short of physically restraining him, which was not an option, we could not prevent him from leaving. This is a school, not a prison camp. To prove it, I'd like to show you around, if you're willing."

I told him I'd be happy to take a tour, and over the next half hour Santopietro guided me through a pair of classrooms, a small but well-equipped science lab, and a gym with a basketball court and some benches and free weights at one end, the weights either very well used by the students or acquired after heavy use by others. In the kitchen, two women prepared pasta and Bolognese sauce for the evening meal, and I smelled cookies baking. In the dorms, boys sat around in groups or on their beds, most staring at phones or screens. One or two of them acknowledged us, but only briefly. We were of little interest.

"Do they have internet access?" I asked.

"Only after the first two weeks, if they behave: one hour a day in the afternoon and longer on weekends. But the content is restricted, and phones and tablets, which are school devices, can be taken from them if they misbehave. Of course, they can ask to borrow someone else's device, but if you have only an hour's screen time, you may be reluctant to share."

"And they can call anyone?"

"Each student has five contacts," said Santopietro, "agreed to in advance with the school. If they want to call anyone else, they have to ask permission to use a school phone."

We left the students to their screens and walked to the back of the main building, where there was a football field, a track, and a large section of furrowed ground cordoned off with rope. The smell of compost came from the rows. Next to them was a trio of high tunnels for growing plants, a greenhouse, and a toolshed with its door standing open. A long line of plastic milk jugs by the greenhouse had been filled with earth in preparation for winter sowing. This was how one cultivated produce in a state that could be fierce with cold.

"We try to produce as much of our own food as we can," said Santopietro. "We have spinach, lettuce, and kale planted, some cabbage and broccoli too, and we're hopeful for carrots and beets. We're also overwintering scallions and leeks. The greenhouse is mostly herbs. We grow enough to supply some of the local stores and a few restaurants in Madison and Skowhegan. We encourage the boys to get involved, and they share in the proceeds of what we sell. It supplements their pocket money and aids their personal development. They can also earn extra cash by taking on chores like painting and maintenance, even cooking if they're interested."

"I thought a lot of them came from wealthy families," I said. "Is pocket money an issue?"

"Comfortable," Santopietro corrected, "not wealthy, or not all, but the well-off can be funnier about money than the poor. We don't want competition or envy among the students, so each boy receives an appropriate amount weekly, based on age. I know it may not look like it from the outside, especially to you, but everything we do, we do with the welfare of the students in mind."

"And to make a profit?"

"Less of one than you might think, but yes. We don't take state funding, so if we start losing money, the school will close. I don't want that to happen, for professional and personal reasons. This industry has an unfortunate reputation, some of it deserved. There are bad actors out there, but we're not among them. So far, we're in the black, and I plan to use those profits to expand the facility. Over the next five to ten years, I intend to double our enrollment, hire a full-time therapist, and widen the curriculum."

I watched six teenagers take a soccer ball onto the playing field and begin passing it among them.

"How many of those kids are here for the long haul?"

"If you mean for a full academic year," said Santopietro, "probably a quarter. The rest vary, but our minimum period of residence is a month. If they're flirting with rebellion, that's typically long enough for them to see the error of their ways. As for the more recalcitrant, we make it plain that if they fail here, the next step down can be a steep one. The first thing we do when they arrive is show them a film of what the alternatives involve. Nobody here has his head forcibly shaved or is punished with severe physical labor or weeks of mandated silence for breaches of discipline. We have to remind them of how lucky they are."

I walked the cordon of the farm, Santopietro following a short distance behind. I looked at the wooded hills and thought of Scott Theriault's final moments, when he'd realized too late the mistake he'd made. I thought of Mallory Norton and the conversation with her parents that lay ahead of me. I fought the urge to retreat south to the safety of Portland and leave Ward Vose to his guilt and the Nortons to their pain.

I glanced into the toolshed, because that was rule number one in the private investigator's handbook: If a door is open, look inside; if a door is closed, open it, then look inside. It applied on both a literal and metaphorical level, as long as you accepted that most of the time, the door, actual or otherwise, would be closed to you. Things worth knowing, meaning anything that someone didn't want you to know, were often hidden. Sometimes, though, they were hidden in plain sight.

"Tim Sadlier, our custodian and groundskeeper, works out of that shed," said Santopietro. "It's his den. He's running errands at the moment, otherwise you'd have met him."

The shed contained an old kitchen chair with a pair of plump cushions for comfort. An upturned bucket served as a side table; it was topped by a dirty mug and an empty candy bar wrapper. The rest was gardening equipment and supplies: pots, compost—

And seeds, the bags marked with the name and logo of the supplier: the Smiling Seed Company of Orono, Maine.

"You were at Élan," I said to Santopietro.

"I was. Whatever you've heard about it, however unbelievable, may be true."

"My lawyer was there."

"Really? What's his name?"

"Moxie Castin."

"I don't remember him," said Santopietro, "but there were multiple campuses, and it might have been before or after my time. Does he also represent Ward Vose?"

"No, that's another lawyer. I meet a lot of lawyers. It's an occupational hazard." I took a last look at the shed, but I'd seen what I needed to see. "Tell me about Roger Teal, Mr. Santopietro."

"You've met him. I'm sure he was able to speak for himself."

"He was. I just didn't believe everything he told me. Why does he remain in touch with this school?"

"He believes in our mission."

"Which part, exactly?"

"All of it."

"See, that's what I didn't believe. He participates in your nocturnal raids, doesn't he? He abducts terrified boys from their homes."

"That's a very pejorative interpretation," said Santopietro. "It's an unpleasant component of our work, one that we activate only in extremis. Very few students come here willingly, but the really disturbed ones, those whose parents are living in fear, have to be brought to Spero under duress or in restraints. We take them at night, when they're tired and disoriented, because it minimizes the potential physical harm to everyone involved. Nevertheless, it's very traumatic for the boy—and the team members involved."

"I hear what you're saying," I replied, "but why would someone take on that job unless they were being paid? Even then, it would stain the soul. It would certainly stain mine. But then, I wouldn't agree to do it for any amount of money, and I surely wouldn't do it for free. Yet Roger Teal volunteers."

"That doesn't mean he enjoys it," said Santopietro.

"Doesn't it? Presumably there are other ways he could make himself useful here, ones that don't involve brutalizing teenage boys."

"Again, *brutalizing* isn't the word I'd use."

"I'm sure it isn't," I said. "It would look bad on the prospectus. But is what you and Teal are doing to these boys any less worthy of censure than what was done to you at Élan?"

"I decline to submit to your judgment, Mr. Parker."

"Teal said something along the same lines."

"Can you blame him?"

"I can try," I said. I pointed toward the dormitories. "With your permission, I'd like to speak with any students who might have been friendly with Scott Theriault."

"I can't allow that."

"Why not?"

"It would require parental consent," said Santopietro, "which I'm not about to seek because I know it would be refused. Even if I anticipated a different outcome, an interrogation by a private investigator might be confusing and distressing for the boys."

"What do you think I'm going to ask them? If they killed Scott or know who did?"

"Scott had an accident in the woods. He broke his leg, fell into a river, and drowned."

"Okay, so I won't ask them that. Actually, I was going to ask them whether Scott might secretly have been seeing a girl, someone from Bingham."

Santopietro went very still.

"Which girl might you be referring to?"

"Mallory Norton," I said.

"You really are intent on stirring up trouble for its own sake, aren't you?

Scott Theriault wasn't seeing any girl. How could he? He wasn't even allowed into town for the bulk of his time here because of all the rules he broke."

"She could have traveled up here to meet him. He didn't have to cycle or hitch a ride down to Bingham."

"But she didn't."

"How do you know? Teenagers are clever, and you and your staff have to sleep sometime."

"This is speculation," said Santopietro. "You have no proof."

"If there's proof, I'll find it," I said. "It's what I do, and I'm very good at it. Anyway, I'm starting to like it up here. The fresh air agrees with me."

I rubbed my hand along the wood frame of the toolshed, my fingertips following the grain.

"Who else volunteers to snatch children for you, Mr. Santopietro?"

"It's time you were going," he said. "I have work to do."

I didn't move. "You establish a school way up in a remote area where even the law is nebulous," I said. "Anyone might think you didn't want to be noticed. You want to expand your operation, yet you elected to cease drawing state funding. Declining it gave you independence, but it also meant you could go about your 'mission' without having to worry about supervision by the department. Again, there you go, hiding your light under a bushel. But at the same time, the original department supervisor, Roger Teal, chooses to volunteer his services out of the goodness of his heart."

"I don't care for your tone," said Santopietro.

"And I don't care for your school."

Santopietro took out his phone.

"If you don't leave in the next sixty seconds," he said, "I'll call 911 to inform them that we have a trespasser on the property and I'm worried for the safety of my students and staff. I'll tell them that, due to the intruder's profession, I have reason to believe he might have brought a firearm onto the campus in breach of the law. I'll advise them that I have locked down the students in light of the threat posed by this man."

As it happened, I'd left my gun in the car and parked outside precisely because I'd be entering a school, but an arriving state trooper or county deputy wouldn't know that. At best, I'd end up doing a lot of explaining; at worst, I could get shot. Somewhere in the middle lay the prospect of enjoying the comforts of a cell in Madison or Skowhegan. I raised my hands in acquiescence and walked away. Santopietro stayed with me as far as the main building, where he remained with his cell phone at the ready. Over by the cabins, Renders leaned against the frame of an open door, his arms folded across his chest.

My grandfather—who, like the best of older people, was really a younger person in disguise—taught me a skill he said would prove useful in later life, regardless of the path I chose. Here's how you start: Anytime you walk into a new room, note five aspects to it. After a week or two weeks, you make it six, then seven. Soon, it's second nature to you. On one level, it's a useful way of grounding yourself in the moment, because we live in a world predicated on distraction. But if your job is dependent on spotting what's missing or what doesn't belong, the ability to take in with one glance a room, a house, a property, or a person becomes essential. With practice, the dissonances you pick up may not even be physical, because you've adapted to wrongness in all its forms.

I hadn't learned much from my visit to Spero, but I'd learned enough: The school couldn't have been further out of plumb if it stood on one side, and that went double for Santopietro and Renders.

Here were subtle men.

CHAPTER

XCIII

I picked up two coffees and a bag of doughnuts at Jimmy's on my way back to the Motor Inn. Sabine Drew's car was parked in the lot when I pulled in. She knocked on my door a couple of minutes later. I handed her a coffee and gave her a choice of doughnuts. I sat on the bed, my back against the headboard, while Sabine took the room's only chair.

"How did your visit to Spero go?" she asked.

"I poked a stick through the bars," I said.

"Why?"

"Because it's what I'm being paid to do."

"I thought you were being paid to investigate Scott Theriault's death."

"That too, but poking sticks through bars is fun."

"You're a strange man."

"Says the woman who talks to the dead."

Sabine's eyes softened, transforming her face so her features, which were severe in repose, like a medieval fresco of a saint, were closer to handsome.

"Says the man who also talks to the dead. That makes us quite the pair."

"Except it seems I have competition for your affections. Who is he?"

"Tim Sadlier."

"The same Tim Sadlier who works at Spero?"

"Yes." Now it was her turn to spot a change in me, but it was a tempering, not a softening. "Why does that bother you?"

I saw again the branded bags from the Smiling Seed Company in the toolshed that served as Sadlier's den. "Everything about Spero bothers me," I said.

"Tim has agreed to speak with you. He'll tell you what he can."

"Okay," I said neutrally.

"Okay," Sabine echoed. "But we have a lot to talk about before we get to him."

"Where do you want to start?"

"With what's out there in the woods."

SABINE HAD SET ASIDE HER COFFEE. When she was animated, she used her hands to communicate as much as her voice. The cup was getting in the way.

"Death is inconsistent," she said, "or better to say that it is consistent in its action but less so in its consequences. What persists after, if anything, is not a consciousness entire but fragments, mainly feelings: hurt, anger, confusion, sadness—and fear."

I thought that Scott Theriault's grandfather, with his theories of death and persistence, might have understood, but I said nothing. I wanted to listen.

"You can't conceive of how frightened the dead are," Sabine continued. "Or perhaps *you* can; others, less so. The transition from this life to the next is like standing on the edge of an abyss and being told to step off with no guarantee that the alteration in your circumstances will constitute an improvement. Fear is the most natural response.

"So they have all these emotions but without a capacity for reason. The dead can't be reasoned with, only comforted, so I try to provide reassurance before sending them on their way. It needs to be done quickly or they'll become trapped in a cycle where the dominant feeling becomes so overwhelming that it occludes all else. Have you ever seen an animal in a zoo repetitively pacing its cage because restriction has driven it insane? The dead might empathize."

She pointed to the window and the river beyond.

"The day I arrived here," she said, "I saw a woman with part of her head missing by the shore of Big Island. The wound was very neat, as if her skull had been marked into quarters before one was excised with a blade. She's been out there for a long time, and when the sun eventually dies and our world comes to an end, she may still be present to bear witness, she and those like her. In the moments before the Earth is engulfed by the sun, only the dead will stare.

"But the woman on Big Island has a form, and that's not always so. What remains after death is so primal and concentrated yet so abstract that it might not be able to hold a shape. What I encountered in the woods was formless but composed of emotions from more than one person. How long have people been dying out there in the wilderness? Thousands of years, I expect. It's not surprising that facets of them remain. What is unusual is that they should conjoin, because that's another thing about death: It's lonely. We die alone. And when the dead come searching, it's for the living, not for those like themselves.

"What I'm telling you is that I've never before come into contact with a congregation of the dead bound together with hostile purpose, not like this one. A family, yes, or members of a community—unity in life reflected after—but not disparate souls, some dead for centuries, others barely in the grave, forced together. And in that residue, I sensed Scott Theriault, or the vengeful part of him. The rest is gone—"

I interrupted her for the first time.

"What about Mallory Norton?"

Sabine shook her head.

"Only through Scott."

"What does that mean?"

"Something of her drives his hate—it was fleeting, but it was there—though nothing of her endures."

"Why?"

"Who can say? Because if she's dead her passing was sudden and relatively painless? Or the opposite: It was drawn out and agonizing, and she was grateful when the hurting came to an end."

Sabine picked at doughnut crumbs, wetting a finger to lift them to her mouth. It was such a quotidian act in the midst of an odd conversation, and I was reminded that she lived ceaselessly with what she spoke of, so the extraordinary had become as common to her as the salvaging of the final flakes from a pastry.

"I said that some aspect of Mallory Norton was fueling Scott's hate," she continued, "but that hate has been weaponized by an outside force, the same force that's binding together the lost dead of the Kennebec. It's using them for its own ends—and to amuse itself, because I also felt that from it—but it's not part of those woods. It's trapped in them, but it's learned to reach out from its prison to manipulate its environment, and that reach is extending all the time. It's filled with memories, but it moved so fast that I had an impression only of agelessness. But just as one can identify familiar faces in a crowd, I picked up names from it. Among them was yours. Another was that of your friend Louis."

"What does it want?" I asked.

"An end to its suffering."

"And does it have a name?"

"Yes," said Sabine. "It calls itself Brightwell."

CHAPTER

XCIV

By the lake, Jennifer Parker spoke.

"Brightwell," she said.

Beside her, Martin started in dismay. He knew of Brightwell and his kind. How could he not? They had been responsible for Martin's death.

"Why are you saying that name?"

"It's him," Jennifer replied. "He's the one trying to recalibrate the machine."

CHAPTER

XCV

It was all shadows now. Dusk had waned into early evening, but come winter, dusk would hardly register at all. Come winter, there would be only light and dark.

Sabine Drew and I were seated in the living room of Mallory Norton's home. Mallory's parents sat opposite us, with an empty space between them on the couch. It could have been left for their missing child in the hope that she might yet return home, but it also represented the growing distance between husband and wife. Their daughter's absence was slowly sundering them, aggravating faults and fractures in their relationship that predated her disappearance. Were Mallory to come back, the marriage might survive; if she did not—when she did not, by Sabine's reckoning—the chances were that it would fall apart.

And meanwhile, a name echoed in my mind:

Brightwell, Brightwell.

Sabine had introduced me as someone who wanted to help. Both parents were wary but not hostile. Their clothes were crumpled, their manner resigned. They were losing hope and preparing for the worst.

"We were warned people might come," said T. K. Norton. "You know, looking for money in return for finding our daughter."

"We've had calls," said his wife. "Emails too."

T. K. Norton continued as though she had not spoken.

"Some of them, the police said, wouldn't even ask for money. They'd want to get involved because it made them feel important. But whoever took Mallory might be among them, so we're obliged to report every contact."

He grimaced at Sabine.

"A detective named McKibben vouched for you after your last visit. He said that while he couldn't accept you are what you claim to be, he couldn't explain you any other way. He told us you'd located missing persons in the past, and even if you couldn't help, you wouldn't do us any harm. We just shouldn't get our hopes up."

His eyes flicked to me.

"What about you, Mr. Parker?"

"I don't want your money," I said. "As for harm, the worst has already been done to you."

"Not quite," he said. "God willing, it won't be."

Anita Norton made a small noise, like an animal whimpering in its sleep. Without looking, her husband searched for her hand, found it, and held it. They stayed that way for a few seconds before Anita slipped her fingers from his. The gap between them widened.

"Tell me about your daughter," I said. "What is she like?"

Again, not *was* but *is*; present, not past, until the facts proved otherwise. I did not need to add to their pain through carelessness. And between them, they told me of her, growing more voluble as they went on, even smiling. Childhood, school, work; friends and boyfriends, but few of either, and no real enemies they could point to; a girl content in her own company; reticent, verging on secretive, but not to the point of alienation, not even close. Loving—and loved; they hoped she knew that.

"Could she have been seeing someone without your knowledge?"

"She worked evenings at Colburn's," said Anita. "A couple of times, it was after midnight when she got home, and she said she'd been hanging out with people from the restaurant. They might have had a beer or two. I didn't ask. I know she's still underage, but I was happy for her to socialize."

Which contradicted what the Colburns had told me. I might have to call Mallory's coworkers after all.

"Did she ever bring home food?"

"From Colburn's?" Anita looked at her husband. "I don't recall her doing that. Do you?"

"Once, maybe," said T.K. "I wish she'd done it more often. Those are good ribs."

"I've always wished Mallory had more friends," said Anita, "but a lot of the kids she knew from school have left. They went to college or found jobs elsewhere."

"Why didn't Mallory go to college?" I asked.

"She was accepted to the University of Southern Maine, but she wasn't ready to go straight from high school," said T.K. "She wanted time to think. We'd have preferred her not to delay, but it wasn't like she was sitting around the house doing nothing. She worked hard and was saving money for when she did decide to go."

"Did you meet any of her workmates?"

"Not from Colburn's," said Anita. "They didn't come to the house. I wouldn't have expected Mallory to bring them home. She's shy like that."

Gently, I asked: "Did you ever doubt that she really was going out with them?"

"I thought she might be seeing one of them but wasn't saying."

"Why did you think that?"

"It was just a change in her manner. She was anxious, but not unhappy, if that makes sense. Excited. Also, small things, but important small things: She chose her clothes more carefully, wore a little more makeup, changed her hair."

"I didn't see all that," said her husband.

"You saw some of it," said Anita.

"I just thought she was growing up."

"She was."

The dynamic between husband and wife was shifting, the latter now taking the lead, but I made sure to continue addressing them both as I'd tried to do from the start.

"And you told the police this?"

"Not about the makeup and such, but sure, that she might have had a boyfriend we didn't know about."

"My understanding is that the staff at Colburn's are mostly older women," I said. "If Mallory was dating someone, it wasn't one of them."

"They looked into the Theriault boy," said T.K., "but they found no proof it might be him."

"How did you feel about their pursuing that line of inquiry?" I asked.

T.K. signaled to his wife that she should answer.

"Honestly?" said Anita. "I was glad when they found nothing. Things are bad enough as it is."

With which nobody could argue, but it left Scott Theriault and Mallory Norton isolated in their respective frames instead of becoming part of the same picture. I asked the Nortons a few more questions and wrote down the answers but only out of politeness.

"I'd like to take a look at Mallory's room," I said.

"The police have already been through it," said T.K. "Ms. Drew as well."

"Fresh eyes," I said. "Do you know if the police removed anything?"

"Nothing," said Anita. "They went through her closets, but like most teenagers, she keeps everything that's important on her phone."

And the phone, like Mallory, remained missing.

"I'll show you up," said Anita.

"No," said her husband. "I'll go with him."

CHAPTER

XCVI

Renders and Santopietro were in Santopietro's office at the cottage, leaving Elgot to supervise the evening meal alone. One of the cooks had brought two bowls of pasta to the office but they sat untouched, and the watery red sauce, made from cheap, tasteless canned tomatoes, was already separating. Santopietro made a point of eating the same food as his students. If it was good enough for them, it would do for him also, but he had no appetite after the private investigator's visit. The smell forced him to open a window despite the dampness in the air.

"Parker has nothing," said Renders.

"He has Teal in his sights," said Santopietro.

"That's Teal's fault for telling him so much. I don't understand why he didn't just show Parker the door."

"Because Teal is arrogant." Santopietro ran his fingers through what was left of his hair. "However, in his defense, he may have felt he had no choice but to answer Parker's questions. Berrien put him on the spot. If he refused to cooperate, he might have given the department more reason to be mistrustful of him."

"I thought it was only Berrien who was the problem," said Renders.

"Even if she's a lone voice, you can be sure that people have been listening to what she has to say about Teal and this school. The only reason nobody has made a move is that rumors aren't proof, but I wouldn't put it past Berrien to make finding that proof her parting gift to the department."

Renders still liked the idea of taking Berrien, but Parker's attention was now focused on the school. If something were to happen to Berrien so soon after he'd discussed Spero with her, Parker would have to be a simpleton not to look at cause and effect.

"And there's the dead DEA agent to consider," Renders added.

"Has there been anything more about her?"

Renders had checked the internet earlier. "Not that I could see."

For Renders, hunger finally won out over anxiety. He picked at the pasta, holding a hand under his chin so he wouldn't stain his shirt.

"You need both Teal and Kenney to be gone," he said, "but if we move against one, the other will be in the wind. He might go to the police to save himself."

"Tell me something I don't know."

"How about telling Kenney something he doesn't know?" Renders asked.

"What do you mean?"

"Tell Kenney that Parker is closing in on Teal, and Teal is getting jittery, which is the truth. Parker is up here, with eyes on us, so we can't do anything about it. Would Kenney be willing to kill Teal?"

"Yes, to protect himself and his precious family. Kenney is a survivor."

"So frame it around his family, set him on Teal, and when Teal is gone, I'll take care of Kenney. I never liked him anyway."

But Santopietro was already a step ahead.

"Better yet," he said, "why don't we set them on each other?"

Santopietro picked up his phone and made the first of the calls.

CHAPTER

XCVII

T. K. Norton stood in the doorway of his daughter's room while I pulled on a pair of disposable gloves.

"Why are you wearing those?" T.K. asked. "Is it an evidence thing?"

"A politeness thing. I don't think your teenage daughter needs a stranger touching her possessions directly."

Brightwell, Brightwell.

I started with the bedside table, and even though I had gloves on, I tried to handle Mallory's belongings as little and as tenderly as possible, preferring to use a fingertip to move items. T. K. Norton watched me. He might have been keeping an eye on me—no father wants to give an unfamiliar man untrammeled access to his daughter's environs—but he also wanted to talk, so I stayed quiet until he felt comfortable enough to begin.

"Is she for real?" he asked. "That woman, Sabine."

"Yes," I replied. I was going through the books on the shelves one by one, checking between the pages. I found movie tickets, receipts, a few cards and notes, but all were old and none struck me as important. "Some would call what she has a gift, but she doesn't call it that. If she could, she'd rid herself of it."

A photograph fell to the floor from the pages of an American Girl book: *Meet Molly*, the first in the series. Everyone liked that book. Sam still had her copy. The photo had been taken when Mallory was not yet a teenager. It showed Mallory and her mother, nothing visible in the background, the two of them happy together. I restored it to the book, where it would be safe.

"She says she can't find any trace of our daughter," said T.K., still speaking of Sabine. "That's good, right? Because psychics, mediums, whatever, they deal with the dead. So if she can't locate Mallory, it means she's not dead."

I wasn't about to share with him what Sabine had told me at the motel. It didn't matter anyway. The truth was that no one knew for sure whether Mallory Norton was alive or dead, the exception being the person who had taken her, if there was one.

"I need her not to be dead, Mr. Parker," he said.

I could have offered him a platitude. I could have told him that a lot of people were trying their best to bring about that outcome, which was true, and that it was why I was searching his daughter's room. Instead I said: "I know."

He pulled away from the door.

"I'm disturbing your focus."

"No," I said, "you should stay. I may have questions or a detail I'd like clarified. And my company would be welcome, right?"

If he went downstairs, I knew he would not rejoin the two women in the living room. He would go elsewhere to be alone with his fears. I imagined that T. K. Norton was someone on whom a great many people relied: his family, his employees, his customers. He might even have liked it that way. The problem with being that kind of man was that you fell out of the habit of turning to others when you were in trouble, or you never developed the habit to begin with. You suffered alone, and you suffered badly.

So I asked him about the pictures on the walls and about his business. He spoke more than I did, and when he went silent, I found something else to ask. And all the time I moved methodically through the room, checking not only his daughter's things but also the closet walls, the underside of the bed and mattress, even the baseboards, inspecting each item or section of the room thoroughly before proceeding to the next. I left the clothing until last. To do the job right, I'd have to take out jeans, sweaters, and T-shirts to examine, pat down, and, if necessary, refold. I asked T. K. Norton to help with the refolding. The underwear I did as discreetly as I could, and it didn't take long, but Mallory Norton owned enough sweaters, tops, and T-shirts to clothe fifty teenagers, with enough left over for those feeling the cold to double up.

Sometimes the revelations come fast and easy, and you find what you're looking for right off the bat. Those instances are rare. More usually, you ask ninety-nine questions with no good reply, then the hundredth provides an answer that advances the investigation a single, crucial step. You knock on ninety-nine doors only to be told at each to go screw yourself, then the hundredth is opened by the person you've been looking for, even if you didn't know their name or their face until that moment. And once in a while, you spend an hour painstakingly searching the room of a girl who might be dead and fear you're going to leave with nothing only to learn at the very end that the effort was worth it. Persistence, if you're fortunate, is rewarded.

Among the T-shirts was one more scruffy and stained than the rest. The shirt was off-white and had been folded so it matched those above and below, but it was different. It even smelled different because it was unwashed, so the scent of the person who had worn it, and who had gifted it to Mallory, would not fade. The faintest hint of sweat and cheap male deodorant came from it. I unfolded the shirt and held it to the bedroom light, haloing the logo of the Smiling Seed Company.

CHAPTER

XCVIII

T. K. Norton watched me photograph the T-shirt with my cell phone. I then restored it to where I'd found it, photographing it again once it was in place. Only when I was finished did he ask why.

"Do you and your wife garden?" I asked.

"Not seriously," he replied. "I can mow a lawn and prune a bush, and Anita grows herbs for the kitchen, but we have a company that does the grunt work, plus any planting. I'm too busy and, if I'm honest, too lazy to do it myself. I like sitting in the shade with a beer, but beyond that, I'm an indoors guy."

"Is the yard company local?"

"They're halfway between here and Madison."

"Do you know where they source their supplies?"

"It's never come up. I can ask."

"I'll do it. Give me the name." I took out my phone.

"Ken 'n' Beck Landscape Solutions."

I looked up from my phone. "Really? Ken 'n' Beck, like Kennebec?"

"Ken and Becky Zarin. They were both born here. They didn't move up special just so they could name a business."

I found the company website. It was a bare-bones home page but offered both landline and cell phone numbers. I tried one, got a message, tried another, and got Becky Zarin. I gave her my name, told her I was with T. K. Norton, put him on speaker to confirm, and asked her where she sourced bedding plants, seed, compost, and whatever else she used.

"We have our own beds, greenhouses, and growing systems," she said. "If we bring in stuff from outside, we try to keep it as local as possible. We use a couple of suppliers in Bangor and Portland, but that's still in-state."

"Anyone in Orono?"

"No."

I thanked her, hung up, then leaned against the bedroom wall to compose an email.

"Do you have a printer?" I asked T. K. Norton.

"Yes, but—"

"Give me your email address," I said. "I'm going to send you a letter that I want you to print out. Then you and I will sign it."

He told me the address and I added it to the message.

"Do I get to read the letter first," he asked, "or should I just close my eyes and make my mark?"

I was warming to T. K. Norton, but did my best to suppress it. If Sabine was right and my fears were correct, it would make everything harder later.

"It won't say much beyond detailing the circumstances under which that T-shirt was discovered. I'll send you the pictures I took as well. You can print two copies of everything if you'd like to hold on to one of them."

"I was going to do that anyway," he said, "but I can be open about it now."

I sent the email. T. K. Norton checked his phone, confirmed that the email and attachments had arrived, and went to print them. From where I stood, I could see the Smiling Seed T-shirt, the rounded edges of the letters visible, like massed threads fed through the holes in a tapestry. Those threads now connected Roger Teal and Edward Kenney to each other, Teal and Kenney to Spero, and Mallory Norton to Scott Theriault, because I was certain that if the T-shirt was analyzed, it would be rich with Scott's DNA. It might even bear traces of the sauce used to baste Colburn's barbecue.

Mallory Norton was the girl Scott Theriault was seeing covertly before he died, but she'd disappeared before he went missing. When Scott went north instead of south after fleeing Spero, was he looking for her? They might have agreed to run away together. Mallory could have located a cabin or camp, abandoned or unoccupied, where they'd rendezvous prior to moving on—or, in the short term, where they could hook up for a few hours before Scott went back to Spero and Mallory returned home. But wouldn't it have been simpler for them to use her car, and why was that car then found abandoned by Lake Parlin? No, it didn't fit, and not because I wasn't seeing something obvious but because I didn't have all the information I needed. Now, though, I was closer to finding it.

T. K. Norton came back with the pages and together we signed the two copies. The document wouldn't have the force of an affidavit and wouldn't stand up in court, but it might be important as a link in a chain of evidence, if only to prove that I hadn't planted the T-shirt in the room to implicate Spero. I folded my copy and stored it in my jacket pocket.

"How about telling me what's so important about that T-shirt," said T.K.

"Can you give me twenty-four hours? Will you trust me for that long?"

"Trust you? I don't even know you. And if it involves my daughter, then no, I can't give you twenty-four hours. I won't give you twenty-four minutes."

He was right, of course. I was like a dog with a bone, and I'd let it overwhelm my better instincts.

"Does your daughter have a nickname," I asked, "or a pet name at home?"

"Just Mal."

"Not Smiles?"

"No, never."

"I think Scott Theriault might have given that Smiling Seed T-shirt to your daughter," I said. "He was the boy she was seeing."

"Did he hurt her?" he asked. "Is that why he ran away?"

Because that, of course, was another possibility: a besotted young woman murdered by a troubled young man.

"It's the car," I said. "If your daughter and Scott Theriault were out there together by Lake Parlin, and something happened between them, like an argument that ended badly, how did Scott get back to the school?"

"He could have walked."

"More than twenty miles, in the dark?"

"That's six hours or so, if you're fit."

"And not traumatized," I said, "which he would have been in that scenario. But they wouldn't have wanted to drive so far from Bingham or The Plains to be alone. Time was precious. He would have been worried about being missed, and she needed to be home before you and your wife started fretting. Without trying, they could have found somewhere quiet halfway between Bingham and Spero."

"You don't want this to be Theriault's doing because you're working for his father," said T.K.

"I have no personal stake in it," I replied. "But if you choose to go down that path, you're accepting that your daughter is gone, and the only person who can confirm what happened to her is dead. You can tell the police about the T-shirt, and they'll come to me and ask why I think it belonged to Scott Theriault. I'll give them my reasons; they might decide to send the shirt to be tested, and Ward Vose or Scott's mother will be asked to give a DNA sample for comparison. I don't know how long all that will take, but it could be weeks. And by the end of it, a new narrative will have emerged, and that narrative will solidify: Scott Theriault killed Mallory Norton, and his own death followed. That might be the truth or it might not, but regardless, you and your family will have to live with the uncertainty. And let me tell you, Mr. Norton, it's the not knowing that destroys us."

T. K. Norton sat on his daughter's bed. Had I not been present, he might have lain on it and breathed in what was left of his child.

"And the alternative?" he asked.

"Leave me to do my job. Say nothing to anyone about that shirt and give me a day or so to see what I can find out. After that, I'll go to the police myself."

It was time for me to go.

"I told my wife that I was scared Mallory wasn't ever coming back," he said. "She slapped my face."

"Because she's scared too," I told him. "I'm staying at the Motor Inn if the police need to talk to me. Otherwise, I'll be in touch."

CHAPTER

XCIX

I said nothing to Sabine Drew about the Smiling Seed T-shirt as we left the Norton house, but she was too sharp-eyed not to spot the change in me.

"What did you notice that I missed?" she asked.

"I'll tell you later. Where are we meeting your boyfriend?"

"He's not my boyfriend. We're not nineteen."

"So what is he?"

She stared out the side window.

"He's company."

"No more?"

"I'm working on it."

"Well, that's hopeful," I said. "And you still haven't told me where we're meeting him."

"He suggested the Kennebec River Brewery, up in The Forks. It's not like we have a lot of choices here, and pleasant though our lodgings may be, I'm beginning to feel the walls closing in."

She continued to watch the town go by. Only when there was no more town to watch, which didn't take long, did she speak again.

"Why didn't Mr. Norton come down to say goodbye?"

"Because I don't think Mr. Norton was capable of it," I replied. "He's drowning. What did you and his wife talk about while we were gone?"

"About how her husband is drowning," said Sabine. "If the girl is dead, that marriage dies with her. Everything that's happening revolves around Spero, doesn't it?"

"Yes."

"And now you're worried that Tim might also be involved."

Damn, the woman was good.

"Is he?" I asked.

"Would I be sleeping with him if I thought he was?"

"From what you've told me, you were sleeping with him before you knew much more than his name."

"I hope you're being facetious," she said. "Otherwise, you're just being mean."

"Let's go with facetious. But Spero is a small school. If there was something off about it, Sadlier must have noticed."

"He did, but Spero pays reasonably well, and the work is year-round, which is rare up here. Tim did his best for the boys. It was a job he used to like, even when it was hard."

"So what changed?"

"That's what you'll have to ask him."

THE KENNEBEC RIVER BREWERY was part of a resort called Northern Outdoors. On this particular evening, in the downtime between leaf-peeping and winter sports, it was uncrowded, with only a handful of tables occupied, most of them by men who looked like hunters. Tim Sadlier was in a corner as far removed as possible from everyone else, drinking a dark ale. He stood awkwardly when we approached as though unsure whether the done thing was to embrace Sabine or give her a manly pat on the back. She settled the issue by rubbing his arm affectionately, and he and I shook hands. I realized I was hungry, and this would be my only opportunity to take a break from the Shop 'n Save, so we ordered flatbreads with various toppings to share and a house salad as a sop to our arteries. I drank water; Sabine asked for a fruit beer, and apart from thanking the server when it arrived, she said little more for the next hour. She wanted me to form my own impressions of Tim Sadlier, unmediated by interference.

By the end of the conversation, I had no doubts about Sadlier's character but even more about Spero. Sadlier told me about the incident with Anthony Marshall, about Leonard Levesque and his hostility toward Scott Theriault, and about Scott himself.

"I knew he sneaked out nights," said Sadlier. "He wasn't the only one who did, but Scott would go read with a flashlight or smoke a cigarette if he'd managed to bum one. If I was working late, he might come find me. I'd let him help, and then he'd head back to the dorm."

"What about the running away?" I asked.

"That happened twice in the weeks after he arrived and before I got to know him better. He learned fast that it wasn't worth the effort, and life at Spero was hard enough without losing all his privileges. The first time I caught him wandering around after dark, I thought he was trying to slip out again, but he said he wasn't, that he only wanted to be alone for a while. I made him promise to stay on the property, because if he left and people found out I'd seen him, I might lose my job. He promised he would."

"But he didn't keep that promise, did he? He went north and died."

"I don't understand that," said Sadlier. "No one does."

"And was it just time to smoke and be alone that Scott wanted?"

"I thought so. Other times, when it suited him, he wanted company, or what passed for it with me."

"You liked him."

"I did. He had no business being at Spero."

"Could he also have been sneaking out to meet someone?"

"Like who?"

"A girl," I said.

"The police asked me that same question. I said I didn't know. I stay late at the school one or two evenings a week, and other than that only if I have to cover for staff. I get paid extra for the hours. So I know how quiet it is up there, but it's not so quiet that I'd hear a vehicle if it stopped far enough away."

"Sabine told me that you felt the school had changed for the worse, and you were less happy there now. Why?"

"Apart from dead kids? It's Renders, the new assistant principal. He's a disciplinarian. He's too weak to be anything else. He and Santopietro are tight, though."

"Who else is Santopietro tight with? Roger Teal?"

"I think they go right back to the early years of the school, when Teal was the inspector for the state's education department. He still comes up every month or so or when a tough nut needs to be cracked. That's what they call it when they have to bring in a boy by force: 'cracking a tough nut.' He and Santopietro go on trips together too, outside of school business."

He let that hang.

"Are you suggesting they're in a relationship?" I said.

"They could be. Teal is married, but when did that ever stop anyone? I know they go on trips only because I saw printouts of hotel bookings in Santopietro's office when I was fixing a radiator. They were going to Tampa." He coughed. "I say that I 'saw' the printouts for the bookings, but I might have gone poking where I shouldn't. They don't tell me much at the school, and the only way I can find out what's happening is by being nosy."

I wasn't taking notes. It wasn't that Sadlier was nervous, exactly, but if he saw someone writing down what he said, it might be counterproductive. I'd remember what needed to be remembered.

"Tell me about the Smiling Seed Company," I said.

Sadlier looked puzzled. "What about it?"

"Does it supply the school?"

"Sure. We get a good discount, and they throw in a bit extra for free. The head of the company is another of Santopietro's old friends."

"Edward Kenney."

"That's right. He and Santopietro were at Élan School together. Whatever they went through, it brought them closer. Kenney calls Santopietro 'the Saint.'"

Which was also how Roger Teal referred to Santopietro. Teal had said that one of his friends was once immured at Élan. It would make sense if that friend was Edward Kenney.

"Do the extras provided by Smiling Seed include company T-shirts?"

"Oh, yeah, and Spero's glad of them. Those boys go through clothes like you wouldn't believe."

"Who makes the deliveries?"

"Kenney himself."

"The head of the company makes deliveries all the way up here?"

"It's not a big company, and like I said, he and Santopietro are close."

"Does Kenney also like cracking tough nuts?"

"Not that I know of."

"Does he ever visit the school at the same time as Roger Teal?"

"I've seen them together there, but I couldn't say how often."

"And where does Renders fit in?"

"He doesn't," said Sadlier. "Renders looks at Teal like he's shit on a shoe, excuse my language, and I've heard Renders tell Santopietro that the school should cut its ties to Smiling Seed."

"To Smiling Seed or Edward Kenney?"

Sadlier thought for a moment.

"To Kenney, but Kenney is Smiling Seed, just like Santopietro is Spero."

I had hoped for a revelation, but so far I was coming up empty. I still had the Smiling Seed T-shirt, and the cords linking Teal, Kenney, and Spero were drawing tighter, but it was all circumstantial, with no proof of wrongdoing.

"Why do you dislike Renders so much?" I asked Sadlier.

"It's his attitude, and the way he treats the boys."

"Or is there more to it than that?"

Sadlier's face reddened.

"This happened just a couple of days ago," he said. "I told Sabine about it. Renders keeps his own place between Bingham and The Forks, but each member of the staff has to spend a set number of nights on campus each week, and they sleep in one of the cabins. I heard noises from the one Renders was using when he was on duty. It was late, and I was on my way home, but the sounds were so strange that I was obliged to see what they might be. It helps that I know my way around the motion sensors."

He swallowed and winced as though he'd rather have spit out whatever he'd choked back.

"Renders was sitting in an armchair watching pornography on this big laptop he has. He wasn't playing with himself or anything like that, just sitting there with a beer in his hand. Look, I'm not a prude, and I won't condemn a man for whatever occupies him when he's alone in the privacy of his bedroom, but the girls on that laptop were teenagers, or not a whole lot older, and they weren't enjoying what was being done to them, not one bit. You could see it on their faces, and the sounds they were making weren't ones of pleasure. If you ask me, Renders was getting off on their pain and humiliation at least as much as on the sex, and I don't think a man like that has any place in a school."

"Did you tell anyone about it?"

"No."

"Because you were worried it would be your word against his, and you might lose your job if you weren't believed?"

"Oh, I'd have been believed, all right, although I'd still have lost my job."

"So tell me why you didn't say anything."

"I was about to be on my way when I heard Renders speak," said Sadlier. "A man laughed at whatever he'd said, and I realized Renders wasn't alone. It was Santopietro. They were in there together, watching those girls being hurt."

Sadlier drained his beer.

"Now I really am looking for a new job."

CHAPTER

C

Sabine Drew trailed me from the pub, leaving Sadlier inside.

"What now?" she asked.

"I don't know," I said. "We're still dealing with pieces of the puzzle, but more of them than before."

Sadlier had told us he was prepared to go to the police and share what he'd seen in the cabin. Combined with the Smiling Seed T-shirt at the Norton house, it might be enough to secure a search warrant for Spero, but only if DNA testing confirmed that the shirt was Scott Theriault's. And what then? Santopietro and Renders could deny what Sadlier claimed to have witnessed, turning the tables on him as a troublemaker who resented the assistant principal, and watching pornography together, while embarrassing and potentially damaging to their reputations as school officials, was not illegal, depending on the pornography. What I did know was this: Those who gained pleasure from watching women being hurt and humiliated eventually got to wondering what it might be like to do some hurting and humiliating of their own, and Mallory Norton had drifted into their orbit.

Before leaving the parking lot, I checked the tracker app, but Kenney's vehicle was at his home and Teal's was in West Gardiner. I had run out of ideas, and soon I would run out of time. I could only keep my promise to

T. K. Norton and hope that McKibben and the Major Crimes Unit might have more luck. Back at the Motor Inn, I wrote up my notes, answered the more urgent of my emails, and went to bed. I anticipated having trouble sleeping, but I was out as soon as I lay down. I wanted to escape, and my body and mind permitted it.

CHAPTER

CI

In Detroit, the cross-checking of traffic-camera images with the details of the Airbnb renters from the Hamtramck apartments on the night Gai Cotter vanished finally produced a match. Edward Kenney, co-owner of the Smiling Seed Company in Orono, Maine, was the driver of the Camry whose occupants had discarded Cotter's body in a dumpster of construction waste off I-94. The picture on his driver's license left no doubt. The man in the passenger seat beside him had not yet been identified.

There was no longer any doubt about Cotter's fate. The dumpster and its contents had been taken to the northwest of the city; the contents would be used as landfill for homes being demolished under Proposal N, but they hadn't yet been sorted to remove organic and hazardous waste. When the dumpster was located, the remains of Cotter's body were discovered halfway down, wrapped in garbage sacks.

The FBI preferred dawn raids for the apprehension of suspects, but under pressure from the DEA, it was decided to move on Edward Kenney as soon as possible. Within the hour, the FBI agents in Augusta, Bangor, and Portland had been alerted, as had the task force groups of the Maine DEA. By midnight, they would be ready to roll.

One thing was made clear to them all: Edward Kenney was to be taken alive.

CHAPTER

CII

I was woken by a double buzz from my phone, followed, seconds later, by ringing. The clock read 11:30 p.m. and the call was coming from Tony Fulci.

"They're on the move," he said. "So am I."

He stayed on the line as together we monitored the progress of the two vehicles on the app, one, Kenney's, heading south, the other, Teal's, north. When they reached Pittsfield, they stopped; they had returned to the storage lot. Ten minutes later, only one car left, Kenney's BMW. Teal's Highlander stayed where it was.

"Take a look in Teal's Toyota, then call me."

"What about the tracker?"

State law didn't prohibit GPS tracking, but it could be considered a violation should the monitoring cause emotional distress. If Teal was dead, his distress, emotional or otherwise, was at an end, and we'd be left to explain to the police how we'd managed to locate the body.

"Call me first," I said. "Then we'll decide."

CHAPTER CIII

Edward Kenney called Santopietro from Hartland. He was using a fresh burner, which he hadn't activated until he was out of Pittsfield.

"It's done," said Kenney.

He heard Santopietro breathe a sigh of relief.

"How?"

"Does it matter?"

"I don't suppose it does."

"We need to talk, and you need to help me get rid of a body."

"Of course. I'll be waiting."

I bet you will, thought Kenney.

I WAS WATCHING KENNEY ON THE APP. He was on the 151, driving toward Athens. If I was right, he'd go west to pick up the 201, which was a better road, then north toward Solon and the Kennebec River Reservoir, Bingham, and finally, The Plains.

Edward Kenney was on his way to Spero.

CHAPTER

CIV

Tony Fulci called me again as Edward Kenney neared Bingham. Along the way, Kenney had stopped for twenty minutes at a gas station in Solon, probably to fill up and close his eyes briefly. I was parked off the main road that went through The Plains, almost within sight of the first of the turn-offs for Spero.

"I found the Toyota," said Tony. "It's locked and empty."

"Take a look around."

Tony did, but Teal's car was the only vehicle in the vicinity, and when Tony searched the ground with a flashlight, he saw no bloodstains or signs of a struggle.

"Can you check the trunk?"

"I'll have to bust it open."

"Do it."

I heard the sound of metal on metal, then Tony's grunts as he popped the back of the Highlander. An alarm began to wail.

"Nothing," said Tony.

"Get out of there," I said. "And take the tracker."

"Consider it done."

I went back to monitoring Kenney's BMW. A few minutes later, he stopped again, this time in Bingham where Main Street crossed Austin Stream to become Jackman Road. I wondered whether Kenney was having second thoughts about approaching Spero and, if so, why. Had he even informed

Santopietro that he was on his way, and did anyone go visiting a secure school after dark with good intentions?

Five minutes went by, then ten, before the BMW resumed its journey north. Whatever had provoked the delay, Edward Kenney was over it. The first fat drops of rain hit my windshield, but I didn't turn on the wipers and kept the car dark. Distantly, I heard a rumble of thunder. Closer, I glimpsed headlights.

CHAPTER

CV

From his cottage, Santopietro heard a vehicle enter the lot. The paddock gates were kept closed at night but rarely locked. The fence was low enough that locking the gates made little difference, but Santopietro always kept in mind a fire or medical emergency. He didn't want the police or EMTs to be delayed, but he also didn't want them breaking his gates by driving through them, because they were nice gates.

Santopietro looked out the window and watched the BMW park at the edge of the lot, beside the cars belonging to Santopietro and Renders. It was not Renders's scheduled night, but Santopietro had asked him to switch with Ishan Lal, one of the part-timers. The BMW's driver-side door opened and the interior light went on. Edward Kenney emerged and paused to take in the two vehicles.

Santopietro saw no lights in the student dormitories. It was possible that some of the boys might have been woken by the sound of the car, but they were teenagers, and Santopietro was convinced that most teenagers would sleep through the Second Coming and wake the next morning to discover a stranger with a beard entreating them to behave better. Even if one of them did hear the car, they'd be reluctant to get out of bed to investigate, never mind leave the dorm on a miserable, stormy night.

Despite the rain, Kenney took a moment to stretch after the drive, then began walking toward the cottage. Santopietro left the office and went to the front door to greet him. Kenney kept his hands rammed in his jacket pockets.

"Edward," said Santopietro. "You picked a bad night for it."

"In so many ways," said Kenney.

"What's that supposed to mean?"

"The Game is over—for all of us. There are feds at my home."

Kenney's neighbor Joel Legere had called him on the road to say that federal agents were crawling all over Kenney's property. Either Legere had spotted that Kenney's BMW wasn't in the driveway or he'd seen him leave, but regardless, Legere had never come across a conspiracy theory he didn't believe and regarded all institutions of the federal government as either untrustworthy or actively corrupt. Legere was a crackpot, but Kenney had always gotten along okay with him because Legere was a crackpot who liked gardening. His latest good deed for Edward Kenney was to inform him that the latter's worst fears had come to pass.

"Do they know you're up here?" asked Santopietro.

At first, it struck Kenney as a stupid question. If the FBI knew that, they wouldn't be at his house right now. But he quickly saw that the question wasn't so stupid after all: The Saint was weighing his chances of survival. The FBI had tracked down Edward Kenney, which meant they'd soon identify Roger Teal, if they hadn't already. But if Teal was dead, and Kenney could be silenced, there'd be no one left to incriminate Santopietro. The Game could go on.

But that wasn't going to happen. Kenney wouldn't allow it, if for no other reason than, damn it, he just didn't like Santopietro. He supposed he never had. His right hand emerged from its pocket holding a gun.

"Game over," said Kenney.

He raised the gun as lightning flashed. The glare illuminated a figure standing to Kenney's left, concealed until now by a sugar maple. Kenney did the worst thing possible: He hesitated, and Renders shot him—once, twice, then a third time, the shots indistinguishable from the roll of thunder that accompanied them, Renders advancing with each pull of the trigger so that he was close enough by the last to see a hole appear in Kenney's face, like someone had dabbed the bridge of his nose with dark paint. Kenney fell to the ground and did not move again.

Santopietro left the shelter of the cottage to join Renders. Together they stared down at the body.

"We'll put him in his car," said Santopietro, "and you can drive—"

Renders heard a sound that was harsher and nearer than any thunder. Santopietro reached behind his back as if to scratch an itch, then pitched forward. As Renders caught him, he saw Roger Teal nearby, holding a gun in a two-handed grip, his legs wide, like Angie Dickinson in the opening of *Police Woman*. Teal fired a second time and Santopietro's body bucked with the impact, though by then he was already dead.

Renders didn't drop the body or try to run away. Instead, he rushed at Teal, Santopietro's corpse held before him like a shield, and knocked the smaller man off his feet. Teal went down, the gun falling from his hand, and Renders dropped Santopietro's body on top of him. Teal scrambled on the wet ground for the lost gun as Renders leveled the barrel of his pistol at Teal's head and pulled the trigger. Teal's right eye turned to a dark unseeing star as a corona of red erupted from the back of his skull.

Renders lowered his gun. Another flash of lightning came, illuminating the two bodies, and still there was no movement from the dormitories. Renders had blood on his hands and blood on his raincoat, but the rain was already washing it away. The adrenaline was wearing off as he checked his body for wounds, but Teal's bullets didn't appear to have passed through Santopietro's body. Renders picked up Teal's gun and examined it: a Smith and Wesson Equalizer, a home-defense weapon, probably loaded with frangible rounds to limit collateral damage. That was fortunate, and a man ought to ride that luck; a disaster might yet be avoided. Renders began dragging Teal's body toward the parking lot.

CHAPTER

CVI

As before, I didn't drive into Spero but parked off the road, just behind the tree line. Whatever was happening at the school, I didn't think it would be a good idea to announce my presence. I was halfway to the gate when I heard a series of muffled bangs, the first of them nearly lost against the thunder. Only two big exterior lights burned at Spero, and those were close to the gate, so the rest of the campus was umbrous, the outlines of its buildings barely distinguishable from the night sky except when lightning flashed, though the sudden brightness was so blinding that I was forced to shield my eyes.

Three vehicles were parked in the lot, Edward Kenney's big BMW the farthest away. The others appeared to slouch, and as I passed them, I saw that the right-side tires on both were flat; only Kenney's tires were intact. Halfway between Santopietro's cottage and the BMW, a body lay face down at the edge of the lot. I knelt and turned the head enough to see the features. Roger Teal stared back at me with his intact eye. I restored him to the gravel. Over by a sugar maple, a second body was lying on its back, its mouth open wide to accept the rain—Santopietro—and near the path to the cottage was a third man, Edward Kenney. I checked each for signs of life and found none.

I heard a roar from the parking lot as the BMW kicked into gear. Before I could react, it was speeding off. I was about to go after it when a stream of students appeared from the main dormitory, all barefoot and wearing pajamas, some of them crying. I shouted for them to get back inside, but a fire was blazing in the rooms on the second floor. I ran to the nearest of the kids and asked if there was anyone left in there. An older student did a head count and told me one boy was missing.

"Leonard isn't with us," he said. "Leonard Levesque."

"Where is he?"

By now the fire had properly caught and a window on the upper floor exploded, spangling the night air with glass. The older boy pointed to the main school building, where more flames were visible. Silhouetted against them was a boy.

"That's Leonard. He's the one starting the fires."

LEONARD LEVESQUE DIDN'T MOVE AS I APPROACHED. He was entranced by what he'd done. Only when I was beside him did he acknowledge me.

"Are they dead?" he asked.

"Is who dead?"

"Santopietro. Renders."

"Santopietro's dead. I don't know about Renders."

"Who are the others?"

"Roger Teal and Edward Kenney."

Leonard Levesque wiped his eyes clear of rain and tears.

"Teal was one of the men who took me. Are you sure he's dead?"

"I'm sure."

"Good."

"Why are you burning the school, Leonard?"

"I have to make up for what I did," he replied. "Otherwise they won't ever leave me alone. I think they might kill me."

"Who'll kill you?"

"The dead boys."

His eyes glittered madly, reflecting the flames, as though he were burning up inside.

"What did you do, Leonard?"

"I told Santopietro about Scott and his girlfriend," he said. "I'm sorry now."

"Why?"

"Because he and Renders raped her in the cottage."

"How do you know?"

"I watched them do it, through the window. It felt good at the time, but I was sad later. I wanted to hurt Scott because everybody liked him more than me. I wanted to get him in trouble, but I didn't think they'd do what they did to his girlfriend. You believe me, right?"

"It doesn't matter what I believe."

"I hate this place."

I heard a crash as part of the dormitory roof collapsed. The fire, freed, soared into the night sky, and the flames hissed in the falling rain.

"That's okay," I said. "Once you're done, there won't be much of it left to hate."

I went over to where the older boy was corralling the rest of the kids in the rain.

"What's your name?"

"Jamie Hanscomb."

"You're in charge now, Jamie. Take the boys to the shelter of the trees beyond the campus. I'll call 911."

I didn't want the kids to remain on the property in case the fire spread. I didn't think it would, not with the rain, but I couldn't be sure.

"Are you going to stay with us?" Hanscomb asked.

"I told you, you're in charge. Help will be here soon."

"Where are you going?"

His voice trembled. He might have been older than the rest, but he was still only a child.

"To find Mr. Renders," I replied.

"When you do, will you tell him something for me?"

"If I can."

"Tell him to fuck off and die."

CHAPTER

CVII

Renders was trying to think clearly. He was wet and cold, stained with mud and blood, and if the light in his rearview mirror meant what he thought it did, Spero was going up in flames, incinerating three corpses in the process.

Renders had begun moving the bodies, but at that point, he definitely hadn't been thinking clearly, because his first thought was to hide the dead and clean up the whole mess. It was only after he'd commenced dragging Teal's body across the lawn that he realized he'd be better off coming up with a story to justify shooting Kenney and Teal, which might not be difficult since the two men had arrived at the school in the dead of night armed with guns, and one of them had killed Santopietro. But by then the damage was done—Renders had interfered with a crime scene, which wouldn't square with his explanation that he'd shot the men in an attempt to defend himself, his employer, and the students from armed intruders. Add what Leonard Levesque knew to that equation and a couple of other loose ends, and Renders realized his best hope was to run.

Then he saw that two of the cars in the parking lot, his and Santopietro's, were resting on their rims. He realized Kenney and Teal must have punctured the tires, which was when he'd gone searching for the keys to the BMW. Renders was forced to concede it was smart of Kenney to lie about having taken care of Teal, even though Renders and Santopietro had suspected that, even if it was true, Kenney might be planning to take care of them next. Everyone had been trying to outsmart everyone else, and Renders was the last man standing, which made him the smartest by default.

From behind the BMW, Renders watched the private investigator approach the cottage and contemplated shooting him too. But Parker had done nothing worse than aggravate him, and killing a man for being annoying was harsh even by Renders's standards, though if Parker's death had aided a cover-up, Renders would happily have killed him ten times over. Instead, while Parker was distracted by the bodies and then the fire, Renders set about putting as many miles as possible between himself and Spero while it was still dark.

It was about forty miles from The Plains to the US border, and once he was safely in Canada, Renders could lose himself. He didn't know how long he'd be able to hide, but he had more than eleven thousand dollars in cash back at the house that he'd pick up before he left, and he would find work somewhere. Even if he managed only a few more months at liberty, or a year, it was better than spending those days in a cell; and if he did last a year without being located, the chances were good that he'd manage two, then three. He might even die a free man. But he had one final task to perform before he left the country. He'd have to be quick, but it would be no less pleasurable for that.

Renders parked the BMW in the yard of his rented home, went inside, and commenced stuffing clothes, shoes, and toiletries into a large canvas bag. He added a phone charger, his laptop, and a few books. He thought about bringing his gun and a box of ammunition but was worried about being questioned and searched at the border, and he didn't have a license to transport. Finally, he retrieved a small lockbox from under the floorboards of his closet and removed from it the cash, his late mother's two-carat diamond engagement ring, and a Rolex bequeathed to him by his father, the final item with paperwork but no box. He thought he might be able to get a few thousand for the ring and the watch combined, bringing him close to fifteen thousand in total, and a frugal man could survive for months on that kind of money. A year earlier, Renders had stayed in a one-star motel in Niagara Falls for just thirty-five dollars a night. If he'd said he wanted to stay a week, the guy would have jumped for joy, settled for two hundred, and even thrown in fresh towels.

When he was done, Renders put the bag in the trunk of the BMW, returned to the house, found an empty plastic bag in the kitchen, and went down to the finished basement. A battery-powered lamp shone on a mattress, a beanbag chair, an opened twelve-pack of water, and a crate containing candy bars, bread, cheese, potato chips, and soda. In a corner, a fan heater blew enough warmth to make the space comfortable. On the mattress, tethered to the wall by a chain fixed to a leather cuff on her right ankle, sat Mallory Norton. She was wrapped in a comforter and dressed only in her underwear. Her head and shoulders were exposed, and the lamplight showed bruising around her neck: Renders liked to choke. She watched him approach but said nothing and did not stir because there was nothing to be said and nowhere to go.

"Hey, honey bear," said Renders. "I got bad news. We've had some fun, but our time together has come to a close."

He saw her try to figure out whether this meant her situation was about to get better or worse. Better meant freedom, but worse—

Renders held up the plastic bag. "A new game," he said. "The last one."

Mallory cast away the comforter and held up her hands to ward him off.

"Get away from me," she said.

"I warned you before about using your nails."

She'd scratched him once, deep enough to draw blood. He'd made her regret it, and she hadn't done it again.

Mallory began screaming, but Renders was on her. He put the bag over her head and tightened it around her neck.

"Breathe," he said. "Breathe . . ."

A sound from behind made him turn. Approaching fast was a man nearly as wide as he was tall, dressed in a blue leisure suit and holding a tire iron. Before Renders could react, the tire iron connected with the side of his face, dislocating his jaw.

Mallory wrenched the bag from her head as Renders sagged to the mattress, his unhinged jaw moving strangely. Before he could figure out how to make it move the way it should, Renders was gripped by a massive hand that closed around his neck and lifted him off his feet; the stranger held him against the wall and applied gradual pressure around his neck with his fingers and the heel of his hand.

"Breathe," said Tony Fulci. "Breathe. See how you like it."

Renders was losing consciousness, but his eyes felt as if they might explode from their sockets before he did. Then another voice spoke, one that Renders recognized.

"Tony, put him down."

For a second, the pressure actually increased, and Renders was convinced he was going to die, but then the hand was gone and he dropped to the floor. He lay gasping with his eyes closed, registering sound and movement around him as Mallory was freed from her chain. Renders's mouth, neck, and throat hurt. They hurt a lot. He tried to say so, but nothing came out except a kind of moan lubricated by blood and drool.

Renders opened his eyes to see Mallory standing above him. She took a step back, raised her right foot, and kicked him as hard as she could in his shattered face. There came an explosion of pain, then no pain at all.

CHAPTER

CVIII

I stopped Mallory Norton from kicking Renders a second time. One kick I took as a positive sign of engagement, but two or more would be worrying, even potentially fatal. I told Tony to stay with Renders while I brought her upstairs, lending her my jacket to keep warm. I called 911 and gave them directions to where we were, then went through my contacts until I found T. K. Norton's number. I handed the phone to his daughter.

"Call your dad," I said. "Tell him to come get you."

CHAPTER

CIX

It was a couple of days before Mallory Norton could be interviewed by police. She collapsed in her father's arms shortly after he arrived and was taken to Redington-Fairview General in Skowhegan. Physically, she was doing as well as could be expected, but her considerable reserves of psychological and emotional strength were drained.

She'd been waiting for Scott Theriault when Renders found her. Later Santopietro came; they brought her to his cottage, and that was how it began. When they were done with her, Renders assured Santopietro he would get rid of her, but instead Renders kept her for himself. It was bad, she said, always bad, but the worst was when he told her what he'd done to Scott. It seemed that Leonard Levesque had begun dropping hints in the dormitories after Mallory's disappearance, and Renders and Santopietro hadn't liked the way Scott started looking at them, not one little bit.

"Renders took Scott from the school," Mallory told Detective McKibben. "He used a rock to break his leg, then held him under the water until he drowned. He said it was my fault. He told me that if I'd stayed away from Scott, none of it would have happened." She glared at McKibben, as if he were the one who had said it. "But that's a lie."

Renders maintained that he had buried Scott in a shallow grave. He could not explain how the body subsequently washed ashore miles downriver.

"Nature rebels," said Sabine Drew when I told her.

Meanwhile, Renders, as part of a plea deal to avoid a sentence of life without parole, was sharing all he knew of the Game, though he was forced to do it in writing because of the wiring in his jaw. Members of the media reported on the four men's involvement in the troubled-teen industry, and a few wondered whether the fact that two of them were former students of Élan might have had some impact on their actions, but no conclusions were ever reached. Had I been asked, I might have shared another thing Sabine Drew once told me: Evil finds its own. It forms clusters.

Sometimes, matters don't end well, but they end.

AT 26 FEDERAL PLAZA, the New York field office of the FBI, Special Agent Edgar Ross finished reading the file from the homicide investigation unit of the Boston PD on the murder of D. Francis Sturgis of Wellesley, Massachusetts, until recently a member in good standing of the Colonial Club, if not the human race. The paperwork didn't tell Ross much that he didn't already know, and what was worth knowing wasn't in it, because he was keeping that detail to himself.

As far as the BPD was concerned, what they had was a clean, well-planned kill, possibly carried out by individuals who shared Sturgis's sexual tastes and feared he might rat them out as part of a plea bargain. No one paid much attention to reports of a Black man who, earlier on the day of the murder, had apparently paused within sight of the Sturgis residence to take the Wellesley air. Only Ross had discreetly followed up on the reports, which took some time because the man was both careful and skilled, with a sixth sense for surveillance. What Ross discovered wouldn't have been enough to justify further investigation—it wouldn't even have been enough to merit sending an email—but it was sufficient to satisfy him.

The man was Louis.

And Ross said nothing.

6

They shall cause lamentation. No food shall they eat; and they shall be thirsty; they shall be concealed, and shall not rise up against the sons of men, and against women; for they come forth during the days of slaughter and destruction.

The Book of Enoch, 15:10

CHAPTER

CX

I asked a favor of Sabine Drew, one to which she was reluctant to agree because she was frightened. I told her she was right to be, and I was frightened too, but we would not be alone. Angel and Louis would be there, and Tim Sadlier said he would come with us.

Finally, Sabine agreed to help us locate Brightwell. We had to do it now, before winter set in. Once the snows came, we would not be able to enter the woods so easily, and all the time his reach would grow.

We drove north to where the wreckage of a small plane had long lain lost in the woods by the site of an old fort. As we drew nearer, Sabine became noticeably more anxious. She was sitting in the back of my car with Sadlier. In the rearview mirror, I could see her holding his hand tightly. Louis and Angel were in a car behind us, staying close all the way.

At last we came to the point on the road from which we could hike the shortest distance to where last I'd seen the child: Brightwell in his new incarnation. Louis and Sadlier had brought axes and knives, while Angel and I carried pistols. Each of us had a small pack with water and snacks, but Sadlier had also put together a larger backpack with an emergency medical kit and more should we end up spending longer in the woods than we intended.

"Well?" I said to Sabine as we stood by the tree line.

"Yes, he's in there, but he's not alone."

"Who's with him?"

"A little girl, or what was once a girl. She's the one holding him captive. It's odd."

"What is?"

"I can hear him calling. I think he wants to be found."

"Is it a trap?"

Sabine regarded the woods, listening for voices audible only to her.

"Oh, he'd harm you if he could, and he did try to have your friend killed. But he failed, and now you represent his last hope for freedom."

"We're not here to free him."

"Aren't you?" She grasped her walking pole. "Because he says you are."

WE WALKED FOR AN HOUR, and while progress was slow—there were no trails—it was not uncomfortable. The air was cool, not cold. Only as we reached our destination did I notice that the singing of birds had ceased.

Sabine stopped, but before she did, I was already shrugging off my pack, and Angel was doing likewise. We felt it, all of us: the stillness and a kind of charge in the air, as if we had wandered too close to an industrial power cable. The air smelled of decay, and I heard a sound like leaves whispering, but there was no breeze. Before us stood a rotted American sycamore, a species of tree now virtually extirpated in the wilds of the state, so this was a relic of an older time, even though it was no more than a trunk and branches, all heavy with toadstools; decomposers breaking down wood and organic matter for nutrients. Yet despite how singular the tree was, I had almost missed it. It was both there and not there, like an optical illusion, a projection of light on air. It was real, but its reality was tenuous. As it decayed, it embraced evanescence.

"He's inside," said Sabine. Her eyes darted over the trees as though following a sprite. "And the girl is nearby. She's watching us. She doesn't want us to take her pet."

Her "pet." If the girl had ensnared Brightwell, we should be more scared of her than of him.

Louis and Sadlier went to work on the tree with the axes. Though rotten, the trunk was thick, and the bark and flesh clung to the blades, so once a cut was made, the two men struggled to free the axes and start again. Sadlier broke through first, revealing a hollow heart and releasing the reek of decomposition. From then on it was easier, and they used the axes like crowbars, wrenching chunks of bark and cambium from the whole, slowly moving downward until—

"My God."

Sadlier dropped his ax and backed away, coming to a stop by Sabine. Louis stayed where he was, and Angel and I moved forward to join him.

From the core of the tree, a face stared out at us. Its eyes were open but milky, its skull hairless, its skin translucent. On the neck, collapsed but still apparent, was a goiter. The head was held fixed in place by tendrils, as though the root system had grown up instead of down, allied to ivy with bloodred leaves. The tree might have been corrupted but it was not completely dead, just as it existed on the periphery between the seen and the unseen. As we stood before Brightwell, his lips moved, but his mouth did not open and he could not speak. One of the tendrils had pierced the soft tissue beneath his chin to impale his tongue.

"He can't be alive," said Sadlier.

"But he is," I said.

"He wants it to stop," said Sabine. "He wants you to bring it to an end."

I thought I glimpsed movement in the undergrowth, but when I looked in that direction, there was nothing. Still the girl was close. Sabine had warned us.

"Show him mercy, Mr. Parker," said Sabine. "Please."

I put my hand on my gun, but Louis stopped me. He took an Elk Ridge hunting knife from its sheath. The blade was less than four inches long but wickedly sharp.

"It has to be this way," he said. "It has to be, if Epstein is right."

"I'm not sure I can do that," I said. It is a terrible, intimate thing to take a life with a blade.

"Not alone," said Louis. "All of us."

"Why?"

"Because I don't want to know for sure."

He placed the tip of the blade against Brightwell's throat. I gripped the handle, and Angel's fingers closed over mine. Brightwell's sightless eyes blinked once.

"Now," I said.

The blade sank deep, stopping only when the quillion touched the skin. A thin trickle of blood wept from the wound, mixed with a yellowish, viscous sap. Brightwell's lips ceased moving, but there was no revelation, no confirmation. I felt only regret, and a sickness inside. From the forest, I heard a child scream. I let go of the knife at the same time as Angel, leaving it for Louis to wrench the blade from what remained of Brightwell. I reached out to close his eyes, and only then, as I touched the eyelids, did a void open, the place of nonbeing, the nothingness that was before everything, and I knew then that Brightwell was truly gone, his existence forever expunged.

"It's over," I said.

No one spoke. We gathered up our belongings.

"Are we just going to leave him like that?" asked Sadlier when we were ready to go.

"What do you suggest?" asked Louis.

Sadlier reached into his pack and withdrew a small bottle of white gas, the liquid fuel used in camping. It would burn hot and clean.

"The ground is damp," said Sadlier, "and there's no wind. I reckon we'll be okay, but if it shows signs of spreading, I have an Element fire extinguisher in my pack."

"Best to be prepared, right?" I said.

"I don't believe anyone could have been prepared for what I just witnessed," said Sadlier.

He let Louis spray the white gas inside the tree before handing him a box of InstaFire matches. Louis struck one, tossed it, and retreated fast as the fuel ignited. We stayed to watch the tree burn long enough for what was inside to be rendered unidentifiable. Sadlier stood by with the Element, which resembled a foot-long baton, but the blaze only licked at the exterior wet bark, and finally the flames began to die down. Sadlier smothered what remained of them with the extinguisher and we left the clearing, left it to the weeping of a child.

CHAPTER

CXI

Sabine Drew and Tim Sadlier walked behind the rest; Sadlier deliberately slowed so they would be out of earshot.

"Whatever it is," said Sabine, "say it."

"What kind of men are they?"

"Do you really want to know?"

"I wouldn't have asked otherwise."

Sabine took his hand and kissed it.

"At least one of them," she said, "may not be a man at all."

FROM THE WOODS, THE CHILD WATCHED THEM GO. She did not recall any longer the manner of her passing, only the pain of it, and her hatred was pure and uncorrupted because she had died so young.

A voice spoke from beside her. She had not heard the woman approach. This surprised the child, who heard everything. The woman wore a summer dress and her face was a skinless mask of red.

you've been out here for too long, said the woman. *i've come to take you away*

where am i going? asked the child.

to the sea

and after?

you'll forget

i'd like that

The child saw another woman standing nearby, older, with a portion of her skull neatly excised.

who is she?

she is your grandmother

The child gazed at the woman with the ruined skull but made no move toward her, and the grandmother stared blankly ahead, so each might have been a stranger to the other.

and her? asked the child. *who is she?*

By the smoldering sycamore stood a girl no older than the child. Her face, too, was bloodily despoiled. She was peeking through the hole in the tree at what remained of the angel.

she is my daughter, said the woman. *but she's dangerous*

dangerous like me?

no, said the woman, *dangerous like her father*

She took the child's hand.

would you like to hear a story while we walk to the sea?

yes, said the child.

once there was a being that asked the question the rest of its kind feared to ask

go on

can you think what that question might be?

no, said the child.

that question, said the woman, *was "Why?"*

ACKNOWLEDGMENTS

I'd like to thank Marshall Mintz and all those involved with PubKey in New York for having a sense of humor, thus permitting their bar to be taken over by criminals for an afternoon. May their PubKey enterprise bring them continued success. Professor Benjamin Wold, Director of the Centre for Biblical Studies at Trinity College Dublin, kindly provided the thoughtful Aramaic translation used by Rabbi Epstein in the novel. Chloe Teboe, director of communications for the Maine Department of Education, suggested various sources of information on private schools, but any errors made, or liberties taken, are all my own. Leo Hylton's columns on prison life for *The Bollard*, Portland's free paper, are always informative and provided some of the details about the Maine State Prison used in this novel. Some special copies of this book are accompanied by a map of Parker's Maine, for which I am indebted to the extravagantly gifted artist Rob Ryan.

As always, I'm grateful to Emily Bestler, my long-serving/suffering editor at Atria/Emily Bestler Books, for her advice and support, and to all the staff in New York, including Gena Lanzi, Dayna Johnson, Hydia Scott-Riley, Lara Jones, Kayla Slusser, Dana Trocker, Sarah Wright, David Brown, Tracy Roe, Samantha Hoback, Vanessa Weiman, and more. I'm similarly thankful to Jo Dickinson, my editor at Hodder & Stoughton, and to all at Hachette, including Katie Espiner, Jen Wilson, Swati Gamble, Alice Morley, Catherine Worsley, Rebecca Mundy, Eleni Lawrence, Oliver Martin, Dominic Smith and his sales force, editor emerita Sue Fletcher, Jim Binchy, Breda Purdue, Siobhan Tierney, and Elaine Egan—and Laura Sherlock, that fine publicist. Meanwhile, Dominick Montalto does his best to save my blushes at the copyediting stage. My agent, Darley Anderson, and his team continue to keep me solvent and in print, while Steve Fisher, my film and TV agent at APA, and his assistant Chip Draper have spent many years patiently but determinedly guiding my work toward the screen. Ellen Clair Lamb acts as the acceptable face of the operation, looking after social media, promotion, and proofreading, aided in the last by Cliona O'Neill, while Cameron Ridyard maintains my blue-chip website. Finally, love and thanks to Jennie, to Cameron and Megan and Sam, and to Alastair and Alannah for being there.

John Connolly
Spring 2026